PRAISE FOR #1 BESTSELLING AUTHOR

LINDEN MacINTYRE

"A masterful storyteller."
—*Toronto Star*

"One of our country's most vital writers."
—Craig Davidson, *The Globe and Mail*

"His gift is capturing the poetic thrum of life's
unanswered questions and ragged endings."
—*Maclean's*

"A terrific grasp of dialogue . . . [and] cannily
builds tension and mystery."
—*NOW* (Toronto)

"The man can write."
—*The Gazette*

"Powerful and compelling."
—Robert J. Wiersema, *National Post*

"Linden MacIntyre proves once again how adept he is at dealing
with the topical and the taboo." —*Winnipeg Free Press*

"Engrossing."
—*The London Free Press*

"[MacIntyre writes with] impressive delicacy and understanding."
—Scotiabank Giller Prize jury citation on *The Bishop's Man*

ALSO BY LINDEN MACINTYRE

Punishment

Why Men Lie

The Bishop's Man

Causeway: A Passage from Innocence

Who Killed Ty Conn (with Theresa Burke)

The Long Stretch

Published by Vintage Canada, a division of Penguin Random House Canada Limited,
in 2018. Originally published in hardcover by Random House Canada, a division of
Penguin Random House Canada Limited, in 2017. Distributed in Canada by
Penguin Random House Canada Limited, Toronto.

Vintage Canada with colophon is a registered trademark.

www.penguinrandomhouse.ca

This book is a work of fiction. Names, characters, places and incidents either
are the product of the author's imagination or are used fictitiously. Any resemblance
to actual persons, living or dead, events or locales is entirely coincidental.

Library and Archives Canada Cataloguing in Publication

MacIntyre, Linden, author
The only café / Linden MacIntyre.

ISBN 978-0-345-81207-0
eBook ISBN 978-0-345-81208-7

I. Title.

PS8575.I655O55 2018   C813'.54   C2016-908254-7

Book design by Terri Nimmo
Cover images: (café interior) © Sonny Abesamis/Arcangel;
(coffee stain) © Igor Dutina and (paper texture) © Kamyshko from Dreamstime.com
Interior image © Pixelshow1 | Dreamstime.com

Printed and bound in the United States of America

2 4 6 8 9 7 5 3 1

Penguin
Random House
VINTAGE CANADA

To Darrow and Daniel
who have but to ask

Secrets, silent, stony sit in the dark palaces of both our hearts: secrets weary of their tyranny: tyrants willing to be dethroned.

James Joyce, *Ulysses*

Shatila Camp, Beirut

September 18, 1982

She lay there as if she was sunbathing in the heat, and the blood running from her back was still wet. The murderers had just left. She just lay there, feet together, arms outspread as if she had seen her saviour.

ROBERT FISK, *Pity the Nation*

∿

According to Lt. Elul's testimony, while he was on the roof of the forward command post, next to the Phalangists' communications set, he heard a Phalangist officer from the force that had entered the camps tell Elie Hobeika (in Arabic) that there were 50 women and children, and what should he do. Elie Hobeika's reply over the radio was: "This is the last time you're going to ask me a question like that, you know exactly what to do"; and then raucous laughter broke out among the Phalangist personnel on the roof.

Kahan Commission report, February 8, 1983
TEL AVIV, ISRAEL

ONE

CYRIL

I.

The reading of the will was a formality. Pierre's widow had been running things for years, five years and two months, to be precise, since June 26, 2007, the day he'd vanished.

Pierre Cormier had led a complicated life, much of it unknown even to his closest friends and kin, and so the mystery of his disappearance lingered. But by the summer of 2012 investigators had concluded to the satisfaction of insurers that he was dead. It was time to lay the mystery aside, embrace administrative closure—imperfect though it was from an emotional perspective.

And so his little family assembled in a lawyer's office late on a Wednesday afternoon in August. It was, all things considered, a congenial gathering, the young widow, the amicable ex, the adult son, all more or less resigned to the fact that how he died would remain

forever unresolved. Financial realities had long ago been accommo-
dated by the power of attorney Pierre had granted Lois in the days
before his disappearance. She had been, these past five years, scrupu-
lously fair.

The son, Cyril, didn't really know why he was there. He was
working as a newsroom intern at a television network and an early
departure from a busy office didn't look good. But the lawyer had
insisted. Formality or not, it was a necessary bit of business.

From the corner office on the forty-second floor of the Draycor
Tower they could see Lake Ontario and, through the late summer
haze, at least a hundred boats—sailboats, powerboats, ferries.
Presumably it would have been on everybody's mind that Pierre
Cormier had spent his final days on a boat. The visitors were unaware
that the vast office they were meeting in had once been his, so dili-
gently had he kept his corporate and private lives apart.

The lawyer, Ethan Kennedy, was personable and frank. It was all
straightforward, a matter of some explanation and some signatures.
There was, however, one small item that they might find amusing,
what seemed to have been an uncharacteristic bit of mischief by
Pierre. It had been so out of character that Kennedy had forgotten all
about it by the time he'd found the piece of paper in the file.

It was a brief instruction for a post-mortem celebration. In the event
of his death, Pierre wanted no funeral, no memorial service. He made
no reference to the preferred method for the disposal of his mortal
body, burial or incineration. But he did want a small social gathering
of his family and closest friends, the format to be styled on a function
he had once watched with interest on television, a celebrity roast.
Those present at the roast would each give candid assessments of his
character and life and by the end of the event each would hopefully

have achieved an understanding of Pierre that no individual among them had fully known. He included a short list of people he wanted to attend.

None of this made sense to Cyril. His father even contemplating a memorial event, let alone a roast? The father that he knew had been a very private man, a paragon of professional and personal discretion, an introvert, in fact. His only socializing had been work or golf related.

"So, who's on that list?" he asked.

Everyone in the room that day was on the list, including the lawyer, and also a police officer named Nicholson. The lawyer vaguely remembered who he was. There were familiar names from Pierre's time at Draycor, including a former Draycor chairman, M. J. Brawley, since deceased. The only name that no one recognized was "Ari."

"Ari what?" Aggie Lynch, the ex-wife, asked.

"That's it. Just 'Ari.'"

Kennedy resumed his examination of the one-page document. "He was someone he knew from a restaurant or pub they frequented, somewhere in the east end. There's an address—Danforth Avenue."

Aggie was skeptical. "I never ever heard him mention anyone named Ari. And a pub? I can't imagine Pierre 'frequenting' some dive in the east end. What did you say the name was?"

Aggie was a snob about the geographic destination "east," though she'd been born and raised on Canada's East Coast and her ex-husband was of Middle East extraction. For Aggie Lynch anything east of the Don Valley meant vulgar and not a little unpredictable.

Kennedy glanced again at the single page he was holding. "The pub is called the Only Café. I think I've driven past it. By the way, it's also where he wanted this event, however we describe it, to be held. Furthermore, he wanted this man named Ari to preside."

"The east end," said Aggie Lynch. There was a vaguely incredulous expression on her face. "When would he ever have been in the *east end*? Lois?"

Lois Klein, the young widow, nodded. "I recall that there was someone he'd meet up with occasionally at a little pub I'd never heard of. Someone from back home, I thought. He wrote that, what, five or six years ago?"

"It's dated . . . six days before he disappeared," the lawyer said. "In June 2007."

"Back home? You mean Nova Scotia?" Aggie asked.

"No," said Lois. "Lebanon."

"It *was* five years ago," Kennedy said. "We all know the kinds of pressure he was under. But I think we can assume that this was whimsy on Pierre's part, his way of making light of a sad event, whenever it transpired. He was a young man—I'm sure he thought this was far, far down the road."

Aggie Lynch presumed to speak for all of them: "Well, whim or not, I think we all agree on what you can do with that document." Lois was nodding. The lawyer was already reaching toward the shredder.

"I'd like to have that," Cyril said.

∼

The neighbourhood was unfamiliar to him. At the bar Cyril asked for Ari, not really expecting anyone to know him—not after five years— but the man behind the bar nodded and told Cyril that Ari hadn't been in that evening, though he was a regular.

"He comes and goes." The bartender shrugged.

"How long have you worked here?"

"Eighteen months."

It was a noisy place, long and narrow. It was dark, mostly lit by a row of candles jammed in bottles along the bar and old lawn-sale lamps on small wobbly tables against a wall. He sat on a stool and ordered a beer. The music was from the eighties and the crowd, mostly men, was also of his father's generation. He recognized the Clash. "Should I Stay or Should I Go."

It had been the question at the forefront of Cyril's mind for three weeks, since the meeting with the lawyer. He now knew that single sheet of paper off by heart. Roast. The Only Café. Ari. He knew the words but not the purpose. The mystery behind the words intrigued the journalist he hoped he could become. But he couldn't escape a sense of menace. Finally he shook himself: *Come on, wake up—it's just a pub; he was my dad. What am I afraid of?* He went.

The décor was self-conscious kitsch. A Rolling Stones poster, Mother Teresa, Che. Faded prints of old Impressionists. A portrait of Van Gogh with a bandaged ear. The bar seemed stocked with affordable hard liquor, Scotch and rum and rye. A few bottles of predictable single malts. But there was an impressive display of bottled beer, many brands he'd never heard of. A sign above the cooler read: *The Hall of Foam*. There was absolutely nothing about the place that would have appealed to the father that he knew.

He sipped his beer, eavesdropped on a quiet conversation about city politics. Cyril hadn't voted but was interested in the drama. The bartender paused in front of him and nodded at his glass but Cyril said that he was fine for now. Then he asked, "What's over there?" He pointed toward a heavy curtain just as someone walked through carrying a mug.

"Coffee shop," the barman said. "If that's your thing."

"I think I'll check it out," said Cyril. "Can I take my beer?"

"No problem."

Though it had the same seedy ambience, it was a quieter place. There was more room and more comfortable furniture. He could see the potential on this side of the establishment for a small private gathering. The Only Café was, Cyril decided, exactly the kind of place that would appeal to him and his friends. Relaxed, ironic, respectably grungy, unassuming and cheap. Many of the tables were occupied by young, pensive people staring at their laptop screens, mugs of coffee growing cold, lager growing warm.

He settled into an overstuffed armchair, more mystified than ever about what might have drawn someone like his father to this unlikely place.

He drained his beer, was sorely tempted to have another, to roost for the entire evening in this antiquated armchair. But he quashed the temptation, which he recognized as just another flight fantasy. He'd been having a lot of them of late—peculiar impulses to disappear. He had no destination in mind, but that wasn't the point. The thought was comforting to him.

Cyril took a notebook from his backpack, tore out a page and wrote: *Ari. I think you knew my father, Pierre Cormier. Can we talk sometime?* And signed it. *Cyril B. Cormier.* Then he returned to the liquor side of the establishment and handed the note to the bartender.

"Can you give this to Ari when you see him," he said. The bartender nodded and placed the note on a shelf beside a bottle of Teacher's Highland Cream.

"By the way, what's Ari's last name?"

"I don't know," the bartender said. "How do you know Ari?"

"He knew my dad."

"Ah. So why don't you ask your dad?"

"He passed away."

"Sorry to hear that." Then the bartender leaned closer and said in a low voice. "I don't think Ari has a last name."

∾

His mother often said that Cyril was the spitting image of his father, tall and lean, a mop of curly hair, fashionable glasses. He lacked his father's intense ambition, but he shared his curiosity, his fascination with intrigue. He didn't know much more about his father's nature than what his mother shared, which was brief and usually bitter. When he was only twelve his dad became a stranger who would reappear occasionally from the opaque world of big business and a relationship, soon to be a marriage that, for a while at least, shut Cyril and his mother out.

Pierre never forgot a birthday, though, and the Christmas gifts were always lavish. Once when Cyril was fourteen his father had taken him on a hiking-camping holiday but the experience, as it unfolded over three days of a Thanksgiving weekend, seemed to propel Pierre into a funk that could have been boredom or resentment and was marked by a series of lengthening silences. Silence was not uncommon during their encounters.

Pierre was not a talker, at least where Cyril was concerned. Cyril had learned that he was powerful in a courtroom and a terror when it came to dealing with troublesome investors who sometimes tried to take him on in public. He was vice-president, legal, for Draycor PLC, a mining company with far-flung properties. But Pierre never talked about his work when Cyril was around. And he never talked about his boyhood or, come to think of it, any aspect of his past.

When Pierre engaged at all with Cyril, he had conveyed encouragement about the value of hard work and vision. Minding his own business, appreciating his good fortune to be growing up in a stable, civilized society like Canada. Old-fashioned nostrums, earnestly delivered. Cyril always paid attention, listening attentively for warmth.

He remembered asking, by the sizzling campfire on a drizzly night during that camping trip, if Pierre had ever gone camping with his dad when he was a boy. Pierre was silent for a minute, then laughed. No, he said eventually. There was no camping. He'd grown up poor.

"Do you know what a refugee is?" his father asked.

"There were some in my school," Cyril replied, and waited. "I didn't know them, though." And waited. But his father had relapsed into silence.

He recalled that brief exchange with painful clarity. He now knew that his father too had fled the chaos of a distant war, becoming a refugee in an unlikely place—Cape Breton Island—before moving on to the big time in Toronto.

He said good night to the bartender, slung his backpack over a shoulder and stepped outside. The street was busy and suddenly exotic with clusters of men in deep conversation, men of all ages wearing skullcaps and baggy white cotton trousers, sandals, smocks to their knees; women head to toe in black, faces covered. And then he noticed, just along the street, the mosque and for a moment he had a sense of what might have drawn his father to this unlikely neighbourhood.

～

It was poker night, a ritual each Thursday for Cyril and his friends, guys he'd known since kindergarten. "Poker night" had a ring of innocuous masculinity. "Poker" was a euphemism for escape from work and kids and women.

They didn't always play cards on poker night but when they did it was inevitably blackjack. You only had to have the clarity and concentration to count to twenty-one and that was usually possible no matter how much beer you drank. The guys were in the middle of a hand when Cyril arrived. Poker night always started out at Leo's place. He, like Cyril, was single. But, unlike Cyril, Leo lived alone. The others at the table were married and had nicer places, but at Leo's, you could be loud and clueless. Conversations could be inappropriate and dumb and dirty.

They made space for Cyril at the table, but he fetched a beer instead and receded into a quiet corner of the room. From his backpack he retrieved the document Ethan Kennedy had given him. "Let me know how it all turns out"—the lawyer seemed to mean it.

The guys ignored him, which was protocol. They knew that Cyril was going through a few things and would consult them if and when he had to. They all knew the generalities of his distress: the uncertainty of working as an intern; friction with his mom; a rocky patch with Gloria, his girlfriend; and, of course, the missing dad who had recently been sort of found.

"News?" said Neil.

"None," said Cyril. "All good."

Answering nods and murmurs, everybody studying the cards.

∽

The others were gone and it was just Leo and Cyril.

"I really appreciate you letting me crash here for another night," Cyril said. They clinked their bottles.

"No problem. As long as you like," Leo said. Then the unasked question: What next?

Cyril sighed. "I'll go to Mom's place tomorrow, hang out there for a while."

"You don't have to . . . I mean, your *mom*?"

"She's ordered me to move back in and sort out the mess Gloria left on her doorstep."

"What mess?"

The mess was mostly boxes of his father's books—not a huge collection, but enough to clutter up his mom's verandah with unwelcome reminders of her past. Two days after he'd walked out on her, Gloria had dumped the boxes when Aggie wasn't home. Aggie had never cared for Gloria and it was mutual.

"I can't believe that Gloria would do that, dump everything on Aggie's verandah." Leo was shaking his head.

Cyril laughed. "Everything doesn't add up to much. My clothes. Some books, personal papers. A bunch of diaries or daily journals that Dad kept. I haven't really had the stamina to look at any of it closely. I kinda understand the gesture. Gloria's way of telling me to piss or get off the pot, right?"

"Still, it was a witchy thing to do."

"Don't be too hard on her," said Cyril. "She's been putting up with a lot."

"It's none of my business, but besides the roast . . . ?"

Cyril nodded. "In the will he left me enough to keep me going for a while, at least til I get my shit together. And the books."

"You said diaries?"

"I think so. Journals, day-timers, they're in his handwriting anyway. Maybe someday I'll get up the nerve to take a closer look."

Leo stood and stretched. "Okay." He yawned. "It's time."

"Leo," Cyril said. "I have this nagging feeling . . ."

Leo seemed perplexed. "What about?"

"That my father is still out there somewhere."

"I thought you said there was proof . . . he isn't."

"Yes, but people make mistakes. I think he had secrets. I've dis-covered this pub where it seems he used to hang out."

"Whoa! Your dad hanging out in a pub!" Leo laughed. "You need some sleep. And look, don't feel you have to go to Aggie's. You can stay here for as long as you need to. Consider this your home."

"I wish I could," said Cyril.

∼

Leo rented the second floor of a house on a quiet residential street in Parkdale. It backed up against a high chain-link fence that enclosed a junior high school playing field. There was a scrim of spindly pine trees between the backyard and the fence and because the school left a light on until midnight, the trees cast creepy shadows on the wall above the couch that was Cyril's temporary bed. When there was a breeze the shadows moved like ghosts.

Cyril had been at Leo's for four days, waking up each morning to the tweet of a gym instructor's whistle, the carefree sounds of boys gal-loping around the running track or going through their soccer drills. The percussion of a basketball on asphalt seemed to originate some-where in his pillow. He didn't have to think that far back to find himself among them, when the air and sunshine and the moment were eternal. Something else that changed when Pierre moved out, half his life ago.

Then, when he was nineteen, his father disappeared for good, an open-ended absence that had left him stranded somewhere between sadness and anger. The most comforting scenario was that Pierre was on the run, but if he was, from what or whom?

There were a few facts and they were shared and parsed repeatedly, but they had only yielded other questions. There had been a wharf-side explosion in a remote place, Mabou Coal Mines on Cape Breton Island. There was a sunken, shattered boat. It looked like a propane explosion. But what about the missing body? And what about the rumours of a looming crisis in what had been a magical career? And what about his health, the guarded hints of cancer? Questions adding up in the minds of lawyers, corporate accountants and other cynics to an imaginative disappearing act. Suicide was a tempting answer, too, but in the absence of a body or a note, Pierre Cormier was just gone.

For Cyril the mystery had been a source of hope, a heartbeat that kept Pierre alive, at least in his imagination where he could invent scenarios of reconciliation and even revelation. Basic knowledge— like who his father really was.

And then, on a warm Saturday in June that year, a single bone turned up in an East-Coast lobster trap. His friends had been unable to suppress incredulous chuckles when he told them. But the fisher-man who'd hauled the trap up from the depths quickly understood that he was staring at what the media would delicately call "human remains." There was a fine gold chain entangled in a fractured joint that had once connected the bone to some other part of a skeleton. The chain, a gift from Lois, confirmed that he was dead and the family concurred that this bone fragment was all that anyone would likely ever find of a gifted man named Pierre Cormier.

The moment marked a turning point in many ways. Cyril was living with Gloria and she was taking a rare weekend off. Her work, and his lack of work, had become a matter of tension between them.

She was a first-year associate with a prominent Bay Street law firm. He was in limbo.

But the tension had been set aside that morning. It was a day for lingering, a soft lilac-scented day of idleness and intimacy. And then the phone.

It was Lois and she sounded tense. "Something has come up. About your dad. Can you meet me at your mom's place?"

He felt a flash of fear that swiftly turned to hope: "He's surfaced?"

There was a long pause, then a suppressed ironic laugh. "No. I'm afraid not. I'll explain."

∼

Gloria went with him, though she always found Cyril's mother to be judgmental. She could understand why Aggie had ended up alone. She didn't know Lois but she could imagine the contrast— Lois young and modern, Aggie a container full of prejudice and anger.

His mother's door was open and they'd walked straight into the commotion. Cyril had experienced a deep emotion, somewhere between revulsion and despair, witnessing the two women who had once despised each other now clutching, weeping, comforting. His mother saw him first.

"There you are," she said, wiping her face. "It's all over, dear. He's really gone."

Lois turned and walked toward him, blue eyes flooded, searching his. She seized both his hands, lightly kissing both his cheeks.

"Oh Cyril," she said.

"I'm okay," he mumbled. "What . . ."

"They've turned up proof. A part of his remains."

He was distressed by his lack of emotional reaction to the news. "I don't think you've met Gloria. Gloria Frame."

Lois held her arms out toward Gloria. Her warmth was genuine and it sealed what Gloria had suspected—between Lois Klein and Aggie Lynch there would have been no contest for any healthy man.

"So what's the proof?" asked Cyril.

His mother ignored the question. "Poor Pierre will not be coming home. That's all that matters now."

∾

Leaving there that afternoon he'd tried to engage, to draw Gloria out of what had become an awkward silence halfway through the visit.

"Can you believe it? A fucking bone, it comes down to that."

She wagged her head from side to side, said nothing.

"I mean, it would be funny, in a sick way, if it wasn't real." He looked in her direction, awaiting a response. She was frowning, walking with her arms folded across her chest. She sighed.

"I remember that little chain. Lois gave it to him. I think he said some Holocaust survivor—"

"Cyril. Jesus Christ, I know I shouldn't be so self-absorbed, not on a day like this. But why do I feel invisible around your mother?"

"I'm sorry," he said.

"No," she said. "I'm sorry." And she took his hand.

2.

A phone was ringing on the coffee table. The merry chime of his new BlackBerry. He was sweating, still caught in the anxiety of a dream that evaporated in a sudden panic. Something about him and Lois, or maybe Gloria. They'd kept shifting shapes and faces. He grabbed the phone realizing that he was late for work. He missed the call—he was still trying to figure out the mysteries of the new stupid smartphone, a gift to himself when he first got the call inviting him to intern. There was a message. It was his producer-mentor, Hughes, wondering if he'd forgotten the meeting scheduled for—half an hour from now.

He'd have to take a cab. He quickly washed his face, pulled on jeans and sandals. Sniffed through T-shirts in his backpack until he found one that was odour-neutral. Grabbed a jacket and the backpack and headed out the door. Luckily a cab was dropping someone off across the street.

∿

The meeting was already underway when he arrived. There were ten people in the room and they all turned as he closed the door behind him, nodding and mumbling apologies. It was obviously important because the anchor, Lloyd Manville, was on the speaker-phone from home. Cyril's face was flushed and underneath his jacket the T-shirt was already soaked. He could imagine noxious fumes creeping out of his armpits. Doc Savage, the executive producer, was staring at him as he clumsily sat down, then pointed at him with his pen. The sweaty T-shirt suddenly felt clammy. Savage turned toward the speaker-phone that sat like a large and menacing insect on the middle of the boardroom table and spoke to it. "Suzanne, he's here now . . . what was it you wanted to ask?'

Suzanne Reynolds was the network's star correspondent. She was in London, on her way to cover some aspect of the civil war in Syria, an expanding story that, for the whole month he'd been working as an intern, he'd been struggling to understand. The prospect of being asked a question by Suzanne in front of everyone was terrifying.

"Hello, Cyril." Her voice crackled through the speaker.

"Hi," he replied.

"You'll have to speak up," Doc said.

Cyril leaned forward, pulse racing.

"Cyril," Suzanne said, "I'm trying to remember something you told me just before I headed for the airport."

There was no trace of the annoyance he was braced for. He felt a flood of warmth.

"Something about Lebanon," she said. "Some family connection."

"My dad." He had to clear his throat. He repeated more loudly, "My dad. He was from there."

"That was it," Suzanne said. "I can't remember if you told me whether you've ever been, yourself. I'm sorry. My brain is tired."

"No," he replied. "Never."

"But you'd have family there."

"I suppose so," he said. "My father never mentioned . . ."

"Can I ask something personal?"

"Sure," he replied.

"Is your dad a Christian?"

"I know he was a Catholic, but he wasn't much for religion."

"Uh-huh. And do you happen to know where he came from, exactly."

"I'm afraid not."

"Would you mind asking him?"

"My dad is, uh, dead."

"Oh Jesus, I'm sorry." She seemed to mean it. "You didn't mention that."

"It's okay," he said.

"But there was something else," she said. "I asked you about your name."

"Cyril Cormier," he said.

"No, no," she continued. "Your middle name. Where it came from. The 'B.'"

"Oh," he said. "Bashir?"

Someone in the room exhaled loudly.

Cyril stared around the table but nobody bothered to explain the significance of Bashir, assuming that he was familiar with the violent politics of his father's homeland. He had no idea why his name was interesting and became quickly lost as the discussion shifted to Syria and its potential to cause havoc in Lebanon, maybe even reignite a civil war that seemed, Hughes observed in passing, to have been going on intermittently since the dawn of time.

Mercifully nobody asked him to contribute, and he was relieved when they decided to send Suzanne to Beirut where she'd prepare a long analysis of how Syria was exacerbating old sectarian hostilities in Lebanon, splitting up communities and forging unlikely alliances between . . .

Cyril maintained an attitude of rapt agreement, reinforced by the occasional strategic nod. As soon as this was over the Google-oracle would help him to discover everything he needed to know, starting with the name Bashir. Then he remembered the BlackBerry in his pocket. He opened up the browser, went to Google, typed in *Lebanon Bashir*. Google answered quickly with *Lebanon Bashir Massacre*.

"And there's a great story," Hughes was saying, "if we can get at it, about the weapons trade. Beirut is probably crawling with Saudi and Iranian arms dealers who are supplying the militias in Syria."

Suzanne asked, "What about a look-back at the Sabra and Shatila massacre? We're coming up to the thirtieth anniversary."

"I don't think so," said the exec. "We did the twenty-fifth anniversary and I don't think there's enough new to say about it."

"Whatever," said Suzanne. "Let's keep an open mind if I'm going to be there anyway."

"Right, then," said Doc. "Check in when you get to Beirut and we'll see where we go from there." He stood and turned toward Cyril. "You okay?"

Cyril tried to smile. "Yeah, great."

"Come see me in half an hour. I have some ideas to run by you."

∾

Alone in his cubicle with Wikipedia he discovered that the name Bashir is Arabic for "the one who brings good news." Perhaps an omen. *Bashir.* The perfect name for a reporter. His spirits lifted, but then his phone rang and he saw Gloria's name in the display. He let the call ring through to voicemail. Not a chance there would be good news there.

He winced remembering their final confrontation just five nights earlier. There had been growing tension. Unemployment does that. Then he got the internship, but the strain between them only worsened and he realized it came from somewhere deeper. "All you fucking do is work," he had complained. "But at least you get a paycheque. At least they have something real invested in you, they have you working in reality . . ."

"Well, quit," she shouted. "For Christ's sake quit and find something else to do. But for God's sake stop the whining."

It was just a word, but it hit him like a hammer. Whining? What more emasculating word might she have used?

"Good idea," he shouted back. "Maybe it's time for a lot of things to change."

"Fine," she'd said, arms folded. He'd walked toward the door and she'd said nothing. And then he was on the wrong side of the door, panic rising. Everything he owned was inside. Hastily he'd patted his rear end, felt the wallet. Well, at least he had that. Reached into his jacket pocket. Cellphone. Thank God, the lifeline. He'd walked off into the night.

He'd been wandering for about an hour when he realized he'd rather die than face his mother. He considered suicide but realized he really didn't want to die, and even if he did, he was at a loss to think of a method that wasn't grossly messy, not to mention painful. He sat in a small park for a while but felt vulnerable there. Then he thought of Leo's.

There were moments in the days that followed when the billows of regret would leave him gasping like a beached fish. Small zephyrs of elation would catch him by surprise—a future unhindered by any obligation. He could become a world traveller. He could live his fantasies of sexual philandering. No ties. No emotional connection *to anyone*. He could become anything he wanted. But such freedom flashes were nothing more than pinpricks in the more pervasive darkness.

He'd look at himself in the mirror in moments of real vertigo and groan. Twenty-four years old, no home, no job, no class. Loser. All his friends had lives, even Leo who had been considered all through school to be the slow learner. "Developmentally delayed," was how the system phrased it. Bullies pestered Leo, nicknamed him "the retard." Not now—Leo the ironworker, high rigger, fearless.

Cyril was, supposedly, the bright one. But Cyril was nothing. Zip. An unpaid zero at the age of twenty-four. Lack of purpose, as his father often commented, is a waste of life.

~

Okay, loser. Just admit it. You miss her. Yes. Painfully. He studied his cellphone for a moment, the small red light winking, daring him to listen. In spite of the dread of even deeper pain, he opened voicemail, entered his password.

"I hope you're okay," she said. And after a long silence, "I hope you'll get in touch when you feel up to it." Long pause. "Anytime you want to talk. And look . . . about the books and things I dropped at your mom's . . . I didn't mean it to be what it looks like. Okay?"

He felt lighter, instantly. And then the desk phone interrupted. It was the boss. "I'm free just now. Come on by."

~

Doc Savage was standing at a window in his corner office, hands in pockets. "Come here," he said. He placed a collegial hand on Cyril's shoulder, pointing out. "Do you know what that building is?"

It was a bland, mustard-coloured building across the street, about seven storeys high. "That's where the Canadian spies work," he said. "The Canadian Security Intelligence Service. Right next to the SkyDome, or whatever name it goes by now. And the CN Tower. The symbolism, eh. Authority and amusement, cheek by jowl. A few years ago a bunch of young jihadists had a scheme to blow the whole fucking thing up, including us. Sometimes—just between you and me and the lamppost—I can understand the impulse. You might recall it. We broke the story."

He turned his back to the window. "So what do you think? Those Lebanon ideas." He walked around his desk and sat, gesturing toward a chair. "I guess I don't have to tell you. Poor old Lebanon. Downstream from all the shit in Europe and the Middle East. Even Africa. All shit-streams flow toward Lebanon. And Syria is no exception."

A small internal voice instructed Cyril to say nothing. Easier to look intelligent than to sound intelligent when you know bugger all. But the boss was watching him, reading signs.

Doc's real name was Arthur. Arthur Savage. He'd picked up the nickname from an old-timer who was a fan of an American writer, Doc Savage, who specialized in heroic novels based on the wild frontier mythologies that everyone believed back in the day.

"I think it was a good call," Cyril said after a long pause. "Suzanne in Beirut." He was careful with the pronunciation. *Bay-root*. First week on the job he'd pronounced Hebron *Hee-bron* and realized that everyone was staring at him. He'd also screwed up Buenos Aires. *Boynas Airies*. He was corrected: *Bwaynose Eye-rays*. "Beirut," he said. "Historically a window on the region. And a better place to get perspective than in the middle of the conflict." A summary of what he'd heard several others say at the meeting.

"Good," said Doc. "Keep an eye on it, read the wires. You might try to get a sense of the sectarian splits. Use whatever personal contacts you have. Everything in Lebanon is personal. Especially the grudges. But why am I telling you?"

Cyril was nodding. *Wires?*

"Work with Hughes on this. He knows the place inside out. I think he was born over there, back whenever. The other stuff, I wouldn't waste my time. Arms dealers . . . nothing that we can contribute from this end. And Sabra and Shatila? Anniversaries of massacres bore the snot out of me." He stood. "One other thing. The better story might be here in our own backyard. Those young guys who got caught plotting to blow up the spies next door—I'm sure they weren't the only ones with something like that in the back of their hot little heads. Think about it."

Cyril stood. "Sure," he said. "Thanks."

"I'll get the library to send some stuff to your desk and you can go through it. Summarize it for me. We're going to be needing a lot of archival stuff. Boil it all down to say, a page, and shot-list the best footage. I think it would be useful for you, just getting to see what other people do. Right?"

"Sure," Cyril repeated.

"And don't be shy about saying what you think."

"Not a problem," Cyril said.

3.

Cyril walked from the office to Aggie's place, which gave him forty-five minutes for reflection on how he was going to handle her. She'd see his homecoming as some kind of moral victory. Of course she would. It would have been a stretch to say he loved his mother. The mutual dependency of a single-parent household made them more like siblings. But he respected her. She was tough and sentimental in the way of Irish women. Her anger had an overlay of sorrow that made her volatile and difficult to read when she was riled.

She'd regarded his departure from their home so he could live with Gloria as nothing short of a betrayal, which had led to an epic shouting match about society and sin. It might have left him feeling guilty had he not been so familiar with her tearful rage. He wasn't exactly afraid of her. He just didn't like to fight with her because he always lost.

Cyril knew of only two people who could intimidate her—*his* father and *hers*, Pius Lynch, an old coal miner who had learned to channel a natural aggression through murky union politics in Nova Scotia, where she was from. What Pierre and Pius had in common was an ability to impose an overbearing silence on the most agitated situations. With little more than an unflinching stare, they could drain a moment of its passion. The stare would say: this really isn't worth continuing because of what might well come next.

Cyril envied that quality, but didn't have it. He was, as his mother often told him, "*too* Irish and *too* Mediterranean." His flight from Gloria's had been typically impetuous. Now what?

She'd said, in the phone message: "I hope you're okay . . . I hope you'll get in touch when you feel up to it . . ." She'd almost apologized about the books. The beginning of reconciliation? Or mere kindness. No matter. He was on his way back home, to Aggie's, square one. He couldn't have imagined this a month ago.

He was walking through a small urban park, not far from the university. The mid-September air was still heavy with the smog of summer. The park was busy. Students burdened by debts, anxieties and backpacks; a circle of boys, kicking a soccer ball; two black women curating a flock of white kids who were throwing water at each other. On a bench, an older man sat with a pretty blond woman who was conspicuously younger, maybe even Cyril's age. They were staring straight ahead at nothing in particular, his arm relaxed across her shoulders. Her hands were folded on her lap. Colleagues? Her father? Her lover? Their expressions were too calm to be revealing.

Cyril stopped, fished his phone from his jacket pocket, speed-dialled Gloria's number. Got voicemail. "Hi. You've reached Gloria Frame. I can't take your call just now . . ."

He was instantly jealous. Where was she? Then he remembered: Friday night, drinks with other first-year associates in commercial litigation. It was routine. Team building, she called it with a roll of her lovely emerald eyes. "Hi," he said into his phone. "It's only me. I miss you awfully." And instantly regretted that he had said it.

~

Mary Agnes Lynch lived in a neighbourhood where people mostly left their doors unlocked. Her street was lined with sheltering maples that were ancient, and grand houses built for large families, constructed uniformly of weathered brick but subtly distinguished from each other by a corner tower, or wooden dormer, or verandah. There were oak trees somewhere, probably in backyards, judging from the distinctive leaves that would mysteriously show up on lawns and sidewalks every autumn. Cyril noted that the dead leaves, the great annual ordeal when he was living there, were already starting to appear.

Growing up on Banting Avenue he'd always been conscious of how few kids there were, which, now that he was older and more obser-vant, probably explained the lack of contact among the residents. Some streets, he knew from friends, become communities. Without children, a street like Banting was just another pretty urban road.

He'd never seen a fire truck on the street. People aged, ailed and failed here, but never seemed to need an ambulance. He was never able to determine how stricken people, not to mention dead ones, were evacuated without anybody noticing. Families broke down and marriages broke up but when people left the street they did so quietly. The only time that Cyril ever saw a cop car on his mother's street was on a day in late June 2007, when they got the news that Pierre Cormier was gone.

Aggie's door was locked, something new since he'd moved out, perhaps a rare admission of vulnerability. He knelt, tilted the heavy cast-iron planter by the front door, felt under it for the hidden key. No key. He then wrestled it aside impatiently, revealing the rusty circle that marked the spot the awkward ornament had occupied for decades, but there was nothing. He had to ring the doorbell and would wait a good three minutes before he heard her footsteps on a stairway.

He noted that she had dressed for him in a black turtleneck and dark brown slacks that accentuated her slimness. Aggie paid a lot of attention to her appearance, as is frequently the case with women who are strong, even after abandonment. She had a fine feminine figure maintained by careful eating habits and long daily walks. She also smoked cigarettes for appetite suppression but was beginning to suffer subtle consequences—microscopic lines around the mouth, underneath the eyes—nicotine effects she recognized but, so far, was able to mitigate with cream and powder, though the powder now seemed to highlight facial fuzz he'd never noticed. Her hair, a healthy mass she usually kept bundled high on the back of her head, was auburn, but, it seemed to Cyril, trending toward a more dramatic shade of red.

He leaned in, she turned a cheek, closed her eyes, he kissed. She turned without a word, took his hand and led him in. He sensed maternal warmth and it made him feel like running.

∾

She offered a drink and he accepted. "A Scotch. Neat." Neat meant strong and he felt he needed reinforcement. He sat and waited. And when she came back she had two glasses and the decanter which she placed between them on a coffee table that never ceased to remind him of the terrible spring day twelve years earlier when Pierre Cormier had exited their lives the first time. She stared at him for what seemed to be a long time. Then poked at an ice cube with a long forefinger.

"I'm glad you're back," she said.

He held up a cautioning hand, smiling. "I don't know for how long. I've been staying with a friend. He said I could move in."

"However long," she said, "I'm glad to see you. We really have to try—"

"You don't have to say—"

"No, I mean to say . . . I . . . have to try harder."

He sipped his drink, trying to suppress resentment. Her contrition couldn't quite conceal an irritating smugness. He put the glass back on the coffee table. It had a heavy glass top set in a stainless steel tubular frame. There was a book of paintings by Ken Danby. Kid in a hoodie sitting on a shore, looking out. He remembered his father's feet, firmly planted there. Pierre standing on the coffee table. The golf ball where the book is.

"When are you going to get rid of this?" he asked, nodding toward the coffee table. "I'd have thought by now . . ."

"If you only knew how much we paid for it."

"I'm sure you could get your price in a flash. Let me put it on Kijiji or something."

"Oh, come on," she said, with a dismissive wave. "Think of all the history . . ."

"Don't."

She was smiling. "You let too many things bother you."

He shrugged, remembering how things had bothered her.

"Do you understand now what I've been saying all along?"

"What have you been saying all along?"

His mother just shook her head, studying him. "I should have left the mess . . . the clothes, the books, boxes of them. Just dumped there . . ."

"You don't know her side of it."

"There's no excuse."

"She's under a lot of stress, starting out at a big law firm. You have no idea."

"I was married to a lawyer."

"You were married to a mining executive."

"Let's not argue. I'm glad to see you. How are things where you are, the new job?"

"It's hardly a job, Mom."

"You have to start somewhere and I'm glad you got your foot in the door. I'm proud. I tell people . . ."

He grimaced but before he could respond, the doorbell rang. "Who can that be," Aggie said, stood and left the room.

Loud female voices. He recognized the laugh: Lois. Then his mother sounding like a little girl. *Petey, give Grandma a hug.* He cringed. Petey. Grandma? His four-year-old half-brother. Quietly he exited the room, through the kitchen, up the back stairway.

∾

The books were neatly piled in banker's boxes along a wall in what had been, and now it seemed would again be, his bedroom. He'd counted the books at Gloria's—there were two hundred and seven of them, textbooks from Pierre's law school days in Halifax, crime fiction, a three-volume history of Irish nationalism, a gift from Pius Lynch. One title caught his eye, *The Most Distressful Country,* which might have accurately described a dozen places he was now trying to become familiar with. There were many books about the Middle East. Lois had suggested he take them off her hands when it became clear, at least to her, that Pierre was never coming back.

He noticed that the lid on one of the boxes had been opened. The diary box—he hadn't really examined any of them, other than to count them. He carried it to the bed and dumped the journals out. There were twenty-four of them. The earliest were cheap stenographer's notebooks, the first from 1983. The writing was squiggly Arabic. By book four his father was writing in English that was equally indecipherable to him. He searched through the pile for the year 2000.

It was a real book with a hard black cover. A daily planner for the epic year. His hand was shaking when he turned to May 26. The entry was written clearly but it was just as unrevealing. *Cool clear Friday. Home early.* That was it, except for one loaded phrase at the bottom of the page: *Over and out.*

He turned the page. May 27. *Royal York. Long talk with Ag. Acrimonious. One of those days you don't forget. Rocket Richard died today.*

Cyril sat for what felt like a long time, staring through his bedroom window. He hadn't even realized that his father followed hockey. Then he remembered a Christmas when his dad presented him with skates. But he was unable to recall if he'd ever worn them. There was a hockey stick but he did remember that he'd given it away, to someone.

A massive maple tree stood just outside his window and at night it seemed to breathe aloud, a calming sound that invariably led to a merciful unconsciousness. *Over and out.* Three words that would sum up the next seven years of all their lives. He took a deep breath, then fished through the pile for the 2007 journal, but he couldn't find it.

Cyril waited on the landing at the top of the stairway, listening for voices. Silence. But when he entered the living room they were still there, Aggie and Lois sitting quietly, studying their coffee mugs. The little boy, Pete, was on the floor with a colouring book, scrawling. Cyril was about to retreat but his mother spotted him. "I was wondering where you got to. Say hello to your little brother. Petey, will you look who's here?"

The little boy scrambled to his feet, went to his mother, pressed against her thigh. She hoisted him onto her lap. "That's Cyril," Lois said. "Your big brother. Say hello to Cyril." Petey glared. Cyril took a seat just inside the door. "Hi, Lois," he said.

Lois smiled and nodded and, as she often did, responded like a ventriloquist, through Petey, now Petey the Puppet. "Hi, big brother Cyril. Someday I'm going to be as big and handsome as you are." Cyril forced a smile. Pete squirmed out of his mother's lap and returned to his colouring book.

At the meeting in the lawyer's office Lois had seemed tense, distant. A little bit uncertain. Even though she was only, what—Christ, still only twenty-nine—she'd looked much older, very much the melancholy widow. Now she was refreshed, a new hairstyle that flopped off to one side and obscured much of her forehead and right cheek, a side part on the left.

"You look good, Lois," he said.

She smiled. "How is the new job working out?"

"It's interesting," he said.

"I can imagine." Her look was an appraisal—of what, he was not entirely sure.

"Let me refresh your coffee," Aggie said. "Cyril, can I get you something?"

Cyril remembered his whisky glass. "I put a drink down somewhere."

"It's on the kitchen counter. You can get us some fresh coffee while you're up."

Lois said, "No more for me. We have to be going. I have a babysitter coming and I want to get him settled down before." She turned to Cyril. "So have they got you working on any interesting stories?"

"They've got me following the stuff in Syria, the Middle East."

"My God," said Lois. "I hope you aren't thinking of going."

"No fear of that. We have someone in Beirut."

"Beirut," said Lois. "Your dad so wanted to go back there to visit. We were in the middle of planning a trip in 2006, when everything erupted." She studied the floor for a moment, then remembered Pete. "What do you think, Pete? Should we be going?"

Aggie's face had become expressionless. "One thing I never heard him talk about, the old country," she said.

∽

"You were gone a while," his mother said, picking up the coffee cups. "Lois was asking where you'd disappeared to."

"What was that about?"

"Just touching base about the will. Everything is fine."

"No fine print? No surprises?"

"Nothing has changed. She's been perfectly fair and up front all along. You know that."

Cyril laughed. "I remember when you weren't quite so charitable, when she first informed you she had all the legal power."

"That was then. She came through. She really is a good person and you should make an effort to—"

"I didn't feel like socializing."

"You were upstairs?"

"Yes."

"You saw where I put the books?"

"Yes."

He spotted what was left of his whisky on the counter, near the sink. He found the bottle, refreshed the drink. "You?" he asked. She shook her head.

"I was looking at the diaries," he said.

"Oh God. Maybe that isn't such a good idea."

"There seems to be one missing."

"Oh?"

"The last one, 2007."

She shrugged, turned toward the sink. "Don't look at me. By the way, she has a boyfriend."

"Oh?"

She turned the tap on. "Somebody she met over the Internet. If you can imagine. The risks people take. And for what." She was shaking her head.

"Mom, what do you remember of the day he left?"

She turned off the tap, studied him. "Why do you ask?"

"Do you remember him standing on the coffee table, with the golf club?"

"Golf club? Standing on a table? You must be dreaming."

~

Cyril was alone in the living room, nursing a third glass of whisky. And Pierre was there again, blind to his son's existence as it seemed he always had been. Strange how Cyril had so often felt invisible in his father's presence. Pierre hadn't even noticed Cyril near the kitchen entrance to the living room. He seemed to be entranced, standing on the precious coffee table. Bare feet, but just the same. The coffee table he wasn't even supposed to put a drink on without a coaster. His father standing on it. Unbelievable. Perhaps, for once, Cyril wanted to be invisible, cringing there against the wall.

His dad in jeans and a T-shirt, bare feet. He had a golf club clutched before him. Cyril wasn't much into golf but it looked like a nine-iron. And there was a ball on the table. Pierre kept tapping at the ball to keep it from rolling, swaying his hips. Then he swung the golf club, swift and hard.

There was the familiar *click* and the ball was gone. Cyril cringed before he realized that the patio doors were wide open. The ball sailed through. Then he heard the *whack* as the ball bounced off the high wooden fence that surrounded their backyard.

Pierre fished another ball from his jeans pocket, bent low, placed it on the glass before him, tapped it into position, then swung again. *Click. Bam*, off the fence. His face was calm, the expression satisfied. He bent again. Another ball, another swing. This time a slight metallic scrape and a less clearly articulated *click*. And no responding *bam* from the back fence. Instead, a brief silence as the ball cleared the top of the fence, and then a shocking crash, glass shattering next door.

Pierre hefted the golf club, studying the shaft with an accusing expression. Then Aggie was in the room. "*What* in the name of *Jesus* . . ."

But Pierre was now down from the coffee table, walking toward the door, the golf club swinging like a vaudeville cane. Bare feet, no sound, no backward glance.

TWO

PIERRE

4. *June 23, 2007*

The days since his arrival in Cape Breton had been awash in early summer sunshine, but now as he scanned the distance for the elusive pilot whales, the sun was dim behind a low scrim of cloud. The darkened sea rolling gently in a light breeze had tricked him at least a dozen times into thinking that he'd spotted a glistening dorsal fin. He turned off the motor, let the *Miriam* drift, struggling to clear his mind. He'd attended yoga classes with Lois but had never succeeded in finding that empty inner place where he might experience enlightenment. She'd repeatedly assured him that such a place exists and he'd been tempted to respond that the people who are able to meditate are probably the people who need it least—people with pure hearts and clean consciences.

Then the whales, really dolphins, according to something he'd read, materialized around him. The arched backs, *shoosh* of mist as the animals exhaled so close that he could smell the rancid breath. First one, as if out of nowhere, then another. And another. Even though he'd been looking for them the intrusion caught him by surprise.

His palatial Draycor office was a world away. Contrast is escape, he thought. Mick Brawley, the CEO and master of that distant world, had put it more directly. *A change is as good as a rest.* It was a phrase that had impressed him when he was still struggling to perfect the language. Even now he appreciated the simple insights in clichés.

He'd produced his phone, scrolling through the photographs. *Let me show you something.*

And Brawley, who kept a sailboat somewhere in the Virgin Islands, was impressed. *A little beauty, what's her name?*

The Miriam. She's not a sailboat, obviously. She gets me where I want to be. Diesel powered. That's where I'll be staying.

Miriam. Lovely. Old girlfriend? He'd cuffed Pierre lightly on the shoulder, grinning.

No. No. I had a sister whose name was Miriam.

Aha.

And there had been a long glance full of questions. *Had?* Past tense? But there was no time and no need to risk the human bonding. Pierre was leaving on a holiday because he had to disappear. Temporarily, at least.

We'll call you when we need you. God willing we won't have to bother you.

There are loose ends.

Nothing we can't handle from here. You've done good work. We've got your back.

I appreciate it. Lois never questioned him—that was the thing. But the last few months had been a strain. And then he'd had to take the sudden trip to Indonesia.

Indofuckingnesia?

We have an issue there. I won't be gone long.

She'd groaned. *Issue? What kind of issue?*

Issue. How he loved that word. Was there a word in any of his other languages, the Arabic, the French, the scraps of Hebrew, with such a functional obscurity? He couldn't think of another word that muddied meaning so strategically, that lacked the urgency of crisis.

We have a situation that needs clearing up.

Well, I surely hope you won't be long. What could be so urgent in Indonesia?

I could ask Cyril to move in, to keep an eye on things while I'm away.

Cyril? I don't think so.

It is easy to feign accommodation in a marriage but the real test is in the willingness to put up with absences and mysteries. He'd loved her for her acceptance of the travel, the lost weekends, his past life. At least the past she knew about—his connection to Cape Breton Island, a place that didn't interest her.

And when the issue didn't go away in Indonesia, when the issue turned into a human tragedy and, eventually, a potential corporate catastrophe, his absence from the office and the city had become a matter of some urgency. *Out of sight, out of mind, hopefully.*

He remembered how her eyes had welled up. *My God, Pierre. Is this really necessary?*

From her point of view, the timing couldn't have been worse, but her perspective was entirely personal. Health and family and future, personal security.

I can't explain it now. They're worried about controversy. They're trying to protect us. Me, you. Anyway, I need a break. And how far away is Cape Breton anyway?

Have you talked to the doctor?

Yours or mine?

Don't be funny. You know what I'm talking about.

Like I said, I'm just a phone call away.

If truth were told, and he hoped that it would be told some day, the idea of Cape Breton made Lois insecure. It's where Aggie came from, where Pierre had found a home with Aggie's help at a time when Lois was still a toddler in Forest Hill. Aggie and Pierre. Lois hated to be reminded of that old bond but Aggie was a central part of his reality. Lois had no choice but to accept her, just as she had come to terms with Cyril, not only as a stepson but as a friend. She never challenged Pierre about the need for playing second fiddle to a job. Not even now, as she sat alone in the swelter of an early summer in the city, hot and heavy with their unborn child.

∾

How did it begin? As with so many large events, a phone was ringing. He was near the door on his way to work. He'd let it ring. It was in mid-February. He was preoccupied—the urgencies of corporate executives, board members, shareholders, other lawyers.

Lois called him at the office later. "I just checked the answering machine . . . there was a message from the doctor's office. You should call him. Some test they want you to repeat."

"He didn't say what test?"

"No."

He was sure it was the piss test. Something in his blood sugar. He worried constantly about diabetes, the plague of men who lived as he did—too much alcohol, too little exercise, too much comfort food. At least once a week he promised to clean up his act, go on the wagon for a while, join a gym. He had to take better care of himself. His wife was almost twenty years younger than he was. Just twenty-four years old, he thought with a mix of joy and apprehension. He'd looked up his doctor's number right away.

It's your PSA . . .

He had to ask. He hadn't even realized that among the blood tests after his routine physicals, so blandly reassuring time after time, there was one that tracked a part of his anatomy he'd never really thought about. He'd heard of prostate cancer but associated it with the many ailments of old men.

What about my PSA?

The doctor wants you to do another one. It's probably an error, or anomaly. When can you come in?

Synchronicity. Another word he loves. English is so rich, an endless revelation of its power to convey meaning or obscure it, nothing he could have guessed from the rudimentary English he'd acquired while growing up in Lebanon.

Two synchronized crises in the past six months, pulling him in opposite directions, personal survival pitted against the interests of shareholders and corporate executives. A humiliating process he could never have imagined, strangers digging in his ass, extracting tissue; his own forensic dig into the anatomy of corporate and political misconduct at the ass-end of the world.

Perhaps, he thought, Cape Breton isn't far enough away.

And, as suddenly as they'd appeared, the whales were gone. A light breeze stirred and the only sound was the soft smack of water on the rocking boat. He went below to fetch binoculars. He scanned the puckered sea around him but he was alone again, alone with his secrets and his fears.

~

The doctor had a kind face and the eyes of a statistician. His specialty was cancer, so a large part of his job was calculating odds. He was a European, maybe French or Belgian, and he reminded Pierre of someone, someone from the distant past who had warned him about optimism, how easily it can become delusional.

He thought of Lois as he listened to this cancer doctor, studying the eyes, struggling to concentrate on the words, listening for realistic hope to take away, to sustain them both. Listening for optimism. I'm a gambler now, he thought. Our lives, from now on, will depend on luck. And lies. Merciful evasions.

"You have cancer," the doctor said. "Okay? Cancer is serious. Let's not minimize that. I'd rather tell you that you didn't. But the biopsy results are clear. So let's talk about what you have and what we're going to do about it going forward. Okay?"

Going forward? A phrase that always sounded odd. Going forward to success. He heard condescension in the phrase. *Con/de/scen/sion*. One of the first big English words he'd absorbed because it captured perfectly what he'd been hearing in the voices and seeing in the faces of his new countrymen in those confusing early days in Canada. Until he was able to make Canadians forget that he was foreign. But here it is again. The patronizing tone. Another English word he liked: *pat/ro/niz/ing*.

But Pierre was really focused on that one loaded word. *Cancer*. A word that until recently was a synonym for death. He could have handled that. *You're going to die. Soon.* He had experience in contemplating death as an immediate possibility. More than once, a probability. Death he could deal with. It was uncertainty that daunted him and in the instant that it took for the doctor to say that one word, two stunning syllables—*kan/sir*—all certainty had drained out of his existence. And for the first time in many years he felt vulnerable. He had cancer. He was, once again, a foreigner.

"The good news, I suppose," Pierre said, "is that I'm relatively young and healthy."

"Yes," the doctor said. "But it's an aggressive cancer and it's widespread in the gland." He consulted a sheaf of documents. "Nine out of the twelve core samples are cancerous. In four cores the Gleason score is eight. Not good. The others show a cancer we call 'indolent,' low Gleason. I'll be discussing this with the team but I'm hoping we can move forward quickly and . . . aggressively."

"Can I see what you're reading?"

"It wouldn't mean anything to you."

∽

The urologist had been generous with his time. He spoke clearly and carefully, setting out the treatment options. They had to face the likelihood of surgery. Very soon. Pierre scanned information handouts while the doctor spoke. The boilerplate was meant to be reassuring but horrifying words leapt from the pages: depression; incontinence; impotence. Unpredictable.

"We have every reason for optimism," the doctor said. "If I was a betting man—which I'm not—I'd not hesitate . . ."

Later, standing in the vast car park, Pierre wondered why the doctor had stopped short of finishing his sentence. Not hesitate to what? Bet a bundle on the outcome going forward? So why couldn't he have said so? And then Pierre, the lawyer, realized: liability. The doctor caught himself before he committed to a possibility he couldn't guarantee. He'd started to say something human but remembered that compassion might come back to bite him.

Wow, he thought. Liability, his specialty. He was a lawyer. He could relate to that. And he was perplexed then, wondering exactly where he'd parked his car. And then he remembered that he'd arrived by taxi.

∾

He'd called Lois from the cab and she picked up even before he heard the ring.

"What are you doing?" he asked.

A thousand phone calls had started playfully: *What are you doing? What are you thinking? What are you wearing?* Playful was their norm.

"Where are you?" she replied.

"In a cab."

"So what was all that about? Nothing serious, I hope."

"Oh, it's about my PSA . . ."

Silence.

"You know the—"

"Yes, what about it? You've had how many of these tests now? How long does it take anyway?"

"I need some more tests."

"Shit."

"It's really nothing to worry about. The way he explained it, half . . . more than half . . . the male population is walking around with scary PSAs they don't even know about."

"What do you mean by *that*?"

"Joking," he said.

"So what's next?"

"No big rush to do anything."

Lie number one.

"So what exactly did he say, Pierre."

"He said it's too soon to say anything for sure."

"Come home."

"I have to go to the office." It hadn't really been a lie, he told himself. What is cancer, anyway? Rogue cells. Everybody has them.

~

The meeting was already underway. Brawley was sitting at the head of a large oval table. He had his jacket on, a sign that he was there to listen. Shirt sleeves were a sign of hands-on micromanagement. M. J. Brawley was a legend in the mining world, the self-made Draycor CEO and chairman of the board. He was a tough man, fond of telling how he'd started out on an old-fashioned mucking machine on rails in some long-forgotten scab copper mine in northern Quebec back in the sixties. He paid particular attention to international operations.

"Ah, there you are, good," Brawley said.

"Medical appointment," Pierre explained, sitting down.

"Nothing serious?"

"Routine. What's happening?"

"Shit is what's happening," Brawley said.

"Work stoppage at Puncak mine," Ethan Kennedy added.

"Work stoppage? How'd they manage that? Puncak is a model of industrial harmony, for Christ's sake."

"It's what we used to call a 'wildcat strike' in the old days," Kennedy said grimly.

Brawley said, "I just want to get a sense of where this came from, where it's going. Just in case I have to brief the board. Okay? So you guys just talk."

Puncak mine in Indonesia was the golden goose in Draycor's international portfolio of mining assets. The talk around the board-room table acknowledged that they had always been uneasy—in principle—about the disparity in wages between the locals and the "professionals" from outside, many of them Canadians.

Western New Guinea was a complex place at the best of times, half of a divided island with a decades-old insurgency that was repressed by Indonesia's heavy-handed security apparatus. Draycor tried hard to stay above the politics, but where there is systemic exploitation, distinctions between the human and the mineral are often blurred. The wage disparity had become the issue and the issue had become political.

Ethan Kennedy was pragmatic. "It's apples and oranges compar-ing our guys with the locals. But it doesn't take much to stir people up and conditions have been ripe for political agitation. And that's what's going on. We have to consider that we could be caught in the middle of something nastier than a pissing match about money. The money we can deal with, I think." He looked toward Brawley, waiting.

"How much of this is getting picked up by the media?" Brawley asked.

"None of it," said Kennedy. "And if it continues to play out the way it's going now, it isn't going to hit the radar anywhere. Certainly not here."

"So what are we suggesting?"

"Pierre?" Kennedy smiled at him.

"We have good people on the ground," Pierre said. "They're talking, right? We might want to throw some money at this at some point. I've been thinking of a sweetened bonus system. But that isn't up to me. For my part I think we keep close tabs on the negotiations, get them back to work and hope, fingers crossed, that the place will be up and running fairly quickly."

"I think we should set a time frame," Brawley said.

"Not a bad idea," Pierre said. "As long as it stays flexible."

"I say we give the fuckers until next Wednesday." Brawley stood. "Every day we lose is lost revenue plus it will make the start-up harder. Idle equipment underground goes to rat-shit in a hurry."

"The union is letting maintenance in," Kennedy said. "They're being reasonable in that regard."

"Good for them," said Brawley. "Pierre, get your bags packed. We may want you on the ground sooner rather than later, and be prepared to stay there for as long as it's gonna take to make an assessment. I worry our guy Harrison is losing control of this and I'm gonna recommend a stronger company presence at the table. Okay, Pierre? All due respect to Harrison, I need someone on the ground with bigger balls."

"Sure," Pierre said. "Whatever's best."

He was already calculating—the Puncak mine problem was real; the peril in his body was hypothetical, the prognosis offered by the doctor, speculative. Even if it wasn't, cancer works slowly. Often hibernates.

This much he knew for sure: he couldn't afford to be an invalid— and surgery could knock him out of action for months.

"Any preference when?" he asked.

"Just be ready," Brawley said. Then he announced, almost as an afterthought, that it was his birthday and invited everyone to join him for drinks at the National Club after work.

Pierre briefly considered going home after the meeting, telling Lois the truth about the tests, the biopsy that he'd managed to keep secret. Instead, he placed a call to Puncak. He got the mine manager who sounded sleepy since it was the middle of the night there. But he could tell that Paddy Harrison wasn't happy with the news that he was coming, the lack of confidence implicit in Brawley's strategy.

"I don't see the need to push a panic button," Harrison said. "We're still talking. I have a good working relationship with these guys. Everything is in good shape and if I can mention money, I think we're going to be okay."

For a dozen reasons he could think of on the spot, Pierre wanted this to be the truth. "Brawley wants a deadline," he said. "Next Wednesday."

"Well, we should keep that to ourselves. No need for threats. They won't work here. But if I haven't worked it out by next Wednesday, you come on down and we'll do what we have to do."

"All due respect, Paddy, if you haven't got this thing ironed before next Wednesday your balls and mine are cat food."

"Oh, I hear you."

∼

"Not coming?" Ethan said. He was frowning. They'd met up in the men's room.

Pierre had totally forgotten Brawley's birthday party.

"Something's come up. Personal."

Ethan shrugged. "I'll say you're feeling feverish."

"Actually, that'll be the truth."

~

He'd driven his new toy, a vintage Mustang, north to Bloor. He might have then turned west, toward home. But he'd turned east instead, crossed the Don Valley and entered what he'd always thought of as the city's European microcosm, Danforth Avenue. He drove past the teeming patios, the Greek restaurants, Greek street signs, Greek statuary, Mediterranean enthusiasm. He drove slowly, absorbing all the images of pleasure. Too much pleasure. Too many thoughtless people. He could feel a headache starting.

He drove until he entered another world. No more patios and pleasure-seeking throngs, no more shish kebab and booze. The signs were now in Urdu, the shops proclaiming halal meat. He drove until he saw the mosque, the unmistakable minaret, the silver crescent, the emerald domes.

He parked the Mustang, locked it, stepped back, admired his car, felt his spirits lift but only for a moment. The car was a reminder of why he endured days like that day, a day of bad news, double-talk and spin. The car was a reward, like the boat he kept in Nova Scotia. Car and boat, vehicles for fantasy, for flight. But now he needed distance from his car, distance from his day. He needed to escape even his escapes.

He started walking. And then he spotted the little bar with the peculiar name in this unlikely neighbourhood. He went in, ordered a beer. He sat trying to imagine what awaited him in the days to come. The patio was just outside and beyond it he could see the domes that made him feel at home.

~

He'd spent maybe twenty minutes on the first beer, then he'd gone to the bar and fetched a second. Perhaps because he appeared to be out of place in his expensive suit and tie, a stranger came and gestured toward the empty seat across from him.

Pierre nodded toward the chair. The stranger sat.

"Have I seen you here before?"

The agitation of the day was undiminished and he didn't answer right away. But there was something about the stranger's accent. Agitation was replaced by curiosity. "I doubt it."

The intruder said, "I'm Ari," and held out a beefy hand. Pierre stared at it.

Perhaps it was the face. Or maybe it was something deeper, a voiceprint in the memory. Or maybe it was just the similarity to another name that loomed large in memories Pierre had buried.

Ari started to rise. "Sorry. I don't mean to interrupt." Pierre quickly grasped the hand. "It's okay . . . sit . . . Harry?"

"Ari. Short for Ariel."

"Pierre Cormier. I've never been here before. A bit different."

"Cormier? Yes. I find the atmosphere relaxing. Casual."

"Ari. Interesting name. Ari what?"

"Roloff. An old Quebec name."

"But you aren't French."

"True." Ari shrugged, looked away briefly. "Nor are you," he said. There was a trace of aggression in the look, the tone of voice.

Pierre could feel the agitation creeping back as he studied the face before him. It was broad and smooth, fleshy, friendly, open, the eyes interested but weary. What a bizarre coincidence. He felt a flutter in his stomach. Ariel. The same name. There was even a bodily resemblance. The man in front of him was short and overweight, borderline obese. The hair, the colour of ash, was thinning at the front but effectively combed over.

"You come here often?" he asked.

Ari smiled, shrugged. "Maybe more often than I should."

"So how long have you been in this country?"

Ari laughed. "Where do you think I'm from?" The subtle thickness of his consonants.

"I know exactly where you're from."

The smile was cautious now. Ari nodded.

"You could say we were neighbours once," Pierre said.

"Ah. Neighbours north? South? East?"

"North," said Pierre.

"Yes. Pierre? *Yimkin kenna as-hab.* Perhaps we were even friends."

"Perhaps. You speak like an Arab."

"Maybe not so much. I've been here five years," Ari said. "You?"

"Quite a bit longer."

"You're from Beirut," Ari said.

"No. A bit south of there."

Ari hesitated. "Damour?"

"You know Damour?"

Ari nodded. "I've been there."

"I had family in Damour. But I was born in Saida."

"Ah. Sidon. But you had family in Damour?"

"Yes."

"I'm going to order a drink. Would you like another beer? Or something better."

"I'll have what you're having."

Ari returned with two glasses. Scotch.

"And you? I'm going to guess Haifa."

"Why Haifa?"

"Just a feeling. You've lived with Arabs."

"Yes. But not Haifa. A kibbutz near Hebron. You never heard of it."

"Probably not. I suppose you hear this a lot, but you bear a remarkable resemblance to someone famous."

Ari laughed. "I don't hear it anymore so much. Someone no longer visible. Someone slowly being forgotten, yes?"

"Forgotten here, maybe. But not so much in other places."

"When did you say you came?" asked Ari.

"I didn't say."

"And you've been back?"

"No."

"Not once?"

"I have nobody left there."

"You said you have family in Damour?"

Pierre shook his head. "Past tense. You know the history."

"The important parts." Ari reached across the table, clasped Pierre's hand again, held it gently for a moment. "Such a tragedy, Damour. And all that followed."

Pierre stood abruptly, light-headed. "I think I have to leave now." He took a quick mouthful of the Scotch. It was strong. "Thanks for the drink," he said, setting the empty glass back down.

Ari nodded and looked away.

And that was how it started.

Just like the old days he made a date with Lois for a Saturday. Hugging her goodbye as he left for work on Friday morning, he suggested it. "What do you say? Scaramouche?"

She laughed. "Scaramouche? Is it still there?"

"I'll make sure," he said.

And, over dinner, he'd reassured her, about health, about work. How the trip to Indonesia (which was by no means certain yet) was mostly optics, a show of company support for Harrison, the manager who had managed to contain a hundred of these crises in the past. It was that kind of place and Harrison was that kind of guy, a veteran of projects in South Africa, Guatemala, Eritrea.

"If I do go, it'll be for a few days. That's all."

She laughed. "Okay." Sipped her wine, stared into space for a few moments. Caught his hand.

"I don't want to get into this right now but I want you to promise something. When you get back, if you go, I want us to get serious about you-know-what."

"I-know-what what?" He laughed, but of course he knew what. It had come up many times before.

Lois worked from home. Her business was hospitality, organizing events and conferences for a small but well-heeled corporate clientele. It was employment that was completely compatible with motherhood.

Pierre smiled and listened. And he nodded. And he verbally agreed. How could he not?

~

Sunday morning he was at his desk at Draycor when the call came through from Indonesia. It was Harrison. He sounded calm but Pierre had an ear for reading stress. Under pressure and against his better judgment, Harrison had mentioned Brawley's deadline, told the union guys that he was getting heat from Toronto but, more ominously, from local bureaucrats, including hardliners in the security forces, to sort this out. By Wednesday.

"They walked out."

"Fuck," Pierre said.

"They blocked the maintenance crew this afternoon. Maybe you'd better get here as soon as possible."

"I'll get back to you."

He called Brawley at his cottage. "It's getting out of hand," he told him, then, briefly, he explained what was happening. Brawley remained silent for a long time after Pierre had finished speaking. Pierre eventually asked, "Are you still there?"

"I'm here," Brawley replied wearily. "It's your call, Pierre."

"I need some direction. Where do I go from here?"

"Pierre, don't bother me with questions. Bother me with information, yes. Anytime. But don't ask stupid questions." There was another silence. Then: "You know exactly where to go from here. This is the last time you'll ask a question like that. Am I making myself clear?" The line went dead.

Pierre was sweating, his hand shaking when he placed the call to Harrison. "Do what you have to do. But use restraint. Okay?"

"I'll do my best," said Harrison. "But you should be here."

"I'll be there as soon as I can."

But he just sat staring at the telephone, weak with nausea, the words boiling back from memory, from the worst days of his life: *This is the last time you're going to ask me a question like that, you know exactly what to do.*

He would love to have responded—*I know exactly what to do, you bastard. Put a bullet between your fucking eyes.* Words he should have said in 1982 but didn't. And in his heart he knew he should have said them now.

~

The doctors were unhappy. They could only offer an informed prognosis. The decisions were up to him. "You need treatment, preferably surgery," the senior doctor told him sternly. "And it should be sooner rather than later." There were two of them. One talkative, Pierre's age, the other younger, silent.

"We want to book you for an MRI."

"The timing is awkward to say the least," Pierre said. "I have to go out of the country in a day or so. It's rather urgent."

"I see. And for how long?"

"It could be days or it could be weeks."

"We don't want to overstate the urgency of your problem here, but timing is an issue. You understand metastasis . . ."

"Yes. Yes. Look. I've been researching . . ."

"You've been googling?" The doctors exchanged smiles.

". . . and there's a link between prostate cancer and testosterone. I think we can gain time by . . ."

"You're referring to ADT, androgen deprivation therapy."

"Whatever it's called. I've got testosterone, tons of it, right. Almost off the scale, I'm Lebanese."

"You have a high level . . ."

"So what I want to do is bring it down, way down. To zero if I can. There's medication, I understand."

"ADT is something we would only consider after primary therapy, surgery or rad—"

"I don't have time for primary therapy right now."

"In the circumstances, Mr. Cormier—"

"In the circumstances this ADT stuff can slow things down and I have no choice but to try that."

The elder doctor sighed. He dropped his pen, picked it up, rolled it between thumb and forefinger. He studied Pierre for just a moment. "It's your call, Mr. Cormier."

Pierre stood, picked up his briefcase, and left.

~

The Wednesday deadline passed, but he felt uneasy, and on Thursday morning he told Lois, "I have to go. Tonight."

He booked his flight. He packed. He headed for the office.

Ethan Kennedy was waiting for him outside his office door. "Harrison's been trying to reach you. He's on the phone right now. You'd better talk to him."

~

"Eight fucking people . . . dead? How? Who . . . ? You must be mistaken. And women? Jesus Christ. You're not telling me . . ."

Harrison was quiet. "When can you get here?"

"I'll be on a plane tonight. I want every detail. If there's video, I want every frame."

"I'll have it ready for you."

He called Brawley. There was no answer so he left a message. *We have a problem.*

He paced. He stopped, stared out over Lake Ontario. The sky was grey, contemplating snow. *Eight people dead.* Puncak would be in pitch darkness now but for the twinkle of light around the camp, the headframe, administration buildings. Midnight there.

He kept a bottle of cognac in a cupboard. He fetched it, set it on his desk. He couldn't find a glass. The coffee cup would do. He poured, then called Lois. He described the latest crisis.

"Come back safe," she said. "We have a life."

"The limbo is waiting," he said.

She laughed. "The what?"

"The limo," he said. "What did I say?"

"Never mind," she said. "Hurry back."

"Love you."

5.

For the week that he'd been at the Puncak mine site he'd lived among the Western workers in the camp inside the fence. His room was simple, a single bed, a small writing table, faint scents of aftershave, disinfectant, stale cigarette smoke. A television set with clear reception. CNN. The BBC.

Paddy Harrison gave him an office in the administration building where he had access to high-speed Internet, a sat phone and a machine for playing video recordings. Harrison's assistant handed over banker's boxes full of tapes and documents—contracts, transcripts, maps and property descriptions, both underground and surface.

Harrison lived in an apartment set up to feel like home. He had a housekeeper and a cook, local people, and he invited Pierre to dinner on his first night there. There were drinks. Harrison impressed him, friendly, open, honest. They were about the same age. What had happened here at Puncak disgusted both of them. Eight people dead. For what, exactly?

Harrison admitted that he was on the verge of quitting, starting out again from scratch. Maybe working for some non-profit, giving something back. But he had a daughter in her second year at Princeton and there was, of course, the burden of the family tradition. The Harrisons, as everybody knew, were mining pioneers, like Brawley.

"So where did this all start?" Pierre asked.

"It's been brewing for a long time but I've heard a rumour, some incident involving miners. Something between the locals and the guys from Canada—we have quite a few here. I understand you're from Nova Scotia."

"Yes," Pierre replied.

"We have a shift boss from Cape Breton. Top-of-the-line miners from there, as you'd know."

"Where in Cape Breton?"

Harrison excused himself, then returned with a folder. "A place called . . . Mabou."

"I know the place."

"Sandy MacIsaac. Good man. Maybe if you have an in. They're a pretty tight bunch. I'd be curious to know what they know."

"So, Paddy, tell me what *you* know," Pierre said.

On the day of the riot the tension had finally erupted in a confrontation with a truck. A large transport truck approached the security perimeter, moving slowly toward the gate; it was early morning, just after sunrise. Harrison remembered waking up to crowing roosters, then hearing angry voices; dressing quickly, driven by a kind of panic—knowing with uncanny clarity exactly how things he couldn't see were unfolding and how they'd continue to unfold when he was in the middle of them.

By the time he'd got outside someone had mounted the driver's side of the truck, got the door open, dragged the driver out. The driver fell to the ground, wind knocked out of him. He couldn't get up and was soon being kicked and beaten. The truck lurched forward, heading for the gate, picking up speed. A squad of security opened fire, but not before the truck rammed the gate. The hijacker at the wheel was killed instantly by the gunfire and the truck, now uncontrolled, smashed through, coming to rest against the commissary.

Everything after that was lost in chaos, facts buried in sensory impressions that in the aftermath fuelled contradictory accounts that were expressed with ever-escalating certainty and passion.

Harrison led him through a file folder full of still photographs lifted from surveillance pictures shot from inside the fence in the days prior to the riot. One of the geologists, an amateur photographer, shot a video during the actual confrontation. It was hard to watch, Paddy warned him. Several photographs of a man called Ramos, believed to be the leader; one extreme blow-up of his hand and a dark object that Harrison believed might be a gun. The way he was holding it, standing, arm cocked as if he was about to throw something, Pierre was doubtful.

"Maybe a grenade," said Harrison.

"More likely a rock or bottle."

"There have been arrests. I suppose they have ways of finding out who did what."

"Arrests?"

"Several of the ringleaders are in custody."

"But not Ramos?"

"Not yet. This one," said Harrison, pointing to a pretty woman, "is Ramos's girlfriend, or mistress. We think he has a family in Jakarta or somewhere."

"Where's she?"

"She's in jail but we have no idea where he is."

"Maybe I should talk to her."

"Suit yourself but you'll get nothing out of her. Just abuse and rhetoric."

"I suppose."

"I think we should leave the questioning to the experts. If anyone can get these people to talk, they can. Right?"

"Well, we should stay on top of—"

"Pierre, it isn't just our call anymore. There are larger issues. Political issues."

"Fair enough. But let's make it very clear to the local powers that they've fucked this thing up quite enough already."

~

The men in the Puncak cafeteria had been exceptional only for their unusually pale complexions, the pallor of men who work long shifts underground. One had a rucksack hooked over the back of his chair with a faded maple leaf stitched on it.

"Canadians?" Pierre said, and smiled.

The four men at the table went silent, looking up at him. One nodded.

"Cape Breton?" Pierre said. All four laughed.

"Pierre Cormier," he said. "I'm with Draycor. Can I join you?"

"Cormier," said one, gesturing toward a chair. "That's a pretty common name where I come from. What Cormier might you be?"

"New Waterford," Pierre said, offering his hand. "But my ex-wife's people are from near Mabou. I spent a lot of time there. You know the place?"

"Well fuck me," the miner said. "Know the place?"

"You fuckin' people," said one, laughing. "You're all related."

"I'd heard there was someone here from Mabou," Pierre said. "A MacIsaac?"

"You got it. Sandy MacIsaac from Mabou Harbour." He held out his hand.

"I'm sure I've seen you at the West Mabou dance," Pierre said.

"Quite possible."

∽

The story of the strike that had turned into a riot and a massacre came out slowly, and that it came out at all was because they'd trusted him. He was a company man, a lawyer, but he was a Canadian and he had a coincidental tribal link with one of them.

Over coffee Pierre explained that he and his ex-wife had spent many happy summers back where Sandy came from and, in their better days, they'd schemed about retiring there. That the marriage had ended (amicably) only added to his credibility. These miners understood such things, the demands of work, the absences.

Sandy agreed to walk him through the battle scene, an open space just outside the chain-link fence that separated the mine property from the cluster of shacks where local workers lived with their families. He and the other ex-pat miners had watched the confrontation from a second-storey window inside the compound. They had been able to see some of the action outside the fence and they'd definitely heard the helicopters and the gunfire.

Sandy said he'd never witnessed anything like that before, the brutality. And he'd worked all over, Indonesia, the Congo. "They usually keep the lid on pretty tight in places like this."

"So what went wrong?"

Sandy shrugged. "It was ridiculous from the get-go. If we had known . . ."

"Known what?"

Sandy was uncomfortable but told the story anyway, as well as he could remember it. One of the local miners was getting married. The Canadians on his crew passed the hat and collected maybe two hundred dollars—hard currency. Some shit disturber heard about it and started agitating about the differential in wages paid to the white guys and the earnings of the locals. It went from there.

"It was nuts," Sandy said.

"Yes," Pierre agreed. "Quite so. Eight killed."

"Even women," said Sandy bitterly.

Pierre nodded.

"Life means fuck all around here," Sandy said.

"How many people know about this, Sandy?"

"Most people here. We don't talk about it, though."

"That's wise." He grasped Sandy's arm. "Nobody would believe it anyway."

"There's also a rumour here that the order for the military crackdown came from Canada. From the company. Is that true?"

"Where did you hear that?"

"It's the talk."

"Talk where?"

"Among the guys, mostly. Makes sense. What we did, passing the hat, didn't have to end like that."

"But where's the so-called information coming from, about Toronto?"

Sandy stepped away, stared off into the distance for a moment. He shrugged, laughed. But when he turned to face Pierre, he wasn't smiling. "I feel like I'm in a witness box."

"Sorry," Pierre said. "I didn't mean to put you on the spot. Forget I asked. Okay?"

"I'd better mosey," Sandy said. "I'm on graveyard all this week. Need to get a bit of shut-eye."

Pierre called after him as he walked away. "I'd like to keep this conversation between the two of us. Okay?"

Sandy just kept walking.

~

He left the geologist's video to near the end of his investigation. Pierre was not naïve about the objectivity of cameras. The camera was another point of view—the perspective of the man behind it. But the information on the recording would be raw, unedited and uncorrupted by human memory and the distorted retrospective of self-preservation.

Footage from the incident was mostly silent. He wasn't sure what had happened to the sound and the camera operator was unable to explain. In any case, the audio would have disturbed the information because sound disturbs emotion in the listener. What Pierre wanted was the simple physical detail of what was happening in the moment.

He paid particular attention to the women. The death of women in a war or any kind of conflict always complicated explanation. Who shoots women? Savages.

Fucking savages, you people. Oh, how well he knew the phrase.

The woman with the laundry basket caught his eye on his first time through the video and he'd stopped the tape. He'd stared in disbelief. A laundry basket?

He'd leaned back in the chair, staring at the screen. A chill rippled through his shoulders. He rewound, pressed play.

There were other women, but she was so incongruous, hurrying around the perimeter, trying to get by, carrying the wicker laundry basket. She was wearing a baggy blouse and an ankle-length loose skirt. Her feet were bare. There were women wearing jeans and baseball caps but some were dressed like the woman with the basket, obviously local. But unlike her they were engaged and angry, faces furious. Some of them were throwing stones. The woman with the basket was clearly not involved. She was on the edge of the action but she dominated Pierre's attention, activating memories of another woman with a laundry basket. On her toes. Arms extended as if in supplication or about to fly.

The images converged and became one picture. A woman lurching forward, arms extended, laundry basket tumbling.

He stopped the tape again. The image was blurry, the woman ghostlike, and that was worse. He pressed play again and she disappeared. The wandering eye of the camera had moved on to action that was more relevant. Later in the video he was sure that he had spotted her, a crumpled figure among others. But he wasn't sure. And it shouldn't have mattered. She wasn't part of the event that he was attempting to reconstruct or deconstruct. She was an element in the statistical account but she wasn't relevant. But he was unable to stop thinking about her.

That evening he had a drink with Harrison. Cancer diet be damned.

"I watched the video. There was another woman . . ."

"Yes," said Harrison. "There were several women. At least two of them from town—I've seen them at the public meetings. Politicals, without a doubt."

"There was one with a laundry basket." Pierre tried to smile, to convey a sense of weary disbelief.

Harrison seemed puzzled. "Laundry basket? I didn't notice that."

"Maybe I was seeing things," Pierre said. And for an hour or so he savoured the possibility that the woman was imaginary. But even if she was, she came from somewhere, a memory he'd managed to suppress for decades. Now revived, threatening to unlock other memories.

Before he'd gone to bed he went back to his temporary office and rewound the tape, played it again in slow motion until he found her. He played it again. And again. And when he returned to Toronto he took the tape home with him. And watched it again and again and again.

∾

He could easily have ducked. He could have delegated this to Kennedy. He could have played the health card. *I've got cancer.* Lois would have put her foot down, insisted. *We don't fuck around with cancer.* Even Brawley would have understood. He was obsessive about what he called "plumbing." But Pierre really had no choice. Early in his life he'd learned the importance of control. Had he taken charge decisively when he should have, this might not have happened, this fiasco. Had he been in control in September 1982, would that catastrophe have happened?

This is the last time you're going to ask me a question like that. You know exactly what to do. Was that what Brawley said? Or were the words from another time, another place? Or do time and place make any difference to destiny?

He tried to imagine the violence at Puncak but the imaginary scene was eclipsed by memories. Beirut. He is again staring into darkness broken by starbursts of light above the flat punctured roofs, the rutted, littered streets. He can even hear the pop and rattle of the gunfire, the shrieking, the grinding clanking Merkava changing its position, gun turret swivelling toward the wretchedness. *You know exactly what to do.* They'd all laughed manically, everyone in the observation post. Including the Israelis who were staring at the carnage through binoculars. *Exactly. What to do.* They'd laughed and he'd laughed with them.

Too much. Too much to think about. He could not afford indulging in self-doubt. There were facts to find, a libretto to prepare for what would be a stern process of accountability. Draycor had his back, he knew it. He had the confidence of everyone who mattered. They told him it was his call. And it was his job to get the facts, report back. And, if necessary, let Communications work with Legal to refine a Strategy for Going Forward.

Your call, Pierre.

Three words. The lawyer, never mind the warrior, should have recognized the potential peril in those words. But he hadn't anticipated that a distant Draycor manager would transmit panic to a minister of government who would in turn relay it to a roomful of paramilitary commanders anxious to unleash their over-armed, overstimulated thugs who were overly impatient for any kind of action, especially against a rabble of undisciplined protesters backed up by wives and kids.

Your call, Pierre.

And he made it. *So suck it up,* he told himself.

∼

There had been a three-hour wait at the airport in Jakarta and he'd spent the time in a bar reflecting on the consequences of a careless act of generosity by some sentimental miners from Canada. A story to be reserved for the special moment when a human interest angle might leaven the predictable investigative thrust. A story that was human in its warmth, though tragic in its outcome. It didn't take him long to finish his report, the last part of which was forensic in the detail of how eight people died in a violent rampage by a unit of the Indonesian special forces, the notorious Kopassus.

For the company, the story would be exculpatory. The media would move on. It was unlikely that in these days of tight budgets an editor would undertake to send reporters to a place so far away, especially when the incident had hardly caused a ripple in the market. Gold was hot and getting hotter. Eight shit-disturbers gunned down by a squad of psychopaths could easily be written off as another minor example of the inhumanity of distant places ruled by cops and soldiers and dictators. But for Pierre a single image would continue to roil the darkest places in his memory.

The woman's body flung forward, the shocked expression on her face. A pretty face. A young face. And whatever she'd been carrying, suddenly suspended in mid-air in front of her. A basket. Clothing. Clothespins. The spinning body, the expression of astonishment. Perhaps the videographer, amateur and frightened, judging by the shakiness, didn't even notice her. What was she doing there? Returning from the river maybe? Rushing to the shelter of a nearby hovel over ground that had always been a part of her safe, unchanging place.

She was on the edge of the frame, the important action was happening about fifty feet away—men with clubs and stones confronting armed commandos. But Pierre couldn't stop staring at her, and the flung basket, what looked like children's clothing. The flurry of clothespins suspended in the nothingness around her.

6.

He'd been home two days, much of the time holed up in his den. He was thinking about deception, truths untold, and lies. *Is there a difference?* Yes, he answered. There is a difference that requires perspective that only time provides. *But what about deception that becomes a lie because of the chemistry of self-preservation? Is it a lie if a listener is hearing what he needs or wants to hear? Who is morally responsible, the liar or the listener?*

He was near the bottom of another Scotch. The bottle was down by about a third. True. No denying that. He picked it up to pour another but put it down again, capsized by untold truths from the dark side of the memory wall, 1982. And the recent truths from Western New Guinea. Truths untold from a cancer treatment centre.

Once again he fished the prescription from the pile of paper on his desk. He squinted. It was still illegible. But he knew what the doctor had written there because he had asked for it. Demanded it, in fact. Androgen suppression. Chemical castration.

He sighed and put the prescription back on the pile, stood and walked toward the bedroom, sat on the side of the bed. Lois woke, rubbed his back. "Come to bed."

"I've been thinking," he said. "We should see a gynaecologist."

She chuckled. "Could we talk about it later?"

"I might have a medical issue in that department."

She sat up. "What?"

"Nothing major, but we should be thinking about clinical options. Go back to sleep."

"What are you talking about?"

"Like I said, nothing major. Man stuff. Testosterone, libido. Nothing that concerns you."

"Excuse me?" She got up, walked around the bed, stood looking down at him.

So he explained late into the night, merciful deceptions concealed in half-truths. Because, after all, nobody, including Pierre, could know the whole truth.

~

The Only Café was quiet. He stood at the bar, ordered a beer, watched the door. He wasn't sure what brought him back. Perhaps the wall of memory, 1982, perhaps the suspicion that the fat stranger, Ari, might know something from behind that—so far—impenetrable wall. There was no sign of him.

The young bartender seemed friendly so Pierre asked him how well he knew Ari.

"As well as anybody knows him."

"Has he been around?"

"Not lately. How do you know Ari?"

Pierre was startled. That accent. It couldn't be, but it clearly was.

"I met him here, a few weeks back. I've been away, on business."

"What kind of business?"

There could be no mistaking either the accent, or the wary manner.

"Mining. I'm guessing you're Israeli too?"

The young man frowned. "I'm a Canadian."

"Ah."

"Do you know Israel?"

"I know Israel. Where did you meet Ari?"

"Like you, here. And yes, I was born in Israel. But I wanted to see the world. I needed a job for a while. Ari knows the owner. We talk now and then. You're from?"

"Nova Scotia."

"And how do you know Israel?"

"I have roots in Lebanon."

"Ah, Lebanon." The bartender smiled. "I've been to Lebanon."

"What were you doing in Lebanon?"

The bartender shrugged. "What do Israelis usually do in Lebanon?"

Pierre drained the beer glass and stood. "Tell Ari if you see him that Pierre was here. The Lebanese guy." He smiled.

"Pierre. I'll tell him."

"And your name?"

"Tal."

They shook hands.

∾

The chiming telephone caused him to rise quickly from where he'd been sitting at the cabin table, staring at his journal. He staggered, light-headed, perhaps from the rocking motion of the boat. The missed call was from Lois so he called her back.

"How are you?" she asked. He could hear the tension in her voice.

"I'm fine. Drifting offshore. I just saw the most amazing pod of whales."

"Ah," she said. "I don't suppose you're getting the papers out there."

"No."

"Just as well," she said. "The company has been in the news a couple of times. Your name came up."

He sat. "What about me."

"Nothing to worry about," she said. "Just keep doing what you're doing. I miss you."

"How did my name come up?"

"Oh, that thing in Indonesia. Something about shareholders."

"What paper," he said.

"The *Globe*. Business section. Now don't go getting anxious. You're supposed to be resting."

"Okay," he said. "We've been in the papers before. How are you feeling?"

"Never better," she said. "A little queasy in the mornings but when I remember what's causing it I get all blissy."

"That's great," he said, now anxious to get off the phone. "I miss you too."

"Love you," she said. "Come home soon."

He opened up his browser, found the story: *Draycor Shareholders Demanding Answers*. All predictable but for the anonymous source quoted four paragraphs down: *A management committee, alarmed by a potential hit in share prices . . . an internal investigation to determine the sequence of events that led to the massacre at Puncak Mine in Western New Guinea . . . sources . . . anonymity . . . not authorized . . .*

He called Ethan.

"I just saw the story in the *Globe*. What the hell . . . I did the investigation. I wrote the complete report and I briefed everybody on everything there is to know. Everyone signed off on it. What's this?"

"A story from out there somewhere. Where you are, I think. Somebody talked about Puncak. Some eyewitness. Stirred things up a bit. It'll blow over."

"But an internal investigation? What's that about?"

Ethan sounded calm. "They have to say something to cover their ass. When the time is right they'll release your full report and it'll be the investigation they're talking about. Okay? Otherwise everything is cool."

"If everything is cool, I might as well come home."

"Look. We've been down this road before many times. This too will pass, as my grandma used to say. You're okay?"

"I'm not especially okay."

"Come on. What's it like out there?"

"It was lovely out here until now. I'm going to come home."

"I don't think you should. Give this a couple more days to die down."

"No, Ethan. I'm not going to sit on my ass a thousand miles away while they decide whether or not I'm expendable. I don't intend to be a scapegoat."

"Nobody's going to make a scapegoat out of you, Pierre. You're too important to the outfit."

"I'll catch a flight back tomorrow. Can I call you? Maybe a late drink?"

"Yes, of course. But I think it's a bad idea, coming back."

"Just don't tell anyone I'm coming."

~

Why had he gone back, a third time, to this hole in the wall, the Only Café, this memory hole, this wormhole, to a place that he had consciously, strenuously, sealed off? An instinct told him it was a mistake to go, but the instinct didn't tell him why. Was it futility, a waste of time, or actually perilous? So he returned.

Blocked memory is a product of the mind's resilience, a benefit of a healthy mental immune system. This was what he told himself. But his immune systems were breaking down. Rogue cells in the body. Rogue memories threatening the soul.

Maybe Ari wouldn't be there.

But this time Ari was the first person he saw, leaning on the bar, talking to Tal, the young bartender.

When he came through the door they both stopped speaking and looked in his direction. Ari nodded and walked toward him.

They shook hands. "It's Pierre, yes?"

"It is. I felt I was a bit abrupt the last time. I think I owe you a drink."

Ari's expression was impossible to read. "Sure, sit," he said.

They picked a table near the large window at the front.

"So?"

The drinks arrived before Pierre had ordered. Two double Scotches.

"It's supposed to be my turn," Pierre said.

"There will be another time, I think? You're a lawyer?"

"Yes. I work for a mining company. Perhaps you saw our name in the paper? Some controversy about an incident in . . . Asia?"

"Maybe."

"I don't know about you, but I sometimes get these nagging feelings that I've been somewhere before, somewhere I know I've never been, or met somebody before who I couldn't possibly have met. You know what I'm talking about?"

"Déjà vu."

"Yes."

Ari chuckled. "So maybe you feel we've been here before, in the Only Café, maybe in another life?"

"Yes," Pierre said. "Something like that. But not here."

Ari's face was blank. The music seemed louder than usual. The din of lubricated, shouted conversation. Ari shook his head, then raised his hands in supplication.

"Beirut city stadium," Pierre said.

Ari shrugged. Looked with clear annoyance up at a speaker on the wall above Pierre's head. "Come outside," he said.

On the sidewalk they were caught between the diminished inside sounds of music and the rushing street sounds, the distant city cries of sirens. Ari lit a cigarette, exhaled smoke toward the traffic. When he looked back at Pierre his face was serious.

"You said where?"

"The city stadium. Beirut."

"Really? And when would that have been?"

"It would have been September '82."

"Not possible." Ari chuckled. "September '82, I remember. If you saw me at the stadium in September '82 neither of us would be standing here now, would we."

Pierre smiled. "I hear what you're saying."

"September. A very difficult month in '82. The Green Line, remember? The stadium was west of the line. Yes?"

"But on the eighteenth of September . . . the Green Line was gone."

"Ah. September eighteenth. Yes. I remember that date. A very sad day. Impossible to forget."

"So you *were* at the stadium that day."

Ari frowned. "Oh no, no, no. I couldn't have been at the stadium. I was at home. I had been in East Beirut. I was called home on the sixteenth. My mother. I remember the eighteenth because it was the day we buried her."

"Ah. I'm sorry," Pierre said.

"It was twenty-five years ago," Ari said. "But days like that you don't forget."

"Yes," Pierre said, disoriented. "I met your namesake there."

Ari frowned. "My namesake?"

"Ariel Sharon."

"Aha. Arik, the minister of defense himself. I heard that he'd been there. How interesting. So *you* were there in West Beirut that week? And you were at the stadium on the eighteenth?"

"Yes."

"And what was your involvement at the stadium?"

Pierre paused. "It doesn't matter if you weren't there."

"True. It doesn't matter. Let's finish our drinks. We can talk about something else. The years have been good to you. You have good health, obviously."

Pierre shrugged. "Outward appearances can be deceptive." He waved, caught Tal's eye. Held up two fingers.

∽

When he rose to leave Ari stood and embraced him. "I admire your outlook," he said. "There is nothing we can't overcome, going forward, with the proper outlook. Even cancer. Not such a big deal anymore, cancer. Yes? But looking backward? Regret, remorse, guilt? Such a waste of time. There is nothing we can change."

∽

He could never forget the date. September 18, 1982. In so many ways it was the day he died, or perhaps, like an insect, metamorphosed from one life into another. September 18. Shatila camp. Beirut. A charnel house. And in a quiet place, in the midst of the devastated camp, the beautiful young woman prostrate, as if asleep, laundry basket on its side, children's clothing scattered, soaking up her blood. Images now back in the forefront of his memory because of a video recorded a quarter of a century later in New Guinea, Indonesia.

The day came back to him with clarity and he now struggled to recall particular details of the less important moments. Two men talking quietly over coffee at a small table in a darkened room somewhere in the bowels of Beirut stadium. Who was the Israeli having coffee with Pierre's commander, the Phalangist, Elie Hobeika? He had a mental image: shaved head; five-day stubble; surprising corpulence for a soldier in a special unit. An officer, in all likelihood, although he could clearly remember thinking that the uniform lacked certain insignia that might have identified the Israeli rank. What was the name of the unit?

Hobeika might even have said the soldier's name, which would explain Pierre's lingering impression that the soldier had been an officer. But the name, the soldier and the unit, had swiftly fled his mind because of what Hobeika said next.

"Those two over there," he said to Pierre. "Take them away. Take them back. We're finished with them."

"Who are they?"

"Such questions." Hobeika laughed. The Israeli laughed. The men were hooded, hands tied. They seemed young. They were gasping.

"What will I do with them?"

"You know exactly what to do. Why must you ask such questions? Elias will go with you."

It would be the last time Pierre ever questioned Elie Hobeika. It was the last time he ever saw him. But it would not be the last time he thought of him, or heard of him, or thought he saw him, or turned away from strangers who resembled him.

~

The sun broke through a sudden gash in the cloud, reminding him that it was noon already. He craved a drink but knew it was the last thing that he needed.

How rare it is that we recognize an unexpected moment as the beginning of an ending. We are almost always taken by surprise by events that, in retrospect, could so easily have been avoided. A moment on September 18, 1982, was such an ending. An instant nearly six years before September 1982 was such a turning point. An unplanned, unforeseen occurrence that transformed everything, set the course for everything that followed.

Remember this, he thought. *Do not forget again.*

7. *January 8, 1976*

It was two days past the Epiphany. The beginning of the annual family excursion to Damour for the reunion of his mother's clan. It would be of an indefinite duration this year because of the unsettled situation in Saida. Who could have known on that quiet morning, January 8, 1976, that shots fired on local fishermen on a noisy day a year earlier would start a war that would last more than a quarter century? Who could have predicted that this thriving, ancient city would become a slaughterhouse?

Brittle winter sunshine. The little yellow car was piled high inside and out with boxes of belongings, heavy carpets tightly rolled and strapped to the roof rack. Mother amid the baggage in the back seat. Miriam, her baby and her husband in the front. He and his father were staying back, afraid to leave their home unoccupied. And there was work to be done at the harbour, fishing gear and boat in need of repairs for having missed most of the autumn fishing because of the political unrest, the rising throb of violence all around.

Freezing drizzle fell that evening as he and his father made their way home from the shore. He can't remember conversation, perhaps because there was none. His father was a quiet man, taciturn and unafraid. They took no particular notice of the Fatah gunmen. For weeks they'd been venturing out of squalid Ain el-Hilweh. Wolf packs on the prowl, flexing their authority. But his father saw no need for caution. He belonged here. These men with guns were aliens.

They approached quietly. He remembers that there were seven, weapons casually slung.

They stop, the barrels of the weapons slightly raised. The leader beckons. He is young. Come. Papers. Pierre's father is sullen as he removes an ID card from his pocket, hands it over.

A boy a little older than Pierre now stands before him, a hostile barrier that separates him from his father. The boy is perhaps seventeen. His voice is raw. *Fuck your sister. Kess ikhtak!*

Pierre understands instinctively the need for silence. He has grown accustomed to existential peril since this pestilence began, the expanding menace from the south. Ain el-Hilweh. Mieh Mieh. He has heard his father speak of the peace and the civility before the Palestinians arrived, this flood of garbage, flushed into Jordan by the Jews, and now into Lebanon, fugitives from King Hussein. *Fuck your sister and your mother*, the boy repeats, waving the barrel of the AK-47.

The leader speaks sharply to the boy. *Ekhra! Shut your mouth.*

Pierre suddenly feels more secure, even though he can hear the rising indignation in the conversation between his father and the leader. And the angry voices of the others adding to the tension. His father shouts back at his accusers, accusing them. Pierre feels panic but senses there is still an element of reason that will turn down the flame before this pot boils over. The leader: he is slim with dark hair clipped short; he has the drawn, bewhiskered look of poverty, but also a certain commanding dignity.

Pierre stares at the boy in front of him. There is something unusual in his face. And then he realizes: one eye is seriously out of sync with the other. One eye looking left, the other right and slightly tilted toward the sky. He is suddenly less menacing. Pierre feels a sudden, crazy impulse to mock him. *Eban sharmouta. Ahwal. Cross-eyed motherfucker. I wouldn't touch your sister if she looks like you, fucked-face.*

He feels better, redeemed by his own aggression, if only in his imagination.

The boy in front of him is sneering, as if he reads Pierre's mind. *Piece of shit. Afraid to say it. I will show you.*

He cranks the weapon. *Clack-clack.*

Stay with him, the leader says to the boy. One of the others shoves Pierre's father roughly and they walk away, propelling Pierre's father before them until they are gone from view.

The wall-eyed boy now looks uncertain. He looks behind him to see where his companions have gone. Then he turns back to Pierre. *Run*, he whispers.

Pierre hesitates, straining to see where they have taken his father.

Fucking run, the boy says, now angry. Pierre backs away, hands raised. The boy raises the assault rifle. Pierre turns and runs on legs that are perilously unsteady, knees of jelly nearly buckling beneath him. Behind him, a sudden burst of gunfire. He stumbles, then recovers and sprints around a corner just as a second burst of gunfire sends a spray of concrete fragments into the side of his face and down the right side of his body.

Down a darkened alleyway, he sees a cellar door ajar. He shoulders through, down a stone stairway into darkness. He slips, falls backward, and reaches instinctively to break the fall, but his hand is now plunged into what he knows is human shit. Overpowering stink. He realizes he is not alone. A child whimpers. A baby starts to wail. Two women in the darkness, children huddled round them. He flees back up the stairs, furiously wiping his contaminated hand on his pant leg, too terrified for nausea.

The streets are silent. There is a rising wind and the icy drizzle stings. He stoops, scrubs the befouled hand in a puddle. Fights an impulse to go looking for his father. In his heart he already knows the futility.

He makes his way in the darkness back through the port, through passages and byways familiar to the fishermen, until he finds his father's boat among the others on the beach, upside down. He crawls under.

∽

In the cabin of the *Miriam* he filled a glass with water. He opened a can of sardines. In the cooler there was bread and cheese and beer. The phone had been silent for what felt like hours. This was what security should feel like. *Yes*, he told himself. *I feel safe here.*

Perhaps Kennedy was right: give it a few more days. He thought of his son and had a sudden overwhelming urge to call him. But he had no idea how to start the conversation.

His diary was on the table beside the cellphone. He opened it. There were two hundred pages left in his 2007 journal, one hundred and ninety-one days, nine blank pages for significant addresses, notes. He would use them all. A letter to a stranger. Cyril Bashir Cormier.

He wrote: *I would rather be remembered as an interesting father than a good one.*

He set the pen down, rubbed his face. Picked the pen up, bent the journal back until it cracked, then set it down, now flat. Wrote: *Maybe we will talk. Yes? Would you even want that? Someday, perhaps, if there is time. If so, remember this. And tell me that I'm wrong, that it wasn't enough for me to have been an interesting parent and a bad one. I am open to persuasion. But you will have to tell me first—what are the qualities of a father who can accurately be described as "good." That is the deal. Because if I can believe that it might have been possible to have been a good father then it might be possible to believe that anyone, father, mother, sibling, stranger can be considered "good" in any role. At this moment, I have doubts.*

Then he wrote: *To understand your father, you must know and understand another man. His story is, in many ways, my story. I cannot tell you with any confidence even who he is. Is he a "good" man or a "bad" man? I do not know. He lives in a world of unreality. He is close to who and what I was. He goes by "Ari."*

THREE

ARI

8.

Cyril could only think of one phrase to describe what he was seeing on the screen. Freaking out. The women, terrified and terrifying, were freaking out. The sound was a high-pitched warble punctuated by screams.

They all looked the same. Head scarves covered their hair and fore-heads, and black shapeless robes made them all seem bulky and uni-formly old. There were soldiers but he could only see their backs. They seemed to be restraining the hysterical women, but he could barely hear their shouts because of the screams and that godawful warbling. Then a bare-headed soldier who looked American or European appeared in front of the camera waving some kind of pistol and he was shouting in unequivocal English: *Get out of here or I'll shoot the lot of you.* Then he raised the gun and fired a shot in the air. *Crack.*

The women howled. And then they started dancing, faces drenched in sorrow, dancing and chanting, hysteria barely in control. The soldier fired off three more shots. *Crack, crack, crack.* They ignored him, his gun, the camera and crew. And they danced as the scene dissolved.

The picture went black for a moment, then came up on what appeared to be a heap of garbage mixed in with clothing and shoes. The camera zoomed slowly and he realized he was looking at dead bodies. There might have been five or six. There might have been a dozen. Some seemed huge, black and bloated bursting out of clothing. Some were only little piles of rags. Up close flies were swarming on the empty faces. There was narration but he didn't recognize the language. Then a voice behind him said, "Norwegian," startling him. Hughes was standing behind him, hands in pockets, jingling his change. He removed his headset.

"How could you tell?"

"I know that piece. You know what that hollering is?"

"No," said Cyril. "There's an English transcript but I haven't read it yet."

"Those women . . . Palestinians. They were ululating. It's how they grieve. You hear it in Africa too." Hughes turned to leave.

"What was it about?"

"A massacre. The women had a lot to scream about."

"You know this place?"

"Lebanon?" He chuckled. "I grew up there."

"But you don't look or sound . . ."

"Because I'm not."

"So what happened here?"

"It would take me all day to explain. When did you say your father left Lebanon?"

"1983, I think."

"I'm sure he knew all about it."

"You grew up in Lebanon but you're . . . ?"

"Irish, I suppose, if I'm anything. I'm not much for ethnic labelling."

He turned. Just outside Cyril's cubicle, he stopped. "Tell me sometime, if you want to—why would anybody name a kid Bashir?"

"I have no idea."

"Don't spend too much time with that stuff."

~

The images stayed with him, and the sounds. Riding the subway north he noticed silent women wearing head scarves in the car and he couldn't suppress a feeling of anxiety. The unavoidable linkage between the images and sounds of the wailing, dancing women and the heaps of silent human refuse, no longer recognizable as individuals and all the more appalling because of that. The animated grief of the women, who were being restrained so roughly by the frightened soldiers, contrasting with the quiet squalor of the dead. The still reality of these women, sitting in this subway car in the middle of Toronto, staring into nothingness, faces partially concealed. He looked away, turned his mind back to his own life.

~

His mother was in the kitchen with a glass of wine. There was an open bottle on the counter. "Help yourself," she said. "How was your day?"

He shrugged. "What are we having?"

"I'm doing a roast," she said. "I hope you're hungry." He hated it here. Everything from the vinyl-covered padded toilet seats to the fake art deco furniture in the living room, the gloomy drapery, the landscapes on the walls, mass-produced but in elaborate gilt frames; the fussy souvenirs, a soapstone puffin, green-tartan coasters, expressions of nostalgia for where she came from—a place as foreign and mysterious to him as Lebanon. Photos of herself, Cyril as an infant, as a schoolboy, an awkward adolescent; the glaring absence of his father.

He hated the manipulative formality of dinnertime. Even the knives and forks: too heavy on the handle end, always falling off the plates when he cleared the table. Tacky Laura Ashley placemats. He couldn't imagine her going to such pains to create an atmosphere of cheap elegance if she were eating alone, which she'd been doing mostly since he'd moved out. And he really hated the gusts of self-reproach he felt when he'd allow himself to recognize that this was her way of showing feelings that she would have considered to be love.

"Somebody at work today made a strange comment about my name," he said.

"What?"

"That he couldn't understand why anyone would name a kid 'Bashir.'"

"I never cared for it," she said. "It sounds so . . . violent. The *bash* in it." She sipped her wine. "But your father was determined. It seems you're named after someone back in the old country. I gather there was a Bashir big shot, but it might not have been him your name came from. I wanted to name you after my father. But your father could be very persuasive."

"Pius?" He chuckled. "Cyril Pius Cormier. Or Pius Cyril."

She laughed with him, but then became serious. "Don't make fun. Your granddad is a marvellous man."

"Don't you think it's strange that Dad never talked about his family, back in Lebanon?"

"He did, a little, when we were planning to get married. The basics, as he put it. But he was determined that his family here would be his only family. I suppose it was to reassure me, in a way. He said once he admired your granddad because Pius is strong and he's honest. A rare combination in Pierre's experience. Strong meant corrupt where he was from."

"So there was nobody he would talk about."

"Just Miriam. His older sister. What happened to her bothered him. A lot."

"And did he say what happened?"

"Just that she was murdered."

He emptied the wine bottle into his glass. "Do you mind if I open another?"

~

He dreamed that night that he was in a large, unfamiliar city, walking along a silent street that was full of rubble. He was with two men. The younger of his two companions said, "Look, we can take a shortcut through here." Cyril was transfixed by the voice, the face so like his own. "No, wait," said the older man. But the strange young man who was so familiar was already heading into what might have been a construction site, or perhaps a demolition project—mounds of earth piled high with massive slabs of broken concrete and shafts of rusted reinforcing rods protruding. He quickly disappeared.

The older man grabbed Cyril's arm. "Come, carefully," he said. Then there was a shout from somewhere beyond the rubble. He couldn't speak or move, only stare at the man beside him. Then Cyril broke free and started running. The screaming was from a deep hole. He stopped, then crawled toward the hole on hands and knees, looked down. It seemed bottomless. He heard a whimper from somewhere beneath him.

He stood, ran back toward the street but the older man had vanished and he saw for the first time that he was surrounded by sheared-off buildings with dangling balconies, uprooted trees, weeds and dusty bushes growing out of craters in the pavement; windowless walls, smoke-stained from fires that had raged inside, punctured as if by giant fists; heaps of trash; rags with blackened arms and legs and faces without eyes; swarms of flies, all green and black. And now there were more strange men there, long lines of silent, hostile, whiskered strangers with guns and belts of bullets strapped across their chests, heavy weapons on their shoulders, ignoring him as he screamed silently for help.

Help me. *Help.*

He woke drenched. Consciousness returned slowly. He was in his mother's house, the bedroom that had been his since infancy. Suffocating safety. He switched on a bedside lamp, flopped back on the pillow.

Then he remembered, or imagined he remembered, sitting in a living room beside his father on a sofa, watching television. Identical images of destruction. Cars abandoned on a highway; throngs of people with babies on their backs, belongings on their heads; roaring clanking lumbering tanks and trucks with grim soldiers glaring. His father pointing the remote, the images and sounds vanishing. For some reason he remembers he was twelve. Yes. Of course. It was just before his father left from their home, never to return.

∼

He stood in the doorway to Hughes's office, one of four along the far side of the newsroom. Hughes was the foreign editor. Cyril occupied one of a cluster of workstations along the opposite wall.

"When did the civil war in Lebanon end?"

Hughes looked up from his computer screen, rolled his chair backward, stared straight ahead for a moment. "Which one?"

Cyril shrugged. "Whatever was going on in 2000."

"Ah," he said. "Spring 2000. As good a date as any. The Israeli pullout. I suppose you could call that a kind of end point. Why do you ask?"

"No reason. Just trying to get my head around it. In case I need to know. What were the Israelis doing there?"

"Someday we should have a beer," said Hughes.

∼

The handsome young man speaking in the documentary had also been memorable for his flawless English, the slightest trace of a British accent. The pleasant unlined face, the reasonable, affable willingness to chat with a reporter who was also speaking English for a change. He could easily have been a regular at poker night. He had thick brown hair, an untroubled expression and was standing in a space that seemed to have been recently bulldozed.

He was unarmed, wearing an olive-green pullover that moulded to his athletic upper body. He described the action of the preceding days as a precise operation in spite of the resistance, and said that special care had been taken to avoid unnecessary harm to the innocent. Transportation had been provided to remove the civilians to safer places. The refugee camp had been on private property, its unfortunate inhabitants living in squalor, poverty, disease. The armed response from terrorists inside the camp had been quite unexpected and there had been casualties on both sides. Injury and loss of life, unavoidable and always tragic. Yes.

The scenes before and after this flattened moment of lucidity in the documentary were jarring. The smashed remains of buildings; smouldering heaps of refuse; and in every shot, it seemed, a human form, sprawled and still, invariably blackened; a bulky woman in a black robe and white flowing head scarf, pleading tearfully. The terrible sound of her querulous appeal to the stolid fighter brandishing the automatic rifle in her face. The boom and crackle of the guns; the rushing vehicles; men in awkward poses shooting wildly at the unseen enemy. All at odds with the smooth familiarity of the young man whose name Cyril had failed to catch because the narration was in Norwegian.

But now the English transcript told him the suave young man was named Dany Chamoun, the commander in an operation that had killed more than a thousand inhabitants of a pathetic shantytown within Beirut, a place called Karantina, named for its earlier purpose, as a place of quarantine for new arrivals in the once-thriving city.

The information in the transcript was appalling. A thousand people exterminated. Maybe fifteen hundred Palestinian refugees. Women, children and, yes, fighters who were attempting to defend this miserable concentration camp, a slum surrounded by people who despised them, a place they never chose but where they ended up. That was the gist of the documentary, and how grievance leads to retribution and further grievance, each growing in magnitude, but never outgrowing the simple, venal banality of its origins in the darkest regions of human nature. Greed. Fear. Hate.

The heavy-handed moral tone was profoundly disturbing to Cyril. He'd screened half a dozen of these documentaries, in French, Italian, Norwegian, English. But he realized that his response to this one had been distorted by a personal identification with that pleasantly articulate commander. How blithely the commander, Dany Chamoun, heir to the prestige of a noble family in Lebanon, had managed to transcend the reality around him, the human consequences; and how easily Cyril had believed him, had accepted him as a reassuring cultured presence in the midst of savagery. Such a contrast in civility to the unstable victims who all looked and sounded alien, hysterical and dangerous.

Cyril set the transcript down, stared at the now-blank monitor for what felt like hours. When, finally, he stood he realized that he'd just experienced a moment in his father's secret life. He felt slightly ill.

9.

He was standing in the newsroom with his backpack. He couldn't bear the thought of going home. He desperately wanted to call Gloria but knew there would be no relief there either.

He heard a door close—Hughes had his coat on, briefcase in hand. He stopped and studied Cyril for a moment.

"You okay?"

"Yes. Sure. You're off?"

"Yes. Good night." Hughes stepped away, then paused, turned to him. "Maybe I have time for a quick pint. You?"

The pubs closest to the office were crowded and noisy. It was a baseball night. So they went to a hotel bar where it was dark and quiet. A waitress brought them a wine list. Hughes frowned at the prices. "This'll be my treat," he said. "A belated welcome." Cyril protested just enough to be polite.

"You don't seem to know much about your dad," Hughes said, after they'd ordered.

"My parents split up when I was twelve," Cyril said. "Even when he was around he wasn't very communicative. I assumed that he and Mom were from the same place, on the East Coast. But then he told me once that he was a refugee. I suppose I thought that was kind of cool. But he wouldn't talk about it so I eventually lost interest."

"You mentioned that he died."

"He went missing about five years ago. He was on his boat and the boat exploded. Afterwards there was no sign of him or any hint about what might have happened to him. Apart from the obvious. But that wasn't good enough for the lawyers and the insurance companies. Things were up in the air until recently. We got confirmation a few months ago."

"Any idea what caused it?" Hughes asked.

"Speculation that it was the propane tank and that the explosion blew him off the boat—the tide carried him away I guess. I gather the place is pretty remote."

"He was there alone?"

"Yes. Taking a bit of a break from a rough patch of work. He was a senior lawyer with a big mining company."

"He did well for himself."

"Yes, he did. He was a VP. Draycor PLC. You've heard of it?"

"Of course. This remote place? You've never gone there?"

"No."

"I can understand that," Hughes said. "He would have been how old when he left the old country?"

"Early twenties. I think twenty-two."

"A refugee."

"Yes."

The wine arrived in a carafe. The elegantly pretty server poured carefully, smiled at Hughes, and left.

Hughes raised his glass toward Cyril, nodded. "Well, here's to dads. In the end they're always mysterious. Probably because we can never know as much as we want to know about them. So you're unique only in the extent of what you don't know. Which might be a blessing. So anyway." He sipped.

"But you seem to know pretty well everything about your father."

Hughes laughed. "I know the obituary details. Born in North Belfast. Married. Went to Cambridge. Recruited to the foreign service. Postings here and there. Eventually Beirut, where I came along. I remember a man in a necktie. Even when we'd go for strolls on the Corniche or on excursions into the mountains, he'd wear a tie. Which is probably why I've always found work where you didn't have to wear one."

"He was a diplomat?"

"For a while. My mother told me before she passed on that he couldn't really deal with all the cloak-and-dagger stuff that went on there during the fifties and sixties. The Cold War stuff. So he switched careers. Taught at the American University of Beirut. I take it you don't know much about Lebanon."

Cyril shrugged. "I've been learning."

"It's pretty simple," he said. "Lebanese corruption. Tribal wars. Exploited by the neighbours, Syria and Israel. It's all you really need to know." He signalled to the server, muttering, "This wine isn't doing a thing for me." He grabbed a fistful of nuts from a bowl, shoved them in his mouth, and chewed rapidly as he studied Cyril's face with unfamiliar intensity.

"Take that young guy in the doc you were watching, the guy talking English. His name was Dany Chamoun and he was head of an

outfit called the National Liberal Party Tigers. Ruthless but not nec-
essarily the worst of the lot . . . pretty typical. Murdered in 1990 along
with his wife and their two kids, one seven and one five."

"Jesus."

"The most revealing part of what happened to him was that he
was killed by fellow Christians, Phalangists acting on behalf of
Syrians. Or Israelis. It doesn't really matter which. One of many
power struggles. That's the way it works. I wouldn't be surprised if
he and your dad knew each other."

"But how?"

Hughes shrugged. "So I'm gonna go out on a limb here, Cyril."
He swallowed and took another sip of his wine. "A whole lot of what
you and I don't know about our dads is because, one way or another,
they got mixed up in all that shit. And I'm gonna go another few
inches out on that limb and suggest that maybe it's just as well they
left us in the dark. We're a whole lot better off than they were." He
sat back.

Cyril took a deep breath. "So how did *your* dad die?"

Hughes laughed. "You won't believe this. We were on a holiday
in Belfast. It was 1978. A bad year in Beirut. Turns out it wasn't such
a great year in Belfast either. Anyway, he was standing at the bar at
our hotel, having a nightcap, minding his own business. Couple of
guys walk in and shoot up the bar. End of story."

"Who . . . ?"

"Who knows? What difference would it make, knowing?"

The waitress arrived at the table but Hughes had changed his mind
about another drink. "Just the cheque, please," he said.

～

Cyril watched him walk away in the direction of the subway station. He might have headed in the same direction, but he didn't feel like going home. He watched Hughes disappear around a corner. He wasn't a big man. He walked with short, quick steps, head tilted slightly forward. He was wearing a tweed jacket and cotton slacks and carrying a briefcase. From behind you could easily have assumed that he also wore a tie. He thought of calling Gloria again. He called his mother instead.

"I'm working late," he said. "Don't wait to have dinner."

"It sounds like you're on the street," she said.

"I just stepped out to grab a bite. Everything okay there?"

"Sure," she said, sounding dubious.

The wine had left a dry feeling in his mouth and his mind was humming with images from the Norwegian documentary. His mother's disapproval completed his determination to have another drink. And suddenly he knew where he would go to get it.

∼

It was like a summer evening on the Danforth. Wandering throngs on the sidewalks and flickering candles on crowded patios—he imagined a European capital. Street signs in Greek. Wine bottles, beer steins, fragments of conversations in foreign languages. He stared briefly at burly men in light leather jackets who stared back silently as he walked by one patio. Short hair, swarthy, calm, appraising faces. They had tiny espresso cups and glasses of water and nervously tapped cigarettes on ashtrays. So unlike his own neighbourhood west of the Don, just beyond the university, where the ethnicities were mostly white and deeply rooted.

And then he seemed to cross another line of demarcation. No patios here but bins of produce on the sidewalks, many shops advertising goods in scrawls that he would later recognize as Urdu. Men of all ages, most of them bearded, hurried eastward. In the distance he could see a minaret. There was a family walking ahead of him, mother swaddled head to toe, dad in a skullcap, knee-length jacket, baggy cotton pants and sandals, tall and quiet and aloof. Little girls, miniatures of Mom. And a little boy chattering and dribbling a basketball.

The Only Café was relatively quiet. There were just two men on the small fenced-in patio. One had a glass half-full of beer. The other man was large, elbows on the table, studying something he was twisting in his fingers. A small book of matches. There was a coffee mug beside his elbow and a cigarette smouldering between his fingers. Neither man paid attention to Cyril as he walked into the bar.

There was muted music. The Band. *Virgil Caine is the name and I served on the Danville train . . .* Cyril stood at the bar for a full minute before anybody noticed. The young man he had spoken to a week earlier was at the far end talking to a woman who was leaning close and smiling. Eventually she nodded in Cyril's direction and the bartender turned, smiled apologetically and approached him.

"I was here a week or so ago and I had a pint of something dark, like Smithwicks, but I think it was local."

"10W30?"

"Could have been. I didn't catch a name. I'll try that anyway."

The spigots were close by and as the bartender pulled the pint, Cyril said: "Last time I was here I left a note for a guy named Ari."

"Ah, yes," the waiter said. "I gave it to him."

"So he's here?"

"That's him outside." He placed the beer on a coaster in front of Cyril who stepped back, looking through the door toward the patio.

"The big guy," the bartender said. "Smoking. I'll send him your way when he comes in."

Cyril sat at a small wobbly table a few feet from the bar and from there he could clearly see the profile of the man called Ari, someone who had known his father. He was halfway through his beer before Ari came inside, filling the door frame with his bulk. He nodded at Cyril as he passed his table, then proceeded to the end of the bar where he engaged the bartender. Cyril kept his eyes down, knowing that he would be inspected. But when he stole a glance in their direction the big man had disappeared.

A small nudge of resentment. He fished his BlackBerry from a pocket, scrolled through messages. One from Leo: *How goes it where ever U R? Gonna make it to poker tonite?* He'd forgotten poker night. He was about to respond when a presence loomed.

"Cyril?"

"Yes." He put the phone back in his pocket and looked up.

Ari sat and sighed heavily, or perhaps was simply exhaling. He studied Cyril briefly. "So what can I do for you?"

The music volume suddenly cranked up. Herbie Hancock. "Watermelon Man." Ari looked annoyed, seemed about to shout a rebuke toward the bar, but then stood. "Let's go outside."

They sat where Ari had been sitting when Cyril arrived. Ari lit a cigarette, blew the flame from the match, exhaling smoke. "I suppose you're here about Pierre. Actually I had to do a bit of thinking before I remembered. It's been what? Years?"

"He disappeared just about five years ago."

"Yes. That sounds about right. And I think I read something lately."

"Confirmation that he was deceased."

"I'm sorry," Ari said, extending a thick hand. Cyril clasped it briefly. "How?"

"Nobody knows for sure. A boating accident. There was an explosion."

"Hmm. Yes. Boats can be dangerous. You must have been relieved, at least, to be able to start putting things behind you."

Cyril nodded. "Yes. But he left another mystery, a document in a file his lawyer had. You were mentioned in it."

"What kind of document?" Ari frowned.

"It suggested that you were important to him."

Ari raised his eyebrows, looked away. Shrugged.

"So can I ask? How did you come to know my father?"

"I noticed him when he came in here once. I'm basically nosy. He wasn't a regular and he wasn't typical of the clientele. He was a Bay Street lawyer, right?"

Cyril nodded.

"Yes. And now I remember. He was from Lebanon. We talked about the old country. I grew up in Israel and I've been to Lebanon. Many times."

"So you're not Lebanese."

"No. I'm more Canadian than anything else. Born in Montreal. My parents decided to do the kibbutz thing in the sixties. So I came of age in Israel, you could say. But I've been back here for quite a while now. Your dad was somebody intelligent to talk to. So tell me, if you don't mind, why do you say he disappeared when you knew there was a boating accident?"

"We know the boat blew up. But they never found his body. Until recently, when they found a fragment. It was how they confirmed that he was dead. There was speculation for a while that he just made himself disappear, or that he killed himself."

"So they've ruled out suicide?"

"Yes."

"But you still have doubts about how he died?"

"I wouldn't call them doubts. Just a feeling that makes me want to find out more about him and what was going on back in '07."

"He had a lot on his plate when I last spoke to him."

"The controversy over what happened at the mine in Indonesia?"

"Yes," he said. "That bothered him a lot. And then of course the cancer diagnosis."

"Cancer?"

Ari studied him carefully, a slow flush rising in his face. It was a kind face, Cyril thought—especially the eyes, dark and deep and warm.

"You didn't know about that?"

"There were hints. What kind of cancer?"

"I shouldn't. But I guess it doesn't matter anymore. It was prostate."

"Prostate."

"I remember people talking about him here, when he disappeared, that maybe he just flew the coop. You hear about it all the time."

"You think . . ."

"I think nothing. I knew about the cancer. I knew what he was going through. Pressures of work, pressures of home. Something snaps."

"You think that's what happened?"

"Like I said, I think nothing. What's to think? Nothing changes, no matter what we think." Ari peered off into the distance. Then made eye contact again and held it, unblinking for what felt like minutes. Then he rubbed his hands over his face and massaged his eyeballs with clenched fists. "Okay." Paused again. "I'm going to have a drink. Your dad enjoyed his Scotch. How about you?"

"Yes."

"I will tell you what I know, which isn't much. But we can enjoy the drink. In his memory."

~

Later, when Cyril stood to leave, Ari remained seated. "One question, if I may."

Cyril sat.

"You referred to a document, that mentioned me?" He smiled, his expression cool.

"Of course," said Cyril. "Sorry. I almost forgot. He didn't want a funeral or a conventional memorial of any kind. But he wanted something here, at this bar."

Ari frowned. "Here?"

"Yes. He said he wanted a little gathering for people who were close to him. He said it should be like a . . . roast."

"A what?"

"A roast. Like when—"

"I know what a roast is."

"He left a list of people. I really didn't know anybody in his circle, but you were on the list. And he said you'd know what he meant and that you'd help arrange the roast."

Ari sat back with his hands across his stomach and studied his fingers. When he looked up he stared at Cyril as if seeing him for the first time.

"Let me think about it," he said.

Cyril sighed. "Do you think he was serious?"

Ari laughed. "I think he was serious. But I'm not sure what he had in mind. All due respect, you can never tell with an Arab. It's how they manage to survive."

10.

He was at the subway stop where he'd normally transfer to a south-bound bus that would take him into Leo's neighbourhood when he admitted that he really couldn't face his poker buddies. Not after what he'd heard from this odd stranger, Ari no-last-name.

He left the station, briefly considered heading home, but walked up to the street and just stood there staring at the traffic, the strangers passing, oblivious. Everyone oblivious. In his mind an image: his father standing on a street like this on one forgotten evening long ago, marooned somewhere within himself, and for lack of any immediate purpose or destination wandering into an establishment he'd never heard of, a place with an intriguing name. A café that was really just a bar with coffee on the side.

Standing there on the corner at—he looked upwards toward the street signs—Bloor and Ossington, Cyril knew that from the moment when Ari had disclosed the most shocking details of his father's cancer treatment, there was someone in particular he had to talk to and he had no idea how or where he could begin.

He had the cellphone in his hand, scrolled through contacts. Found a number but knew that it was at least five years old. He poked it anyway.

She answered merrily but went silent when she heard his voice.

"Lois?" he repeated.

"Yes."

"Hi."

"Hi."

"Look. About the other day, when you were at Mom's. I was thinking afterwards. I'm sorry I bailed out for a while. It must have seemed rude."

"I didn't make anything of it. Where are you?"

"Just out and about."

"Okay."

He knew what he needed but had no idea how to approach the subject tactfully. So he blurted, "Look, I know it's late but . . ."

She laughed. "You call this late? You must lead a quiet life."

"Well, since you brought it up . . ." He tried to laugh too.

"Cyril, what do you want?"

"I want to talk. Sometime. It doesn't have to be right now."

"Talk about what."

"About Dad."

"What about Dad."

"I met Ari, the guy who was mentioned in Dad's note about the roast. We talked about stuff." There was a long silence until finally he asked, "Are you still there?"

"What kind of stuff?"

"Well, about that roast idea. And about his health. You know he had cancer."

"I lived with him. What do you think?"

"I didn't know. I'd like to talk about it."

"What's to talk about? It's hardly relevant anymore. Is it?"

"It could be. I just want to talk."

She sighed. "Where did you say you were?"

"Bloor and Ossington."

"You remember where I live."

"Of course. You're sure it's okay?"

"No."

She opened the door and stepped back, then walked down the hall-way toward the kitchen. She was wearing baggy sweatpants, woollen socks, a light blue cotton turtleneck. He passed the dining room, which had been transformed into a playroom. There were miniature vehicles and bits of Lego scattered on the floor, a stack of kids' books on the table.

There was a bottle of wine on the kitchen counter, Chardonnay, just out of the refrigerator. "I was about to have a glass."

He looked around. "You haven't changed much here, though I think the paint is new?"

She stood, arms folded, saying nothing.

"It's kind of strange, being here," he said. "It's been a while."

"It has." She turned to the counter, picked up a pill vial and removed the top. "Excuse me a sec." She popped something into her mouth.

"You okay?" he asked.

She waved a dismissive hand. "Never better. Just need something to help me sleep. If I don't take something I'm half-awake all night listening for Pete. Of course he sleeps through the night now, but I haven't got used to it yet. You look tired."

"Work is kind of stressful," he said. "I've been digging into Lebanon."

"Lebanon."

"Yes. The civil war stuff. I had no idea."

She nodded, then picked up the bottle, unscrewed the cap and poured slowly into a glass. "Would you care for some?"

He shook his head.

"He never talked about it, you know." She turned, leaned back against the counter.

"I know."

"Just that he figured that the place had settled down and he wanted to go back, to touch base, I guess. Then the Israelis invaded in 2006. He said he wasn't concerned for himself. It was mostly about me being Jewish, etcetera."

"What's that got to do with it?"

She laughed. "You really haven't done much research, have you?"

He felt the blush. "Well, I know about Israel . . ."

"That's a start." She sipped. "Anyway, after the Israeli bombing campaign . . . well, that was the end of that."

"Maybe I will have a glass," he said.

She turned, reached up toward a cupboard door.

He watched her as she stretched on tiptoes, withdrew the glass, then set it down slowly, unscrewed the top again, tipped the bottle, poured carefully. When she turned he blushed because her glance convinced him she could read his mind. She sat, crossed her legs, leaned forward, elbows on the table. Swirled the contents of her glass.

"So," she said.

"You never met this Ari?"

"I think Pierre mentioned him once or twice but I'd forgotten all about it before that piece of paper turned up. Who is he?"

"I don't know much. He still hangs around that little bar in the east end. He says he was born in Montreal but grew up on a kibbutz in Israel. Seems to know a lot about politics, says he worked in Lebanon and knows the place."

"I'm not surprised."

"Oh?"

"It'd be the one thing they'd have in common. The war."

"How do you know that?"

"Everybody knows that, love. In my humble opinion, Lebanon is potentially the ruination of Israel. Never mind the West Bank. When we think of Lebanon, we have to think Iran."

"Iran? I thought Syria."

"Oh yes, that too. And Saudi Arabia and Egypt and Gaza and you name it. Don't expect to ever understand it. I don't, and I've been hearing about it all my life. Mom and Dad are classic salon Zionists."

He wobbled his head. "Okay. But there was something else."

"Oh?"

"This Ari guy. Dad told him about his prostate cancer."

"And so?"

He emptied his glass, then held it up. "Do you mind?"

"Help yourself," she said, and got up, brought the bottle to the table. "Pierre didn't want to worry you or your mother about the cancer. He thought he was on top of it."

"I'm going to look through his diaries to see if he mentioned anything there, but I doubt if I'll find anything. The weird thing is, the one diary where you'd expect to find stuff like that, the work problems and the cancer—I can't find it. 2007 is missing."

"Hmm."

"You didn't happen to . . ."

"Nope. I was pretty thorough when I packed his things."

He reached for the bottle of Chardonnay again. "You don't mind?"

"Be my guest. So what did Ari have to say about the cancer?"

"He told me how he wanted to treat it, and the side effects."

"Okay."

"Testosterone blocking, he said. Shutting down the prostate. Right?"

She stood. "Boy. You and this Ari sure bonded in a hurry."

"I have to ask . . . did he?"

"Did he what?"

"Did he take medication to . . . ?"

"Why would that be any of *your* business? Even if your father was still alive, I suspect he'd have the same response if you asked him."

"Well . . ."

"It really isn't any of your concern. Look. I'm suddenly feeling kind of tired. I have an early start." She turned away from him, turned on a tap and rinsed her wineglass.

"I think it *is* my fucking business, what happened with you and me . . ."

"I think you'd better leave," she said.

"If Dad was impotent . . ."

"I don't think I like where this is going."

He felt a pounding inside his skull, the same sensation that he'd felt just before he'd walked away from Gloria.

"Just go," she said.

He put his glass down carefully and stood, struggling for control, and failing. "Okay, I'm going," he said. "And you can go fuck yourself with your attitude."

She stared at him coldly.

~

Once outside he'd realized that it was only a fifteen-minute walk from where Lois lived to Aggie's—just about the time he needed for a total reassessment of his life and the role of women in it. The clarity was as if someone had lit a floodlight in his brain. Women: crucibles of misery. *Without exception.* He remembered reading about an insect that fucks her mate then eats him. Excellent. At least the insect victim didn't have to stomach the humiliation, the self-reproach. The *emasculation*. As Cyril strode up Banting Avenue a raccoon waddled out of the bushes in a neighbour's yard and stopped, oozing insolence. He ran at it, tried to kick it. The raccoon reared up, hissing, forcing Cyril to retreat. "Fuck you too," he said.

He sat on his mother's doorstep. How tragic if his father had been emasculated physically by some oncologist and then emotionally by that witch and—this is where Cyril's outrage wobbled, started slipping down the anger scale toward guilt—if Pierre had known about the treacherous involvement of his son. He bent forward over his knees and rocked, hands covering his face until the red wine and beer and Scotch and white wine roiled and shot up into his burning throat. He dashed around the corner of the house and heaved.

∿

Breakfast was the other thing that pissed him off about living with his mother. Aggie was an early riser, made a point of telling him ad nauseam how wonderful the world was just before the sun came up. How fresh the city smelled, how serene she found the expectant silence just before the rosy blush of dawn illuminated the eastern horizon, an image that she'd probably read somewhere. He descended from his room into the snap of bacon in the frying pan, the cloying smell of it. Breakfast was the only thing that Cyril found more repellent than getting out of bed. And never more than on the morning after his lamentable encounter with the woman who was, legally, his stepmother.

"Good morning," Aggie said cheerfully, pouring orange juice.

He nodded. He liked his coffee black but Aggie insisted that the flavour would be significantly improved by some oil-based coffee mix. He sat. The mug of ruined coffee was awaiting him.

She put the plate down. "You'll have toast." She rubbed a hand across his back, squeezed his shoulder. He winced.

"Eat up," she said. "Breakfast is the most important meal of the day. What did you have to eat last night, by the way?"

"I grabbed a sandwich," he replied, poking at the egg yolk. Halfway through the effort to force the food down he stood suddenly. "I just remembered. I have an early meeting. Shit. I'm sorry."

"My God, for a job that doesn't pay you anything they like to keep you hopping. Isn't there anybody else working down there?"

"Bye, Mom." He kissed her swiftly on the cheek, and fled.

～

When he arrived at work he was pleasantly surprised to see Suzanne Reynolds standing in the middle of the newsroom. She smiled and waved at him.

He noticed there was a DVD in his mailbox. Seeing his name above the little slot never failed to lift his spirits even though his name was hand-lettered on a scrap of paper that was Scotch-taped on. There was a yellow sticky-memo on the DVD: "East Timor. You should bone up on this. Doc." *Another uplifting story*, he told himself as he sat down. He set the disk aside and picked up the transcript of the Norwegian documentary but couldn't suppress the urge to look around the room for another sighting of Suzanne.

She was standing with the anchor, Manville, who to Cyril seemed much taller and more bald than he'd imagined from watching him on television—not that watching newscasts had been a large part of his life before Gloria had suggested that he might have a latent flair for it. Suzanne and Manville were behaving like old friends and she gently pushed him at one point, laughing at something he had said to her.

In his heart a little tremor—envy, or a sudden recognition of the yawning space between where he was in the journalistic cellar and the Olympian plateau on which Reynolds and Manville were established.

He returned to the English transcript of the Norwegian documentary for the distraction of confronting human circumstances a whole lot worse than his. And if Lebanon failed to do the trick, he had East Timor to look forward to.

He felt light fingers on his shoulder. "What'ya got there?" Suzanne was staring down at his transcript.

"Lebanon," he said. "Translation of a Norwegian documentary I watched."

"Ah," she said. "Any good?"

"Interesting," he said. "A bit one-sided."

"That's Lebanon," she said. "Impossible to find the middle ground."

"When did you get back?"

"Last night," she said. "They got nervous about the cost." She grimaced. "The way it is today—frigging accountants calling the shots for *everything*. Can I buy you a coffee?"

"Actually, that would be nice," he said, remembering the corrupted mug he'd left cooling on his mother's table.

In the elevator he was aware of being noticed and knew it was because he was in the company of Suzanne. But that was okay. Hardly anybody spoke to her but there were nods. Her glow seemed to warm the crowded space.

Lined up at the coffee shop he said, "I've never seen Lloyd in this early." He wanted to add lightly: *Must be because of you.* Thought better of it.

"Have you met him yet?" she asked.

"Um . . . no."

"We'll remedy that," she said. "Great guy. A real trooper. What'll you have?"

When they sat close together at a very small table in a corner, she returned to the subject of the anchor. "There's nobody quite like him, not even in the States, when it comes to live coverage . . . conventions and elections and the like."

"How often does he have to do that?" Cyril asked, and was instantly afraid he shouldn't have.

But Suzanne smiled. "You're naughty."

Emboldened by the smile, he said, "What does he do in between elections, besides read the news?"

"It's a whole lot more than reciting what he sees on a teleprompter. You'll soon find that out."

"I doubt it," he said. "I'm just an intern, a ship . . . more like a canoe . . . passing in the night."

She laughed. "Yeah, right!"

"Seriously," he said.

She placed a hand on his briefly. "Don't be negative," she said. "I hear you've made a strong impression."

"Okay."

"That's what counts around here. Impressions." She stood. "Bring the coffee with you. We can talk more later. Maybe after work. A drink?"

"Sure."

~

Mercifully nobody seemed to notice that he was at the story meeting, not even Hughes. He loved the intensity of these sessions but dreaded being asked for input that would reveal his utter ignorance of most of what they were going on about. Long conversation with the chief political reporter in Ottawa—maybe a reality check regarding new federal regulations for coal-fired energy but please, pretty please, don't make it sound like another slap at the Tory government; Washington guy somewhere in Ohio arguing for a story about Obama leading pre-election polls in that important state; a follow-up to the murder of the American ambassador to Libya in a shootout in Benghazi.

Suzanne chimed in at this point, challenging Hughes who had attributed the Benghazi incident to an outrageous new film by right-wing Americans attacking Islam. "That is such bullshit," she announced. Hughes looked startled.

"Are we really going to waste airtime on that propaganda? Keep your eye on the big picture, guys. You want to talk about insulting Islam? Try trivializing their outrage by attributing it to some fifth-rate piece of American bigotry . . ."

And she went on. Cyril was mesmerized. Hughes was studying a file, plucking at the end of his nose.

"You aren't even fucking listening, Ian," Suzanne accused.

"I am," Hughes replied. "Really. I'm really listening for something new in what you're going on about. Something that might offer us a peg for putting something on the air. Today. Okay?" He slapped the folder down. "You haven't been away so long, Suzy."

"Don't fucking call me Suzy."

"Excuse me, Suzanne. But you haven't been away so long that you've forgotten we are a daily show and that it's an old, old convention in our business to let people know right off the top why we're asking them to pay attention to a particular story . . ."

"Don't lecture me."

Hughes sighed heavily. Manville was smiling slightly. Doc was tapping the end of his ballpoint on the table, calculating where creative tension might turn into conflict.

"Sorry," Hughes said. "Didn't mean to make it sound like a lecture."

"Okay," said Savage. "Lloyd?"

Manville cleared his throat.

～

They decided that Suzanne would take some time quietly exploring an issue that had slipped right off the radar—the whole phenomenon of homegrown terrorism. It had been a big news story six years earlier when eighteen people were busted over plans to blow up places like a stock exchange, Parliament. The hit list was long and ludicrous. Cyril remembered the hullabaloo but questions lingered about whether there had ever been a real threat and, if so, had it been extinguished. And if not . . . it was time to pick up the story where it left off after the conviction and imprisonment of the ringleaders in the terror plot. It was doable and cheap and, just before the meeting ended, Doc Savage declared, "For those of you who don't already know him, I want to introduce a new member of our team, our ace in the hole. Stand up, Nader."

Nader stood. Cyril hadn't noticed him. He'd been seated at the table, back turned. He was young and brown with black-framed glasses and a wispy beard along his jawline. Hair unfashionably long. He looked studious. His lips moved slightly in what could have been a smile. He bowed to the room. Cyril tried to stifle a primal stirring in a dark region of his limbic system—his paleo-mammalian survival complex. Irrational resentment. Insecurity.

"Nader's back with us after a spell away brushing up his Arabic. Morocco, wasn't it? We're thrilled to have him back. He's going to be busy, though we won't see him around here much. He has a lot of contacts, let's just say. Mosques and the security establishment. So that's where he's going to be spending most of his time, cultivating sources. He'll report directly to Suzanne. We'll assign a producer later."

Cyril was surprised when Nader turned to him directly as everyone was leaving, smiled broadly and held out a collegial hand.

"Nader Hashem."

"Cyril Cormier."

"We should grab a cuppa tea sometime," Nader said. "You can give me the lay of the land. Like the man said, I've been away."

Cyril laughed nervously. "Well, sure, Nader. You're an intern too?"

"Nah. Worked here as a temp once before. Got a year-long contract this time. We'll see at the end of that."

"Ah," said Cyril.

"We can talk about the War on Terrible."

"The what? You mean the . . ."

Nader winked and walked away.

Suzanne and Hughes were standing in the corridor outside the boardroom. She hailed Cyril. "Come over here. I hear you've been talking to this fossil."

Hughes ignored her. "Did you get up to anything interesting last night after I left?"

"Actually," said Cyril, "I hit another bar. A place on the Danforth. You got me thinking. I met up with a fellow my father used to know."

"Ah," said Hughes. "Somebody from the old country."

"Actually, no. Some guy from Israel."

11.

The caller ID provided neither name nor number, so Cyril was surprised to hear Gloria's voice when he picked up.

"Hi."

"It's me," she said, "in case you don't remember."

"Of course I remember," he said. "It's just that I wasn't expecting . . . where are you calling from?"

"Work."

"How is work?"

"The usual. Did I get you at a bad time?"

"No."

"You sound distracted."

"Well, I'm in the middle of something. But how are you?"

"You know, nothing spectacular," she said. "I was wondering about later, maybe after . . ."

"I think I've got something on . . ."

"Oh? Okay then . . ."

"What about lunch?" he said.

"Let me call you back."

She called back minutes later. "I'll have about half an hour at one o'clock."

They agreed to meet at a small burrito place where service was efficient. He was surprised by a confusing buzz after he hung up that he would later break down to its particulars: anticipation, anxiety, a tingle of uncertainty.

∽

Suzanne had been standing in the doorway to Hughes's office, arms folded, leaning on the door frame. Now she was chatting at a workstation halfway across the newsroom. She's like the queen bee in a hive, he thought—always seems to be idle but really the most important worker in the place. He could feel her curiosity about him and wondered what it could possibly be based on. Surely nothing more than generosity. He tried to estimate her age. She'd been around for decades, so maybe fifty. His mother was only a few years older than that, but, Jesus, this Suzanne looked good. It's all in outlook: Think young, act young, be young. His brain lurched into a forbidden zone: what would *that* be like. An older woman. A grown-up. Then again he'd once considered Lois to be an older woman when she was only, what . . . twenty-four. Same as he is now.

"Hi you," she said when she got over to his cubicle.

One of those open-ended greetings that seemed to be loaded with insinuation. Insinuating what, though?

"Hey."

"You look busy."

He laughed. "I'm glad you think so. I don't know yet the difference between busy and confused."

"Just to know there's a difference between confused and busy puts you way ahead of most of us," she said. "So, you have time to indulge me in that drink a little later, right?"

"Of course," he said.

"Maybe pop into that place you mentioned, where you met the Israeli guy."

"You might find it a little funky."

"Funky is good. I came of age on funk. So what was the connection between your dad and this guy?"

"I have no idea. My father mentioned him in a paper about the kind of memorial service he wanted. It was with his will."

"He must have known this guy pretty well."

Cyril shrugged.

"You have a name?"

"Ari."

"Ari what?"

"No last name that I know yet."

"Your dad didn't give him a last name?"

"Nope."

"Ari. Interesting. Later then."

"Right on," he said, realizing immediately that it sounded adolescent. *Right on.* Christ. But she hadn't noticed, just smiled. He watched her walk away, admired the fluid movement.

~

Gloria was waiting for him just inside the door of the burrito place. She was pale and looked weary even when she smiled. Hair swept back in a ponytail that didn't really suit her. High heels and a pantsuit on someone who looked best in jeans and running shoes.

"You're okay," she said, eyes searching his.

"All things considered," he said. He knew better than to tell her she looked tired because he wasn't sure if she would take it as a compliment. "You're all dressed up," he said. She blushed and instantly looked healthier.

They lined up. Trampled on each other's efforts to begin a conversation. Laughed self-consciously. Went silent, studying the menu that was pasted on the wall.

"You'll be having the usual," he said.

"You remember?" She ordered a burrito bowl, vegetarian. "You'll be having yours with chicken?"

"I guess."

She had her wallet out. "My treat."

"No, no."

"Yes, yes. Unless you can tell me truthfully that they've started paying you."

"Not exactly."

"Maybe you need a good lawyer. Launch a class-action suit against those companies who exploit the young. Internship, my eye. It used to be called indentured service."

"Actually, indentured would be a form of job security. We don't even have that. And they used to feed and house the servants."

"I'm only half-joking about the lawsuit."

"Maybe after I get through the door."

"See. That's the problem," she said, turning toward the cashier. "They hold your future hostage."

When they were seated, she said, "And how is Mom?"

He winced. "Mom is Mom."

She giggled then. "I can't imagine it."

"Can't imagine what?"

Gloria was studying her bowl, poking at the rice. "You and Aggie, cohabitating again."

"Under the circumstances I don't have many options."

"You want to talk about the circumstances?"

He leaned back, threw an arm over the back of his chair and let her talk.

She missed him. He interrupted once, to tell her that he missed her too. She had surprised herself discovering that what she missed most, and he shouldn't take this the wrong way, was the companionship. Everything else was great. The fun, the intimacy. But knowing, coming home, that there would be someone there to talk to—just talk. That was what she missed.

She smiled but her eyes were serious and searching. "Just talk about the little things like, oh I don't know." She pretended to ponder, then smiled. "Like the rest of your life?"

He laughed, picked up a fork, then put it down, dismissed an impulse to comment on the futility of life in general.

"Am I boring you?" she asked.

"God no. I'm just listening."

"You know what I'm saying?" Her eyes were briefly pinkish. She looked away, crossed her arms, seemed suddenly interested in the strangers at the tables all around them.

"I suppose we should be getting back," she said.

He felt terrible. There was such truth in her sentiments, so much more integrity than the facile "I love you" that was rattling around in his conflicted brain.

"What does your weekend look like?" he said.

"My weekend?" She managed to chuckle. "My weeks don't end. What did you have in mind?"

"I dunno," he said. "I want to continue the conversation because . . ." He stopped, rubbed his face. "Because I do love you."

"I know you do," she said gently. "But that isn't really the point, is it?"

"No," he said. "It isn't the point. But I'd like to have a longer conversation about 'the point.'"

"I have to work tomorrow," she said. "But I should be clear on Sunday. At least Sunday morning. We could go for a run together."

"I haven't been doing much running lately."

"I could make you brunch."

"Or there's the old diner on College. I could meet you there."

She paused. "Okay. Let's touch base beforehand. That sound good to you?"

"Sounds good."

They hugged on the sidewalk, then went off in different directions.

12.

It was the rush-hour peak when he and Suzanne left the office so it took a while to catch the attention of a cab driver. Suzanne had warned him, "I'll probably be fading fast by eight o'clock. I ain't as young as I used to be."

"If you want to leave it for another time," he'd responded, trying not to show the twinge of insecurity at what he felt to be a tiny hint of ambivalence on her part.

"No, no," she'd insisted. "Let's do it."

Her Facebook page, which he'd checked that afternoon, revealed that she was a Gemini, May 19, 1962. He was both amazed and impressed to see her birthdate in such a public place. That would make her fifty years old, which meant that she was twenty-six when he was born. Physically she could have passed for mid-thirties.

In the back seat of the cab Suzanne asked playfully, "So what would you be doing on a Friday evening if you weren't going on a date with someone old enough to be your mother."

"Come on," he said, and laughed. "Who are you kidding?"

She looked out her window for a while as the taxi manoeuvred through the gridlocked city, then said, "No, really—what would you be up to?"

"I don't know," he said. "I'd probably have stayed at the office for a while. Screening stuff."

"Probably you would," she said. "I'm going to talk to Savage about that. Aimless screening is a waste of your time."

"It's interesting just the same. I'm studying production technique."

"You should be shooting higher than production technique. Let other people worry about that stuff."

Then, sliding across the car seat to be closer, she said, "But you didn't really answer my question. Say you weren't with me and you weren't immersed in 'production technique'?"

"Hard to say."

"Hard what . . . deciding which of your many lucky girlfriends would get to spend the evening with you?"

He knew that he was blushing and that she could see it. She laughed and grabbed his hand, snuggled closer.

"Really," he said, "no girlfriends at the moment."

"Hah."

"So what would *you* be doing?"

"Well, I wouldn't be at the office. I'd probably meet up with Bruno somewhere, maybe hear some music, take in a movie, a bit of dinner. Nothing major. Or more likely, into my jammies early."

"Bruno?"

"That's what I call him. He's away, though, so you don't have to worry."

Worry about what, he wondered. "He travels a lot, does he?"

"Not really. But he gets asked to literary things and sometimes he accepts. This one's on the West Coast and he's wild about Vancouver. Keeps talking about us moving there."

She released his hand. He realized that she presumed he'd know who Bruno was since her life was more or less transparent as it was for most celebrities.

"So, does SHE have a name? Come on, I'm not buying this 'no girlfriends' business."

"Well. We're on a kind of hiatus," he said. "But her name is Gloria."

"Gloria," she said. "So what's with the hiatus?"

"I don't know," he said, uncomfortable. "She's trying to start a career in law and I'm here. I guess we're both trying to figure things out."

"That's where people make the big mistake," she said. "Too much figuring. Life is short."

"So I hear."

"So how old would your dad be now?" she asked.

"Fifty-two or fifty-three," he said.

"What a waste," she said and grabbed his hand again, squeezed, then held it in both of hers for the rest of the taxi ride. "Dads." She sighed.

When the taxi finally pulled over she already had her wallet in her hand and was leaning forward.

"Let me get this," he said, fishing crumpled bills from the pocket of his jeans. "Come on, wait."

"A receipt, please," she said to the driver. "Add five bucks."

As the driver wrote, she patted Cyril's knee and said: "I'll expense it. This is work."

The café was full, all the little tables occupied, people standing all along the bar. Music loud. The Clash, again. They passed through the crowd, people noticing Suzanne, then through the curtain to the other side, where they found a place to sit. Cyril returned to the bar to order drinks, scanning faces to find Ari.

"He stepped out," the bartender told him. "If I see him I'll tell him you're here."

"Appreciate it."

~

"You must get noticed a lot," Cyril said as he put the drinks down. "How do you feel about that?"

"The secret is to avoid eye contact," she said. "Eye contact instantly removes a barrier."

"It must be a nuisance."

"No," she said. "It goes with the job. The public is the boss. Really."

Going to the washroom he took the long way around, passing through the bar. No sign of Ari. When he was paying for the second round, the bartender assured him, "He'll show up. He always does, sooner or later."

"So, your dad," she said, when he sat back down. "What do you know about him and Lebanon?"

"Not much. All his connections were gone by the time my mother met him. I gather a lot of them were killed in the war. I've only heard about a sister. Name of Miriam. That's all."

"Cormier," she said. "Not really a—"

"He changed his last name when he got here. Making a break, I guess."

"The name he was born with, I don't suppose—"

"Yes," he said. "Haddad. I remember thinking, 'My dad Haddad.' It kind of stuck."

"Haddad. It's a common name over there among the Christians. Especially in the south. There was a notorious warlord named Haddad, a Greek Catholic. I wonder if —"

"I don't know anything about Lebanese politics or religions."

"The main Christian religious group is Maronite. A branch of Catholics. Very big in Lebanon, pretty well controlled the economy and the politics until the civil war."

"My dad wasn't religious. He told me he grew up poor."

She laughed. "That's probably a good thing. Religion and money are at the root of everything that's wrong in the world. In-my-humble, anyway."

"So what did your dad do?" he asked.

"Ah. My dad." Her gaze shifted to people at other tables, wearing headsets, studying laptop screens, chattering. "Dad was a career soldier. I'm an army brat. We lived here and there. A stint in Europe. When he moved from Germany to Cyprus in the mid-seventies, Mom and I and Willie—he's my younger brother—moved back to where Dad came from, in Prince George."

"And your dad, now? Must be retired."

"My dad killed himself," she said.

"Fuck. I mean . . . sorry."

"That's okay," she said. "It was exactly my reaction at the time. Oh fuck."

She sipped. Cyril waited.

"It was after Somalia," she said. "Mercifully it was called an accident. But it was pretty obvious. He must have been going a hundred and forty when he hit the bridge abutment. Not a skid mark on the road. Ah, well. He went through a lot. The strange thing was that he was pretty high up. A lieutenant general."

"I'm so sorry," Cyril said. "I don't know what to say."

"You don't have to say anything. I suspect you know all about it." She caught his hand, then let it go and sat back, studying her drink.

"Your Gloria," she said. "How serious is that? Or was that?"

"Difficult to say," he said. "I thought it was serious. I suppose it always is, when you're in it. Right?"

"I suppose," she said. "I didn't think about relationships when I should have. All I thought about was work. And then it's too late and you always wonder."

"So Bruno?"

"Bruno?"

"So what does he do?"

"Right, you wouldn't know. It's Frank Anderson. I'm the only one who calls him Bruno."

"Okay."

She tilted back and laughed loudly. "You never heard of him? He'd be devastated."

"So he's in the media?"

"Well, yes and no. Not our media. He writes books and freelances magazine pieces. He had a piece in the *New Yorker* a few months back."

"I've been meaning to start reading the *New Yorker*."

"You must. The voice of reason in that crazy country. So, where do you live?"

"Annex, just now. With my mom." He rolled his eyes, sighed.

"She must be pleased to have you back."

"That's half the problem." And then he spotted Ari staring through the open curtain. He waved to get his attention. Ari nodded and disappeared. Moments later he was standing by the table.

"Hello again," he said.

Cyril stood, they shook hands. "I want you to meet a colleague, Suzanne Reynolds. This is Ari," Cyril said.

Ari extended his hand and Suzanne grasped it, smiling warily.

"A colleague," Ari said. "I'm sorry . . . I don't remember where it is you work."

"I might not have said. Television," he said. "Suzanne is . . ."

"I know the name," said Ari. "But I don't watch much. I don't own a television."

Suzanne continued smiling, appraising, interested, civil. A smile that could have led the moment anywhere she wanted it to go. "I didn't get a last name," she said.

"No? I suppose you didn't." Ari laughed and turned away. "I'm with a friend just now but I'll come back. Can I get you anything?"

Cyril looked at Suzanne and she shook her head. "We're fine," he said.

Ari nodded and walked away.

"I know him from somewhere," Suzanne said as he disappeared through the curtain.

"Really?"

"But then again." She picked up her drink, then put it down and clasped her hands, chewing on the corner of her lower lip. "Just my imagination, I expect. He's out of central casting."

"How so?"

"IDF. Israeli military macho. The confidence, the poise. Hard to imagine these were the most vulnerable, paranoid and victimized people in the world until just a few generations back."

"IDF . . ."

"Israeli Defense Force."

"I don't think I've ever met an Israeli before."

"No? You should see the women. The young ones." She pretended to leer.

"You've been over there a lot."

"Oh yes. Probably why I can't shake the feeling that I know him from somewhere. Oops, there he is again—I think he wants you."

Cyril looked toward the curtain and Ari nodded toward the bar side. Cyril excused himself.

~

"What do you know about her?" Ari said.

"She's one of our star correspondents . . . she's nice. She's been to Israel a lot, she says. You two should . . ."

"I don't like reporters very much. Especially reporters like her. Vultures. Anti-Semites."

"Anti—"

"Whose idea was it, coming here? Hers?"

"No. I just thought you two would have a lot to talk about."

Ari laughed. "Yes, probably. But I have no interest in talking to her. So, convey my apologies." He turned away, then stopped and faced Cyril once again. "One more thing. You should be very, very careful. If she finds out who your dad was, I can safely say you're finished as far as she's concerned. And take it from me, she can do a lot of damage."

FOUR

TESTOSTERONE

13. *June 23, 2007*

Pierre was just outside the mouth of the little harbour, approaching the breakwater, when the phone chimed. He recognized Ethan's number and throttled back, reversed briefly. He answered, letting the boat drift in the stiff offshore breeze while they spoke.

Ethan sounded tense. "How's the weather out there?"

"Passable." He let the silence hang.

"Really hot here and humid. I keep wondering how Lois is coping. You'll let us know if there's anything . . ."

"Ethan?"

"What?"

"You didn't call to talk about the weather or Lois. What's up?"

"I'm afraid this is turning into a story. Some little rag out east got onto it. I'm surprised you haven't seen it. Anyway. They're picking up on it here and it's been making waves. The timing is bad."

"What else is new."

"I shouldn't tell you this but they're onto torture now."

"What?"

"You heard me. Silly bastards. Now they're saying we're implicated in a torture scenario."

"Who is saying that?"

"Communications is getting blitzed now by the media."

"For Christ's sake, where's this coming from?"

"This Ramos guy . . . the ringleader. He gave them the slip and now he's in Australia telling anyone who'll listen that he and several other troublemakers were tortured—get this—on our behalf and under pressure from Toronto."

"Come on. Who believes him?"

"It gets worse. One of these dirtbags died in custody. Who knows why? But Ramos—I believe they call him Rambo—is saying it was during an *enhanced interrogation*. His words. Enhanced-fucking-interrogation. That's what we're up against now—a whole new vocabulary. And the media just laps it up."

Pierre's mind was racing: What could possibly have been construed by anyone in Puncak as "pressure" to extract the truth at any cost? He could think of nothing, spoken or written. Then he thought of MacIsaac. *Some little rag out east got onto it.*

Sandy MacIsaac. *There's a rumour here that the order for the military crackdown came from Canada. From the company.*

He could see a figure standing on the end of the wharf, hand shading eyes, watching him. The figure waved, turned and walked out of sight.

"As far as I'm concerned," Pierre said, "there's absolutely no factual basis to support anything he's saying. I think we should prepare to sue the sons-of-bitches who report this. I can tell you, absolutely, that I said nothing and wrote nothing that could possibly be construed as anything more than legitimate inquiry. For Christ's sake, I was determined to make sure that everything was above board. And what's this about a fucking story out here? I've heard nothing."

"Well, that's been part of the fallout from the Ramos shit."

The story was a heavy-handed feature in a local weekly about a Nova Scotia miner and his brush with violence in a distant land, his personal response to what he'd considered an atrocity.

Before he'd left Toronto Pierre had confidently assured Public Affairs that the story would remain dormant, buried in the larger context of circumstances particular to Indonesia, a place where institutions were evolving, to say the least.

Now, however—thanks to Sandy MacIsaac —the Puncak story had a credible Draycor hook. A former Draycor miner—never mind that he had been working on a subcontract—was a witness and he was talking. A Toronto journalist who kept in touch with home through a subscription to the little weekly paper in some place called Inverness had spotted the breathless tale: unreported massacre; local miner witness. *Exclusive.*

"Do you know this Inverness?" Ethan asked.

"Yes, it's just a few miles from here."

"And this guy MacIsaac, is he the guy you mentioned?"

"Yes. I talked to him when I was there, at the mine."

"Right. And have you ever talked to the reporter? Margaret Rankin?"

"No. I've seen her byline, though."

"Well, check your emails. She found this MacIsaac dude in the fucking phone book. He mentioned you. It seems he has your business card. I wouldn't be surprised if Rankin's been trying to get through to you. Of course, you know the drill."

"Why don't you remind me?"

"Come on, Pierre."

"I'm starting to smell brimstone here."

"Look, Pierre. Listen to me. Nobody here is in any doubt about your work on this. And we can handle this Rankin bitch and MacIsaac. But this Ramos? This is just me being me, and speaking as your friend—it looks bad and it sounds bad. So I'm just suggesting you stay put a little longer. It can't exactly be hardship, right? I see by the weather channel that it's almost summer out there."

"Okay, okay," Pierre said. "Screw it. But I'm counting on you to keep me posted about every little detail. We both know how these things blow out of proportion. Got it?"

"Got it. What time is it?"

"One hour difference. Getting onto seven o'clock."

"I know it's one hour difference, asshole. I just don't have my watch on."

∽

After Pierre ended the call he noted that he was now about half a mile away from the entrance to the harbour, drifting to the north. The wind was picking up. He turned on his VHF and dialled the marine weather channel. Strong wind warning in effect. Twenty-five knots out of the southeast, gusts to forty. Diminishing late tomorrow. Rain, at times heavy.

He actually enjoyed rough weather when the boat was safe. He'd spent many days on the water with his father. There were harsh days then, of course, especially late in the fall with the beginning of the cold winter rains. But he remembers only sunshine, warm breezes, the gentle swell of the Mediterranean. His ancient city, older than Moses, a city Jesus walked in, sparkling in the distance against the Hills of Sidon. The crumbling Crusader castle on the seafront a reminder of endurance. His father squinting landward, munching his *manakish zaatar*, gulping water, lost in private thoughts. Even now, with all he knows, with all that he remembers, life before January 1976 is wreathed in sunshine.

Boat rocking insistently now, rising wind abeam. He turned and drove toward the harbour mouth.

He dropped fenders, tied up, then went below. He poured a drink and settled back, reviewing what he had written. The words had come with surprising difficulty. *I have no idea when or if you'll read this. Or how circumstances will have changed the meaning of what I want to tell you now. So let me begin with everything I know about this man, Ari, and all he represents. There is so much and I want to get it all down in the space and time available. I have a pessimistic view of time. The only time we can be sure of is the present moment.*

He was startled by a loud thump, someone jumping from the washboard to the deck. He stopped reading and peered out. Angus Beaton. He'd been wondering if he'd show up since he'd seen Beaton standing at the end of the wharf. He shouted, "Come in."

Beaton slid the glass door open and stepped inside. "It's beginning to blow," he said.

"Some weather tonight and tomorrow, according to the forecast."

"I didn't mean to interrupt."

Pierre laughed. "What do you think you're interrupting?"

"A fella never knows." Angus Beaton sat, studying the floor. "You were gone all day."

"It was lovely on the water. Spent hours watching a big pod of blackfish."

"I'd heard they're out there. Early this year."

"I just poured myself a drink of Scotch. Will you have something? There's beer in the cooler."

"No, no. I'm good."

And then the silence that Pierre had become accustomed to in the few days since he'd met Beaton. He'd noticed the little travel trailer and the half-ton near the end of the wharf but hadn't realized someone lived there until he saw a light on his first night in the harbour. Later, because he was having trouble sleeping, he'd been sitting near the stern studying the stars when he heard a footstep crunching on the wharf above him. It was Beaton standing there in the dark, hand raised, the glow of a cigarette faintly illuminating his face.

Beaton was a large man, once clearly muscular but now overweight and flabby. For twenty-two years he'd been a soldier. This much he had disclosed when they'd exchanged brief introductions. He still had the soldier haircut, the soldier gaze. Pierre had asked him where he'd done his soldiering but the response was unrevealing. "All over the place."

Pierre inquired whether Beaton knew a local hard-rock miner named Sandy MacIsaac.

"Can't say it rings a bell," he replied, after giving it some thought. "But I've mostly been away from here since I was about nineteen. MacIsaac's a pretty common name." Another, longer pause.

"So you were with the whales," he said, looking directly at Pierre and smiling.

"You should come out with me. Maybe the day after tomorrow. I don't think this weather is going to last."

"You're still going to be around?"

"A few more days, it seems."

"It'll be hard to leave the peace and quiet, I imagine."

"I suppose."

"I could never hack Toronto."

"You lived there?"

"Petawawa was close enough."

"You're sure I can't get you something."

"That's okay." He stood. "There were people here today."

"Oh?"

"In a cop car. In suits. Two of them. The car was unmarked but I could tell by the hubcaps. And you could see the flashers in the back window. They were looking at your spot."

"My spot."

"Where you tie up. And they were checking out your car."

"Strange," Pierre said. "Did you talk to them?"

"They asked me if the guy belonging to the car was still around. I told them I had no idea. Which wasn't a lie. You could have gone anywhere, right?"

"You didn't get a card or anything?"

"No. I don't talk to those people unless I have to."

"I understand," Pierre said. "Sit down. I'll make some tea."

"No. I have to be somewhere."

"By the way," Pierre asked. "Do you get the local paper?"

"The *Oran*?"

"I think that's what it's called."

"I have one in the trailer. I'll drop it off."

After Beaton left, Pierre tried to write some more but he couldn't get the call from Ethan off his mind. Sandy MacIsaac resurfacing and a big league business reporter from here. Margaret Rankin. They'd probably grown up together, this Margaret and Sandy. Goddammit. And a cop car? He had a fairly good idea what that was about, but why wouldn't they just have phoned to set up a proper meeting? They had his number. "Sit tight," they'd instructed. He was definitely sitting tight. Why skulk around?

∼

He checked his watch. It was 4:00 a.m. He considered getting out of his bunk, putting on his rain gear and braving the weather to retie the boat. It was chafing against the wharf, lightly but enough to wake him. He listened carefully. No damage being done. The rattle of the anchor chain that he'd left unsecured. The rain was loud against the roof. Not going out in that, he thought.

He let his mind drift back to where he'd left off the writing.

He picked up the pen.

14. *January 10, 1976*

For two days he made his way along the seacoast, keeping to the shoreline, foraging for food. He travelled cautiously with frequent stops when it was daylight, avoiding everyone. He would trust nobody until he reached Sa'diyat, twelve miles away, stronghold of the warlord, Camille Chamoun, the former president; protected by his private army. He would be safe there, and soon join his mother and his sister in Damour.

But the Chamoun enclave in Sa'diyat was silent and now he cowered in a citrus grove below Damour. Billows of smoke floating away from the hillside above him, frequent flashes, followed by the roar of slamming mortar, rockets crashing, the crackle of automatic rifle fire. He sank to his knees in the sandy soil.

During the night there had been a lull in the bombardment. As the dawn approached, the hill above the grove was quiet. On the hillside he could see light flickering. Maybe lamplight, maybe cooking fires. He was stiff and sore and hungry. The density of darkness in the grove around him was reassuring but at the same time unsettling, a primitive darkness, moist and heavy with the musk of compost and damp soil. His eyes were fixed on where the homes and churches were supposed to be. Damour. He'd convinced himself that they were safe there, even after this. His grandfather's house was like a fortress, thick stone walls, seemingly as old as the hills themselves.

He'd slept somehow until the silence woke him. He had no idea what time it was. He heard a vehicle moving quickly, sound increasing to a crescendo not far from him, then diminishing. And then the sound of another vehicle approaching, slowing down, stopping. A faint blush marked where the sky began. He tried to calculate where the truck was, tried to guess who might be in it.

By the time he reached the highway it was illuminated by blue-grey light. No sign of life in either direction. He crouched in the ditch, straining to spot movement in the village sprawled against the hills in front of him. Then he saw the Range Rover pulled off into a gully, barely visible but for the unmanned .50-calibre machine gun on the roof. No sign of anyone. The silence and the stillness of a grave. Then somewhere—and maybe he imagined it—the squalling of an infant. In his mind there was only one infant, his sister's child. He stood and dashed across the road, bent low.

Then he heard the clatter of boots behind him, felt hands roughly grabbing, overpowering him, a blow that split his consciousness. Flashing light in screaming darkness. The pavement rushing up to meet his face, the taste of blood and asphalt. Hands dragging him backward, off the road, through weeds and nettles. He thought of dogs, large, wild, hungry.

A boot flattened his ear, crushing his flashing skull. The taste of sand. The metallic clacking of rifles being readied. Through one eye he could see the Sacred Heart of Jesus on a rifle stock. Someone's hands were in his pockets.

"Papers. Where are your papers?"

He struggled to speak, but no words came.

The boot lifted, paused, came down hard, heel first.

Returning consciousness, barrel of the Kalashnikov with the Sacred Heart hovering above his face, cold muzzle pressed against his forehead. His eyes were glazed. Twisted mouths were moving furiously, silently, he heard only a rushing roar. Saw the fingers of the gunman caress the fire selector. The barely perceptible motion of a stranger's hand obliterating an entire lifetime. He imagined the bullet readied in the breech. Fingers shoved the selector down all the way to semi-automatic—a single shot for him. A *coup de grâce*. He squeezed his eyes shut, then felt a hand grabbing roughly at his throat. The cutting pressure around his neck from the small gold chain he has worn since boyhood.

He opened his eyes. A bearded man crouched beside him, examining the little crucifix—a First Communion gift from Miriam. The man grasped his chin between a filthy thumb and forefinger, turned his face this way, that way. Lips moving, still silent. The gunman stood and reached down a helping hand, and gently pulled Pierre upwards until he was sitting. It was still too soon for standing. Sound returned in hollow murmurs and the gangsters gathered around, no longer hostile, just curious. One of them handed him a plastic bottle full of water. They laughed as he retched.

∼

He studied the looming Mabou hills and above their dark profile, the glow of dawn. And he was amazed at how he'd awaited death that morning more than thirty years before, face to face with the wall-eyed boy who had saved him with a single word. *Run.* And the feeling he remembered as he ran was sorrow. Often, he'd imagined such a moment in the safety of home or school or on the open sea. Violent death was Lebanon's communal narrative. Heroes. Victims. Martyrs. Massacres. He had never thought of sorrow as the dominant emotion in a final, violent crisis. He'd imagined a paralyzing terror. But, in the reality, unexpected as such moments almost always are, he'd only felt a kind of bitter sadness. He thought of Cyril, three years older than he was on that day.

Yes. He is old enough to know the truth.

He set the pen down, went below, stretched out on his bunk, hands behind his head. Staring at the low cabin ceiling, he imagined lying in a coffin. At home, when such insomnia descended, he would retrieve a small bag of marijuana from the bedside table drawer. It always helped. But he had no pot here. Lois had told him, as he was leaving, "I think you have enough on your plate without an airport bust for dope."

You have enough on your plate. Yes. An understatement. Controversy. Scandal. Health. And the fat man and the history he'd all but forgotten.

Ari Roloff was the name the fat man used. But there was another name in another lifetime. A name from Greek mythology. Charon. *A coin for Charon.* A coin for the ferryman who transports souls across the river separating life from death. He rose from his bunk, fumbled through the thin light of the emerging day, into the main cabin. Peered out through a window. The tide was high and he could see beyond the long, rain-washed expanse of wharf a faint light inside the travel trailer. The light seemed to flicker in the gusts. He was briefly tempted to knock on the door. The lashing rain and hurtling wind were daunting. But the real distance between them was the primal isolation of strangers in a temporary place.

Light. He switched on a lamp. Returned to his journal. It was time now. It would not be easy. He felt the return of an aching sadness. Above the thrashing wind he could hear the rattle of oarlocks, the *plash* of oars, the approach of Charon's ferryboat.

15.

He was leaning up against the wheel, staring out. The rain was streaking sideways on the windshield, obscuring vision, but he could see the white spray rising over the breakwater, silently disintegrating, disappearing, then rising again, more furious with each surge. He turned the ignition key, heard the rumble of the engine, felt the gentle tremble. Reached up, activated a windshield wiper. Then he saw a man standing near the end of the breakwater, hunched forward in resignation or defiance. It was impossible to tell.

Pierre didn't bother with the rain pants. Just rubber boots and slicker. To reach the breakwater he had to fight the wind and rain down the length of the wharf, past Beaton's trailer. He struggled onward, along a storage shed that briefly offered shelter on the lee side. On the breakwater he had to clamber over boulders the size of cars. No longer able to walk upright, he was practically crawling, bashing knees and shins. *How did he get out there? How the hell will we get back?*

Then Beaton turned toward him, raised cautionary hands. *No, no, don't* . . . Then he was moving tentatively toward Pierre, arms spread wide like a tightrope walker. Within reach he extended a hand and Pierre grasped it and they stood there neither knowing who was saving whom. Beaton was now laughing and shouting: *Brilliant!*

Pierre shouted back: *You're insane.*

I know, I know, but isn't this fantastic!

~

Now the man was quiet, shivering and dripping, clutching the mug of coffee in both hands, looking lost. Pierre had taken charge when the footing was secure, seized his elbow and propelled him past the little trailer. He offered no resistance. Beaton climbed down to the boat without a word. Entered the cab and sat. Pierre was thinking, is he drunk? But nobody with impaired balance could have made it to the end of the breakwater in that wind, survived there for however long and then made it back.

He'd filled a kettle. Boiled water. Prepared coffee in a French Press. "You take milk?"

"No. Black. You mind if I smoke?"

"Smoke away."

Beaton's hands were trembling as he unwrapped a package of cigarettes from a bread bag. The smokes were dry but the little book of matches was soggy. "Hang on," Pierre said. Held out the propane ignitor, flicked a flame.

Beaton inhaled deeply, exhaled, a kind of sigh. "I didn't mean to drag you out there. I was okay, you know."

"I couldn't tell from here. I wasn't sure that you could get back."

"Ah," Beaton said. "You didn't have to worry. I'm used to the rocks. I think there's some mountain goat in me. That's what they used to say. In basic training. Obstacles courses were my bag. You'd never know, looking at me now." He laughed, studying the floor. "I was in good shape once. I used to be a runner."

"I could never get into running," Pierre said.

"They used to have local races in the summer. Five miles. I never won any of them but was always in the top five or so."

He puffed on the cigarette, sipped the coffee. Then he looked at Pierre, eyes appealing: "You wouldn't happen to have anything stronger?"

Pierre produced the bottle of Scotch from a supply cupboard. Poured for both of them.

"A fella lets himself go," Beaton said. "It just sneaks up on you. You look like you're in pretty good shape."

"For now," Pierre said.

"So what do you do to stay fit?"

"I play golf. That's about it."

Beaton chuckled. "Golf." Shook his head. "You'd be what age?"

Pierre hesitated, remembering the bluntness of these people. "Going on forty-seven," he said.

"You sure don't look it," Beaton said.

"I have a young wife," Pierre said. "And you? How old are you."

"Forty-one."

"You had some years left, in the military . . ."

"I suppose."

"Burned out?"

Beaton studied him for a while, puffed the cigarette, then ground it out.

"Just for the record, I don't believe in this PTSD bullshit, if that's what you're getting at."

"Not getting at anything," Pierre said.

"I had it easy compared to some."

Pierre turned to the stove, poured coffee for himself, held the pot out to Beaton. "More?"

"Nah. Do you mind?" Beaton picked up the bottle, poured. "Take this officer that I knew. There was this day in Panjwai—"

"Panjwai?"

"Afghanistan. A forward observation base . . . we've all been there one time or another. There's this nearby hill. Big rocks and steep. You'd go up between the rocks and over them. A race to the top. You get bored, eh? Anything to kill time. At the top you had to fire one shot with the nine mil just to prove you got there, then head back down. Coming down was just as hard. Sliding on your arse as much as anything."

"So how was your race to the top?"

"Oh, I never did it. Not me."

Pierre nodded.

"Anyway, this day, the guys were racing up and down the hill. Captain was on his way back down. Heard a shot behind him. Then maybe a hundred shots. From automatics, eh. And there were still two guys up there."

"Did you get them back?"

"Oh yeah. That night. We went up. The bad guys were long gone, though."

"How's the drink?"

"Good. We caught up with the ragheads hiding in a village. We fucked them up good."

"You knew it was them?"

"Didn't matter, really."

"So this officer, who ran up the hill. He was with you in the village?"

"No, no. He was back at the Kandahar Airfield by then. See, he was the senior officer. Should have known better. So he was hauled up on charges. But they bought his excuse."

"Which was?"

"Reconnaissance."

Pierre nodded. "It could have been."

"Yes. And the guys backed him up. The army finally decided he had PTSD. Charges went away but they kept him on the base, which was worse than the guardhouse. Unfit for command, they said, due to trauma accumulated over a long time. He told me, 'Don't believe that PTSD shit, man. I just fucked up. That simple.'"

Pierre walked to the sliding glass door, studying the weather.

"So what did it for you?" he asked, back turned.

"What do you mean?"

"Made you give it up."

"Just figured it was time. Gave it a lot of thought in Kandahar. I been in Cyprus, Golan Heights, Bosnia was the worst. Never felt so fuckin' useless in my life. Doing nothing is worse than anything in a situation like that. Worse than the killing even."

Pierre turned, nodded. "I can imagine."

"You do queer things sometimes, just to remind yourself that you're a soldier, what you're trained for. I was in Somalia too. You probably heard."

"I might have read something."

"You'd have to know what it feels like to kill another person."

"I hear you."

"If you don't mind me saying so—it's Pierre, isn't it?—you have a little trace of an accent yourself."

Pierre smiled. "Look who's talking."

"I mean foreign."

"I grew up in Lebanon."

"Ah, Lebanon. Then you'd know what I'm talking about."

"Not really."

"It's afterwards that it gets to you. I mean if you're normal, you start thinking. Right?"

"But I thought you guys were all about peacekeeping."

Angus coughed, then looked up and raised a finger to his lips. "Shhh." He stood then and stretched. "Thanks for that." He nodded toward the empty mug.

"Come back later," Pierre said. "I have a couple of T-bones I have to get rid of."

"I might do that."

∿

By noon the storm was diminishing. Jagged clouds raced across the sky but there were periodic flashes from the sun and the heaving sea was settling. He stepped outside and climbed up onto the wharf. The wind was fresh with the mingled sea and forest fragrance that was unique to this pristine hidden place. He felt, if only for a moment, safe.

He heard an engine and turned in time to see Angus Beaton drive away in his half-ton. He tried to remember the line from the book, *Ulysses*, from long ago in university. The line about dark places and secrets. *Secrets weary of their tyranny: tyrants willing to be dethroned.* Or was it dark palaces. How many secrets was this Angus Beaton carrying?

Back on the boat he briefly considered a glass of wine, but then filled the kettle. Tea for now. He dialled home. No answer. Visualized his wife, missed her, missed the intimacy, longed for the once predictable sensation of arousal. It was gone, of course. The doctor had reluctantly agreed that blocked testosterone could help. Chemical castration. A cruel description, but a small sacrifice in his fight against the silent cancer cells. No big deal, considering the alternatives. The kettle squealed and he turned off the stove and sat, suddenly overwhelmed by weariness. He considered crawling back into his bunk, but knew the ache that felt so much like fatigue was from a specific place, a place of inescapable awareness.

The journal was open, face down on the table, and he told himself that he should make an effort to resume the writing, but the impulse was blocked by a feeling of—and the word came out of nowhere—impotence. He smiled at himself and thought of Lois and the mystery she carried in her body. Something to anticipate. Creation. The potential of a new life, a second chance.

∽

By early evening the sky was clear, the sun shimmering. Beaton's truck had not returned and Pierre was not surprised. Even when he was physically present Angus seemed to be adrift, wallowing in memory. Pierre told himself it was a blessing in a way, meeting up with this damaged man—a reminder of the need to focus on the now, the present, the only true reality, and how it might evolve. Memory is sentiment. The future, impenetrable. Anxiety a waste of time and energy.

He checked his watch. Seven. He thought of his friend Fadi. It was a long time ago but Fadi's words came back. *The future is a harvest of consequences.* They were in Fadi's office near the port, watching a group of stoned Kata'ib outside firing automatic rifles in the air, randomly and for no reason.

"A harvest?" Pierre said laughing. Fadi, everybody said, was far too educated. The rattle of the automatic weapons resumed.

"It's raining bullets somewhere," Fadi said.

"It's crazy," Pierre said.

"But it will be worse afterwards, when we try to return to what we think is normal . . . that's when they'll be a problem. *This*, for them, is normal. They think this insanity is freedom. A licence to do anything they want. I don't want to be the one to put that back in the box."

"Put what back?" Pierre had asked.

"Anarchy," Fadi said. "That's the harvest that we've planted here."

Then Pierre heard the truck returning.

Angus put a bottle of wine and a bottle of rum on the table. He seemed cheerful. The level of the rum was already down near the top of the label. "I got a head start," he said. "Anyway, I don't think you're much of a drinker. Am I right?"

Pierre smiled. This curious habit of English speakers amused him—always looking for concurrence. *Right? Eh? You know? You hear what I'm saying? Am I right or am I wrong?* Meaning, please agree with me. Arabs and Frenchmen rarely worry about concurrence, tone.

"Right on," he said, handing one of the glasses to Angus. *Right on.* Another of their odd agreeable expressions. He didn't particularly

enjoy rum, but he poured two large wallops. He felt a surge of adrenalin before he tasted his. He was in the mood to drink more than he
should and felt a tiny pulse of warning.

Pierre took a sip. "You can mix it however you wish."

"You got any Coke?"

"I have. There, in the cooler."

Angus rattled in the cooler among the bottles and the cans and
packages. "You're out of ice. You should have told me," Angus said.
"I'm just back from town."

"Ah," Pierre said. "A shopping trip."

"Nah. Visiting the war department."

"The war department?"

"The ex-wife," he said. Raised his glass. "May she rot in peace."

~

Angus liked his steak well done. "Jesus," he said when Pierre cut into
his. "I expect that thing to moo."

Dinner conversation was mostly about wives. Pierre didn't know
enough about Aggie's family history to be helpful in identifying her
for Angus Beaton. "All I know," Pierre said, "is that her mom came
from here. A MacDonald."

Angus laughed. "MacDonald here is like Mohammed in the Arab
countries. Tells you nothing."

"You've been to the Arab countries?" Pierre asked.

"Egypt, Jordan, Turkey."

"Lebanon?"

"Stayed away from there."

"Just as well. You mentioned the Golan Heights."

"Not sure what that is. Arab. Israeli. Whatever." Angus pushed his plate away. "So how do you get along with the ex? You mentioned you tied the knot again. I see you wear the ring."

Pierre extended his left hand, the ring and the loose gold chain around his wrist glinting, a wedding gift from Lois.

"It looks fairly new, the ring."

"About two years. But I don't wear it all the time. I don't like rings. The chain I always wear. It was a gift from my wife. It has a special history in her family."

"My old lady would go crazy any time I took my ring off," Angus said, refilling his wineglass. "I'd leave it home when I'd be going on a tour. Guys got robbed for their jewellery. But she'd assume I was looking for pussy when I was away. Thinkin' the ring would matter." He laughed. "As if."

"Kids?"

"Two. They're great." He produced a wallet and two photographs, which he examined before passing them across. The little boy about nine. An awkward-looking prepubescent girl.

"That was a few years ago. She's fifteen now," Beaton said, pointing at her photo. "The young fella is twelve. We called him Bradley. We weren't into the old-fashioned names. She's Melissa. What about yourself?"

"One. And one on the way."

"Hah. Congratulations. When's the big day?"

"December."

"And the one you have already. How old?"

"Nineteen," Pierre said. "He was twelve when I left his mother. His name is Cyril."

"Y'all get along?"

"I suppose so. You?"

"We got issues." He stood. "I'm going to have another shot. What about yourself?"

He nodded and Angus poured for them both, topped up his own with Coke.

He sat. "See she did a bit of a number on me. I won't bore you with the details. But when I came back from my last trip there was nobody there to meet me. And when I got to the house, it was cleaned out. No forwarding address. No nothing."

"I'm trying to imagine."

"It took a few days to track them down and I just decided to arrive at her new place without notice, which was probably a mistake. It didn't go too well. Now there's a restraining order." He shrugged, then laughed. "Here's how stupid it is: I can't be with the kids alone. She has to be there. If there's anybody in fuckin' danger, it's her, but they can't see that."

"You went today, though?"

"Yeah. Melissa's birthday."

"And that went okay?"

"Actually, yes. The ex was half-civil for a change. In a way that's worse, though. I find it's easier to be pissed off than sad. You know what I'm saying?"

"I hear you."

They both drank and sat in silence for a while. Angus lit a cigarette, then stared at him with half a smile. "I'd bet money you could tell a few stories yourself."

"Why would you make such a bet?"

"Just looking at you. Your age. I was in Cyprus once, on leave. I met an Irish UNIFIL fella. He was based in the south part of your country. Man, the stories out of him."

Pierre shrugged. They sat. The boat was still and silent. Angus crushed the cigarette. "Why don't I do the dishes?"

"Leave them," Pierre said. "There's just a few. It'll only take a few minutes in the morning. Something to get my day started."

"So tomorrow," Beaton said. "What do you think? You'll be going out?"

"Weather permitting. Maybe a little handlining. Judging by the whales the mackerel are out there. You're welcome to come along."

"I might take you up on that."

Pierre drained his glass, then stood and walked back to the glass door and stared out.

"Are you expecting someone?" Beaton asked.

"No, why?"

"You keep looking out, like."

Pierre turned and Beaton was standing, pouring another drink. "You?"

"I'll get my own," Pierre said. Sat and reached for the bottle of rum. There was something liberating about talking to a stranger, a stranger who is safe because he will inevitably disappear back into his own entirely separate existence.

Angus said, "If you don't mind me asking, how'd you end up in Cape Breton?"

"That's a complicated story."

Angus just stared, waiting, then said, "We can talk about something else."

"No, no, no," Pierre said. "There's really nothing to *not* talk about. You know about the civil war, I guess."

"Wasn't very civil, from what I heard."

Pierre laughed. "Well put. Long story short. A priest from here, from over in the Waterford area, was in Lebanon looking for some family history. I guess he hadn't been following the news that closely. For whatever reason, he got stranded there. The airport was closed."

"So he'd have been connected to your family, this priest from Waterford."

"No. No. My family was pretty well all gone."

"Gone?"

He could feel the familiar buzz of caution, but it had been so long since he had talked about it. He splashed some liquor in his glass. Nodded to Beaton. "Let's just say I was at loose ends when I met the priest from here."

"Loose ends?"

"Well, as you know, the country was upside down back then. People's lives on hold. You were either a fighter or a wheeler-dealer. You had to be one or the other."

"And so which were you?"

"A bit of both." He sipped from his glass, then projected a broad smile, reminding himself that Beaton was a soldier. "I'm Lebanese, man. What can I tell you?"

"So this priest."

"Aboud. Father Cyril Aboud. We hit it off and stayed in touch when he finally got out."

"So why did you leave?"

"I suppose it was the Israeli occupation. You know about that. After '82."

Beaton laughed. "The IDF. Cunts, those guys are. Smartest people in the world. Great soldiers. But boy, don't trust them. The stories this Irish fella had. And even when I was in the Golan. Man, oh man. So they did it for you, the ol' IDF."

"Oh, it wasn't just that. It was an opportunity to change my life and so I grabbed it."

"It must have been quite the change."

"Well. It was quiet. Took a while to get used to the fact that nobody wanted to blow up the house that I was sleeping in. Or that I could go to school and figure on finishing the year. That was a big change. Or that I didn't have to carry a gun wherever I went."

"You had a gun?"

"Everybody had a gun."

He stood, grabbed the bottle. "How's your drink?"

"Not sure which I'd find the biggest adjustment," Beaton said as Pierre poured. "Lebanon or Waterford. Always felt foreign over on that side of the island."

"I felt right at home with all the ethnic people. You Scotchmen think you're the only people here."

"Anybody else come over with you?"

"Just me."

"So they're back there."

"What's left of them."

"Anyone close?"

"No."

A light breeze stirred outside. The boat shifted.

"I think the wind is coming back," Angus said.

"It won't amount to anything," Pierre said.

He felt woozy, the start of edginess and impatience. Angus carried his glass to the wheel, leaned against it, looking forward. "That was a wicked sunset before. Maybe I'll go out with you tomorrow."

"That would be great."

He turned to face Pierre. "Why do you think those cops were sniffing around your car yesterday?"

"You should've asked them."

"They seemed to know who they were looking for."

"But they said nothing?"

"You aren't some kind of a fugitive, are you? Not that I'd give a fuck one way or the other."

Pierre laughed. "Why would you ask that?"

"It's a queer place for a holiday here."

"What's queer?"

"Oh, I don't know. Guy by himself on a boat in Mabou Coal Mines. In June."

"I have history here, man. Like I said." His guard was up now and he was almost grateful—adrenalin was neutralizing the effects of liquor. "Do I look like a fugitive?"

Beaton stepped back, sipped from his glass. He was unsteady on his feet. "Nah," he said. "You look more like one of those cops who was around here yesterday." He put his glass down. "Don't mind me, sometimes I talk too much." He held out his hand. "Thanks for putting up with me." He stumbled slightly at the door.

Pierre climbed up the wharf-side ladder behind him, concerned that he might lose his footing. At the top Beaton was breathing heavily.

"The fags," he said quietly. "I swear one of these days I'm gonna quit. Cold fuckin' turkey. Get back in shape while I still got time."

"See you in the morning, then," Pierre said.

He thought of Ari as he watched the damaged soldier walk off into the darkness, erect and careful, conscious of being studied and perhaps evaluated.

Pierre climbed back down into what seemed to have become his world. And for what felt like endless time he just stood staring out over the stern, suspended in the overpowering silence. A lone gull settled briefly on a bollard, then fluttered off.

As sanctuaries go he could have done worse, he thought. He had at other times done much worse. He winced at the sudden memory of sand leaking out of musty rotting burlap, of burning garbage, shit and piss and the intermingled gassy smell of putrefaction. He turned away from the silence and the moonlight and went inside, hoping to find rest there, knowing that he wouldn't.

He sat in the large captain's chair tilted back against the wheel, alone and going nowhere. There was an old moon, one sliver away from fullness, hanging heavily over the Mabou hills and it flooded the cab with light. It was a distraction, if only briefly, from the hovering anxieties that Angus Beaton left behind.

He shifted his position and the chair tilted, springs in the rocking mechanism squawked. He struggled to quell a feeling of regret for having gone too close to irrevocable disclosure. To blab or not to blab, that is the question. Whether or not 'tis in the mind nobler to disclose. But disclosure is rarely noble. Disclosure is transactional. Disclosure is a ruse to create trust. He had heard so much disclosure of "facts" that were lies, emotions that were false. Deception through disclosure. Engagement. Empathy. The best interrogators were the ones who were capable of manufactured empathy.

Pierre had watched and listened while strong, strong men slowly lost the will to resist the pull of empathy, to fight off the creeping, comforting, enervating promises of trust, even when they knew what lay in store. Empathy, a kind of gravity.

He felt guilty, having learned so much so easily from Angus Beaton.

16.

He wasn't accustomed to the subway car, the rocking motion, the human variants around him. He felt sleepy. There was a system diagram on the wall above the carriage door. Nine stations to his stop.

He'd lied again to Lois. "I'm just going to walk around a bit, see if some fresh air will clear my head." Maybe the fact that she wasn't listening made a moral difference. Is it a lie if no one hears it spoken? But why hadn't he told her: that he was going back to the Only Café to see what he could learn there. But that was not the whole truth either. And how could he explain the whole truth—that for a quarter of a century he'd longed to talk to someone who might understand his guilt? And now it seemed as though he'd finally found someone.

He hadn't really expected to find Ari when he got there but he was on a bench out in front of the café, drinking coffee, smoking a cigarette, the embodiment of relaxation.

"You look tired," Ari said.

"I am tired," he'd replied. "I don't know if you've been following. I work for a mining company called Draycor."

Ari shrugged. "Maybe. I don't much follow the news."

Pierre sat. He'd felt the empathy, the opening. "I don't sleep well."

Ari looked away.

"I think I'll try a cigarette," Pierre said. "Do you mind?"

Ari raised his eyebrows. "You sure?" Then he laughed, a deep laugh from somewhere in his girth and Pierre realized he hadn't heard the laugh before. "I wouldn't want to corrupt you." Ari fished a pack of cigarettes from a small leather satchel that he carried.

The reaction to the cigarette had been instantaneous. Pierre felt his head lifting off his shoulders, his stomach roiling. But he didn't cough. He inhaled carefully and concentrated on the cigarette between his fingers. It looked good there. It felt good in his hand. It took him back, and it seemed to steady him.

"Sleep is important," Ari said. Ground out his cigarette, studied passing cars, people ambling away from the mosque. It was a Friday evening. People emerged from the nearby 7-Eleven with slushies, strolling toward the halal restaurants and butcher shops. "I've never had a problem sleeping. Or eating. My secrets of survival."

"You should share your secrets," Pierre said.

Ari looked at him then smiled and turned away to study the passing crowd of believers. "Come Ramadan in mid-September they'll be gorging themselves in the halal restaurants at night. You said you were Christian?"

"I don't remember saying. You keep track of Ramadan?"

"The culture interests me, obviously. Clean living keeps the conscience clean. They sleep like logs, I'm sure."

Pierre puffed. "I can see your interest in Islam. Not just the politics. Faith interests me too. Anything I can't have intrigues me." Another puff. "I'm not much of anything anymore. You?" He dropped the cigarette and crushed it.

Ari shrugged. Cars drifted by. A siren sounded, then the hoarse hooting of a fire truck. Ari opened his mouth to speak, but out of nowhere three speeding Harley-Davidsons appeared and geared down deafeningly right in front of them. Ari stared with obvious contempt, but said nothing.

"Assholes," Pierre said. The motorcyclists were staring back at them. You could read their minds. *Pathetic old men.*

Ari nodded. One of the motorcyclists smiled wickedly.

Pierre said, "Once upon a time we could have made this moment interesting. Yes?"

Ari laughed. "Yes. Very interesting." Together they watched the Harleys roar away, through a red light at the corner, narrowly missing a pedestrian.

"Jesus Christ," Pierre said.

"We're getting old," Ari said.

"Speak for yourself."

"Religion," Ari said. "I guess for some it holds everything together."

"Or blows everything apart." Pierre's brain was soaring on the waft of the tobacco drug.

"You can make that argument, yes. Lebanon, of course."

Ari resumed his study of the passersby. "I worry about them," he said. "They have a big problem now, their young people, influenced by fanatics." He nodded toward the mosque. "But on a personal level, in moderation, it's like everything else. It can be an asset."

"I didn't think you were religious."

"I'm not."

"Well."

"My mother was sick for a long time. I watched her suffer. Her religion was a great comfort—it made her unafraid. And look at these people." He nodded toward the mosque again. "Death as a road to paradise, imagine having that."

"Your mother died twenty-five years ago. You still think about her?"

"Twenty-five years ago, yes." Then he looked at Pierre intensely. "How did you know that?"

"You told me. September 1982."

"You have a good memory."

"It was a memorable time."

"Yes."

"Many things to keep a person awake at night."

"I suppose. But awake is still alive, isn't it?" Ari stood and stretched, shoved his hands deep into his pockets.

"I was Damouri Brigade," Pierre said.

Ari sat, fished out the package of cigarettes, held it toward Pierre. He shook his head.

"Damouri Brigade," Ari said, his expression puzzled. Then, "Ah, yes. Damour. Terrible."

"Elie Hobeika. You know the name?"

"His girlfriend was from Damour. I remember it seemed to justify so much of what he did. He had a funny nickname, didn't he?"

"HK. Not so funny."

Ari laughed. "HK, Heckler Koch."

"His weapon of choice."

"You knew him?"

Pierre felt a tightening in his chest. "Who didn't?"

"Damouri Brigade. It's coming back. Something about the camps."

"Hobeika became head of intelligence for the Phalange."

"I see."

"The last time I saw him he was with someone from IDF intelligence. At the stadium. But you don't remember."

"What was HK doing at the stadium?"

"I'm more curious about IDF intelligence."

"You should ask Hobeika, yes?"

"Hobeika is dead. You didn't know that?"

"I'm not surprised. There are many people who would not be surprised or sad. He was your friend?"

"We had a falling-out."

"Of course. So much falling out in Lebanon. Friends today, enemies tomorrow. But on September eighteenth you were still friends?"

Pierre knew he'd said enough.

Ari sighed deeply. "I wish I could help you, but as I said, I was in Tel Aviv."

"Your mother."

"My mother was a wonderful woman. Born here but a true Sabra. She raised us mostly on her own. Did I tell you that?"

Pierre decided to keep silent. But in the silence, long-suppressed images began resurfacing. Shaved skull, unshaven face. He struggled to refocus. Failed. Time to leave. He stood.

Ari caught him by the forearm. The grip was firm, persuasive, not coercive. Pierre sat. He looked around as if the bar had suddenly become unfamiliar. "I should go."

Ari said, "Wait." Waved his hand at the bartender whose name was Tal. Turned back to Pierre. "You should try harder to forget about 1982, Beirut, Hobeika, the camps, the stadium. It is unhealthy."

"It's not so easy," Pierre said.

"You want to know the secret that enables me to sleep? It is to understand that it's always dangerous to think as an individual when you are in a war."

Tal appeared, smiling. "Yes."

"Two double Glenfiddich, neat," Ari said.

"I'm not sure," Pierre said.

Ari ignored him. "We are not individuals in a war. We are compo-
nents. Do you understand? The responsibility for what happens is
collective. Am I clear?"

"Sometimes . . ."

"No." He had Pierre's wrist now and the grip was almost painful.
"Not sometimes. Always. Collective responsibility, yes. Individual
responsibility? No. That's sentimental. Sentiment is dangerous."

"If you weren't at the stadium, you don't . . ."

"Listen to me. Fuck the stadium. We killed terrorists."

"Women and children?"

"The children were tomorrow's terrorists. The women, incubators
for terrorists."

"Do you really believe that?"

"It is the only truth that matters. They were not individuals but a
concept called terrorism. We were not individuals, but an opposing
concept—counter-terrorism. Soldiers. We were not people then. We
were weapons in the service of our people."

"We were all terrorists."

"Please, spare me the . . ."

"*Faquat esmaani lahza*," Pierre said. "Just hear me out for a moment."

"No. I know all about the fucking stadium. I've heard the stories.
I read intelligence summaries, okay? Listen carefully. *I wasn't at the
fucking stadium.* But I know. Okay? You keep that in mind." He stood
abruptly. "I have a clear conscience. I sleep soundly."

His phone rang, he answered and walked away but not before
Pierre realized that he was speaking Arabic. He quickly ended the
conversation but kept on walking, disappeared.

Pierre assumed that he was gone. But he returned. "The bladder,"
he said, and sat again. Then he was fumbling with the leather satchel,

extracted what appeared to be a photocopy of an item from a newspaper.

"Just for the record, look at this," he said, jabbing the clipping with a stubby finger. "*Jerusalem Post*. September fifteenth, 1982. Read it."

He read. *Edit Burman, beloved mother* . . . "You carry her obituary?"

"And here I am," Ari said. *Left to mourn, Ariel.* Other names obscured by the fingertip.

"So, Ariel *Burman*?" Pierre said.

"Her *maiden* name," Ari said impatiently. "My father had been out of the picture for a long time by then. Are you satisfied now? I was in Tel Aviv when you claim you saw me. Okay?"

"She died on the fifteenth. And they didn't bury your mother according to—"

"Let me repeat: I wasn't at the stadium on the eighteenth."

"Wouldn't they have buried her on the fifteenth or the sixteenth? And in 1982, wasn't September eighteenth Shabbat, and the first day of Rosh Hashanah?"

Ari laughed. He was folding the clipping carefully. "So you're a rabbi now?"

"I'm just trying to work out—"

"Fifteenth, sixteenth, eighteenth. Just listen to me. I know all about the stadium, who was there, what was going on there. Fucking savages, you people."

He leaned across the table, jabbed Pierre's chest, just above the sternum, just below the windpipe. He was smiling, then spoke slowly. "Anybody who was at the stadium on the seventeenth or the eighteenth should shut-fucking-up about it. Take that from me. As a friend." He stood, stuffed the exculpatory clipping back into his satchel. "Good night," he said without looking back as he walked away. "Get some sleep. You have your health to think about."

Tal arrived at the table with the drinks, looked confused.

"Leave them." Handed Tal a twenty. "Keep it."

He downed both drinks quickly. He was tired. He was very, very tired. But now he knew.

~

Thoughts of death come almost naturally to people who have spent real time among the dead—doctors, undertakers, soldiers—those who have seen death's overwhelming presence and then the disconcerting banality of what it leaves behind.

Aggie insisted on dragging him to wakes when they were first married. Showing respect, she called it. But what is so respectful about staring at a prettified cadaver? Death that neither looked nor smelled like death depressed him even more than the reality.

He put his glass down and entered the forward cabin, raised the mattress on his berth, opened up a small storage compartment, felt inside, carefully rummaging among the ropes and flares and charts until he felt the reassuring metal. He spoke softly. *Ari, I believe that I have the solution for our difficulties. I think you've met my friend before. I know you'd recognize each other even after twenty-five years.*

He returned to the captain's chair, put the Browning on the table.

17. *January 17, 1976*

He was a captive but he was not a prisoner. He was among fighters but he had no weapon. He knew who his companions were. But they were not his friends. They shared nation, family, religion. They shared victimhood, a common enemy—the aliens, the Palestinians and Syrians and the traitors who supported them. But while there was hatred, there was no passion. He was surprised by the docile patience of their idleness. He would eventually learn what they already knew, that the alternative to idleness was chaos. Looking back from a distant future, he'd wonder how he could have spent the greater part of seven years waiting, always waiting, rarely knowing what he was waiting for.

"What is your name?"

"Pierre."

"I am Elias. What did you do before?"

"I am a fisherman."

"I was a hairdresser."

"I am Bashir. I was a schoolteacher."

For days they'd hardly paid attention to the periodic crackle of automatic weapons on the hillside. It didn't matter who was shooting, who was being shot at. The sound was random, recreational. Damour was under siege and they were waiting. Then the bombardment would resume. *Whoosh, whump*. Unexpected, unpredictable. Day and night. Smoke lingered over the cringing hillside. At night there was the distant flickering of flame. They waited.

They reassured him: Not to worry, the siege is stable for the moment, people are hiding in their cellars, sheltered in the strongest buildings. There are three churches, built like fortresses. There are more than a hundred fighters there—maybe more than two hundred—strong, well-armed men, men who would lay down their lives before they'd allow the terrorists to defile this Christian enclave, this asset so strategically astride the highway south. "Where are you from?"

"Saida. You say you are Bashir? You have the same name as—"

"But I come from the Bekaa. Deir el Ahmar."

"My mother is from over there, Damour. She's there now, with my sister and her baby and her husband. Why are we waiting here?"

"They're safe. They will be fine."

～

Damour was under siege because of a highway and because of history, geography and destiny. But soon there would be reinforcements with orders to end this miserable provocation. Have patience.

After days of sitting there below Damour, his impatience had subsided. His family, or what was left of it, was safe. His mother, his sister. He believed that. He grieved for his father. The unexpected encounter, the brutal climax. How can murder happen almost whimsically? No apparent prologue, no ritual, no drama. Death, as sudden as a stumble and as meaningless. He studied the sky, the pewter January sea, felt the sting of rain and sorrow.

The town was only half a mile away but he had no choice but to wait like the others. The young commander, not much older than Pierre, the man they called HK, knew why they were there and what they were waiting for. Of that everyone was certain. HK knew and that was good enough. HK was the leader. His youth was seasoned by experience and a brooding hatred. This, to Pierre, seemed more normal than the foolishness he heard among the other men. The talk of women, alcohol and drugs. Endless fantasies. HK was as desperate to reach the Damour as he was, but HK was disciplined. He too had loved ones in the town but he was waiting for the moment—a moment shaped by tactical significance that was larger than any personal consideration. Everyone had loved ones somewhere. Pierre knew that he could trust HK and that he could follow him.

∾

He recognized the sudden clatter of weapons being readied, men shaking off their idleness. He stared where everyone was staring—toward the highway. Two men, more like boys, came toward them carrying a white flag. It was near dusk but they were clearly visible, waving the white flag that turned out to be a sacramental vestment belonging to a priest. The priest had sent them down.

They had weapons slung across their backs and moved cautiously, calling out comradely greetings, as they came closer. Then HK appeared. Pierre had never seen a weapon like the one HK was carrying. It might have been an American M16 but seemed larger, more terrifying.

HK moved forward, spoke briefly to the boys and then returned. He wanted two men to accompany him up the hillside for an assessment.

Pierre stepped forward. "I will go."

HK stared at him for a moment, then smiled and shook his head.

Pierre felt a sudden surge of fear—they are in greater peril than he thought—but the fear evaporated quickly. We are their deliverance. Those boys are their deliverance. His family was safe. His mother. Miriam. He knew it. Elias nodded in his direction, then he and Bashir headed off with HK toward the hillside.

∾

They were gone for no more than twenty minutes. HK was silent as he walked past everyone, and went to sit in the Range Rover alone.

The others crowded around the men who had been with him. They just shook their heads, faces empty of expression. Pierre was now confused.

Then HK was back among them. "People will try to leave and will come in this direction. Starting tonight. There is nowhere for them to go, except by sea. We need boats."

"I know where there are boats," Pierre said. "I walked from Saida, on the shore. I know boats, I was a fisherman."

Two other fighters raised their hands. "He's right," one said.

"You three go. Get the boats," HK instructed.

Pierre started walking toward HK, but Elias blocked him. "No," he said. "You must not ask. The terrorists are massing in the hills. Thousands of them. Damour is lost."

~

They came through the darkness, silent, slowly—individuals and little groups, old men and women, children, women carrying infants, families. Small boys struggling with luggage, sacks of household implements. They moved more quickly as they crossed the highway, shadows flitting. There had been shooting. The priest explained that they'd been noticed as they left the church and the terrorists had attempted an attack but the two boys covered their escape.

Pierre was overwhelmed by the anxiety he'd managed to subdue for days. He ran among the refugees, peering into faces. He accosted women carrying infants until finally someone grabbed him from behind.

"What are you trying to do?" HK demanded, furious.

"My mother. My sister. I have to find them."

HK frogmarched him away from the procession. "They aren't here."

"You don't know."

HK stepped back. "Come."

They were now among the trees. HK was studying Pierre with an almost indiscernible flicker of emotion. "I knew your mother's family," he said. "They will not be coming out."

"You don't know," Pierre cried out. HK stood silently. Then Pierre was on his knees.

HK lifted him.

"What is your Christian name?"

"Pierre."

"Listen to me, Pierre Haddad. We will see an end to this. Together. That is my promise to you, to them. Blood for blood. Remember."

∼

Elias handed Pierre a Kalashnikov with two loaded magazines taped together. "It's from HK. Do you know what to do with this?"

Pierre nodded. "Yes," he lied.

"You'll need it in the days ahead."

"What day is it?"

"January seventeenth. Why does it matter?"

"It doesn't matter. Who is HK?"

Elias just stared at him.

"What does HK stand for?"

"Everybody knows that."

"What does that mean, though?"

"You'll know soon enough."

"Where are we going?" Pierre asked. The question was instinctive, the answer wouldn't matter.

Elias smiled.

"Karantina."

FIVE

TIMELINE

18.

There was a faint vertical glow of light on the wall beside the unfamiliar drape. It was obviously morning, maybe late morning. Cyril had to reflect for a moment to recall what day it was. Saturday. He was sitting on the edge of a strange bed and he was unable to remember where he'd left his clothes. He hadn't made it home and he recalled the lie he'd told at some point the evening before to reassure his mother.

She had called at about 7:30 Friday evening. Ari had just walked away from him, leaving him seriously rattled. *She can do a lot of damage.* Suzanne was at the table waiting for him. Then he'd felt the vibration in his pocket, fished out his phone, saw Aggie's number and walked outside where it was quieter.

He'd called back and got his mother's answering machine. He felt a spasm of relief. He told her he was with the guys and would probably be out late—might not be home at all. Went back inside to find Suzanne scrolling through her messages. She smiled at him and put the phone away. "So what did Ari have to say?"

"Nothing interesting. Just that he's too busy to talk. We should come back another time."

"Busy? Friday night in a pub?"

"That's what he said."

Outside the Only Café she'd seemed stressed, increasing his confusion. "Where now?" he'd asked.

"Let's just walk."

They'd walked slowly, heading nowhere in particular. Her arms were folded, her bag looped over her shoulder. She was mostly silent.

He'd been grateful for the silence. He'd assumed he knew Suzanne, but now he wasn't sure. But then, who was Ari anyway?

∼

The restaurant was called Lolita's. They'd been walking for about fifteen minutes when Suzanne spotted the place and laughed. "Role reversal," she said, and it took a moment for him to realize the comment was flirtatious. Lolita. Right. Ha! She grabbed his arm, pressed herself against his shoulder. She was smiling and he welcomed the sudden change in mood. "I could use a proper drink," she said. "But you must be hungry."

The restaurant was busy so the hostess led them to the bar to wait until a table became available. He was happy at the bar, perched on a stool, Suzanne beside him, almost touching. Closer than they could ever sit at a table but with a neutral place to stare when the conversation lapsed. Shelves of bottles and behind the bottles, barely visible, a mirror in which he could see their reflection.

"I'll drive myself crazy all night," she declared while they were waiting for their drinks. "I know I've seen him somewhere but I just can't place it. How long has he been here?"

"I don't know," said Cyril. "I don't know anything about him."

The drinks were set down in front of them. She turned sideways on the stool, elbow on the bar. "You don't even know his name?"

"Just Ari."

Her smile was crooked, skeptical.

He shrugged. "I told you that."

"Maybe you did. Tell me again."

"There isn't much to tell. Dad dropped by that place one night, I don't know why. They met. They had something in common, maybe just the Middle East. Maybe something more. Dad mentioned him in a note attached to his will so it must have been more than a casual connection."

"Maybe we should think about eating something," Suzanne said. "Are you okay staying here at the bar?"

"This is perfect."

"Okay." She asked for menus, then turned to him again. "Do you know what year your father came to Canada?"

"I think it was the early eighties. Maybe '83 or '84."

"I was over there a lot in the eighties," she said.

"I have his diaries," Cyril said. "They start in '83."

"Diaries?" She laughed. "So how come you don't know exactly when he came?"

"Well, the first couple are written in Arabic. But even the English ones . . . I've just glanced. It's a bit creepy. Right?"

"Yes," she said.

"And the one I really want, the one that covers his last months in 2007—that one is missing."

"Really?"

"Which is partly why I keep wondering if he's still alive somewhere."

"How so?"

"If he ran away from something, he'd take it with him. Right? It would have had clues about what was going on."

She nodded.

"Anyway. It seems my father had a lot of secrets. It's possible that Ari might know some of them."

"I'm sure he has his own secrets, this Ari. In fact, I'd put money on it. Damn, I wish I could place him."

"What kind of secrets would Ari have?"

"Real ugly secrets, if my vibes are accurate. Ugly, ugly. Someday I'll explain my theory about secrets."

"A theory."

"Yes," she said. "Here's the short version. Secrets are invariably motivated by something shameful. Like a betrayal or a crime. When the shame becomes too much, it leads to self-destruction of some kind." She tossed back what was left in her glass, then again turned sideways on her stool. "Look at me."

He looked. Her eyes searching. Then she smiled.

"What?" he asked.

"You're how old again?"

"Twenty-four."

"Twenty-four. I bet you have your own secrets," she said. "Interesting secrets."

He laughed, but realized he was blushing. "I'm an open book. Okay?" Then he asked, "Do you think *your* father had secrets?"

"Big heavy secrets. Don't we all?" She waved a dismissive hand, turned back to the bar. "I'm going to switch to wine. What do you say we get a bottle and order up some grub. Red or white?"

"I'm easy," he said. "I like red. Anything."

She rummaged in her bag, retrieved a pair of reading glasses and began examining the wine list.

"About suicide," he said. "I used to hope it was that. It's easier to understand."

"Malbec?"

"What?"

"You okay with Malbec?"

"Anything."

~

They stood outside the restaurant watching for a taxi. He didn't know what time it was but it felt late, city sounds subsiding. "That was fun," she said.

"Fun?"

"I don't get to do that much anymore," she said. "Just hang out. Talk about stuff."

He caught her by the wrist but he was unsure why he'd done it and suddenly he wished he hadn't. Maybe he'd expected that she'd instantly withdraw her arm but she didn't. She reached out and touched his cheek.

"We could share a cab," he said.

"I'm walking distance." She checked her wristwatch. "Hey," she said. "It's still early. At the risk of seeming forward . . ."

"No fear of that," he said.

"Come." She looped her arm through his and they started walking. "We'll have a nightcap at my place and then we can call a cab from there. Okay?"

"Sounds great."

~

He dropped to his knees and fished around beneath the bed, felt the fabric of a T-shirt. And he remembered how deftly she had stripped it off him, how carelessly she'd tossed it.

He could hear a shower from somewhere up above. Then it stopped. A footfall. He tossed the bedclothes, searching. Ah. Underpants. But what about the trousers? The socks are probably caught up in trouser legs somewhere. A sudden wave of despair drove him back into the bed and he dragged the blankets up. Fragments of the night before floated freely. How she'd grasped his hand, guiding his fingers. "There," she sighed. "Yes there. Yes. Oh my . . . perfect."

He buried his face in the pillow. What did she think? It was like she had to tell him *everything*. Like it was his first time. Christ oh Christ oh suffering Jesus. Never again. Ever.

Then Suzanne was standing in the bedroom doorway, swaddled in a towel, smiling at him, roughing her hair with one end of the towel as she clutched the rest of it in front of her.

"Ah, there you are," she said. And dropped the towel. "May I join you?"

~

He must have slept again because he was surprised by her tone of voice when, finally, she spoke to him. "So what are your plans for the day?" She was kneeling on the bed beside him, wearing a light dressing gown. The tone was friendly, almost collegial, with no trace of the intimacy that had seemed, at least to him, so recently to have been irreversible.

"Come on, sleepyhead. Time to rise and shine." She tossed his trousers at him, laughing.

He shook them off his face. *Of course*, he told himself. *What did you expect?* She had drawn back the drapes and the room was bright. The impersonal sparseness told him that it was a guest room.

A phone chimed. "That'll be mine," she said and dashed out into the hallway.

He put his pants on, then the T-shirt. He stood and stretched, then left the room. Suzanne was leaning against a wall, one bare foot rubbing the other. She was patting her unruly hair, which she had gathered up and clasped with a large, amber-coloured clip.

"Love you too," she said into the phone, then shoved it into the pocket of her dressing gown. She stood for a moment and studied Cyril with what he took for sympathy. "I have the coffee on," she said at last. He followed her toward where he now remembered they'd sat the night before, at a rustic harvest table Bruno had designed and built for her before they'd lived together.

"You take yours black?"

"Please," he said.

She busied herself at the kitchen counter. "I'll make toast," she said. Then she turned suddenly, stared at him and frowned. "Are you okay?"

He always felt reassured when women asked that. *Are you okay?* "I'm a notch or two above okay," he said. And he was gratified to see her blush before she turned her full attention to the toaster.

∿

At the door she took a handful of Cyril's hair, shook his head a little. Smiled. "Less said the better, I find."

"Yes," he said. "But thank you."

"You're welcome." She grinned and stuck her tongue out. For a flash she seemed to be about fourteen years old and he didn't want to go. "Oh," she said. "You mentioned the diaries your dad left. That the early ones are in Arabic."

"Yes."

"Hughes reads Arabic. I'm sure he'd take a look if you're up for it."

"I like Hughes," Cyril said. "He's been helping me. I'll mention it."

"You can trust Hughes. He's the most decent man I've ever known."

He was puzzled by her tone, by the expression on her face. Thoughtful. Then she smiled. "You might as well hear it from me. Everybody else knows anyway. For a couple of unproductive but otherwise contented years I was Mrs. Hughes. Does that shock you?"

He thought about it for a moment. "No," he said. "In fact, it makes perfect sense."

He smiled, turned, skipped down the front steps and jogged off down the street.

19.

When he figured that he was out of sight he slowed to a walk. Early on a Saturday Danforth Avenue was still quiet. He felt his spirits sag, the post-coital emptiness of everything, the pointlessness. Women think it's only them.

He checked his cellphone. It was twenty after nine and there were messages. Email, voicemail. He was near a coffee shop and he went in. An old song playing softly in the background was one his father liked. A hoarse, hungover voice like he imagined his would be at that moment: *Sunday morning coming down.*

Three voice messages. Aggie. Leo. Not unexpected. But Lois? A text from Leo. *Hey bro, you planning to crash here? I left the door unlocked just in case.* There was an older man alone with his Saturday newspaper seated near the front window. Cyril tried to guess his age. How old would Pierre be now? How long before he'd have looked like that? Dry, thinning hair, sallow, furrowed skin.

He listened to his mother's message. "Lois called, looking for your number and I gave it to her. Okay? Also the number for that apartment, where you were staying before you moved back home. I suspect that's where you are. I'll see you when I see you. By the way I put your supper in the fridge." He put the phone away. Lois?

Cyril could remember how he'd resented his father in the early days of his abandonment, how it clouded everything, how it contaminated their encounters. He resented the cars, the luxury condo, and then, of course, the fancy house. He came to resent the tablecloths in the restaurants Pierre would take him to, comparing them to greasy paper placemats at the McDonald's and the Chuck E. Cheese's establishments that Aggie patronized. He developed a resistance to the smallest gestures he considered to be false.

He had eventually warmed to Lois. Maybe it had something to do with puberty. Almost overnight he'd come to see her as an extraordinarily attractive woman. Sexy. Awful thought, he told himself. But the resistance to Pierre's rare and superficial gestures lingered. The offer of a pint of Guinness when he was only seventeen along with the insinuating wink: *Your mother doesn't have to know.* He knew his dad was working hard at establishing a connection of some kind but the teenaged Cyril fought it all the way. What was that perverse resistance based on?

Lois. Lois was the problem. Lois sister. Lois stepmom. Lois woman.

He listened to Leo's message. "Some woman called. Lois or Lulu. I think it was your stepmom. Someone told her you were here. Not sure where you are but you better call her, okay? Touch base when you get this."

His stomach was beginning to protest the coffee but he got a refill anyway, then stared at his cellphone. Had he really told Lois to go fuck herself? What brought that on? He hit play.

"Hey you. Can't imagine what you're up to this late on a Friday night." A light laugh.

Why was it that Lois almost always caught him by surprise.

"There's something I've been wanting to talk to you about. I was wondering if you could come by some evening soon. And don't get all paranoid. I think it's something that will cheer you up. Plus I really want Pete to get to know you. He needs a man around. A father figure sort of. You *are* brothers after all. Okay? Call me. Bye."

Jesus.

Then there was Gloria. He should call her, confirm tomorrow morning or call it down. But he couldn't. He just couldn't. He felt the sudden weight of everything. He realized he hadn't showered. He decided to go home. Maybe Aggie would be out.

∽

He unlocked the door, held it ajar for a moment, listening, felt his spirit rising as he entered. The coast was clear. He was thirsty. Passing by the kitchen he was drawn by the hum of the refrigerator. He drank orange juice from the carton the way he knew she hated. Belched and put the carton back. Then he went to his room, dumped the diaries on the bed, stood for a while surveying them.

The two written in Arabic were for 1983 and 1984. That much was clear from the numbers on the covers on the spiral notebooks, carefully inscribed in that foreign style where ones resemble collapsing sevens. He tried to imagine his father's hand actually printing those numbers on the cover and writing the impenetrable flowing oriental dots and squiggles on the pages. It was impossible.

1985. The English was simple and unrevealing, crudely rendered in comparison with the fluid scrolling Arabic. Details about the weather. Uneventful days. Homework. Television programs, watched presumably for the education they offered. *Sesame Street*. *Dallas* references were plentiful. He was really into *Dallas*. Had a thing for Pam. Popular songs. Many unfamiliar names. A priest whose name Cyril could recall from references by his mother. Aboud. The "father" carefully printed in large capitals. *FATHER Aboud*. Frequent phrases in Arabic. He flicked through the pages. There was so conspicuous an absence of revelation that Cyril soon decided it was deliberate. His father didn't even trust posterity with secrets.

Could he imagine it himself—taking pen to paper and writing down the most significant events of the past twenty-four hours? Suzanne? Honestly? No way. He flopped onto his bed, felt guilt, then a creeping excitement that hardened him again, remembering how she unbuttoned her blouse halfway, then stopping, as she slowly settled on a footstool, extended her leg. "Help me with my boot," she said and he knelt in front of her.

"Now help me with my buttons."

Imagine writing that down somewhere, oblivious to the likelihood that someone might discover it and read it and exploit it the way everybody takes advantage of the power of information. He rolled over on his stomach, thrust himself against the yielding bed. Imagine writing this down!

∾

He returned to the diary of 1985 and this time sensed a sadness that had to be regret, probably homesickness.

January 10, 1985: Today FATHER A say Mass today for Miriam and mother. 9 years ago.

He fetched his backpack, retrieved a writing pad. He made a note. *January 1976. Check back, Norwegian doc—something in it—pretty sure.*

He stuffed his note and the two Arabic diaries into his backpack so he'd not forget to take them Monday morning when he went to work. Fell back on his bed and drifted off to sleep, wishing he could simply dream the truth.

∼

He knew, as soon as he'd stepped out of the shower, that she'd come home. The ambience had changed. Then came the unmistakable gritty howl of the coffee grinder. A good sign maybe. Hospitality.

"There you are," his mother said. "I was going to call out search and rescue." She presented a cheek for kissing. "I was starting to make coffee but decided that I'm going to have a drink instead. You?"

"Sure," he said.

"I suspect you had a hard night. But we won't go into that."

"Whatever."

He opened the cupboard below the sink where she kept what she called the drinking bottles. He wielded a half-full plastic jug of vodka.

"The usual?"

"Take the good one out of the freezer," she said. "I want it really, really cold and straight."

~

They were on their second. The chit-chat had been superficial, pleasant. Cyril admitted to himself that he was actually glad to be home, and decided to forget the complexity, not to mention volatility, of the personality in front of him at the kitchen table.

"Tell me again. What was he like?"

"You're asking the wrong person," she said. She swirled her glass, studying the contents.

"You knew him for a long time. You lived with him."

"It wasn't such a long time, looking back. And I don't think anybody knew him."

"Hard to believe," Cyril said.

"Yes," she said. "Hard to believe these days when everybody is trying to be noticed. All this Facebook stuff and gabbing constantly. Everybody looking for publicity. I remember one day a reporter showed up looking for him. I went to fetch him from the classroom but he wouldn't come out. He seemed upset. That's just the way he was. Private."

"So, when did you two get involved?"

"Involved?" She laughed.

"Some hot older guy—a foreigner—in the high school?"

"Oh stop," she said, blushing. She stood, picked up their empty glasses, turned toward the sink.

"Mom. What do you think happened to him?"

"I don't want to think about it. What I am thinking is we'll have leftovers from last night," she said. "Okay?"

"Sure."

"I had a really nice dinner prepared."

~

It was nearly midnight when he texted Gloria: *Just checking in. Looking forward to tomorrow. But maybe a nice long walk, okay? A little out of shape for running. Your call re breakfast. xo*

He'd been browsing in the journals for about an hour when he found the photograph. June 15, 1986. The picture was taped to the page. There were about twenty in the graduating class, all gowned and looking awkward in their mortarboards—except for Pierre. He held his in front of him, against his chest, his free hand clutching a scroll that was, presumably, his high-school diploma.

He was in the back row because he was one of the tallest. Cyril calculated that Pierre would have been twenty-six, or close to it. He was conspicuously older—even at twenty-six there was a hint of grey in his unruly head of hair.

He was smiling but the eyes were serious, wide and wary as if he didn't trust the photographer.

He carefully removed the photograph, resolved to frame it. There were so few. His dad, as Aggie often hinted, was always reticent when there were cameras around. He leaned the photo against the base of the reading lamp on his bedside table.

He gathered up the diaries, started putting them away, year by year, in the space he'd made on a bookshelf. He would have to study them, correlate the information, cross-reference with other sources. Pierre could not have—would not have—gone to all the trouble of recording the mundane details of his existence for the span of twenty-four years unless it was for some practical purpose. The only purpose Cyril could imagine was to assist him in remembering what could not be written down.

He took one more look at May 2000. *Over and out.* There was no memory from Cyril's experience that had greater clarity than

May 26, 2000. *Cool clear Friday.* Indeed it was. A day that was unremarkable until he found his father standing on that precious coffee table with a golf club. *Home early.* Cyril could confirm that: it was precisely what he'd thought. *Dad's home early for a change. Must have an early evening golf commitment. But why is he standing on the coffee table for a practice swing?*

He shelved 2000, then 2001 but as he picked up 2002 he noticed a marker of some kind wedged between the pages. It dominated late January. It was a press clipping carefully torn from a British newspaper, the *Guardian*. According to the entries, Pierre had been in England for weeks. Cyril had no memory of that trip—his father was always working somewhere. The pages before and after January 25 were filled with detail about weather and appointments. Except for the page on which he had taped the clipping. Part of the entry on January 26 was in Arabic.

Cyril carefully detached the clipping and unfolded it.

JANUARY 24: ELIE HOBEIKA
Lebanese Militia Leader Who Massacred Civilians.

It was a news report but also an obituary, of sorts.

Elie Hobeika, who was killed in a massive bomb attack at his house in the Beirut suburb of Hazmiyeh, was one of Lebanon's most controversial figures. His death at the age of 45 comes at a time when he had agreed to testify against Israeli prime minister Ariel Sharon in a war crimes trial that may be held later this year in a Brussels court. A leader of the Christian Maronite Lebanese Forces (or Phalanges, as they were known) during Lebanon's bloody civil war, Hobeika acted

as Israel's liaison chief during that country's invasion of Lebanon in
1982. He was the leader of the Phalange forces in the Beirut
Palestinian refugee camp of Shatila when the Maronite president,
Bashir Gemayel, was assassinated in September 1982.

When Cyril finished he read it a second time. Why would his
father care enough to cut this out and save it? Maybe it was for the
reference to the man he now presumed to have been his namesake,
Bashir. Or maybe not. He read it for a third time, all the way through.

Hobeika claimed that there were 2,000 Palestinian terrorists hiding
in the Sabra and Shatila camps. When given the green light by Israel
whose defence minister was then Ariel Sharon, to enter the camps,
the Phalangist militiamen slaughtered more than 1,000 men, women
and children.

   Born in Kleiat, in the Lebanese province of Kesrwan, Hobeika
left school after completing his exams . . .

He tucked the clipping in a pocket of his backpack. He would take
it to the office, follow up, check if there was archival footage of this
Hobeika. He turned out the bedside light. He lay in darkness, mind
struggling to reconcile conflicting images. His father looking out of
place in a group graduation photo in Cape Breton. His father standing on an expensive coffee table positioning a golf ball. A street lined
with crumbling buildings, smoke-blackened holes where windows
were supposed to be, vegetation growing out of craters in the pavement. Wailing, ululating women. His father with a gun.

In the darkness he could detect a small red winking light.

He sat up, switched on the lamp.

It was a text from Gloria and it was brief: *B' fast not possible. Didn't hear from u so made other plans. Ttyl.*

20.

Nader was half sitting on Cyril's desk, leg hooked over one corner, arms folded. They were both watching Suzanne who was standing in the middle of the newsroom talking to Hughes, clutching a sheaf of paper in one hand. "I wonder what that would be like," Nader said.

"What," Cyril said.

"Don't tell me you haven't wondered too."

"Not sure what you're getting at," Cyril said, knowing exactly.

"I'd be petrified," Nader said.

Cyril laughed. "Petrified? Petrified means hard."

Nader laughed. "Man, you're worse than I am."

"Whatever you're driving at," Cyril said, opening a file folder.

"I bet she'd want a full debrief afterwards," Nader said. "She's big on . . . um . . . context."

Cyril looked up, studied Suzanne, struggled to control his face before the wistfulness revealed itself. "She might surprise you."

"I'm sure she would. You know that she and Hughes were once—"

"Yes."

"I'm trying to picture it."

"I can see it. Look at them."

"Really?"

"Sure."

Nader stood, stretched, yawned. "Maybe just once, I'd take my chances. A little humiliation could be educational for a dude like me."

"Let me know," said Cyril. "Or on the other hand, don't."

"I hear Manville took a run at her," Nader said, "and couldn't get to first base. But a fella can dream. Right?"

Nader started to move away but Suzanne called out, "Don't go anywhere." Then walked over to them.

"How was everybody's weekend?" Her tone was flat, uninterested.

"My weekend was busy," Nader said.

"I'd like to hear about it. Hughes's office in ten?"

"Sure."

∾

Hughes's desk was piled with folders, newspapers, books and DVDs. He was leaning on his elbows, hands cupping his face. His eyes were weary.

Suzanne patted a place beside her on the couch, said to Nader: "You sit here. I've been hearing from Hughes. You *have* been busy."

"After Friday prayers, I hung out for a while," Nader said. "I think we're making some headway but everybody is being super cautious, as you can imagine."

She nodded. She looked at Cyril. "And what about you, young fella. What did you get up to?"

Cyril felt the warmth in his face. "Very quiet weekend," he said. Then he remembered his father's diaries. "Just a second," he said. He went to his desk and fetched his backpack, returned to Hughes's office. "Suzanne mentioned that you read Arabic."

Hughes tilted his head and made a face. "I suppose," he said.

Cyril retrieved the two notebooks from the backpack, put them on the desk. "These were among my father's things. Sometime when you have nothing better to do . . ."

Hughes picked one up, examined it. "1983," he said. "Is that when your dad came to Canada?"

"Around then."

"Hmm," Hughes said, flipping through the pages. "Can I hang on to these for a while?"

"Of course," said Cyril.

"Great," Suzanne said. "Look. I've got some news." She was smiling at Cyril now. "Good news and bad news."

"Let's have the good news," Nader said.

"Cyril has been reassigned to work with us. I talked to Doc on the weekend. He agrees and he's pretty sure that he can swing a contract down the road a bit."

"Wow," said Cyril. "You're kidding."

"Don't get too excited," Suzanne said. "It'll be a temp contract. Maybe, if you're lucky, for a month. But these things have a way of putting down roots if you're any good."

"So what's the bad news," Hughes said.

"Same as the good news. Cyril has been reassigned to work with us. As an intern for the moment. What do you think?"

"I can't see any downside," Cyril said.

"Right answer," said Suzanne. "So let's get busy."

"Oh," said Cyril to Hughes. "And there was something else. It was folded up in the diary for 2002." He rummaged in the backpack until he found the clipping from the *Guardian*.

"What's that?" said Suzanne. He handed it to her.

She scanned it quickly. "Holy shit," she said. "He knew Hobeika, obviously. You know who Hobeika is . . . was?"

Cyril shook his head. "Just what I read there."

"Well, you can look him up," Suzanne said, laughing. "What a piece of work he was. I'd forgotten someone took him out. I sure hope that they weren't friends."

"Let me see," said Hughes. She handed the clipping across the desk to him and he read it quickly. "Wow."

~

Cyril listened carefully to the conversation as it unfolded, and when he started to become confused by details that were contingent on half-remembered background facts, he pulled a notebook from his backpack and started writing down fragments so he could reconstruct what he was hearing later. Radical voices in the mosques. Fundamentalists attacking the pragmatic secularists. Visiting imams, some of them dangerously persuasive. Young folk bored, and in many cases, insulted by a Western culture that manipulated style and taste and values for crass commercial reasons. Kids raised in homes with firm, faith-based convictions being pulled this way and that by the materialistic culture.

As Nader analyzed the situation, Cyril began to see and hear another Nader—engaged, a little bit outraged. He was describing young people caught in the middle of an age-old dynamic: older people brainwashing and recruiting young idealists to fight their wars.

But there was something new and sinister in the political equation— a violent medieval vision plotting to replace modern corruption with something probably worse. A fundamentalist dictatorship. Young idealistic people were responding sympathetically.

"As if," Hughes interjected, "corruption was unheard of in the caliphate." He shook his head.

Nader smiled. "People have had six hundred years to forget the inconvenient part of history—six centuries of colonial oppression."

"Talk to the Jews about oppression," Hughes countered, "and the Armenians, the Serbians. The Irish. Don't get me wrong but—"

"So how do we get people to talk about this?" Suzanne interrupted.

"Not so easy anymore," Nader said. "They've been burned so many times. Right? They're hyper-vigilant about spies."

"So what about you?"

"They know where I work so they probably assume I talk about it to you. But they trust me. So far."

"But they're going to be careful, right? When you're around."

"Yes. But in a way I take attention away from the people they really should be worrying about. Man, some of these mosques are so infiltrated," Nader said. "They have no clue. I know three guys who are actually *working* for CSIS right in the middle of everything. One of them is a real agitator. There are times I want to expose the bastard."

"You were going to talk to your spy contacts about a meeting," Suzanne said.

"Yes. I think it's going to happen. They're getting worried. There are rumours about youngsters making plans to go to Syria, young Sunni guys who are really, really upset about what happened in Iraq."

"Fucking Iraq," said Hughes, tossing his pen down.

"Why Syria?" Cyril asked.

They looked at him, suddenly remembering his presence. "Who wants to go first?" Suzanne said, smiling.

"It's okay," said Cyril. "I can look it up. But so what if young guys want to go over there to get involved. Better there than here." He smiled, feeling slightly confident for the first time.

"And what do we do with them when they come home more fucked up than when they went?" Suzanne asked.

Hughes rescued him. "Cyril has a point. I remember young warriors all fired up about the menace of communism, going off to Vietnam—young *Canadians*. And back in the thirties, we forget the MacKenzie-Papineau Battalion. Idealists and young communists heading off to stop the fascists in Spain . . . they came back, joined the army, fought Hitler, came home again, had babies, got jobs and mort-gages. Got old and died. Oldest story in the world."

"We're trying to do a *doc-u-mentary*, guys," Suzanne said wearily. "Not the history of boys . . ."

Hughes gave her a sour look.

"Nader," said Suzanne, "my takeaway is that you're close to get-ting that background briefing from CSIS. Am I right?"

"I'm close. They've asked for names. Who'll I say?"

"Tell them you, me and Cyril."

∽

"I don't know how you do that," Cyril said, outside Hughes's office.

"Do what?"

"Come and go in the mosque, walk that line."

"No problem," said Nader. "I'm a believer. People know that. There and here. I believe in what I'm doing, both places. Sometimes that works. The big word nowadays, I hear, is authenticity."

"It's that simple?"

"Who said anything was simple?"

∽

"Coffee?" Suzanne said, smiling at him.

They walked together toward the elevators. Waiting there, Cyril said, "Thanks."

"Like I said, it's temporary. At least for now."

"Isn't everything?" he said. She did an exaggerated double take.

"Wow. You sound like Hughes." Poked him playfully, then sobered. "Let me say just one thing. If your dad was, in any way, tied in with Elie Hobeika then maybe you're better off not knowing. Okay? Take it from me. He was one bad dude."

"Okay," he said. "But look . . . I hope you're going to be okay with this."

"With what?"

"Me, working on the team."

"Why wouldn't I be?"

The elevator dinged in front of them before he could answer. It was crowded. They squeezed in. At the bottom she plucked his sleeve, led him off to one side as the crowd dispersed.

"Why wouldn't I be okay with you working on the team?"

"Well, you know . . ."

"Wait now," she said. "Let me guess—you're asking if our working relationship might be affected by, um, recent events?"

"Something like that."

She studied his face for a long uncomfortable moment. Finally she said, "I wouldn't lose any sleep over it. That was then, this is now. Okay? *Now* let's go get that coffee. It's your turn, by the way, *now* that you're nearly on the payroll."

He dialled Gloria's number but it rang through so he left a message. "I've got some good news. Call me back."

But she didn't call him back, so he sent a text: *Got some exciting news today. Can we get together?*

The reply was prompt and it was brief: *getting 2gether prolly not a good idea just now. Wots the news?*

He studied the cryptic words for what felt like a long time. The casual coded lingo acknowledged history and intimacy. But the meaning was clear.

He texted back: *Understood. News not all that exciting. Be well.*

21.

Gloria hadn't even noticed him. She had cantered by, face flushed with the exertion of her run or by the momentary merriment she was sharing with the man who was beside her. Cyril had been trudging through a little park not far from the office on his way home—a lovely evening for a walk, or for a run. And runners were not uncommon in the parks or even on the sidewalks. So he hadn't reacted when he'd heard the running feet behind him. The thought that passed through his head had been of all the places in the world where running feet behind him would have paralyzed him. Then as she swept by he recognized the hair, the golden ponytail threaded through the open space on the back of the familiar ball cap.

His first reaction was the kind of thrill he always felt when he saw her unexpectedly. He'd almost called out. But he caught himself in time. They were estranged. The thought hit him like a sucker-punch. The bond between them had stretched and frayed. He'd never doubted that the bond was intact, but at some point, it had obviously broken. Any stranger would have seen that there was a connection between the two runners, something comfortable and clearly physical.

Then they were gone, God knows where—it occurred to him that it might well have been to her place and he had a fleeting, nauseating image of them in the shower. She had looked lithe and lean, head high and proud and the glistening flush of pleasure on her lovely face. He realized he had never truly given her full credit for the bodily perfection that he had just observed in motion, a product of intelligent self-discipline.

It was as if he had just seen her for the first time and then he realized that this was partly true. He'd never really *seen* her running because he would have been beside her (or a bit ahead). Whenever he had been fully conscious of her body they were so close that the only sense that really registered was the sense of touch.

He hadn't noticed much about the man she'd been running with. Slightly shorter than Gloria, thick in neck and torso, broad of shoulder, scalp shaved and shiny. Possibly a weightlifter, synonymous, in Cyril's view, with shallow, narcissistic. No, this can't be serious, he thought. He was the opposite of Cyril, clearly not her type.

He felt an almost overwhelming need to run after her, to pound on her door. He had his cellphone in his hand, scrolling through the numbers. A slight poke of a finger would restore the connection, would bring her back.

"Don't be such an idiot," he said aloud. And then he was angry at almost everyone he knew, starting with himself.

～

Aggie was in the kitchen, the counter littered with bowls and pans, knives and wooden serving spoons. "Ah, there you are."

Cyril went straight to the cupboard below the sink, extracted the plastic jug of vodka. "Will you be having the usual?"

"Supper's almost on the table," she said.

"I'm not hungry," he replied. He half-filled a water glass, plopped in two ice cubes and retreated from the kitchen.

"What about . . . ?"

"Don't bother," he said, and climbed the stairs.

He sat on the side of his bed for five minutes, sipping the vodka. "Fuck her," he said finally. "Fuck everybody. Gloria. Aggie. Pierre. Lois. That thick-necked bald-headed fuck she was running with. And Suzanne, for fucking with me and fucking up my focus." And then he felt a momentary elation, maybe from the vodka or maybe from a thought: "I have a job. Thank God for work."

He randomly pulled several of his father's diaries from the shelf.

∼

It was like trying to learn about a chef by reading recipes. The one revelation Cyril could take away for sure was that his father didn't trust anybody in those early days in Canada. But not even in a diary? Written only for yourself?

After morning class, to Macdonalds with AGNES for burger. She has new car.

Pierre made no record of how they'd met. There were frequent references to Agnes, but nothing to suggest an emotional trajectory, or intimacy. Then, out of the blue, on May 30, 1987—*Marriage Agnes today. Fr. A, Pius, Peggy, Al M, Sam W, Johnny Abbas. John MacNeil. B. Shebib. Irving. Reception at Cedars. J Campbell from*

CB Post show up. Sent away. Drove Halifax late. Lord Nelson Hotel.

The next three days were blank.

Then it was back to the delivery of furniture and appliances. It seems he drove a truck in those days for a family named Schwartz. There were frequent references to Irving, who owned the truck and seemed to be a friend. *Irving many questions. V. interested wars.*

June 5, 1987. Three trips Eskasoni w. irving. Indians all get new stoves. Irving friends of Indians. Jews and indians all same history, irving say.

He was interrupted by a knock on his bedroom door. "Everything okay in there?" Then the door opened.

He stared at his mother.

"Sorry," Aggie said and started to close the door. "It's just—you really should eat something."

"I was just looking at the day you guys got married," he said.

"Are you sure you should . . . ?"

"I wouldn't worry," he said. "He didn't reveal much."

"There wasn't much to reveal. A small ceremony in the vestry at St. Anthony Daniel in Sydney . . ."

"The vestry?"

"He didn't have any proof of baptism or confirmation or anything and, anyway, he didn't really care about religion. But he wanted Father Aboud to marry us. Only Mom and Dad and a few friends came. And then there was a little party at the Cedars Club. That was nice."

"And you had a honeymoon in Halifax."

"Let me see that."

"I don't think so. It gets pretty steamy in Halifax. The Lord Nelson, eh?"

Now she was in the room. "I don't believe a word of it. Even if it were true. Steamy, for God's sake. Give me that."

He handed it to her.

"Right," she said. "The Lord Nelson." Face flushed, she flipped through the next pages. "You're nothing but a big liar." She tossed the book at him. "I'm going to bed. But you should eat."

"Wait. June '07. Help me remember."

She sighed. "So we're back to that, are we?"

"Just work with me."

"I had the one visit from the police. They only wanted to know when I had last seen him or spoken to him."

"But weren't they interested in earlier in his life, when you were . . . together?"

"Why would that have anything to do with anything?"

"Maybe there was something in his past. Maybe he had enemies."

"They might have asked if he had any connection with Lebanese people here but I would have said that was highly unlikely. He wasn't like that. He had no time for that stuff. He had friends all over. Jews, Scots, French, Micmac. You name it."

"What about . . ."

"You have to understand. In many ways, your father was always a stranger. To me and everybody else. I find even talking about it difficult. You live with somebody for years. You think you're sharing everything. Then one day you realize you really didn't know that other person. And it dawns on you, that you only know what another person wants to let you know."

"Which makes everyone a stranger?"

"More or less."

Wednesday, March 30. 1988. Son born. 8:30. I am in del. room with Ag and doc and nurses. Hold baby to see and there is eye contact. V. dark eyes stare at me, no blinking. I see recognition, but also curiosity. Very happy day.

Wednesday's child. He struggled to remember the nursery rhyme. Monday, fair of face. Tuesday something about grace. Then Wednesday.

He googled: Wednesday's child . . . *is full of woe.*

He turned out the light, climbed into bed with his clothes on.

~

Timeline. The word brought him fully awake. He checked the bedside clock. It was 4:00 a.m. There was a soft breeze shifting a drowsy curtain, usually enough to send him back into slumber. But the word just sat there. *Timeline.* He swung his legs over the bedside, remembering a research tip that Nader had given him.

"What you need is a timeline, man. It requires you to take stock of everything you know and when you do that, it's amazing how much you'll discover that you don't know. And when the picture becomes clear, you see what you need to know and just how much you don't need to know."

They'd been killing time on a sidewalk patio on King Street. Cyril was nursing a beer. Nader was rattling the ice cubes in his much-diminished Coke—his third.

"Do you really think you're better off drinking that stuff?" Cyril asked. "By my calculation you've had almost a gallon."

"It's the culture, man. I'm not averse to a discreet shot of Appleton Dark to improve the flavour. But I never developed a taste for the pint or even wine. Just don't see the attraction. Though I do get a kick out of watching other people getting off on it. Especially when it gets them yakking. You know what I mean?"

Cyril nodded.

"Gotta get our stimulation somewhere. Like when I have coffee? None of this double-double for me. I order four-by-four."

"Four-by-four? Ah . . . never mind."

They sat watching the passersby. It was a warm autumn evening, people heading home or to the bars. Nader shook his head. "Before you know it, all that lovely flesh will be buried in layers of wool and Gore-Tex. What a crime, winter. Crime against humanity."

The waiter paused by the table. "Refill?"

Nader nodded.

"I'm okay," Cyril said. "Timeline, eh?"

"It could be the key."

∽

As he left for work that morning, Aggie asked, "Will you be late tonight? Someone has to plan the meals here."

"Probably," he said.

∽

Nader dropped a thick sheaf of papers on his desk. "Been doing your work for you, brother."

"What's this?"

"I printed off some Lebanon stuff from the '76 to '83 period to get you going on the timeline. Focused on the civil war, how it got started, up until the bombing of the Marine barracks."

"What Marine barracks?"

"October '83. Somebody drove a truckload of explosives through the front gate of the U.S. Marine base in Beirut and blew the whole place up. Hundreds killed. It's all here."

"Marines in Beirut?"

Nader laughed. "Just read it. Make notes of the key dates. Arrange everything chronologically. High points of those days all usually involve mass murder. I'd mostly forgotten about Sabra and Shatila."

"Okay. I heard something about that . . . the clipping from the *Guardian*."

"Good. The Hobeika guy was up to his neck in it. There's more about that massacre here. I'd put a lot of that stuff out of my head. Heard too much about it when I was a kid."

"You had people . . . ?"

"No but my mom was born in Gaza. So."

"And your father?"

"Persian. I'm a hybrid, man."

"So. Tell me more about timelines."

"What you gotta do is pick a starting point and work forward chronologically, dates and developments. So let's say you start in— let's say January '76, and what happened. Then move forward."

"But that's the problem. From January 1976 to 1983 is pretty much a blank."

"Nothing is blank. Your father was somewhere, doing something. You try to figure out where he was and what was going on and you'll probably get a good idea of what he was up to. He was a refugee, man. So he was *not* unaffected by events. You say his immediate family was wiped out? But I gather what you're really after is what happened to him more recently, yes? Five years ago. Why the disappearance. This much you know: he went into hiding, sort of, but you know *where* he was . . . and what happened out there. Right?"

"Not a hundred percent," Cyril said.

"Okay. Maybe you need two timelines. Think back. When was it? June?"

Cyril suddenly felt uneasy. "It's all kind of a blank. I was nineteen, man. He was always absent. I never really gave it much thought until the police showed up."

Nader produced a notebook and a pen, wrote briefly. Cyril watched him, wondering. *Should I tell him? Should I confess that I was relieved that he was absent so much that spring? How even when they told me to anticipate the worst, my first thoughts were of myself? How I felt, in a sick way, safe? From him?*

Nader put the pen away. "Key question, always, right after *what* is *why*. You might be surprised that the answer is sitting there, maybe in bits and pieces, but it's there somewhere."

Cyril struggled to return to the moment, the here and now. He knew too well the why of his feelings in June 2007—and why he'd never be able to confess them to anyone.

Nader said, "Start with the diaries. Correlate with these clippings."

"Diaries are strange," Cyril said. "Coded secrets, sometimes. Don't you think?"

"Yes. But codes can be broken. That's why they're fun."

"In any case, the most important one is gone. Disappeared."

"Someone made it disappear."

"Who?"

"Whoever made the boat blow up," Nader said.

"But if it was an accident?"

"I think we can assume that if it was an accident, he and the diary would not have so completely disappeared. There would be something, fragments. I mean, think of plane crashes in the ocean. They find briefcases, documents, bodies, kids' toys. Somebody made that boat blow up, my friend. Maybe your dad. Maybe someone else. I figure once you've found the 'why' you'll know the 'who.'"

"Okay. I hear you."

"And have you considered going down there? Check it out. Maybe talk to witnesses."

"There were no witnesses."

"Still, there's nothing like seeing for yourself. And surely there was someone who at least heard something. It was an explosion, man."

"Maybe."

Nader looked away, squinted. "Here comes Hughes."

Hughes had one of the diaries in his hand.

"So far I haven't found out much," he said. "Some of the entries raise a lot of questions, though. Everything elliptical. Reading between the lines, lots of torment. I wish my Arabic was better. But I'd like to take another pass. What about you, Nader? How's your Arabic?"

Nader raised his hands defensively. "Conversationally okay. But reading? Uh-uh. I'm learning, though. Now, Farsi . . ."

"So I'll have another stab at it," Hughes said. "Okay with you?"

"Sure," Cyril said. "But why do you say 'tormented'?"

"He's trying to write a poem in one place. About killing."

"About killing in general?"

"Yes, but the hook is something specific. Something personal."

"In 1983."

"Well, the specific killing seems to have been in '82." Hughes hesitated for a moment, then said, "September '82. A woman."

"Sabra and Shatila," Nader said. "September '82. There were lots of women."

"What's confusing me," said Hughes, "is that your father was living in Kfar Matta when he was writing this in 1983."

"What's Kfar Matta?" Nader asked.

"It's an old Druze village in the Chouf Mountains. The Druze were mortal enemies of the Phalange, especially in '83."

"Maybe he was a captive," Nader said. "After the massacre."

"Uh, no," said Hughes. "These people didn't keep captives very long, if at all. Especially somebody like Cyril's dad who was in the Kata'ib. As far as I can tell, Pierre was there for months. Got special treatment. And now I'm extrapolating, but it looks like he left the village near the end of August. Somehow hooked up with the Israelis when they were pulling back. Obviously saw what was coming. Ends up in Canada . . . September sixteenth, 1983. That was one date he was specific about."

"I wonder why," Cyril said.

Hughes studied him for a moment, then sighed. "Well, I guess it was a big moment in his life. Real sanctuary, finally. But it also might be significant that the massacre in the Beirut camps started on the night of September sixteenth, 1982. Exactly a year earlier."

∼

At the top of the long legal writing pad Cyril printed DAMOUR, JANUARY 1976. At the bottom of the page: CAPE BRETON, CANADA, SEPTEMBER 1983.

He stared at the space between, lost in a sudden vapour of anxiety. Seven years to fill. He remembered the DVD, the Norwegian documentary from 1976. Fished through the paper rubble on his desk. Found it. Sorted through a stack of paper until he found the script translation, then the name of the English speaker in the documentary. Dany Chamoun. Phalange Militia Commander. Aftermath of massacre at Karantina refugee camp. January 1976.

He took the DVD to a screening room and watched the documentary again. And then again, without sound, without the script, scanning faces for his own.

22.

What he missed most acutely about Gloria was all the talking that they did. They talked incessantly, in restaurants and pubs, in cars, on buses, jogging, and in bed. She knew his secrets. Did his father have a Gloria, someone that he truly trusted with his secrets, with his codes? Could he have been so isolated that he trusted nobody?

His timeline now had four pages: Damour and Karantina; Sabra and Shatila; Kfar Matta; Canada. Three waypoints. The most daunting gap was from 1976 to 1982. Something happened in that period that would explain his father's life and probably his death. He was now convinced of that.

Who was his father's Gloria?

The answer was obvious.

Lois had called him, left a message. All he had to do was call her back. He remembered the friendly tone, the "Hey you . . ."

Five rings before the machine kicked in but then he heard her voice talking over the recording. "Just hang on a sec."

"Hi."

"Hey."

"You were trying to reach me?"

"Ah . . . yes. How are you?"

"I'm okay. Look. I was going to call you. A hundred times. After that last thing. I was a complete—"

"Never mind," she said. "All things considered, it was nothing. You're sure you're okay, though?"

"You know what? All things considered, I am. The internship is turning into a job. For one thing."

"Wow, that's great. Amazing, actually."

"Well, it'll be a temp position, but isn't everything nowadays. It'll be up to me. And fate."

She laughed. "That's the way to look at it. Life is temporary, after all."

"I wanted to talk to you about Dad, actually. Can I come by sometime?"

"Sure," she said. "Anytime. Plus we have a little bit of business to tidy up, you and I. Okay?"

A jolt of panic scattered all his thoughts and words.

"Don't worry," she said. "I think you'll be pleasantly surprised."

"Okay. When would be good?"

"Come by this evening. Say after eight."

"See you then. And, oh. I just want to say it—I'm sorry about the last time. That was . . . that wasn't me talking. It was pretty gross . . ."

"Not a problem," she said. "Later, okay?"

∼

There was a text message waiting from Nader.

Wot y'up to? We should talk. Face to face.

He replied: *when, where*

our patio in an hour?

cu there

∼

Nader was slouched at the little patio table on King Street, watching passersby through his shades, plucking at the whiskers underneath his chin. He was the epitome of cool. Even the large beer glass full of Coke was cool. Nader had no qualms about being an observant Muslim, no matter where or what the circumstances. The faith was who he was. There was a second glass.

"I took the liberty. It's on me."

Cyril smiled, sat, sipped the beer. "Thanks," he said. "So?"

Nader took a long drink of the Coke. "Look. This guy you know, the fellow who hangs out in that bar in the east end."

"Yes."

"The Israeli."

"Yes."

"How much do you know about him?"

"Not much. Why?"

"Suzanne met him, right?"

"Yes."

"You know she thinks she remembers him from years ago. In Lebanon. We talked about it."

"Okay."

"She's pretty sure it was back in '82 or '83. After the massacre in the camps in Beirut. It was her first big story. Made a lasting impression on her. Anyway, she's been going through her files and she now thinks she saw this guy at a press conference way back when. He was in the background, kind of watching over the Israeli general or whatever who was doing all the talking. But she remembers him because someone told her at the time he was part of a heavy-duty anti-terrorism unit. Sayeret Matkal. Like, what were they doing there?"

"What?"

"Sayeret Matkal. Elite outfit. IDF special forces. Did you ever see the movie *Raid on Entebbe*? Charles Bronson. Based on a real story. That was Sayeret Matkal."

"So?"

"So what would he be doing here if he's the same guy? Some guy connected with that outfit."

"That was a long time ago, Nader."

"I've heard from other sources, Suzanne might be onto something. So I'd like to meet him."

"Do you think he has something to do with our story?"

"I've been picking up some buzz among my contacts, that our security people have signed up an outside consultant to advise them on counter-terrorism strategy. Imagine how that would go over in the mosques? An Israeli anti-terrorism spook? Whoa. Word is they've been bringing him on board their surveillance since '05 when they were monitoring the so-called Toronto Eighteen."

"I wasn't really paying attention . . ."

"The bunch of guys rounded up in '06 by this INSET outfit . . ."

"Inset?"

"Integrated National Security Enforcement Team. They grabbed a bunch of young guys who were fantasizing about blowing up Toronto. Stupid, most of them, but there were a few who could have been dangerous. Anyway, this secret terrorism consultant might have been a part of that, and word is they're using him again. Imagine what the radicals could do with that. Especially if this consultant has the kind of history Suzanne suspects."

"Why now?"

"Arab Spring, man. Everybody has been going on about the lovely revolution. Like it was gonna be all over by summer, fall at the latest—peace and democracy across the Arab world. People haven't got a freakin' clue. I don't blame the spooks for being spooked."

"So what do I do?"

"Let me tag along next time you go to see this Israeli."

"Sure."

∽

Cyril decided he would walk. It would take forty minutes to get from the office to where Lois lived but he needed the exercise. It had been weeks since he'd had any cardio and he could feel it in his chest. He could feel it in his head.

What could Lois want? He knew what *he* wanted: he wanted information. "A little bit of business to tidy up," she'd said. Her tone had been almost parental, which reassured him somewhat.

There was a five-year difference in their ages but they shared perspective on most things, taste in books and music, consciousness of trends. But Lois was from a family that was Jewish and conservative. Her social life had been strictly supervised by parents who had plans and expectations of what they wanted her to be—basically a projection of their ideal selves. They had more or less disowned her when she announced that she was going to live with an older man, a man who wasn't Jewish. An Arab, yet.

His mother had seemed almost relieved when she discovered that Pierre's new girlfriend was working in a restaurant. "A waitress, if you can imagine." She in fact had been a hostess in a high-end establishment frequented by the rich and influential, one of those places that never has to advertise, a place you never went just to eat but, instead, to meet and dine. It was on the forty-seventh floor of a downtown office building and had a dramatic panoramic view of the city and the lake. Pierre had entertained important clients and company directors there and that's where they had met. At the time she was also attending university, learning the business side of hospitality.

His mother's contempt for the waitress who was also just a student, "a child," only made Lois seem more human to Cyril. And so it would transpire that Cyril became a frequent visitor. He was always conscious of her prettiness—that was normal. They were relaxed together and it seemed to make her careless in his presence—the way she dressed and moved around the house.

He kept reminding himself: *She's Dad's wife, she's my friend. She's like my sister.*

"I'd be grateful if you'd check on Lois now and then," Pierre had told him. "She gets a bit stressed when I'm gone. Her family situation isn't the greatest. She likes you. You're good for her."

And then, the incident.

It happened while Pierre was on a business trip to Indonesia. It was springtime. He'd gone to his father's place with his books because Aggie had people in for bridge or for a book club. They were studying.

Cyril was at the kitchen table. Lois was working in a cranny that she used for office space. It was late. And then, unexpectedly, she was behind him, a hand resting lightly on his shoulder. It was a small hand, a hand he had frequently admired for its delicacy. It reminded him of little bird bones. Impulsively he laid his cheek against it. The hand lingered, then withdrew.

"I'm going to put some coffee on," she said.

"Good idea."

Standing at the open fridge, she changed her mind. "There's a nice bottle of Pinot Grigio here. Maybe . . ."

"Better still." He stood. "I'll open it." When he leaned into the fridge to fetch the bottle he brushed against her.

In his memory it was a kind of blur, even immediately afterwards when they were breathless, awkward and embarrassed.

Who started it? He didn't really know. It was frantic, perhaps because of some deep impulse to get it over with before their brains kicked in. They were standing, struggling for balance, knocked the bottle over but he retrieved it just before it toppled off the table and the distraction helped sustain his ardour for perhaps half a minute longer than it would otherwise have lasted. And then it was over. Remorse would follow close behind.

For all of them, it was a turning point when Pierre returned from Indonesia. Cyril couldn't help attributing the change to what had happened between him and Lois. Pierre seemed more distracted, more distant than he'd ever been before. Was it possible she'd confessed to him? Was it possible he knew, and that he was waiting for a proper opportunity to drop the bomb?

Then three months later, in June 2007, Pierre was gone. Cyril grieved, but he finally relaxed. Until the day she announced to him and Aggie that she was pregnant.

∾

She presented a cheek and he lightly brushed it with his own. He noted she was wearing makeup.

"You look good," he said. "You look very good." They both blushed and she caught his hand lightly.

"Come in," she said. "Let me have a look at you. I've just put on a pot of herbal tea if you're interested. I *could* find something stronger."

"No. Tea will be great."

After the tea was poured they sat at the kitchen table. "So," she said brightly. "You must tell me all about the job."

"It's more of a project than a job, though they're telling me that it could lead to other things."

"A project," she said. Her tone was mildly teasing. "I don't suppose it's anything that you can talk about."

"Actually it's interesting. All the stuff that's going on in the Middle East. Syria, the Arab Spring stuff. How it's stirring up young Muslims. Even here."

"That's a story that isn't going to go away for a while. It sounds like you're onto something that could last. Good for you."

"Maybe."

"Everything else good in your life?"

"Well. That's another story."

"Ah." Then a silence. Finally: "Well, I'm always here. To talk."

"And you," he said. "You're happy?"

"Yes," she said tentatively. Paused, sipped her tea. "I think I mentioned, I'm seeing someone."

"You mentioned."

"It doesn't bother you?"

"Why would it bother me?"

"Well. Your dad . . ."

He waved a hand. "It's been five years. I'm surprised you haven't . . . you know. Long before this."

"Nobody could ever replace your dad."

He nodded. Then he said, "You probably knew him better than I did."

She smiled, caught his hand and squeezed it. "We only know what people show. Don't you think?"

"And he was pretty good at hiding things. Not much for showing."

"I suppose it comes down to what we need from someone."

"Yes. Well. But something about this project I'm working on has me wondering who he really was. About his life before he got here. What he left behind. Mom says he never talked about it to her."

She refilled the cups. "Well. Your mom and me—we have that much in common, I guess."

"He never talked to you either?"

She shrugged. "I really wasn't interested. I suppose I should have been."

Cyril said, "It's only lately I got interested. I guess as we get older."

"I remember when he brought up the possibility of a trip back, I asked about relatives. He said that there were none that mattered. I gather they were all gone."

"Gone."

"Yes. In the civil war."

"But did he ever mention anything about how he managed to survive?"

"No."

"I find that odd."

"Really?"

"Yeah. There's usually a reason people avoid talking about whole chapters of their lives."

"Isn't that a bit judgmental?"

"Maybe. But I think I have a right to know who he really was."

"Can I say something?"

"Sure."

"People sometimes have to do desperate things to survive. I know that from my own family. I'm here because of people who survived.

You're here because your dad survived. We're here because people were able to survive catastrophes. We should be glad. No?"

"But knowing how . . ."

"That was his call to make. And it was okay with me. I loved everything I knew. I couldn't have loved him more, no matter what he told me. And I couldn't have loved him less, either." She looked away. "Now," she said. "Some business."

"Before the business," he said. And he caught her hand. "I have to ask this. Did he know what happened when he was away?"

"Why is that relevant?"

"Because I couldn't help wondering when he just disappeared like that."

"You think he would have just skulked away if he'd known? You're right, Cyril. You didn't know your father. Neither of us would be sitting here now if he knew. That much I'm sure of. So what's your point?"

"I don't know what my point is. I'm sorry."

"Don't be sorry. When he disappeared, he was worried about his job, for one thing. About becoming the scapegoat for people who were killed at one of their mining projects in Indonesia. Everybody was looking for someone to blame and he would have been convenient."

"Mom says it was all crap."

"It was. Typical corporate ass-covering. But it bothered him. A lot. And then, of course, the diagnosis . . ."

"What *was* the diagnosis?"

"You know. That guy Ari told you."

"I just know that it was cancer, and about that medication he was taking."

"Well, there isn't a whole lot more than that. He was diagnosed early that year. I knew it was serious even though he kept minimizing it. They wanted to operate right away. But there was this mess in Indonesia and he wouldn't take the time off to deal with his health. The fucking company was more important. Do you really need to know this?"

"I really do."

"He decided he could hold everything off by following an extreme diet and taking this ridiculous medication . . ."

"And what did that do?"

She studied his face, his eyes. Her expression was a mix of sympathy and disbelief.

"So I have to spell it out? It flattened his libido. Okay? Satisfied?"

Cyril just stared at her.

"It made him impotent, okay? Imagine how that went over with his Mediterranean temperament. In any case, we'll never know if it had any effect on the cancer."

"But if he was impotent, how could you get . . . ?"

"Get what?"

"Pete . . ."

She laughed. "Oh for Christ's sake. You aren't thinking . . . ?" She laughed again. "I'll spare you the details. Just thank modern science, obstetrics and gynaecology. Our Pete is a science project. Conceived in a lab. Okay?"

"Okay."

"So you can relax. You. Are. Not. Pete's. Dad. Have you got that?"

"Yes. Lois?"

"Yes?"

"You know, when I first heard that he was gone . . . I was relieved, in a way. Pretty sick, eh."

She was puzzled. "Relieved?"

"Relieved that we were safe, from him finding out the truth. About us."

She smiled. "What was the truth about us? That we behaved like stupid children?"

"Something like that."

"Smart children learn from their stupidity, Cyril. I did. Didn't you?"

"Okay. Yes. I suppose."

"Now get up. I want to show you something."

∾

He followed her down a short flight of stairs. He thought she was leading him into the basement but there was a doorway at a landing and he remembered the garage. She flicked a light switch and opened the door. The space was bright. There had once been a ping-pong table here—one of Pierre's ideas for entertaining Cyril. They'd played once, maybe twice, neither any good at it. Cyril remembered the silly little balls ponking on the concrete floor and vanishing. His dad, impatient, crawling underneath the table. Pierre was never good at not being *very* good at everything he tried, and never very good at concealing his impatience.

Now most of the garage was occupied by a car concealed under a fitted protective tarp.

"Help me take this off," she said, grabbing a corner.

Cyril squeezed around the front, grabbed a piece of the covering and together they rolled it back to reveal a vehicle that Cyril, up close, couldn't immediately recognize. He'd learned to drive but he didn't have a car and never felt he needed one.

"What do you think?" she asked.

"Wow," he said. "It's elegant for sure." And it was. Sleek and sexy, obviously powerful.

He walked around it, stepped back for perspective. It was a Mustang. It was black with a wide white streak along each side, near the bottom of the doors. COBRA 2. "What year?" he asked.

"It's a 1975," she said. "Someone at the office put it up for sale. Pierre wasn't much for toys but he said maybe it was meant to be— that 1975 had been a special year."

"Did he say why it was special?"

"He said it was the last year of his childhood."

"Ah."

"Does that mean something to you?"

"Well. Yes. The civil war started in 1975."

She nodded.

"Did he ever talk about the civil war?"

"No."

"Do you think he was in it?"

She walked along the car slowly, rubbed a finger along a fender, examined the finger, rubbed her thumb against the fingertip. "Why would it matter?"

"It's just something I'd like to know."

"I suspect he was."

"Why do you suspect?"

"You just got the vibe."

He noticed that the car was up on blocks, but before he could ask about that, she said, "The wheels are in storage. I'd have someone put them on for you. Make sure everything is working properly."

"What are you talking about?"

"This is yours," she said.

"What?"

"He'd want you to have the car. I've had this on my mind for quite a while."

"But I don't . . ."

"Like I said, it's yours. And I'd really like to get it out of here. I hope you don't . . ."

"No. I understand. But what would I do with it?"

"I'm sure you'll think of something. Sell it, even. It's probably worth something. I think he drove it once. Maybe twice."

"Okay. If you're sure. But one thing."

"Yes."

"What did you mean about his 'vibe'?"

She shrugged. "How he'd react, how intensely he'd focus on news from there and how he'd leave the room, or change the channel as if I wasn't there, like he was all by himself. He couldn't stand violence on TV or anywhere and yet he had . . ."

"He had what?"

"I remember once we walked into a subway station and you could hear loud voices as we were coming down the stairs. At the bottom there was this guy ranting at a black kid. The kid couldn't have been more than seventeen and he was terrified, pale, if you can imagine. Anyway, this shabby white guy was going at him, threatening, and Pierre just lost it."

"Lost it and did what?"

"Actually, not much at first. He stopped and just stared until the white guy noticed. I had his arm and tried to move him but he was like a rock. The guy started into Pierre but only got about three words out when Pierre had him pinned by the throat against the wall. I thought your dad was going to kill him. The guy's eyes were popping out. Then Pierre let him go and the guy just took off."

"And Dad said nothing?"

"Not a word. Yet he'd nearly faint at a sudden loud noise. Or he'd get anxious at a helicopter sound. Once we went into the fancy cheese place on the Danforth and he got weak . . . I thought he was going to be sick . . . he said he'd wait outside. I never did figure that one out. Loud noises I could understand. But there was something about the smell of strong cheese."

"And so . . ."

"Like I said, he survived a catastrophe somehow. That's all that matters to me. He survived long enough to . . ."

And then she crumpled, put her face against his shoulder.

He rubbed her back but he did not hold her. They were so beyond that.

At last she stepped back. "Do you have a Kleenex?"

He dug in his pocket. "A piece of paper towel?"

She laughed. "Give it to me." She blew her nose. "I'm sorry," she said. "I thought I was stronger."

Then it was his turn. Almost. He struggled. He held his breath.

"The car was a sign of hope," she said. "With everything else going on, he had hope, no, *he was sure* that he could handle everything. The car was faith in the future. So that when they were saying that maybe he . . ."

"Maybe he what?"

She blew her nose again, tossed her head dismissively and looked away from him. "Oh, don't act like you didn't hear it too. That he just . . . gave up on everything. Ran away or killed himself. He had no intention . . ."

"Who was saying that he . . . killed himself."

"*I. Don't. Know.*" She sounded wobbly again. "Just people who didn't have a clue."

"But you saw nothing . . ."

"Of course not. What did I just tell you?"

"There was nothing unusual. No signs . . ."

"Nothing. I spoke to him about the drinking but . . ."

"Drinking?"

"He wasn't supposed to be drinking at all, because of that diet he was on. But he'd come home late and he'd obviously have been drinking somewhere. I actually thought for a moment that he was having an affair." She laughed. "I suppose, in retrospect . . ."

"And what did he say, when you mentioned it?"

"I never mentioned an affair . . . he was impotent, for Christ's sake."

"But the drinking . . ."

"He said there was somebody he knew, from the old days, some guy . . . I thought some Lebanese guy. In a bar. So it all made sense and I didn't push it, especially when he said he was going to go on the wagon."

"And he never mentioned the guy's name. Or where they met."

"No. But it all kind of added up when that business about the roast came up. That place on the Danforth. Now about this vehicle . . ."

"I'll work on getting it out of here."

"No rush. And Cyril?"

"Yes."

"Don't become a stranger, okay?"

"I promise."

"I don't want this frigging car to become the end of something. Again. You understand?"

"Yes." And then he put his arms around her and she put hers around him and buried her face in his neck. And they stood like that, swaying slightly.

23.

He had promised Nader that he'd take him to meet Ari but this was personal. And, in any event, it was impossible to know for sure when Ari might be at the bar. In fact he'd gone twice that week in hopes of finding him and failed. On the second visit he'd left a note with his phone number. "Call me. I'd like to talk." The call came Thursday evening.

"Yes? There is something you want to talk about?"

"It's about my dad, again."

There was a long pause before the response. "Ah, yes. When?"

"When's convenient?"

"Come tomorrow at two. The usual place."

∾

Ari was out front waiting. The street was busy. "What's going on?" Cyril asked.

"Friday prayers," Ari replied. "Can I get you a coffee?"

"Sure."

There was a bench and he sat, fascinated by the scene in front of him, tingling with the realization that he was in his father's world. The bar, the mosque a block away, the Israeli, the contradictions and the tensions that had defined his father's character, determined how his life played out.

Ari sat beside him, handed him a mug. "I didn't put anything in it. I take mine black."

"Me too. It's like this every Friday?"

"Oh yes. And every day, on a smaller scale. The really observant ones show up to pray five times a day. Can you believe it?"

"What do you do for a living, if you don't mind me asking?"

"I'm in business. I work for myself. What I like about this scene is that it takes me back to a time when the whole world was kind of like they are. Synagogue on Saturday. Church on Sunday. I remember, as a kid in Montreal, people streaming out of the churches on a Sunday, heading for the cafés and the bistros. You don't see that anymore. Now it's all materialism." He sighed, sipped.

"You were born in Montreal."

He nodded, placed the coffee mug on the bench between them, fished out a package of cigarettes. "I don't suppose . . ." he said, holding the pack toward Cyril.

"No, thanks."

"I seem to recall your dad didn't smoke either. I think he did once upon a time, but not when I knew him."

"How did you and my dad meet?"

"Here. I see a guy looking kind of out of place. I'm nosy. Turned out we share some history."

"History."

"Like old war vets, I guess. We were in different wars but I guess the farther away you get from it the less important the specifics. It was just an experience we had in common. I guess it would be the same for any war."

"I suppose."

"For him it was something more personal. For me? Duty. Politics.

It makes a difference in how you see things. We didn't talk about it much."

"You didn't talk about the war."

"Not much."

"So if you didn't talk about the war . . . ?"

Ari smiled. "How old are you?" He removed a cigarette from the pack, then turned away and put it in his mouth. Flicked a lighter and inhaled.

"I'm twenty-four."

Exhaled long and slow. "Give yourself another twenty years."

From inside the bar came a Tom Waits ballad, hoarse and mumbled. Ari listened, puffing on the cigarette.

"They say that guy is a great poet but I can never make out a word he's saying."

Cyril laughed. "You could look up the words online."

"Yes. I suppose I could."

Cyril could feel a rising pressure. Frustration. Disappointment. Memories of a dozen aimless, pointless conversations with his father. The sense of being stranded, missing what's important.

"All this online business. We talked about that, your dad and I. Changing times. Technology. Nothing nearly as exciting as you'd imagine."

"So you didn't know each other in the old country?"

"Not at all. But we were in the same general area, same general time. Same general mission."

"Mission?"

"Staying alive, mostly. At least for me."

"And for him?"

"Like I said, it was personal for him."

"How do you mean, personal?"

"He lost family, but you'd know that."

"Not really?"

"Parents, sister, extended family. They were in Damour."

"I've heard of it."

Ari studied him with sympathy. "I guess you didn't communicate much."

"Not much."

"A shame. No continuity between the generations these days." Then he laughed, inhaled. "Listen to me."

"So you were in Lebanon."

"Yes."

"What was that like?"

Ari seemed to take the question seriously, as if he'd never had to think of it before. At last he said, "It was an education." He dropped his cigarette, ground out the remnant with his heel, both hands planted on the bench, leaning forward. "You know what, Cyril? About this roast nonsense? I think it was a way for your dad to make sure that we met up. Maybe pick up where he and I left off. I admire your interest and I'm happy to be getting to know you."

He reached out a hand and Cyril clasped it.

"So let's stay in touch, okay? But we can forget about this . . . roast. Agreed?" He stood.

Some impulse instructed Cyril to refuse to be dismissed. He remained seated. "Basically, I guess I want to know what happened to my father."

Ari sat again. "Of course. But I can't help you there."

"But you were close to him at the end. Maybe he said something."

"He said plenty. But I really don't want to go there. Okay?"

"Why not? What's at stake?"

"Occam's razor."

"What's that?"

"A problem-solving principle—sometimes things are just what they are. Lawyers have a line, *res ipsa loquitur*. Things speak for themselves."

"But I don't understand what 'things' are saying."

Ari squinted at the passing cars. Then he lit another cigarette. "Cyril," he said. "Let me talk straight. Your dad is dead. We know that now. Fact. There was an explosion on his boat. Fact. He was on the boat . . ."

"We don't know that for sure."

"Don't know what?"

"That he was on the boat."

"Come on. Where the fuck do you think he was. It was what, about seven in the morning?" He studied the ground for a moment. "At least that's the time that sticks in my mind."

"Nobody knows why the boat blew up."

"I read somewhere it was a propane tank. He was living on the boat, wasn't he?"

"Yes he was."

"You see. There's another fact. A bunch of facts, in fact. You know why he was living on the boat?"

"Vaguely."

"Well, look into it. Figure it out from there. That's one area we talked about. Man to man. The fucking war? That was history. Just a place to start a more important conversation. About life." For a moment Ari seemed to choke up. "And okay. Here's what still bothers me. I thought it was going to be a long conversation. Two guys with a lot in common. We were interested in the future, not the past. Which is one reason why I never bought into . . ."

He stopped and looked away.

"Bought into what?"

"That he killed himself. I never saw him as the type to bail out on the people who cared about him. You hear what I'm saying?"

Cyril nodded. "I guess I don't know as much as I should about his problems."

"No?" He stood. "I'm going to get a drink. You?"

Cyril shook his head. "A Coke maybe."

Suddenly Cyril wanted to be somewhere else. Ari was at the bar. Just stand up and walk away. There was no purpose to be served by being here.

Then Ari was back, talking as he sat down, continuing a conversation that started in his head while he was away. Or maybe long before. "People never really get over wars when they've been in them. And when it's personal . . ." He grimaced, sipped his drink. "And he was going through some stuff. Flashbacks and the like."

"Like what."

"He was always vague. But I could imagine. Look. Things kept shifting. Your friend today could be your bitter enemy tomorrow. Women, children become mortal enemies. You trust nobody. That's what happens when people are being manipulated from the outside. By Syria. The Americans." He raised his hand: "And I'll be the first to admit it. By us." He shook his head, gulped a mouthful of the drink. "But it would never have been enough to put him over the edge. No."

The waiter appeared, spoke briefly in French. Ari replied in English: "Tell him I'll get back to him."

When the waiter left, Ari said, "This is kind of like my office. Some of my clients call me here."

"We were talking about flashbacks."

"Yes. See, this is where I have a problem with all this talk about war crimes and prosecutions in The Hague and all that stuff. Who decides what's a crime in a war? Some fucking lawyer? Some judge long after the fact? The whole war scenario is criminal. The destruction, death, uprooting people. The infliction of suffering on other people is criminal. Then you've got one side pointing fingers at the other. Usually the winning side pointing at the losers, and talking about justice. Bullshit. How I see it, anyway."

Now his face was sorrowful. "You've got me thinking back." He produced the pack of cigarettes.

"Sorry. Maybe I should just go. Come back another time."

"Yes. We can pick this up again. Maybe this is being helpful? I don't know."

"It is."

"And of course, there was the stuff at work." He shook his head. "And the cancer."

Cyril nodded.

"And the marriage."

"His marriage? What about his marriage?"

"I don't know. Who knows about a marriage? Certainly not a guy like me who's never had one."

"So what about it?"

"Probably nothing. His wife is Jewish? Right?"

"Yes."

"Jewish women." He smiled, shook his head. "They get obsessive about family and I guess she was pretty typical. I forget her name, though he mentioned it a lot."

"Lois."

"Yes. Lois. Yes." He seemed to drift off for a moment. Then: "Last time I saw him he was pretty agitated and I guessed it had something to do with trouble at home. She was desperate to have a baby. But with the cancer and the medication, he didn't think he'd be able to oblige. It was like a deal-breaker in his mind."

Cyril felt a sudden chill that originated somewhere in his back, a warning signal: don't challenge. Acquiesce. Retreat.

"When was this?"

"When was what?"

"That conversation? About Lois? Babies."

"I don't know. A week, maybe two before he went away. She meant everything to him, this . . . Lois."

He almost blurted—she was pregnant when he went away. But he was silenced by the dissonance. And then he was confused. And then he realized that this was exactly how he was supposed to feel.

"You think he killed himself?"

"As I said, it would have been contrary to everything I knew about him. But I suppose we have to keep an open mind, even for what is unpalatable." Ari stood then. "I hope I've been a little bit of help."

"Yes. Maybe we can talk some more. Another time."

"Anytime. You know where to find me."

Their hands were now clasped again and Ari was holding on. "The one thing I want you to take away, though. Your dad wouldn't have done that to us. You understand? He was a survivor. Through and through. He had everything to live for."

Cyril suddenly felt the tears pressing behind his eyes. They hugged. And this, too, he realized, is how he was supposed to feel.

SIX

MEMORY

24. *June 25, 2007*

To the east the sky was the colour of cream, clotted in three places by darkening clouds, residue from the storm the day before. He knew that this is how a sunny day begins. It would be hot. He stood peering into the flat black unrevealing surface of the water, the fatigue like a crust around his eyes, the sound of distant rumbling in his brain. He didn't know if he had slept. He must have slept. Time, according to his wristwatch, had passed.

He'd got up a dozen times, tried to piss a dozen times to fool his brain, to make it think that that was why he couldn't sleep. Overactive bladder.

Overactive memory, his brain replied.

Anxiety compresses memory, as it compresses challenges, leading to paralysis. This is where the night had gone. Trying to unpack the density of a compressed memory, the cascade of crises tumbling around him, demanding resolution. He tried to focus on the eastern sky, groped for the simple comfort of anticipating sunshine, warmth and solitude. Felt only a nervousness that was depressingly close to fear.

The gun was on the table where it had rested throughout the long night, a silent partner in his torment. He imagined that he could still taste the muzzle in his mouth, the acrid smell of expended gunpowder in his nostrils. No, he told himself. That would never happen. But what would it be like, to no longer feel this suffocating weight?

No way. Never. Never. I have not survived so much to end like that.

But.

Briefly he allowed himself to remember Bashir, the teacher who became a warrior. Gentle Bashir, for whom he named his only son. Bashir—who died for principle, if remorse and self-destruction can ever truly be considered principled.

He shivered, hugged himself. Sobbed once. Walked into the cab, sat at the table, picked up the gun again, felt its reassuring weight, thought about their long relationship, the Browning's unconditional promise—protection from his enemies, even the enemies that lurked within himself. Also on the table, his journal, pen clipped to the page where he stopped writing at five that morning.

Where did this need for confession come from and why to, of all people, his son? Cyril. A man-boy who will never know the world as he has known it. Who, Pierre had somehow become convinced, should know it. Yes. But only when he would not be around to answer questions. The inevitable questions. How? Why?

He put the gun down, picked up the pen.

It was time to write about himself.

He wrote: *Karantina, Damour, Tel al-Zaatar, Sabra-Shatila*. Historical compression. But if you have been there for all of it . . .

Damour was under siege before they went to Karantina. Or was it? His family was dead, murdered by their enemies, before he went to Karantina. Or were they? What if Karantina really was the provocation so neatly described in the official historical compression? He was part of it, the crime that caused the deaths of his mother, sister, brother-in-law, infant niece, their relatives and neighbours in Damour, that gave birth to the atrocities of Tel al-Zaatar, that deepened Damour's agony, that spawned the slaughter at Sabra and Shatila. But he, and everyone around him, had been provoked. By something. Sometime. Somewhere.

He put the pen aside, stared longingly at the silent gun. Who would care? Really? Who would mourn?

Nobody.

Cyril, Aggie? Hardly. Draycor, Brawly, even Kennedy would welcome it. Ari? Ari especially would celebrate. Lois? No. No, no, no. And he remembered their unborn child.

∿

Karantina. He was cold, huddled in the crowded truck, feeling the painful dampness of the January night. But in particular he remembered the unprecedented fear. All prior sensations that were variants of fear—fright, apprehension, jitters—replaced by the despair that floods the consciousness when self-control is gone, when you have become an incidental part of something large and incomprehensible.

He remembered with particular clarity the sounds of the truck: the flap of canvas around him and his two dozen companions, the straining motor, labouring in the lower gears, the creaking groans as it clambered over broken ground. The other trucks. And APCs. Range Rovers. The clanking tanks. And then the silence. The darkened figures marshalling in units. Murmuring voices. The clatter of weapons being readied. From inside the camp, dogs barking, a child screaming.

A gunshot. From somewhere.

Then people running crouched toward the awakening encampment. Firing wildly into darkness, into shapes. One desperately endless fusillade. Singing whispers in the air. *Whump* of rockets. Sudden shooting flame and dancing shadows.

Pierre lies flat, face down in dirt that smells like sewage, lost in the confusion, the AK-47 in his outstretched hands. He should be firing it, but where? There is nothing visible to shoot at, but they are shooting anyway. Everyone, it seems, but him. Someone in the camp is wildly, desperately shooting back. The air is full of hissing bullets, full of shouts. Screams of women, children. The dogs have gone insane, howling, barking, yelping. He feels, for the first time, the hysteria of battle.

A startling hand on his shoulder and Elias and Bashir are there, crouched beside him. "Get up," Elias shouts. "Stay with us. Do what we do."

And he does. That long night. And on many, many long days and nights thereafter. He does what everybody did until he no longer could.

In the daylight he stands, listening as the young commander, Dany, tells a television journalist in his flawless educated English that the operation was for everybody's benefit. The unfortunate refugees were on private property, interfering with the nation's commerce. But it was for their good too. It was no way to live. They will all be better off.

Yes, casualties. Regrettable. Panicky irrational resistance by the terrorists who have infiltrated the civilian poor. It is a necessary response by the government of Lebanon. Perhaps, yes, disproportionate. But time will tell.

And Pierre is somehow, like the television journalist, reassured.

Karantina. Fifteen hundred dead. Karantina is a massacre. But he remembered living people, in the thousands, pathetic living people being herded into buses, loaded onto trucks. And he remembered wishing they were all dead. Every miserable one of them. It would be doing everyone a favour, even them, to end their wretched lives. Expunge their wretchedness. He remembers the throbbing hatred he had for them, not for what they'd done—he had no idea what they, as individuals, had done—but for who they were collectively. They provoked in him feelings that he loathed. He hated them for making him feel hatred. And he felt hatred because he hated feeling fear, hated feeling the contempt he had for them and, consequently, for himself.

And now, more than three decades later, he knew that by the end of that chaotic year of sieges and street-battles, destruction and mass murder, the fear would give way to an emotional numbness and a mental clarity—the objective attention to detail that distinguished the work of the bureaucrat, the soldier. He learned how hatred eventually consumes itself, becomes indifference, like smoke.

But on that first night, on that cold lurching drive from Jounieh to Karantina, he was dangerously distracted by his feelings—the grief, the doubt, the uncertainty. He was reminded of a recurrent nightmare: he is walking onto a brightly lit stage, conscious of a vast crowd of spectators. He is carrying a violin and must perform a complicated solo but staring out into the mass of human shapes and shadows, he remembers that he has never played a violin before.

In the days and weeks and months ahead he was sustained by hatred, and he became a competent performer, a professional. And he discovered the peculiar sense of freedom that came from being part of something larger and more important than oneself, a small part of a vast and orchestrated project, the paradoxical freedom of captivity.

That day marked the birth of hatred in Pierre, and it was only slightly mitigated by the departing buses and trucks, hauling the traumatized survivors to—somewhere, some other squalid place. And by the bulldozers and loaders, and dump trucks that within a day or two obliterated the evidence that anyone had ever lived in Karantina, or that so many of them died there.

~

Pierre slept, face resting on his forearm. When he woke there was a spot of drool on his shirt sleeve. He checked his wristwatch. Nine forty-five. He stood stiffly. His body ached. He almost lost his balance walking to the door. Supported himself for a moment against the frame.

It was already hot, the sun shimmering halfway up the blue bowl of the sky. A perfect day for the water. The kind of day that Angus Beaton found to be acceptable for being on a boat. He welcomed the prospect of Beaton's company, another person's demons, the comforting perspective they'd deliver.

He left the cab and climbed to the top of the wharf. Stood, hands on hips, staring toward the little travel trailer for signs of life. But the truck was gone.

Then his phone was ringing. He pulled it from his pocket. It was a number that he vaguely recognized—the boardroom speaker-phone. He let it ring through to voicemail, then climbed back down into the boat and waited.

"Call back on this number ASAP." The message was from Ethan. Pierre could hear that there were others in the room.

He dialled.

Ethan picked up. "I'm going to put you on speaker," he said. His voice was tight, another sign that he was not alone. "How are things out there?"

"Fine," Pierre said, and waited.

"There you are," said Kennedy. "Say hello and then I'll tell you who we have here."

"Hi, all," said Pierre. He could hear the murmuring replies.

"You know everybody," Kennedy said and listed them. And when he heard Brawley's name, heard the hearty shout-out from the boss, he understood where this was going.

"I'm going to let Mr. Brawley do the talking," Kennedy said.

Pierre could picture him. It was early there. Brawley's white shirt, starched and shimmering, would be unsullied. Necktie loose. Bespoke suit jacket hanging on the back of his chair. He'd be in his usual position at the end of the long oval table.

Pierre picked up the gun as Brawley enthusiastically talked about the weather in Toronto. The Blue Jays. New season starting. Great prospects. Pierre aimed the gun out the door. At some point during the long night he'd loaded it.

He toyed with the idea of firing off a round. Wake them up. He smiled at the thought but resisted it, not knowing where the bullet would end up. Someone else's boat.

And he thought again of Bashir. How long had they been together? Six years, and yet he'd been surprised. The last person in the world that he would have expected to take such an exit, funny, philosophical Bashir. He should have seen it coming, but Bashir just walked around a corner without saying anything to anyone.

"Are you still there?"

"Yes, yes. You were saying?"

"Look, Pierre. I'm going to cut right to the purpose of this call and then we can have a longer discussion about what comes next. Okay? What I have to say brings me no joy. No joy at all. But there has to be a parting of the ways here, Pierre. We've weighed all our options . . ."

Pierre asked his boss to spell it out, out of a subtle creeping malice: "What are you trying to tell me?"

There was a long pause. Finally Brawley cleared his throat: "There's no gentle way to say this. But we have to cut you loose, Pierre."

He squeezed the trigger. The windows rattled and a chip of creosote flipped off a timber piling on the wharf. Oops. He hadn't realized there was a bullet in the chamber. For an instant he was mercifully deaf.

"What the fuck was that?"

"Sorry, I dropped something."

"You're sure you're all right?"

"I'm fine. Where were we?"

He could imagine the confused glances, startled eyes seeking clarity in other eyes that were equally perplexed. He could hear the thought: *That* was a gunshot. *Fucking Arabs. Savages.*

The teleconference ended with a promise to get back to him with details of the plan for going forward, followed by a lot of expressions from around the table of respect, affection and concern. Pierre was unexpectedly touched, even knowing that the feelings were cheap and rootless. Still, it meant something to him that they'd risk the kind of insincerity that would bother them later, remind them of their acquiescence to hypocrisy. He suddenly felt sorry for all of them. Ethan Kennedy in particular.

∼

He waited fifteen minutes and decided that Beaton wasn't going to show. Just as well. He untied his lines, tossed them down, clambered back on board and pushed his stern away, backed into the narrow channel of the little harbour. Idling, he eased his gearshift forward, felt the contented thrum of the machinery beneath his feet. He could hear the gentle wash against the hull. He looked back, watched the furrows widening behind. And then he was out on the soft swell, the infinity above him compromised only by some wispy cloud, perhaps a dissipated contrail.

He set the autopilot directly westward, the throttle just past idle. Walked toward the stern, gun in one hand, cellphone in the other. Sat in the sunshine and waited for the call he knew would come.

High above the boat there was a cloud of gannets soaring like confetti in the light breeze, dozens at a time plunging toward the prey that only they could see beneath the surface of the water, countless silent splashes marking their attacks.

And suddenly the pilot whales returned, close enough that he could hear them gasp as they surfaced in rolling loops, indifferent to his presence. Larger, wiser mammals exploiting smaller, dumber creatures for survival. The raw reality of life.

What would it be like, he wondered, to exist in a state of freedom from self-consciousness, spared the burden of reflective memory?

The Draycor move to cut him loose was dictated by the company's survival instinct but would be tempered by contemporary circumstances. In another time or place he'd simply have been eliminated. He'd witnessed it, participated in it, the termination of an individual who had become an inconvenience or a threat, rebellious or intransigent. *Keep him quiet.* They would want to keep him quiet by persuasion rather than coercion.

~

Ethan was on a pay phone in a coffee shop. A security precaution. Pierre understood and was impressed. Leave no footprints.

Ethan couldn't speak at first. Pierre listened to the clatter and the voices, every voice asserting a separate consciousness, lives perhaps as compromised and complicated as his own. He felt oddly solid for the first time in what seemed like days.

"So, Ethan."

"Jesus Christ. I don't know what to say. How are you doing?"

"I'm doing just fine. I know the drill. Okay?"

"Just the same. You must . . ."

"Just fill me in on what they said behind my back."

Ethan told him that Brawley had actually mentioned a recent massacre in Baghdad to explain why someone would have to take the fall for Puncak. He'd referred to the international outcry, how a singular event can redefine a larger mission. Diverse international objections and concerns about a mission in Iraq, Vietnam or a mining operation in Wherever—could harden into focused outrage because of one or two or eight or eighty deaths that happen in the glare of media attention. Never mind particulars. Never mind relevance.

"For the media," Brawley had declared, "controversy is pure gold and they're constantly prospecting for it, turning over rocks, chipping away at promising outcrops, looking for the motherlode. And nothing, I mean nothing, gets a gold rush going like a massacre. Them and their goddamn metaphors."

Pierre struggled not to laugh.

Mercifully, Brawley had continued, Draycor had been spared that misery, at least initially. But the chickens were definitely coming home to roost. There would have to be the appearance of accountability.

Ethan said he had stood up for Pierre. Baghdad and Puncak, absurd. The circumstances were entirely different.

"The circumstances," Brawley had interrupted, "were irrelevant. What we have is eight dead people."

"Jesus Christ . . ."

"Bear with me . . . this is NOT about fact or fairness. This is about optics. And Pierre, you've gotta believe me. I'm sick about this. But you know and I know, sometimes we gotta hold our noses and do what we gotta do for the larger enterprise. Are you with me on this?"

Pierre did not reply.

The pay-phone call, of course, was part of the larger strategy, which he recognized as Ethan was disclosing, in utter confidence, the details of the settlement that he would soon be offered: a generous financial package of money and shares, numbers to be finalized, but certainly in the seven, possibly even eight-figure range. The formal announcement of his departure would be crafted with Pierre's participation.

It was so familiar to him: first the conference call; now the personal touch—the poison pill dissolved in a cocktail of familiarity, friendship, generosity. He imagined that it had been discussed the day before, at a special Sunday caucus.

"You'll probably want someone from the outside to review the final settlement and the usual conditions . . ."

"What usual conditions?"

"Well. Basic confidentiality . . ."

"Non-disclosure."

"You know the drill." Ethan laughed. "I'm sure you've drafted your share of them . . ."

"I'll be thinking about it," Pierre said.

"Look, speaking as your friend, there shouldn't be a lot to think about. Right?"

"I hear you, Ethan. And thank you for this. It means a lot."

"Okay." Long pause. "Let me know what you decide. I'm here to talk. When do you think you can come in?"

"I'll get back to you in a day or so."

"A day or so? Okay. But a heads-up . . . Communications and HR have the bit in their teeth. I'm trying to slow them down, but you know Brawley."

"Talk to you later, Ethan." He stared at the BlackBerry for what felt like a long time. A tired expression was murmuring inside his head. *The enemy of my enemy is my friend.* So true, so clever the *first* time someone thought of it. He tried to remember a name that Ethan Kennedy had mentioned a day or so earlier. The name of the newspaper reporter in the city who came from here. Then he remembered and started scrolling back until he found the last email message from Margaret Rankin: *Your personal perspective is vitally important to the story. Our mutual acquaintance, Sandy MacIsaac, spoke well of you. I'm anxious to follow up.*

He was still staring at the BlackBerry when it chimed again. Lois.

"Hi, sweetie," he said.

"What's it like out there today?"

"It's lovely. I'm sitting in the sunshine, listening to you. You saw the doctor?"

"Yes. She sent me for an ultrasound. I actually saw him."

"Him?"

"I have a feeling."

"I'm hoping for a girl. Can we find out?"

"Do we want to?"

"I do."

"I'm envious of you, on the boat. It's stinking hot here. The city is a mess. When are you coming home?"

"I'm not sure yet. Are you following the news?"

"Not as closely as I should. I'm trying to stay calm, lying down a lot. Moving slowly. I don't want anything to go wrong."

"You're feeling okay, though?"

"Fat and lazy and apprehensive. But healthy. Sleep and lack of alcohol and I'm eating well, which might explain the fat."

"The fat, I'm sure, is in all the right places."

"And you? Still living the regimen?"

"Best I can." He didn't tell her about the alcohol, the meat; he didn't tell her about forgetting, frequently, about the wretched pills; he didn't mention that he'd just ended his career.

"Which reminds me," she said. "I almost forgot . . . you're to call the doctor's office. There was a message."

"Which doctor?"

"With the 'Z' name."

"Zlotta?"

"I think. Anyway, they called."

"Okay."

"What do you think?"

"No idea. But Lois? I've been doing a lot of thinking about what's important. Things will be different when I'm back. Okay? I can't explain right now. But believe me."

"Oh, how I hope you mean that."

"I promise."

"So how much longer do you think they'll leave you out there?"

"Hard to say," he said. "I'll try to get an answer."

"Okay," she said.

He knew she wanted to press him on his promises. She wanted some specific possibility to anticipate, a number circled on a calendar, perhaps. But he couldn't tell her that his reasons for staying put were infinitely more complicated than any aspect of the job that he no longer had.

~

He considered calling the doctor's office but he knew they would ask the question he'd already deflected twice that morning: When can you come back?

The frenzied gannets swirled and plummeted, the whales around him rolled, glistening and gasping.

Pierre watched, as if hypnotized by the spectacle, then stood, picked up the gun and hurled it, watched it sail upwards and away, a black projectile against the flutter of confetti, until it disappeared among the little gannet geysers that reminded him so much of shrapnel.

He examined the BlackBerry, briefly considered sending it after the gun but then sat down and scrolled back to rankinm9@hotmail. com. Wrote: *You can call this number after eight, your time, tonight but not before. Cormier.* And he typed in his private cellphone number.

25.

He'd told Lois he'd be working late and it was only partially untrue. There were arrangements to be made—files to review, emails to be sent, meetings to be had—before he could leave for the East Coast. But he didn't tell her that he also wanted one more visit to the Only Café. Maybe one day he'd explain to her the compulsion to go there, if and when he ever could explain it to himself.

He lingered in the doorway, scanned familiar faces, listened to the now familiar babble, the music—reggae tonight—and he realized that he felt at home there, as if he had been a regular for years. What a shame that this would have to be his final visit.

He hadn't expected to run into Ari, didn't really want to encounter Ari, if the truth were known. But there he was.

Pierre nodded, ordered a whisky, then walked over to Ari's table.

"Sit for a minute," said Ari. He sat. Neither spoke until finally Pierre said, "I was passing by. Thought I'd drop in one last time."

Ari frowned.

"I plan to take some time off. My life is getting complicated. I don't expect to be back here again." He smiled. Raised his glass.

"Anywhere interesting?" Ari asked.

"A place I know on the East Coast. I have a boat there."

"A boat?"

"I find a boat to be the perfect escape."

"How so?"

"You know. Out on the water. You can imagine that nothing happens out there, nothing matters. Just the weather and we aren't responsible for that."

"And what do you do out on the water?"

"Read. Think. Mostly look at the distance between me and the land." He shrugged.

"Yes. The land. Where everything happens. Where we have responsibility."

"Exactly."

"I've never been east of Quebec."

"I lived on the East Coast when I first came to Canada. I think of it as home now. Cape Breton Island."

"I've been following a bit the business with your company in Indonesia. Unfortunate."

"Yes. Very."

"So that's why you were there?"

"I led the investigation. It was exhausting, not to mention distressing."

"I can imagine."

"I'm glad I bumped into you. I'm sorry about how we left things the last time I was here."

"No need to be sorry." He smiled. "We think alike. We understand each other."

Pierre nodded, studying the other man's eyes.

Ari gestured, taking in the bar. "If we could read each other's minds."

"Just as well we can't," Pierre said. "It's hard enough to read our own. Right?"

"Yes. But to be aware of others and their difficulties gives a comforting perspective sometimes. Why do you think people slow down at car accidents? Get off on bad news? The distress of other people is reassuring."

"One way of looking at it." Pierre studied the face, imagined it with dense black stubble, imagined the skull hairless. He was certain, but there was the lingering impact of the denial, so emphatic and sincere, his dead mother his alibi. A lie, but unassailable on grounds irrelevant to reason.

"We survived," said Ari. He grimaced, made a gesture of resignation with his hands.

"Yes."

"Survival sometimes comes at a cost."

Pierre nodded.

"We survive when others don't. There's no point wondering, why or how. It happens. Survival isn't really a matter of choice, so I wonder sometimes about this thing they talk about, survivors' guilt." He laughed, studied his glass. "Survival has no moral quality."

"That's an interesting thought."

"You were in the camps?"

The sudden question startled him. "What camps?"

"You know the camps. You were there. I didn't mean it as a question. You were one of Hobeika's boys." Ari shrugged. "An interesting man, Hobeika. One way or another, if you were with Hobeika, you were in the camps."

"You knew him?"

"Everybody was aware of him."

"Yes. I was with him—in your forward command post . . ."

"*My* forward command post . . ."

"With your General Yaron, the IDF intelligence people, Mossad, watching and listening to what was going on a couple of hundred metres away on that Thursday night. I was with him at the stadium on Saturday morning . . ."

"But you were also in the camps . . ."

"Hobeika wasn't in the camps. I just told you where he was."

"But you?"

"Briefly, on Saturday. He sent me there after his meeting with someone I thought was you." Pierre paused, watching for a telltale flicker. Then looked away. "I'm sorry for the mistake."

"You saw the camps on Saturday?"

"Shatila."

"This person with Hobeika at the stadium. He was IDF?"

"That's what I was told."

"He wore a uniform?"

"There were no markings. As you know, the uniforms were much the same, yours and ours."

"What was he doing there?"

"He delivered two prisoners from the camps for interrogation. Anyway, the stadium was full of IDF, Shin Bet. Surely you knew that."

Ari shrugged and made a face. "Possibly. And these prisoners? Terrorists?"

"I was ordered to take them back into the camps when our people were through with them."

"Saturday morning."

"Before the army moved in."

"Just to take them back?"

"I don't think I have to spell it out."

"So why to the camp? Why not the stadium, like so many others?"

"You know why."

Ari shrugged.

"The reporters. Politicians showing up at the stadium, asking questions. Your people were getting sensitive."

"And that's what you did."

"That's what we did."

Ari sighed heavily, shook his head. "It is not such a big thing. In the circumstances. Two more bodies among the hundreds."

Pierre remained silent.

"But in the present context. To these people, now?" Ari gestured again around the bar. "It would be horrifying to them. Taken out of place and time, out of context, these things become large. People who have never had to think about survival see such events in a different way. Impose their idealism, their morality. They become prosecutors and judges."

"It's why we keep secrets," Pierre said.

"And why we should. I will speak as your friend. I consider you my friend." He paused, searching Pierre's face. Pierre waited.

"Hobeika. He is gone now. Beyond judgment. But some of what he caused, what he did, remains painful for people who survived him. I understand the circumstances as you do. But there will always be people wanting to punish, to harm even people who were not responsible, at least not directly. You understand?"

Pierre nodded.

"For someone to acknowledge, I was with Hobeika here, I was with Hobeika there, doing this, doing that. I was with Hobeika in the command post, or Phalangist headquarters in September 1982, or in the camps—it is like the smell of blood to sharks."

"Or to admit that I was at the stadium on Saturday, delivering prisoners to the men who would do your dirty work . . ."

"The same. You and I, Pierre, we love this country, Canada. The whole world should be like Canada. But Canadians, they are like everybody else. Quick to judge. Quick to demonize people who might not fit their . . . how can I put this? Their sanctimonious self-image." He laughed then. "I need a smoke. Come outside."

They stood and watched the traffic. "In every car there is a secret," Ari said, exhaling. "In that mosque, in the memory of everyone who goes there, secrets. And of course the fabric that keeps the secrets hidden."

"What do you mean, fabric?"

"The lies. Everybody lies. If every immigrant or refugee told the whole truth, there'd be hardly anybody here."

"I was a refugee."

"So you understand what I'm talking about?"

"I didn't lie."

"No? So you told them you were in the camps? You told them you were in the Kata'ib?"

"They didn't ask."

"And if they'd asked: Pierre, where were you on the night of September sixteenth, 1982, or during Friday, September seventeenth, or Saturday the eighteenth? Pierre, what was your relationship with this man, this mass murderer named Elie Hobeika, head of intelligence for the Kata'ib—"

"We were the Lebanese Forces . . ."

"Who ran the fucking Lebanese forces? Kata'ib, Phalangists . . . brutal, savage killers. Merciless, remorseless."

"What about Israel? The weapons, the training, the uniforms you gave us."

"What I think is irrelevant. It's what these people think, these people inside this pub with their laptops and their googling, their piety. It's the immigration people. Border police. Refugee boards."

"Savage killers . . . or patriots. It's a matter of opinion."

"For the Kata'ib, the Damouri Brigade . . . it is a matter of record."

"Israeli record."

"We shouldn't . . ."

"I often wondered, since you brought it up, why our friends in Israel were so clear and specific about what happened in the camps and about blaming the Phalange entirely. Nobody else."

"It was fact."

"But not all the facts."

"True. In war and politics there is a selection of facts."

"Yes. And among the forgotten facts, that Saad Haddad's men— your private army in the south—and the IDF counter-terrorism specialists were also in the camps."

"That isn't fact." Ari sounded weary.

"No? I heard they were."

"You heard what?"

"About Haddad's men, about the Sayeret Matkal . . . In the camps, directing the killing. But I agree. It no longer matters."

"Sayeret Matkal?"

"You've heard of it?"

"Of course. Netanyahu was Sayeret Matkal." He laughed. "You aren't suggesting."

"I'm suggesting what I heard from Hobeika. You were Sayeret Matkal and you were in the camps with our people."

"You heard speculation. Very dangerous speculation. Remember what happened to Hobeika?"

"You're well informed."

"Everybody knows what happened to Hobeika."

"I don't. You tell me."

Ari looked surprised. "I don't believe you." And he laughed, laid a large hand on Pierre's forearm. "He blew up. You know that."

"But who blew him up?"

"It could have been anyone. Palestinians. Syrians."

"Israelis."

"Perhaps. But why would we? There were many people in the line-up ahead of us. Look, we could sit here all night naming them. But I'll just mention one name. A place. Because I know that if you were part of the Hobeika gang you were there."

Pierre felt a peculiar numbness in his hand and realized that he was holding his drink too tightly. He breathed out, put the glass down, folded his arms across his chest.

"Zghorta."

He didn't catch it right away. "What?"

"Zghorta, Ehden. 1978. Tony Frangieh, his wife and kid. The thirty bodyguards. You know about Zghorta, Pierre. Because you were there. Yes? Wasn't it in June?" He was staring at him intently, watching, waiting. "And to your great credit, Pierre, was it not after June 1978 that you had doubts about this psychopath who was your leader? This human weapon, HK."

"I have no idea what you're talking about."

"No? You see, Pierre, and this is no secret. I was in IDF intelligence. A mere cipher, of course. We were a small service. Not like Mossad and Shin Bet. But we knew things and we saw things. And I saved things, things I still have, documents I have recently reviewed. Hobeika? Yes. He was one of us, Pierre. He wore our hat. But he was a man with many hats. But why am I telling you this? You know more about it than I do."

He looked away and sighed. "It is tragic what people do to one another for survival. Yes, tragic for the victims. But also for survivors who have to live with secrets."

Pierre was now unsteady. He should not have come here. He

should not have had the drink. He should not have allowed the conversation to go this far.

Ari sipped his drink. "Hobeika was at Zghorta, yes? One of the commanders. You were with Hobeika. And so, Pierre, if you were asked by a refugee board or, God forbid, the police, where were you in January 1976, or June 1978, or where were you on September eighteenth, 1982, or where were you—?"

"I must go now," Pierre said. "Perhaps we'll get a chance to talk again."

"Let me finish. A simple question. Would you today be a Canadian, with your Bay Street office and your Mustang and your boat? Can you answer that, Pierre Haddad?"

Pierre turned away, then paused and turned back. "Charon."

"Sharon? What about him?"

"No. Charon, with a 'C.' I just remembered something. This man at the stadium. This IDF officer. He gave me a note and he signed it. 'Charon.'"

"Ah. A note."

"Yes. And I kept things, too—I saved things. I still have it somewhere. It was a *laissez-passer* that enabled us to pass an IDF checkpoint at Shatila on the Saturday morning."

"I see. And to do what, on Saturday morning in the Shatila camp?"

"To kill two more people. The two terrorists you delivered to Hobeika. Two nobodies you caught hiding in the Sabra hospital. What had they done, Ari? Why did they deserve to die? Why would they, two minnows in a shark tank, warrant the attention of an officer in Sayeret Matkal? Tell me. Or tell me that you can't remember. That by September eighteenth it didn't matter who they were or what they did or didn't do. We were killing everybody. Right?"

Ari studied his cigarette package, opened it, carefully selected one. Lit it, exhaled. Studied the street.

"Terrible," he said. "It is terrible to live with such a memory. So much killing."

Pierre nodded.

Ari gripped his hand, held it firmly, tugged him close and hugged him. "Enjoy your holiday."

"Yes. Thank you. Goodbye."

26.

Lois was asleep when he got home and that was a relief. It would have been difficult to talk to her about anything else. He longed to tell her everything and one day he would find a way but it wasn't time. Not yet.

Quietly he closed his office door. He kept the journals in a box beneath his desk. He dragged the box out, retrieved 1983, flipped through it. Yes, there it was, tucked between two pages, the note, the Hebrew hieroglyphics. The name. "Charon." No rank, no title, no first name.

Hobeika seemed to have known Charon well. You could feel the chemistry between them. And so Ari knows about Zghorta, that bloody debacle? Charon was IDF intelligence. Hobeika was Phalange intelligence. Blood brothers. Charon would have known everything. Every detail.

He leaned back, thought back. What year did Hobeika die? Pierre had been in England when he'd heard, actually saw it in a newspaper. Clipped the story and saved it, like the *laissez-passer*. He often went to

England. What year? Right. The joint venture in Belize? Contract signed in London. Early in 2002. He retrieved the journal for 2002, found the clipping.

JANUARY 24: ELIE HOBEIKA
Lebanese Militia Leader Who Massacred Civilians.

Yes. There it is.

Elie Hobeika, who was killed in a massive bomb attack at his house in the Beirut suburb of Hazmiyeh, was one of Lebanon's most controversial figures.

He remembered wondering at the time who had done this. But a thousand individuals and groups would have seized any opportunity to eliminate HK, would celebrate his death. Thousands, maybe tens of thousands of people who at any given moment would have killed each other, united now in collective satisfaction.

His death at the age of 45 comes at a time when he had agreed to testify against Israeli prime minister Ariel Sharon in a war crimes trial that may be held later this year in a Brussels court. A leader of the Christian Maronite Lebanese Forces (or Phalanges, as they were known) during Lebanon's bloody civil war, Hobeika acted as Israel's liaison chief during that country's invasion of Lebanon in 1982.

He remembered thinking back then that no one could ever know for sure who had killed HK. Israel. The Syrians. Hezbollah.

Palestinians. Druze. Morabitoun. Amal. The Chamouns. Frangiehs. Gemayels. Every one of them had reasons. It only mattered that he was gone. He was gone, irrevocably. There would be no more of the peculiar tingling, no more the creeping sense of an unseen presence, no more the sudden surge of fear at the sight of a familiar facial feature, the sound of a familiar voice.

They'd spent six years together and Pierre had learned to read Hobeika's mind, read every nuance of expression in the face, the voice. It was not an unpleasant face, not the face of an evil man, if there is such a thing. He understood Hobeika, understood his motivation. In the beginning, vengeance for Damour. They had that in common. The murder of their loved ones. Whenever he felt doubt, he would remember Damour and the need to satisfy the spirits of the dead, to give them peace.

Hobeika was persuasive. Zghorta was to be another holy mission to avenge Damour but Pierre had doubts. So many incidents like Zghorta. He was surprised, thinking back. Had the taste of vengeance begun to sicken him as soon as that? After Zghorta, remorse had lasted, became toxic, inescapable. June 1978, more than four years before the final breach. What could Ari know about it? He would know what Charon knew. Pierre, alone in semi-darkness, in Toronto, almost thirty years later, laughed out loud. Ariel. Charon.

He had purged HK from his mind, purged the flashbacks. Hobeika was dead. But he had seen Hobeika's ghost in that unlikely place. The Only Café. Ari had reminded him that the past is never dead as long as there is memory. Memory is the afterlife, both hell and heaven.

He retrieved a notepad from his desk drawer: *Memo to self—find Brussels lawyer who pursued the 2002 war crimes case alleging Ariel Sharon's complicity in Beirut camp massacres 16/09/82–18/09/82. Ref E.*

Hobeika who had agreed to testify. Assassinated in 2002. Had he been pre-interviewed? Affidavits? Documentary proof?

He studied the note, then added: *What year did Ari come to Canada? Five years ago = 2002.*

He laughed aloud.

He entered "Zghorta-Ehden" into the search box on his laptop and was almost instantly rewarded by photographs from the paradise it seemed to have become—lush vegetation, mountain snows, villas and resorts. Prosperity and peace. The miracle of commercial propaganda. Then, further down the menu: *Ehden massacre.*

∽

June 13, 1978. It was cold for June but there was no wind. The journey by sea to Tripoli was calm. The chill might have been from nerves or hunger or dread. He had been uneasy since the briefing. The mission was to send a message to the Syrians and their collaborators in the north. A message about Lebanon's unity, integrity, determination to be whole and independent. The message would be delivered to a powerful family of northern Christians who had recently been allies but were now traitors because of their continuing affection for the Syrians.

Until that night Pierre had been sustained by the sense of satisfaction that comes from growth and purpose. His association with HK had made him privy to the strategies, the vision, the planning and the intrigues of the inner circle. He had dined with Sheikh Pierre, been drunk with the son, Bashir, who would succeed him, who would expel the aliens—Palestinians, Israelis, Syrians—the interfering lot of them. He would unify the country. But now, this sending of messages? To what end?

There would be resistance, HK had warned. Expect it. Maybe a hundred people who were blindly loyal to the traitor, who would die to keep HK from his goal. This was the reality they faced.

Who is the traitor?

They will speak to him. They will persuade him by their strength, their ability to penetrate the north, that he is dangerously misguided. And they will then withdraw, their objective having been achieved. Lebanon's integrity secured.

Who is the enemy?

Syria.

And that was all they had to know, they who were at the sharp end of the stick. A year ago Tony Frangieh was an ally. Today he is a traitor, but he will understand his folly.

Pierre was cold now in the early morning mountain air. His friend Bashir, the schoolteacher, was silent, always deep within himself at the beginning of an operation; this disturbed Elias, the extrovert, and he complained to Pierre and to HK that Bashir's palpable apprehension was damaging to morale. No one dared to use the word "afraid" for they were all, in a deep and private way, afraid.

They were the vanguard. Bashir was carrying one of the three grenade launchers. Their first objective was to disable vehicles to deter escape.

The cars and trucks exploding launched the main assault.

∼

An almost instant cacophony of automatic weapons. Early morning darkness, lit by flashes, the lightning of the RPG, flaming vehicles. Shadows flitting. Howls of madness, cries of sudden pain and terror. Lights briefly in the windows of the villa. Then gone.

~

Elias slapped his shoulder, pointed toward an entrance. The fusillade was now a roaring continuum, a shield. There was, for the moment, hardly any response from within the mansion. It was still dark enough to move forward without being immediately noticed. Bashir launched a grenade toward the entrance but it exploded against a stone wall. They were running now, and Elias barely paused to lift his boot. The door flew open and he was in the doorway, firing blindly into the room. Pierre squeezed past him and in the dim light inside could see a small thing shuddering against a wall, sprouting small rosettes, disintegrating. Elias paused, changed magazines. Now there was a bundle of bloody rags quivering on the floor. And there was screaming.

The woman seemed to be flying through the air. She landed awkwardly on the bloody pile of rags, hysterically howling, dishevelled, nightgown asunder revealing bare white legs, bare behind. Elias appeared to have frozen momentarily, or wanted to extend the moment of her living horror for a beat, two beats. Three. And then he opened fire again.

Through a doorway from another room a man ran ludicrously wearing only underpants and brandishing a knife, but Elias, intently emptying his magazine into the senseless jerking body of the woman on the floor, couldn't see him coming. Pierre's shout was lost in the din of shooting.

He pointed his Kalashnikov toward body mass, and fired. The man stumbled, turned toward Pierre, pitching forward. Lost. The confused expression on his face seemed to say, *Oh shit . . . I didn't see you there . . .*

Pierre swung his weapon toward Elias, aware now that he was screaming: *stop, stop, stop, stop,* but was instantly jerked off his feet, swung round, propelled toward the door. And out into the blue-black dawn.

He stumbled, foot and ankle tangled, was lifted bodily, and hurled to the ground. Bashir was standing over him, panting, gasping. "Not today," he heard him say. "Not today . . . there will be another time." His face was wet from his exertions. They were now lost in the crowd surging toward the house, Hobeika leading them.

∼

Pierre woke at his desk. He checked his watch. Four thirty. There was whisky in his glass. He quickly swallowed it. He picked up the writing pad, focused. Brussels. 2002. Hobeika.

What could Hobeika have possibly disclosed in Brussels that the world did not already know about the camps? There had been inquiries, one in Israel. The Kahan Commission had all the forensic detail, much of which it published, about the roles of Begin, Sharon, senior IDF commanders, IDF intelligence, Mossad. Fadi Frem. And of course, HK himself. Did HK claim that he had new evidence about the camps? Was there more about Sharon? Was there proof?

Or might he have had other war crimes on his mind, crimes attributed to him and the Phalange alone? Countless crimes in which he knew, as Pierre knows, the Phalange were but accomplices, rough cudgels in the hands of someone infinitely stronger.

∼

Hobeika's face was close enough that he could feel the spittle of righteous indignation, smell the reek of garlic. "Do NOT fucking speak to me about the blood of innocents. Remember who you're talking to." After the fury came the calm, an arm across his shoulder: *"For thirty bodyguards I feel badly. For their families, yes. They were like us, working people. Zghorta was not supposed to be that way. The child. Vera. Even Tony. We were there to talk to him, not to kill him, not to kill his family. It was not the plan. But in the dark, and the confusion . . ."* He shrugged and stepped away.

"To talk? With rocket launchers?"

"You are tired, my friend."

"I am not tired."

"Take time. There are things you do not know, should not know. You don't have to know. But believe me when I tell you—this operation was not in our control. Its execution and the outcome were determined elsewhere. This you must understand."

"Where, this elsewhere?"

"This is irrelevant. The only constant in our history is what happens elsewhere. Now go, take time. Have you ever been to Paris?"

"No."

"It can be arranged."

"I do not want to go to Paris, I want to go home."

"You are forgetting. We have no home."

27.

The Brussels lawyer took his number and said he'd call him back to make sure he was who he said he was. Five minutes later, the phone rang on his desk.

Pierre was brief and the lawyer listened carefully.

"As you know I am a Canadian lawyer. I understand you had an interest in Elie Hobeika."

The listener on the other end said nothing.

"I am Lebanese by birth. I spent six years with Hobeika."

"What six years?"

"1976 to 1982."

"When in 1982?"

"Until mid-September."

"And then you were no longer with him?"

"Correct."

"Was there a falling-out?"

"I would say so. He wouldn't disagree if he could speak."

"This falling-out? Was it over what happened in the camps in September?"

"It was over many things."

"But you were in the camps, during the atrocities."

"At the end."

"At the end?"

"Saturday morning. I was there to make sure that all our people were gone."

"Interesting. How can I be sure whom I'm talking to?"

"Does it really matter anymore?"

"You have a point."

"I was in the forward command post of the IDF the night of the sixteenth. I was beside Hobeika when he got the call from inside the camp, about what to do with the women and children. I heard what he said."

"Everybody knows that story. The famous words, 'You know exactly what to do,' etcetera."

"I know who he was talking to."

"Interesting. You have a name?"

"Yes."

"Would you know—just out of curiosity—how to contact this person?"

"He's dead."

"You seem certain of that."

"I am."

"I see."

Then Pierre asked the questions. How had Hobeika become a potential witness? He had approached the Belgian legal team when he'd heard about the possibility of prosecuting Ariel Sharon, then the prime minister of Israel.

What was he prepared to tell them? He'd been cautious, but he'd assured them that what he had to say would be explosive.

What had they expected from him? Not much. They knew that he would want to deflect blame; he would minimize the involvement of the Phalangists by perhaps inflating the Israeli role. What he planned to say would undoubtedly have been fascinating. Unfortunately, he took it with him to the grave.

Pierre asked what the Belgians had hoped to achieve by prosecuting Sharon.

Clarity, the lawyer said. Finality. "The Kahan report stated categorically that there was no direct Israeli involvement in the killings. Perhaps Hobeika could have challenged that by substantiating rumours that the IDF had people in the camps, actively participating. On the other hand, maybe he had nothing. We'll never know."

"Who killed Hobeika?"

"That's anybody's guess."

"The Israelis had a reason."

"Many people had a reason. It would have been risky for the Israelis, knowing that the finger of suspicion would inevitably point to them."

"The finger of suspicion never seems to bother them. If they did have something to hide, and he was planning to reveal it, the damage would have been greater than the speculation over who might have silenced him and why."

Pierre could hear the deep sigh on the other end of the phone line.

"In any case, the prosecution failed before it started, as you know."

"Why did it not proceed?" Pierre asked. "Was it because of what happened to Hobeika?"

"That was problematic. Yes."

"What if there was an actual document, a record from another source?"

"It would be interesting but no longer from a legal viewpoint."

"There is no statute of limitations for war crimes."

"No. No. But there has to be the political will to pursue such things. We had it for a while in Belgium. We had a law permitting extra-territorial prosecution of war crimes. No matter who, or where. But the law was repealed. So that was that."

"And your case against Sharon?"

"Stillborn."

"A pity."

"Yes. We spent a lot of time, of course, trying to substantiate a motive for the assassination of your friend. There were so many. It might have been very revealing if we'd had time to follow up on at least the more interesting ones. For example, a rumour circulated in Beirut that offered a possible identity of Hobeika's killer."

"Oh?"

"Allegedly, a mysterious bomb-maker who has been implicated in a number of explosions in the Middle East."

"Was there a name?"

"Benarik."

"Israeli?"

"By nationality, but believed to be a freelance."

"Benarik?"

"Yes. It seems he got the name because of a physical resemblance to Sharon."

"No other name?"

"I've heard that he was also known as 'Charon.' You'd know the name from mythology, I presume."

"Yes . . ."

"Appropriate, in the circumstances. Yes?"

~

Pierre sat for a long time staring at the silent telephone. Then he picked it up and rang Kennedy's extension.

"You did criminal law before you switched over?"

"Yes. Why do you ask?"

"I want to contact somebody in the police."

"My contacts were mostly Metro."

"It might be a place to start."

~

"The moving finger writes and having writ moves on, nor all thy piety nor wit can lure it back . . ." Who wrote *that?* Gibran? Khayyam? An Arab to be sure. The irrevocable nature of words, written or spoken. Once out they acquire the same potential for consequences as any deed.

Zhgorta, the camps, Hobeika were history. Even Ariel Sharon, felled by a stroke, inert, without a voice. But words endure, for all witnesses, for all time.

Pierre knew that it was imperative that he be cautious with his words. The detective suggested that he drop by the College Street headquarters at his convenience. Ask for Det. Sgt. Angus Brown.

Pierre had the feeling that the call was mostly courtesy, because he worked at a large company on Bay Street and was a well-connected lawyer. But he had to follow through.

The officer on the front desk checked his business card, then his driver's licence, handed him a visitor's badge, directed him toward the elevators.

Detective Brown listened carefully, making notes. Pierre realized that he was probably too young to recognize the significance of specific details in the background he was laying out. The cop appeared to be in his mid-thirties and to have no knowledge of, or very little interest in, politics.

"This man you worked for . . . how do you spell it, H-O-V . . ."

"H-O-B-E-I-K-A. He had a nickname. HK."

"Aha. What would the K be for. H would be Hobema?"

"Hobeika. No. HK was for Heckler Koch . . ."

"Jeez . . ."

"It was his weapon of choice."

"Heckler Koch. That was the rifle the crazy dude in Alberta used to kill the Mounties two years back."

"I read that."

The policeman, now engaged, had many questions. But Pierre, anticipating how the conversation would conclude, kept the answers general and, where necessary, vague.

"What I really want to discuss," he said at last, "is an individual I met recently in Toronto who might have been involved in the assassination of this man, Hobeika."

The policeman looked up, startled. "Why didn't you say that?"

"I just did."

"What do you mean . . . assassinated?"

Pierre paused, realizing that he was now on the brink. He took a deep breath.

"I believe the man, Hobeika, was preparing to give evidence in a war crimes investigation. And he was killed because of that."

"What kind of war crimes are we talking about?"

"The murder of innocent civilians, including women and children."

"Okay. This individual you believe might have been involved in taking out this . . . other guy? You have a name?"

"I'd rather not give a name just yet."

"I see."

"I'm here seeking guidance."

"Is there anything else you want to tell me?"

"Not right now."

The policeman closed his notebook. "I'm going to have to take this up the line." He stood up. "I'm pretty sure that someone will be getting in touch."

He walked around his desk, shook Pierre's hand. "Thanks for coming in. I'm going to have to do a bit of research but you've given me a good place to start."

Pierre thanked him for his time.

"Just sit tight. I'm sure someone will be contacting you."

∼

And it wasn't long before someone did. Pierre smiled at the cleverness of the acronym on the business card: INSET. Integrated National Security Enforcement Team. Two officers in suits. The older one was tall, had close-cropped grey hair and a four-day stubble. Inspector Nicholson.

"People call me Ron. We're, as the card says, an integrated service. RCMP. Provincial cops. Metro. Andy here is intelligence. CSIS. You know about them." Nicholson smiled broadly and Andy seemed to blush.

"So, anyway, tell us a bit about yourself before we get to the nitty-gritty."

"Sure. What do you want to know?"

Nicholson flipped open a notebook. "Full name, date and place of birth."

"Pierre Joseph Cormier. Born January 29, 1960. Saida, or Sidon, in the southern part of Lebanon."

"And you're what now . . ."

"Canadian citizen."

"Since when?"

"I came here as a refugee in 1983."

"Date?"

"September. The sixteenth. My name on arrival was Haddad. Pierre Joseph Haddad."

"You changed it?"

"I was living in a small East Coast community. I was anxious to fit in."

"I can imagine. And what was the basis of your refugee claim?"

"Well. There was a civil war in Lebanon at the time. I had good reason to believe that my life was in danger. The refugee board agreed."

"So why did you think your life was in danger?"

"I had been a member of a militia. It was a complicated situation."

"A militia?"

"Yes. The central government was unstable to say the least. The military and civil authorities were ineffective. So there were a number of militia groups, officially called Lebanese Forces, quite separate from the national army. The militias were mostly based on religion or family loyalties. I was in a Christian militia group but I defected. I was being hunted."

"You're a lucky guy. It isn't easy for a combatant to get status as a refugee."

"There are exceptions."

The officer flipped through his notes. "We'll come back to that. I believe you said that you were associated with an individual called Hobeika. Elie Hobeika."

"Yes."

"And this Hobeika was assassinated in . . . 2002, January, I believe."

"Yes."

"So how close was the association with this Hobeika?"

"From 1976 until 1978 it was very close, I thought. Then it deteriorated."

"What happened in 1978?"

"A military operation that went wrong. From my point of view."

"From your point of view?"

"Yes. But of course you realize that in a war the individual point of view is irrelevant. Can be dangerous even."

"Not just in war, my friend," said Nicholson. He sighed. "At the time of his death, I understand, this Hobeika was co-operating with a . . . Belgian . . . investigation into alleged war crimes by some fairly high-level political figures in Israel."

"Yes," Pierre said.

"You got in touch with the Belgian investigator?"

"Yes."

"Why?"

"I have certain information that I thought might be useful to them if they wanted to renew their investigation."

"I see. And your information deals with what?"

"Mostly the Israeli invasion of Lebanon in June 1982. The assassination of the Lebanese president-elect, Bashir Gemayel, in September that year. And the subsequent massacre of Palestinians in the Beirut camps."

"You said you might have run across a person here in Toronto who could have been mixed up in the assassination of this . . . Hobeika fellow."

"I have a hunch, that's all."

"That's okay. We specialize in hunches. So where did you run into this fella?"

"In a bar."

"What bar?"

"A little out-of-the-way place in the east end. The Only Café."

"The what?" Nicholson laughed and made a note. "Can you tell us what, if anything, you know about this fellow from the bar?"

"I can only repeat what he told me. He's a Canadian who grew up in Israel. He's a former member of the Israel Defense Force, IDF. Intelligence, I believe. He possibly served in an elite anti-terrorism unit."

"And does he have a name?"

"I'd rather not give it to you just now. In any case, I believe it's not his real name. I suspect that he might be a fugitive bomb-maker who was known in security circles overseas as 'Charon' or perhaps 'Benarik.'"

"Ben what?"

"Benarik. Spelled like it sounds. As you know it was a bomb that killed Hobeika."

The officer finished writing, then looked at Pierre sternly. "So let me ask you this. What was your involvement with this Hobeika fellow?"

"I lost my family early in the war. I was sixteen. I was kind of adopted by the militia group Hobeika belonged to. He knew my mother's people."

"This militia group was what?"

"It was a section of what was called the Kata'ib, which has different spellings."

"I've heard of it."

"You have?"

"We did a bit of homework on our own before we came to see you. Now this guy in the bar. What made you suspicious?"

"Certain things he seems to know. Matters have come up in conversations."

"You're worried about this guy?"

"Not really. A lot of time has passed. But we never know, do we?"

"Well, there isn't much to go on without a name. So when you feel ready . . ."

"Roloff. Ari Roloff."

"Spelling?"

As Pierre spelled the name, Nicholson and the silent officer named Andy exchanged glances and Andy nodded. Nicholson wrote briefly in his notebook, then stood.

"I suggest you keep this under your hat for now. For your own good. Right? We have a few things to check out. We'll be back in touch. Okay?"

"Yes, and for the record," Pierre said, "I wouldn't want my company dragged into anything."

"Absolutely. Just sit tight for now. We'll be able to reach you here at Draycor?"

"No. I plan to take some time off, go away for a while."

"Any place interesting?"

"Probably some boating on the East Coast."

"Ah. Prince Edward Island."

"Why would you think PEI?"

"I guess because there's a lot of Lebanese there. I think the premier is a Lebanese guy."

"The Lebanese are everywhere," Pierre said. "Including Cape Breton, which is where I'll be."

"Ah, Cape Breton," said Nicholson. "I believe that's where my family originated."

"I didn't know that, Ron," said Andy.

Nicholson looked at him and smiled. "People would be shocked, Andy. Shocked by all the things you guys don't know."

They laughed and they all shook hands. Pierre handed them his business card after writing his personal cellphone number on the back. Nicholson wrote a number on his own card and gave it to Pierre.

∽

After they had gone, Pierre sat staring through the window at the sky. His office was spare, unrevealing, the desk almost always clear, but for the photograph of Lois. There was a painting of a stylized cedar, unrecognizable as a tree, hanging on the office wall, along with his framed university degrees. He studied the cedar, remembering the pride with which he once wore that symbol on his shirt pocket, the profound loyalty he'd once felt to the country and the cause it represented.

He picked up the phone and rang Ethan.

When he answered, Pierre said, "I need to see you about something. It's kind of private."

"Sure. Do you want to go out?"

"No. Let's say tomorrow morning here in the office. A couple of things I want to draft for you to notarize before I leave. On a client to solicitor basis."

"Fine. As long as it doesn't involve the company."

"Not at all. Not remotely. A brief instruction in the event anything should happen to me. And a power of attorney to Lois."

"You're sure you're okay?"

"I'm okay. Just some personal housekeeping."

"Tomorrow morning. Say nine thirty. When are you leaving?"

"Soon. I'll bring the coffee."

"Excellent."

"And Ethan." He hesitated. "Let me just say my life is really complicated now. It isn't only Puncak. I'll try to fill you in a bit tomorrow. Client to lawyer, right?"

"Absolutely," said Ethan.

28.

How could he not have understood the fundamental symmetry? Surely what was going on around him had resonated somewhere in his memory. Or was it possible that he had so successfully walled off his past that he had forgotten elementary survival skills? Was it possible that he had come to believe his own deceptions—that he really was a reinvention? That the world that he'd inhabited since 1983 was on another moral planet, unlike the world he'd lived in for the first two decades of his life—the world in which he had developed all the instincts and reflexes that had enabled him to survive so much so long when tens of thousands like him hadn't.

He studied the horizon. The Magdalen Islands were off to the northwest. He could probably blend in there, revive the French he'd allowed to lapse for such a long time now. Or carry on, hook down the inland waterway and really disappear, somewhere in the Caribbean. Briefly he regretted having thrown away the Browning, his one physical connection with the turmoil of his distant past, perhaps a hedge against the unexpected.

No, he thought. That was wise.

Tonight, he told himself, I will speak with this Margaret Rankin off the record, get a sense of her reliability. Tomorrow I will drive to Halifax and from there fly home. He would tell nobody, he resolved, not even Lois. He would surprise her. He would surprise them all. From now on he was on his own.

He asked himself: How much will I tell this journalist when we talk? How much do I really know?

HK told him once: "Our advantage lies not just in what we know, but in what people think we know."

But experience had also taught HK that there is real danger when others think we know more than we should.

What do I really know? I made a phone call. There are eight people dead. But he also knew *why* he'd made the phone call. He knew the context and context is full of variables and as the context expands so do the variables. Each one implicates more people, draws more people into the dark realm of accountability. And he, Pierre, was at the centre of the circle once again.

He checked for messages. There was one. *Will call at nine your time. Looking forward. Thanx. Margaret.*

∾

Beirut, September 7, 1982. He was surprised when HK had invited him to the private dining room, presumably to celebrate with him and half a dozen of his most loyal and trusted commanders. He'd had little contact with HK for years now; there had been a chill between them for too long to remember. But things were changing rapidly and there was much to celebrate. Their sheikh was now the country's president. Arafat was gone and with him thousands of his terrorists; the Syrians were gone.

A week earlier the young sheikh faced down the Israelis who had demanded a peace treaty by year end, the ultimate repayment for chasing out the terrorists. But the sheikh knows it wasn't peace the Jews wanted, at least not peace for Lebanon. They wanted the optics of a treaty, diplomatic recognition by another Arab state. And the sheikh knew that a peace treaty with Israel would mean war with Syria and the ultimate dismemberment of Lebanon. But even in the absence of a treaty they are too close to the Israelis, owe them far too much.

Pierre listens to the animated talk as the wine flows. There are many platters heaped with food. He has lost his appetite for wine and food and politics: these men, his mentors and protectors, once his friends, have grown rich on the fruits of chaos. Peace for them will mean a return to the rule of law, but they owe their wealth and power to anarchy. He knows now, from the liquor-loosened conversation, that this is not a celebration. This, he thought, is crisis management. The sheikh was much too strong. Political stability could cause a crisis worse than war.

Bashir, beside him at the table, was trembling. "I need to talk," he whispered. "Outside."

The night was hot, dripping with humidity and yet Bashir looked like he was freezing. "You know what's going to happen, yes?"

Pierre shook his head.

"They have asked me to find Habib."

"Habib. The bomber."

"Yes."

"Why?"

"There is a rumour. Habib is plotting with the Syrians against the sheikh."

"Why does HK want him?"

Bashir smiled weakly. "I am to bring him in."

"For what reason?"

Bashir shrugged. "To be killed perhaps? To kill? Who knows?"

"Sit," Pierre said. They sat on a low stone wall. Pierre removed a package of cigarettes from his pocket. Bashir accepted one, lit it.

"I am a coward," Bashir said.

"No."

"If I wasn't I would stop this thing at any cost. If I knew how."

"It would be the end of all of us."

"Yes. But it will be the end in any case."

Pierre studied the cigarette between his fingers. "We are pawns in this. Others decide, we follow orders."

"Listen to me, Pierre. HK has kept you close—out of the field.

You must know this. It is because he no longer trusts you. Four years ago you questioned him about the Zghorta operation. Nobody questions HK and survives. You are only alive because you have Damour in common. But I have heard it said that this life insurance will expire for you too. You must be alert. He will find a reason. You have seen and heard too much, as I have. The end will come without warning."

Pierre said, "I will speak to HK. We will send you out for as long as you need. To Israel or France. You have a brother in Boston? It can be arranged."

"No," he said. "There is already an arrangement."

Pierre gripped his arm. "You are nearing burnout."

Bashir looked away. There was a helicopter circling above. "Our friends from the south," he said, "looking for a target that hasn't yet been destroyed." He laughed. Then he sighed heavily. "We are creating a desert."

Pierre draped an arm across his shoulders. Bashir spoke again, his voice barely above a whisper. "About Elias. Watch him carefully. He has spoken against you to the boss. About Chamoun and the Syrians. He has whispered that you have been in secret meetings with Dany and the Tigers . . ."

"Those are lies."

"Yes, of course," Bashir said. "But lies can be helpful for whatever outcome is required. Be careful around him. When your time comes, it will be Elias. If the sheikh dies many others will follow in the aftermath. Be on guard."

Bashir stood, dropped the cigarette, stepped on it. He studied the crushed cigarette, as if it had inspired another thought. He caught Pierre by the hand, stared silently into his face. But his eyes were vacant.

"The sheikh believes he has the Americans behind him. But against the interests of the Israelis, he is nothing. Isolated from the Syrians he is finished before he starts. He will not even survive to the inauguration."

Pierre said, "Come back inside. We will have a drink together. Plan your holiday."

Bashir shook his head and backed away into the darkness. Pierre watched until he was gone, then turned away to go back inside. He was in the doorway when he heard the pistol shot. He paused, heard heavy footsteps, people running. And he thought, how odd that a single gunshot in a place where guns are never silent can cause such a reaction. Anger? Panic? Curiosity? His mind followed the irony until it settled on another thought: that he, Pierre, was feeling nothing.

He had ceased to pay attention, distracted by too many useless thoughts. *The sheikh is finished before he starts.* Could he have imagined it? The sheikh was at the pinnacle of power, the entire country under his control, his inauguration just days away. The Americans needed him, supported him, gave him the confidence to stand up to the Israelis, ignore the menace of the Syrians.

He reflected on the last words of his friend. *The sheikh is finished before he starts.*

He was wrong. He had to be. The sheikh was too experienced, too wily, too well connected to fall victim to lesser men.

∾

HK was terse. *Get Habib. Bring him to me. Tell no one.*

"What am I to tell Habib?"

"You will tell him nothing."

"And what if he resists?"

HK sighed, placed a hand on Pierre's shoulder. "Surely you know how to overcome resistance."

"Why? Why Habib? He is with the Syrians."

HK looked away. "Perhaps. Perhaps not."

"Get someone else."

"What?"

"Someone else can find Habib." For only an instant there was fury in HK's eyes. Pierre turned away. Then HK drew him back and smiled.

"Perhaps we have been together for too long, my friend. Go then. But do not speak of this. It will not be difficult to find Habib."

Habib. The bomber who was blamed by history for what happened on September fourteenth—the explosion that destroyed the sheikh, the saviour; the explosion that brought down an office building and the hopes of more than half the country; that touched off a cascade of consequences that no one had anticipated. No one, perhaps, but HK and his inner circle.

~

September 15, 1982. Bikfaya, the Gemayel stronghold. The place was packed. It was a wake, but it had the atmosphere of a convention. Food, alcohol, floral tributes, important people. Everyone was there, old Sheikh Pierre, grey and sombre and immaculately dressed, accepting condolences and pledges of fealty from family and loyalists, Israelis and Americans, Saad Haddad, the warlord and Israeli proxy from the south. Amin, the younger, weaker brother of the dead sheikh, the president in waiting. Life goes on. War goes on.

And had Pierre imagined it? HK and Elias watching him, then whispering, then drifting off? Was it possible that his bitterness and cynicism had metastasized to paranoia?

If the sheikh dies many others will follow in the aftermath. Be on guard.

Outside, among the dispersing mourners HK approached Pierre, face grave, embraced him, face to his ear, whispered: "If you had found Habib, perhaps we wouldn't be here. This, you must live with." Then took Pierre's face in both his hands and kissed him.

29. *September 18, 1982*

It had been the longest day of his life—a day of nearly ninety hours. Ninety hours that would eclipse every other hour that he had lived or would live.

It was a Saturday. By eight thirty that morning he knew the day was almost over. It had actually started on the fourteenth, Tuesday afternoon, just after four. Elias in his doorway: *There has been a bomb. In Achrafieh. Let's go.* He hadn't slept since then. Not real sleep. Maybe brief restless moments of unconsciousness, in his clothing, sitting upright. Elias, who had gone to school somewhere in Canada, had an English phrase for the state they were in: *Wired but not tired.*

Perhaps it was that first scene on Tuesday afternoon that prepared him for the final scene on Saturday. Elias drove both times. To Achrafieh, to Shatila. *They are saying Sheikh Bashir was in the building.* In his memory, that was when the chill began. And by the Saturday he felt neither chill nor heat.

It seems that he was only semi-conscious when the Israelis stopped them at the entrance to the camp. *You must turn back. Nobody can go in.* The Israeli major spoke perfect Arabic. Pierre had replied quietly: *Move. We have orders to go in to make sure that all our men are out of the camps.* The Israeli studied their papers, shrugged and signalled to his men who slouched away from the front of the jeep.

The difference between Saturday morning and Tuesday afternoon, besides the overwhelming presence of Israeli power in West Beirut, was the silence. On Tuesday, the noise was overwhelming. And the smoke and dust billowing down the streets of Achrafieh were confirmation of catastrophe even before they saw the rubble. The building, all three levels pancaked—pipes and reinforcing rods protruding from the broken concrete; broken furniture and fabric smouldering; scraps of clothing that revealed the presence of a human form or body part. Noise. The shouting, honking, screaming sirens; wailing; the clatter of a helicopter just overhead.

Nobody survived this. We must get back.

A weeping stranger seized Elias by the arm. *Sheikh Bashir is in that helicopter, on his way to a hospital in Israel.*

No. The sheikh is dead. Everything is changed.

Who did this?

Terrorists.

Whose terrorists?

Elias didn't answer.

∼

Now Saturday, weaving through another place of carnage, there is only silence accentuated by the hum of insects. The dead are everywhere, individuals and groups; families; young men sprawled along a wall where they were executed; old men, throats cut; children, their heads cleaved by blows from axes; the silent curiosity of lifeless faces;

LINDEN MACINTYRE

small bodies; large bodies; bodies blackened by long hours in the sun; blackened by the swarms of flies; some still bleeding from a recent knife or axe or bullet; babies; women; dogs; horses. Pierre will ask himself repeatedly, sometimes in astonishment: horses? But he remembered horses. Mostly he remembered his indifference, the self-preserving numbness that sets in after normal senses have shut down.

Elias mutters: *Justice. Justice for the sheikh.*

Hobeika seemed unsteady when he gave the orders, wearily. He'd not slept since Monday night. *Make sure that everyone is out of there.* The Israelis had been adamant, the tone aggressive and contemptuous: everybody out by five on Saturday morning. They were getting questions. There were rumours of a massacre. The media were swarming. The American ambassador was aggressively demanding information. But at seven the Phalangists were still there in the camps, still killing. *Make sure there is no living person left there.*

Elias knew the camp, its narrow streets and alleyways; its breeze-block hovels, many flattened now by dynamite and the bulldozers that have shoved the wreckage, the garbage, corpses, severed body parts, into mounds that only partly hide the savagery. Elias had been there Thursday night, all night, and all day Friday. Pierre sat two hundred metres away, peering through binoculars, from the top of a five-storey building, when Elias called Hobeika.

I have fifty civilians here. I don't know what to do with them.

What do you mean?

They are women and children. What do I do?

This is the last time you're going to ask me a question like that. You know exactly what to do.

Saturday morning. The Phalangists and Israelis were still watching—watching them for they were the only people moving. Shatila camp. A slaughterhouse with a gallery for spectators. Pierre is mercifully unmoved, even now, even a quarter of a century removed from the reality.

He heard it happening. From that observation post he heard the shooting, the shouts and screams; saw the flight, pursuit and murder in the light of flares suspended in the sky, turning night to day. Thursday night to Friday when it escalated in the daylight.

He and Elias drove slowly on that Saturday morning, weaving through the debris. Human debris. What had been, on Tuesday, living, worrying, laughing, weeping, striving, hungry, thirsty, horny. Indolent. Ambitious. Hopeful and despairing. People. Now indistinguishable from broken concrete, litter, the clothing they wore. Crushed water bottles. Rotting garbage from the food that once sustained the bodies that are now bulging, broken, blackened. Inert. Everything inert.

There isn't anybody here alive.

Okay. Wait.

∼

They were sitting in the jeep, listening. "Come," Elias said. "I want to show you something." Pierre felt a flutter in his chest. *When your time comes, it will be Elias.* He stared straight ahead, lest his eyes reveal distrust. "Come," Elias repeated. They exited the jeep, stood listening.

"What was that?" Elias asked, cranking the AK-47. *Clack-clack,* metal upon metal.

Pierre heard only the sound of the Kalashnikov being readied, allowed his hand to slide closer to the Browning on his hip. Then he too heard a sound. A door closing behind a garden wall. Elias was already at the gate, Pierre close behind, their weapons ready.

The woman at the clothesline turned, startled. One arm was cradling a basket full of clothes. On her face, an expression of surprise fast dissolving into fear. Pierre felt an unfamiliar movement in his chest—a response to this evidence of life returning in the middle of an abattoir. She was young, still pretty. She seemed to be unaware of what had been happening just outside her tiny yard, or in denial. Emotion surged in him, something close to passion. He raised a hand. He wanted to touch her. He wanted to pick her up, hold her, carry her away, but he stepped back, intimidated by her fear. He reached toward her, reassuring with his eyes. She cringed. The gunshot startled him. There was a look of sudden shock on her face as she spun away, reaching for the clothesline as if to prevent falling.

Elias was frozen in position, a tight smile twitching at the corners of his mouth, AK extended forward casually, a wisp of blue smoke drifting. It seemed as if she was falling slowly, clothes basket tumbling in front of her, clothes and clothespins suspended in the air, then settling around her head. There was no immediate evidence of injury and for a moment Pierre was able to imagine that she had fainted, that she would stir and he would help her to her feet, take her out of there, preserve her, this beauty, this assertion of survival in the aftermath of Armageddon. It was what prevented him from killing Elias then and there, this fantasy. Until he saw the blood oozing slowly, pooling.

Elias struck him hard, brought him out from the inner place where he'd been caught in a feeling of revulsion not at what he'd witnessed, but at what he now could see and feel within himself.

Get out of here.

~

Driving past the checkpoint he could feel the loathing of the soldiers lounging on their tanks and sandbags; the civilized Israelis, cultured, educated citizen-soldiers repelled by Arab savagery. He stared straight ahead as they accelerated past the waving, shouting officer. Waving them to continue? Demanding that they stop and explain the single gunshot? No matter. They will not dare to go inside and look, and he has had enough of their disdain. He had been listening to it since Tuesday night. Wednesday in Bikfaya. All night Thursday in their command post. Friday, as they pretended to discover what had been happening.

Later they will claim they didn't know. How could they not know? He marvelled at the studied innocence of their inquiries, the patronizing indignation of their warnings. Even Sharon himself, the mastermind. *Your men must not be allowed to run amok.* Run amok? What is that, run amok? They were laughing at fat-ass Sharon on Wednesday when he was there, handing out the orders. Too fat to climb the five flights of stairs to the command post. Deniability through disability. It was funny, almost, the Israeli insistence that they didn't know. Begin, Sharon, Eitan. Even the soldiers and their spies, the Mossad agents. They all knew. They were everywhere. They were the occupiers. As of Wednesday they owned Beirut, West as well as East. Their tanks and half-tracks crunching through the Hamra, officers lounging in the lobby of the Commodore Hotel, infantry patrolling the Corniche. Do the Jews not have ears and eyes like other people? Were they not there throughout it all, on the roof of that five-storey building two hundred metres away, illuminating everything with flares? And yet they acted as if they couldn't see and hear for themselves. *What is going on down there? We've heard a report, three hundred dead. You must exercise control. Discipline. Protect civilians.*

What civilians? He was there when the Mossad spies and HK concurred that there were two thousand terrorists holed up in the camps, that they had a secret arsenal.

He was there Tuesday night when Eitan and Drori gave the orders at Phalangist headquarters: mobilize your Lebanese Forces. Unleash the Kata'ib.

He was there, in the Israeli forward command post when Eitan laid out the rules of engagement—the elimination of the terrorists would be undertaken by the Phalange.

And then the Israeli high command sat back and watched. And listened. But heard nothing, saw nothing. Until Saturday, when all the world saw.

∿

Pierre didn't recognize the man who was having coffee with HK when they returned to the stadium. He could tell that he was Israeli; he knew by the composure, by the absence of identifying insignia on his uniform, that he was from the dark side of their operations. There was no disdain in him, no sign of judgment. Perhaps that's why Pierre remembered him. He guessed that the Israeli was an officer, for it was apparent that he was a leader. He was battle weary, tired and unshaven. But the handshake was firm, the gaze respectful.

Elias briefed the Israeli and HK: no member of the Phalangist forces left in or near the camp. Perimeter still secured by the IDF. All clear as promised. Earthmovers in place for a final cleanup before the regular Lebanese army would arrive in the afternoon to occupy the crime scene. There were no living witnesses. No mention of the woman at the clothesline—the final terrorist to die.

Then Pierre noticed the two men squatting near a wall, hooded, hands tied.

Yes. Them. Take them back to the camp.

There's an IDF checkpoint . . .

The Israeli officer removed a notepad from his shirt pocket. Scrawled something, tore off a page and handed it to Pierre. It was in Hebrew.

This will get you through.

Elias frowned in the direction of the two prisoners. *What are we to do with them?*

You know exactly what to do with them. Don't ask again.

~

They drove in silence, one of the prisoners in front beside Elias, the other in the back beside Pierre. When the jeep rounded a corner, or bounced through a crater in the road he could feel the prisoner's body bumping him or leaning into his, which made it almost impossible to remain unaware of him. He repeated to himself: It is war; they are the enemy. But then he remembered the expression on the face of the man he killed in Zghorta, the last man that he had killed. Four years ago. The look of surprise, of utter vulnerability. The expression on the face of the woman at the clothesline.

He told himself: You must get control; you must refill your heart with the hatred that sustained you, that justified the things you've done, the horrors you've witnessed. Remember January 1976.

The remembering was easy. The seafront; the chilling mist that evening. His father wondering what they would eat when they got home. The Fedayeen patrol. The horrifying sound of gunfire behind him, around him. The smell of shit on his hand that he couldn't wash away for days. And his mother. And Miriam. The last smile, the gay farewell as they drove off toward Damour.

But now it wasn't anger in his heart. It wasn't hatred. It was despair. He gripped the rifle on his lap, squeezed hard to keep his hands from shaking and was glad the prisoner was blinded by the hood.

They were stopped again at the entrance to Shatila by another officer, a captain who demanded that they hand over the prisoners. Pierre was privately relieved but he pretended to resist, sitting there in the back seat. He lifted the rifle from his lap, held it upright, butt resting on his thigh. Elias turned to him. *Show him the paper.* And he remembered: the note from the Israeli officer in his shirt pocket. He presented it.

The captain didn't look at it, kept shouting. *Hand over the terrorists.* And then another officer appeared. This one took the note and read it.

How do you know him?

Pierre shrugged. *He is at the stadium. Go there and ask him.*

The major handed back the note, shouted something at the captain. They both stepped back. Elias put the jeep in gear, accelerated. They bounced forward.

∾

The jeep stopped suddenly. Elias pointed down an alleyway. *Down there.*

Pierre remembered that there were the bodies of young men there, lying among their weapons, blood, congealed brain matter. Bursting out of uniforms, bodies greasy. Four or five of them. They had died quickly Thursday night trying to defend the camp. He thought: two more dead terrorists will hardly matter.

His prisoner stumbled attempting to leave the back seat of the jeep and Pierre caught his arm. He tripped again on some debris and, again, Pierre steadied him. From underneath the hood Pierre could hear a nervous laugh. *Please take it off.*

Pierre ignored him as they stumbled down the shadowed alleyway, his hand on the prisoner's elbow, steering him.

I want to see where I am going.

No. It is better if you don't see.

The stench was overwhelming. The other prisoner gagged and there was vomit from beneath his hood, down his shirt. Elias grabbed the hood, lifted it off, revealed the face of a man who seemed to be in his thirties. He stood blinking, spitting, looking around in desperation, disbelief. Elias pushed him away until he was standing near the dead. Then he grabbed Pierre's prisoner by the arm and roughly dragged him over to where the other one was standing. He snatched the second prisoner's hood and dropped it on the ground.

He seemed young, maybe younger than Pierre. He looked around and he looked upward. He squinted in the blaze of sunshine.

You will do it.

Elias repeated, his voice mercifully low: *You will do it. Two shots. Use the Browning. Quickly.*

Yes.

He removed the Browning from its holster and walked toward the prisoners. The older one stepped back, stumbled on a corpse and Pierre grabbed him quickly, held him upright, could feel him trembling. First the young one. He turned, aimed between the eyes. His mind was blank, hand steady. Damour. Damour. The prisoner was facing him but, at the same time, staring elsewhere. Pierre was momentarily distracted. *What's he looking at?*

And then he realized: *I have seen those eyes before, that wall-eyed face.*

Saida. You were there when they killed my father. He was speaking softly. *You were there, six years ago.*

The prisoner shrugged. *Perhaps.*

Elias was shouting now. *What are you waiting for. Do it . . .*

And suddenly Elias was beside Pierre and with a single shot from his Kalashnikov he felled the older prisoner who stumbled and landed writhing on his back among the dead. Wheeled then to face the younger one but Pierre was faster. He swiftly raised the Browning and shot Elias through the ear.

The surviving prisoner was shaking but his voice was firm. *Quickly. Untie me. Grab that hood. Give me your helmet.*

Pierre was paralyzed.

Wake up. We must go.

Pierre removed his helmet, stooped and grabbed the hood where it was lying on the ground, handed them to the prisoner who was already walking away, back down the alleyway. Left Elias now indistinguishably dead among the terrorists. *Justice,* Pierre repeated silently.

The prisoner was driving when they left the camp. He didn't even slow down for the checkpoint, just raised his right hand in salute, middle finger pointed skyward. The Israelis watched them grimly.

~

Winding up the mountain road, Pierre looked back to see Beirut sprawled below, almost lost in haze. The thought occurred to him that this might be the last time he'd gaze upon the city that he'd fought for, almost died for. Six long, miserable years. Now his fight was ended.

The Mediterranean twinkled, flecks of gold on the azure swells, and there were foreign warships and Israeli gunboats lurking like watchdogs in the distance.

Near Bhamdoun the jeep came to a skidding stop on the roadside.

I am Walid.

Where are we going?

My village. Kfar Matta. In the Chouf.

You are Druze?

I am Druze. The other man was my cousin, Kamal. We were at the Sabra hospital.

You were taken at the Sabra hospital? By the IDF?

Yes. IDF? Kata'ib? What difference?

He removed the helmet, tossed it in the ditch.

Your name is what?

Pierre.

You must trust me now, Pierre. You will let me have your gun, please. And you will wear this hood.

Pierre's hesitation lasted only for a second, maybe two. Beneath the hood the darkness was almost comforting.

30.

And now the sun is twinkling on the Gulf of St. Lawrence, gateway to North America. He realized that he'd been praying. It wasn't the kneel-down-at-the-lap-of-God prayerfulness that he remembered from his childhood, but a rare harmony between his senses and emotions.

He recalled a word that Father Cyril often used: reconciliation. For a moment he had an insight that might have been considered blasphemous: he'd been praying to the spirit of his friend, the priest, a substitute for the God that he was unable to imagine, unable to believe in. But maybe it wasn't blasphemy at all. He thought about their first meeting, in May 1978, and the enigma we call destiny. A saintly priest from Canada, trying to find his roots, to absorb something of his heritage.

Father Cyril didn't know much about his roots but he knew his history, his politics. *It has been the fate of Lebanon, these invasions. From the dawn of recorded time.*

He'd arrived in the country in February with some journalists. He'd travelled with them, north and south. South of Tyre the Israelis had offered hospitality. He would never forget the sophistication, the open-mindedness, the kindness they showed.

Years later Pierre would respectfully suggest, "Perhaps you should have been in Beirut in 1982." Then Father Cyril would remind Pierre of the public response in Israel to the September massacres, the public outcry, the demonstrations, a hundred thousand chanting for accountability. And they would get it—the Kahan Commission boldly naming names, calling for the dismissal of important people who shared responsibility for Sabra and Shatila, including Ariel Sharon.

Imagine that in Syria? Egypt? Iran? Never in a thousand years.

"Are you referring to *Prime Minister* Ariel Sharon?" he'd asked.

Father Cyril had just smiled.

A whale surfaced near the boat, and then another. But they were quickly gone. It was time to move. He had much to do now. It would take a long time to fill the empty pages of his journal, but he'd made a start. And he'd have time for the project, perhaps a real book. Who could tell what new avenues would open up now that he was about to be an idle rich man.

The idea boosted his spirits. But then he thought of Ari and it was as if a cloud had moved in front of the sun. He studied the horizon. The sun was now a scarlet disc hovering, its reflection on the sea a fiery furrow streaking toward the land. The surface of the water was still, viscous, black as he approached the harbour mouth. Beneath the boat small crabs scurried in the sand.

He slowed the boat to idle, retrieved his phone. He called Ethan but there was no answer. He left a message.

"Ethan, call me. Couple of things. I want to give you a heads-up about something. The reporter, Rankin, tracked me down and I'm going to talk to her. Prudently. Just trust me. I can give you my rationale. Call me."

Okay, he thought. I've upped the ante. *Your call, Brawley.*

Because he was preoccupied he didn't notice that his arrival was being observed closely from a car parked on the nearby hillside road. He didn't see a door swing open, a man emerge and stretch after what had obviously been a long wait.

The tide was flat. There was no wind. Pierre secured the boat, then stepped back into the cabin, stowed the journal in his briefcase. He retrieved the whisky bottle, began to pour a drink. He felt the boat move, a rocking motion, from someone stepping down from wharf to washboard. Then a heavy thump as someone large descended from the washboard to the deck.

He turned toward the doorway, the bottle in his hand.

But it wasn't Angus Beaton. It was Ari standing there, smiling, his hand raised slightly in what might have been a greeting, or a gesture of apology.

SEVEN

WAR

31.

"This is excellent!" Suzanne was glowing. She stood behind her desk for a moment, then walked around in front, held out her arms.

Cyril stepped into them. She then stepped back but caught his hands. "Close the door."

He closed the door. She wrapped her arms around him again and this time kissed him warmly on the lips. He felt giddy, the warmth, the fullness of her—what was the word—her *authenticity*. His new contract.

"You had nothing to do with this?" he said when she let go.

"Well, I didn't stand in the way of it. But it was all Hughes and Savage. And yourself, of course. You're on your way, sweetheart."

"Well, it's only for six months."

"Six months here? A lifetime. Cyril, I was a stringer for this outfit for two years before they offered me the time of day. And that was only because I was approached by CBS."

"And of course you let them know."

"Of course I did. Last place I wanted to be was in an American meat grinder but they didn't have to know that."

"Well," he said. "I guess I'd better be good."

"You can start by bringing in that Ari guy. You help us get this Ari fellow on TV and you'll be golden for the rest of your career. Now, where's Nader? Have you told him?"

"No. Not yet. I just came downstairs from signing. But I had a text from him—he's out front."

"Let's go then. Can't keep the spooks waiting, can we."

∼

The hotel was walking distance. Cyril had expressed surprise that the spies would want to meet them in a hotel suite and not at their offices. Suzanne had explained that the CSIS people don't like outsiders wandering around their premises.

"So what if they've wired the hotel room?"

"Not a problem," Suzanne replied. "We have nothing to hide."

The hotel lobby was intense with people checking in, checking out, dragging luggage on tiny wheels, bellhops hauling massive over-loaded carts behind them. Cyril was afloat on a sensation that was almost erotic, a journalist on his way to a clandestine meeting with secret agents. The dim, vast and vaguely intimidating lobby was like a movie set. He had become, on the strength of a couple of signatures on a brief document, a journalist. No, no. Too pretentious. A *reporter*. That's how he'd describe himself, the way Suzanne and Hughes always referred to *themselves*. Reporters. "In our day," Hughes told him once, "journalists were foreigners."

Waiting for the elevator he kept thinking: *If people only knew!*

Suzanne knocked lightly on the hotel room door and there was instant movement on the inside. The door opened. A friendly face, smiling broadly—a hand extended. "Come in, come in. Right on time."

The man turned to Cyril. "We've never met but you must be Cyril. I'm Andy. These two I know only too well."

He grinned at Suzanne, gripped Nader's elbow, led them in.

"Nader, Suzanne, I think you know Bill, and of course you know McGuire. Guys—this is Cyril . . . what was the last name again?"

"Cormier."

A woman who seemed slightly hesitant stood, nodded. "I'm Heather," she said. Shook hands all around, though she paused before reaching out to Nader. He grasped her hand and shook it emphatically.

A tall man in a rumpled linen jacket—Bill—remained seated. He smiled, but his manner was reserved. "We've laid on some lunch," he said. "There's drinks and coffee—why don't we grab something before we start talking."

There was a table with a large silver platter of sandwiches, a second platter full of raw vegetables—cauliflower and broccoli, carrot sticks and peppers; a vast bowlful of ice and water and cans of non-alcoholic drinks. Introductory chit-chat mostly dealt with the current state of the media, the precariousness of the business model and the ongoing revolution in technology. Cyril gathered that McGuire had once been in the journalism business.

The man in the rumpled jacket, Bill, finally interrupted. "We're all busy people," he said. "So maybe we should get on with why we're here. Of course there's the usual understanding, right? Off the record, okay? Understood that we realize certain bits and pieces will lodge in your fertile brains and become part of your general background knowledge. But nothing for attribution in any way, shape or form. Okay?"

"Of course," Suzanne said, her tone slightly starchy. "We wouldn't be in this room if there wasn't a certain element of trust all around."

Andy, his friendliness undiminished, said, "Absolutely. We've been through this before, most usefully in '06, during the Toronto Eighteen thing. And of course nobody is recording. Right?"

"Not unless you are," said Nader with a laugh. "And I think you mean the Toronto *Two* thing."

"I think three is a better number," said Bill. "One casts a wide net sometimes when the specific target is unknown."

"Which is always problematical," said Nader.

Suzanne said, "Okay guys, let's get to the here and now. What can you tell us about your perception of the homegrown radical business six years after the Toronto Eighteen or Two or Three or whatever."

"It's okay if I take notes?" Cyril asked.

They all looked at him and he put his pen back in his pocket.

There followed a lengthy dissertation by Andy on the inflammatory potential of events in Syria and Iraq, the unfocused nature of what had seemed, at the outset, to be a principled rebellion against the Assad dictatorship.

"It's chickens coming home to roost," said Nader, who digressed back to the First World War and the post-war colonial configurations that took no account of the tribal or ethnic or religious realities on the ground.

Suzanne reached out and patted Nader's knee.

"We know all that, love. We've all seen *Lawrence of Arabia*. Let's use our time here to see how these guys can help us advance the story we've been working on. Why don't you go ahead?"

"Sure," Nader said. "Sorry. I get a bit wound up sometimes. But if *I'm* getting wound up then what's going on in the mosques and madrassas everywhere, including here, isn't so hard to figure out. And so, basically . . ."

Cyril listened, struggling to imprint in memory everything that Nader had to say.

"Just to go back briefly to where I was interrupted, the problems in Syria, Iraq and Lebanon and Jordan—let's not get into Palestine— have deep, deep political roots. To the politics add sectarian differences within Islam itself. We understand the challenge of dealing with that from the point of view of national security and the danger of making a security risk worse by using the wrong kind of tactics— surveillance, infiltration—to confront it."

Bill cleared his throat. "Well, hopefully we have the kind of oversight to keep us on our toes . . ."

"And hopefully you accept that we're a legitimate part of that oversight," Suzanne said.

"Absolutely," said Andy. "We're meeting with you because we see no conflict between the interests of security and accountability. The line that's always difficult to establish is where accountability compromises operational effectiveness."

Bill spoke specifically to Nader. "So let's be clear and candid here. We know that you have great contacts in the various Muslim communities and I'm pretty sure you know and probably talk to a number of the people that we have concerns about. So why don't you tell us what, in an ideal situation, you want us to help you with?"

Nader exchanged a brief glance with Suzanne. "You want me to keep on with this?"

"You're doing great," she said.

"People in the local mosques are very aware of the attempts to infiltrate them by the Salafists and other extremists. But there's another concern that's just as large—that there has been an effective infiltration of various mosques by people working for *you guys* and that certain of your people are stirring things up for purposes of— and this is not my word, but theirs—entrapment."

"Understood," said Andy. "Always a hard call. Going back to the Toronto Eighteen-or-However-Many, was your friend, Mubin Sheikh, a concerned citizen or a provocateur when he worked with us while he was gaining the confidence of the ringleaders? Were the original eighteen all potential terrorists or mostly just a silly BOG . . ."

"A what?" Suzanne asked.

"A BOG . . . a bunch of guys. Are we dealing with cultural and sectarian tensions or serious recruitment of young people who will turn into problems for Canadians and Americans and Brits or . . . ?"

"Fair enough," said Nader. After another glance in Suzanne's direction, he carried on. "We could talk all day without a serious disagreement about the problems and the possible solutions. But we're working on a story and, with the understanding that the ground rules here work both ways, background and all that—part of our story, and part of the reason for being here, is getting to the bottom of rumours we've heard from credible sources that CSIS has retained, on contract, a security consultant with deep experience and continuing connections to a foreign intelligence agency. And that this individual is running agents that work for you in the community."

The room fell silent.

"You mention Mubin Sheikh," Nader said. "He did great work. For you, for the community and for us. But I know you had concerns that he turned into a bit of a loose cannon. The word is that the next Mubin would be on a shorter leash. So if you really do have a shorter leash, you know or should know what he or they are really up to."

Cyril could hear the hum of a vacuum cleaner in the hallway just outside the door. Everybody looked toward the door, as if waiting for the noise to go away.

"So what's your question, Nader?" said Andy.

"Okay. The question in the community is who is this guy and what is he up to. And who's holding his leash—if there is a leash."

There was a long silence as the vacuum cleaner faded.

"You want to answer that, Bill?" said Andy.

"Well, right off the top. Normally, whether this were true or false you know we'd never comment. Right? But I'm going to be up front in this case—this is news to us. Just the existence of that kind of rumour is as disturbing to me as it is to you folks. Do you want to elaborate a little bit?"

"Not really," Nader said. "If it's just talk, end of story."

"Can I ask, which foreign intelligence service?"

Nader and Suzanne exchanged a long glance. Suzanne nodded.

"They suspect Mossad. Or IDF intelligence."

There was a round of laughter, Nader laughing with them.

"See," said Nader, when he stopped chuckling, "I don't think these people ever heard of Sayeret Matkal."

"Say what?" said Bill with a broad smile.

Nader stared at him for, perhaps, fifteen seconds. "I think you heard me."

Bill seemed fascinated by some aspect of the ceiling and when he spoke he continued to study it. "When I was a boy, my old dad had an expression he'd use when he thought my imagination was running away with my better judgment."

He stood. "He'd say, 'Billy my boy, you bin' readin' too damn many comic books.'"

Andy laughed. "Stay in touch guys, you know how to reach us if you come across anything interesting."

~

"It was *not* a denial," said Nader.

They were walking quickly along the busy sidewalk. Cyril struggled to keep up with Suzanne and Nader, but was also troubled by two competing instincts—to believe the friendly public servants or his now infuriated friends.

"Suzanne, I can't believe how easily they sucked us into mentioning the Israelis."

"Oh *fuck off*, Nader. I'm thinking and I'd suggest you follow suit."

"Okay. Okay. It's the fact that you haven't said anything since we left that place that's making me nervous."

"Well, Nader, you should be nervous. There's nothing wrong with being nervous. And as far as mentioning the Israelis goes, it was my call, and it was the right call."

"It's a short trip from being nervous to being scared."

She stopped walking so suddenly that Cyril almost stepped on her heel. "Is that what you're thinking? That I'm scared? Jesus, Nader. Really?"

He raised his arms. "Okay. Okay. I'm sorry. I never meant to imply . . ."

"I know that," she said. "But there are certain denials that are unnerving. Either they're dead certain we could never get to the truth if we had a hundred years and all the resources in the world to work on this, *or* they know with certainty that we're dead wrong. We have to think long and hard about which one we're facing here."

She walked on.

"Or," said Nader, "they have their heads in the sand and this guy is rogue or a foreign plant."

"Why would the Israelis take the political risk of planting a spy in Canada?"

"Because Canada is super sympathetic toward Israel right now, so the political risk would be zero. Even when Canada wasn't so friendly they risked forging or stealing Canadian passports for past operations. You know they've done that."

Suzanne stopped again, then turned to smile at Cyril. "How are you enjoying journalism so far?"

"Great."

"By the way, what did Andy have to say when he took you aside as we were leaving? You can tell me it's none of my business."

"He asked about my name, the Cormier and the Bashir. And then he asked if I was related to Pierre Cormier."

Nader laughed. "As if they don't know!"

"Anyway, he told me that shortly before my father disappeared, they'd met with him. He had something he wanted to tell them, something that was bothering him. But Andy said he never got the opportunity."

"Well, that's interesting," said Nader. "Did he mention who met with your father?"

"No, just said 'we.' I guess I should have followed up a bit. Right?"

"Maybe yes, maybe not," Suzanne said. "We have to regroup and figure out where we stand."

"Where we stand," Nader said, "is in the middle of a major story."

"But do we have the goods to tell it?"

Suzanne draped an arm over Nader's shoulder and Nader looped an arm around her waist and they walked on like that.

"We're gonna have to bring Savage into the picture," she said.

"I'm aware of that," Nader said.

~

Cyril examined his new contract, a single page, the pittance he'd be paid. Luckily money wasn't a major factor at the moment. Pierre's will had taken care of that. It was the job description that excited him. Associate Producer. Reality needs witnesses, he thought. Who can I share this with? His mother, but her overreaction would be embarrassing. Gloria? It wouldn't matter to her, not really. She'd be friendly, warm perhaps. But she'd resent the distraction of his call. He could fall through a crack in the earth and she'd consider it a distraction from her all-important files.

Then his cellphone rang. It was Leo. "Hey, what's up? We've all been wondering where you've got to."

Cyril told him that he'd just signed his first contract. It was for six months, but six months was like tenure in the media in the current circumstances.

"Well, I think we should celebrate."

"Maybe just you and I? A drink? How about tonight?"

"I'm tied up tonight," said Leo. "How about tomorrow night? And we should invite the other guys. You can tell us all about it. Maybe I'll ask a few other people. What about Gloria? You guys still on the outs?"

"It's pretty well over," Cyril said. "But I might bring a friend."

"For sure. Bring her . . ."

"Not a her, Leo. A guy from work."

When he'd hung up Nader was standing by his desk scrolling through his cellphone. "So what was your takeaway from our little seance?"

"I wish I could have taken notes."

"They said nothing we don't already know."

"I was surprised when you mentioned the contractor."

"That was a gamble and I'm not convinced we should have been so specific about the foreign connection. But anyway. So we should go to see your buddy at the Only Café. See how he reacts to us. Or if he's even there. If he's their guy, which would be a long shot, they would tell him about the rumours. Man, that would be something. But you know what?"

"What?"

"I'm more worried about our people than I am about them."

"Our people?"

"Suzanne. Hughes. Savage."

"Really? Why?"

Nader sighed and dropped a hand lightly on Cyril's shoulder. "You'll see."

∿

Aggie was effusive. *She hugged him.* "Your father would have been so proud."

"Do you really think so?"

"Believe it. This calls for a toast. Get the Grey Goose out of the freezer."

He poured generously. His mother asked, "Shall we sit in the living room?"

"No. It's only for six months. I think we're still at the kitchen table stage."

"There was never any doubt in my mind," she declared. "You've got your father's brains and your granddad's gumption. I can't wait to tell Grandpa Lynch."

Cyril laughed. "Two things he always said he didn't trust, lawyers and reporters."

"Oh, come on," she said. "He always makes exceptions when he knows people."

"It isn't really such a big deal."

"Here and now, it is a big deal. Let's just celebrate the moment. Top me up."

He stood, retrieved the vodka bottle. "Okay. But easy on the pressure. Please?"

"There's nothing wrong with pressure," Aggie said. "Pressure leads to progress, your grandpa always said."

∼

"When you're free we'll meet in Savage's office," Suzanne said the next morning. "Take a few minutes and think about what we're going to say."

"Who's going to be there?" Nader asked.

"You, me, Cyril, the lawyer . . ."

"What lawyer?"

"Someone from Ottawa. I don't know her. I think she must be new."

Nader nodded.

"You okay, Nader?" Suzanne asked.

"Why wouldn't I be?" He was staring at his BlackBerry, scrolling. "I hate when you go quiet."

He laughed and looked up at her. "Just tell me when."

∼

The presence of the unfamiliar lawyer seemed to change the chemistry among them. Cyril felt a disturbing coolness from Savage in particular.

"Okay. Suzanne," Savage said, "why don't you just walk us through what you've got."

His tone suggested that he was as unconnected to the story as the lawyer. When Suzanne spoke it was as if she was briefing skeptical outsiders. Cyril made a mental note: *the meeting with the spies was friendlier.*

The lawyer's name was Martha and Cyril couldn't help feeling a certain comfort from the fact that she was attractive and smiled a lot.

"So here's the situation," Suzanne said. "We have reason to believe the national security service has contracted out part of a highly sensitive surveillance operation here in Toronto to a foreign operative with a murky history, or that foreign spies are working here without the knowledge of our government, monitoring our mosques. Whatever the case, there are aspects of the surveillance that appear to be borderline instigation."

"Fascinating," Martha said. "Now when you say 'instigation' . . ."

"Yes," Suzanne said. "Nader?"

"Instigation is a good word," Nader said. "It's no secret that extremists are instigating, on the Internet, in the mosques. I think the security folks and the smart people in the community are on top of that. But there's also instigation by our security apparatus . . ."

"Apparatus?" The lawyer frowned.

"Whatever. Mounties. CSIS. Maybe foreigners. To flush out radical tendencies by inflaming them. It's possible that Israel is involved. Here. With or without our say so."

"Hmm," Martha said and made a note.

Nader hesitated until she looked up again. "I'm talking to a lot of young people who see the uprising in Syria as something larger than a rebellion against Assad," he said. "It could ultimately be an attempt to redraw the map of the region to create a new national entity that will become a kind of homeland for people with a shared vision of ethnic and doctrinal purity in a world that has marginalized and humiliated them . . ."

"We've heard all that before," said Savage. "Can you really blame Israel for getting antsy?"

"Of course not," Nader said. "But back to our story—a lot of young Muslims are drawn to what they see as a historical correction . . ."

"Correction of what?" said Savage.

"Well, from their point of view, a hundred years of cultural and economic stagnation."

"What about *your* point of view?" Savage asked.

"I hardly think that's relevant."

"Let's be realistic," Savage said.

Nader stood. "Maybe I should . . ."

Suzanne grabbed his hand. "Sit," she said. He sat.

"You were going to meet with the security people," Savage said.

"We had a briefing," Suzanne said.

"What did they have to say about this supposed infiltration?"

"Well, nothing specific, one way or the other. You wouldn't expect them to . . ."

"I'm hearing denial here, guys."

"I wouldn't go that far," Suzanne said. "Denial by those guys would be confirmation as far as I'm concerned."

"Why don't you just tell me what they said," Doc insisted.

"Look," Suzanne said. "The big political picture is exactly as Nader has described it. We know there's a trickle of people heading for Syria and Iraq. We can safely predict that many of them will die over there or grow disillusioned and come home sadder and wiser than when they went away. Nader, continue."

"Then there are the ones who will come back radicalized and hardened by their experiences. It's unlikely there'll be very many like that but it only takes one or two. And there is real concern in the community that there will be some kind of pre-emptive action by the government to suppress these jihadist impulses and that it will include harassment and detention. And that the perceived bullying will turn a lot of ordinary people into radicals."

Martha smiled. "Harassment? That's pretty strong. We have the Charter."

"Well," said Nader. "Spies and provocateurs don't always respect Charter rights. And we have a government that isn't above creating laws that disrespect the Charter . . ."

"Which is why we have the courts, to defend the Charter," Martha said.

"Politics and paranoia aside," said Savage. "You're really saying that either our security service or someone else has embedded an Israeli spook in a highly sensitive security operation and it's potentially provocative. That's our story, right? What can you tell us about this person."

"Not much yet," Nader said. "We don't have a name. His specialty is counter-terrorism operations. He cut his teeth in Lebanon. Speaks

Arabic. Also French and English. We have a lead on someone who might know him. Who might even *be* him. We're pursuing that just now."

"Okay," Savage said. "But who's going to go on TV and talk about this?"

"It's a problem," Nader said. "In the current climate even the usual public voices are keeping it low-key. Nobody wants to get on the security service radar."

"Yes," said Savage. "And it's a real fucking problem for us. How do you tell a story if there's no proof of anything and nobody who will talk? And on top of that you have what sounds to me like an official denial."

Nader shrugged. Suzanne sighed deeply and shook her head. "Come on, Doc."

Martha spoke. "From a legal perspective this is all premature, though I appreciate the early involvement." She stood. "I have a plane to catch. Doc? Always a joy."

Savage came from behind his desk, seized both her hands, kissed both cheeks. "Martha, next time perhaps a drink?"

"Love to," she said. "Keep me posted. I want to be in on this at every stage."

∽

"She wants to be in on this at every stage. That's a laugh." Nader laughed.

"What are you talking about?" Cyril said. "I thought you were great. And Suzanne, too, the way she laid it out. Savage was just being the devil's advocate."

"I hope you're right," said Nader.

"By the way," said Cyril. "An old friend wants to have a party to celebrate my new job. Why don't you come with me?"

"I don't know, man. I don't think . . ."

"Come on. We need a break. You can be my designated driver."

"Driver? You've got wheels now?"

"Wait until you see."

Nader sighed, then smiled: "Okay. You've talked me into it."

~

Nader told Cyril he'd meet him outside the St. George subway station. It was a clear night with a half-full moon. For the first time since he'd inherited the Mustang Cyril felt that it belonged to him, and that he belonged behind the wheel.

"Well now," Nader said as he buckled up and inspected the car's interior. "Where'd you find this?"

"It belonged to my father. It's been in storage for the past five years. He bought it on a whim . . . it's a 1975."

"Sweet."

"I thought of selling it but I'm getting attached to it."

"Ah, you don't want to part with this, man. This is you. Now who's your friend? What should I expect?"

"Leo. I've known him since kindergarten. He's an ironworker, one of those guys who works in high places. He earns a pile but lives low-key. Real modest."

~

Leo and three others were sitting in the living room when Cyril and Nader arrived. Introductions were exchanged. Cyril promptly forgot the names of the other guests, except for the girl, Megan, who was memorably pretty and seemed to be about nineteen.

He presented Nader as one of the network's investigative stars. Nader shrugged and laughed. "Cyril has a lot to learn," he said.

"Megan's also a journalist," said Leo.

Megan said. "I work at *Metro*, okay? If you want to call that journalism."

It was a tabloid daily giveaway distributed mostly at subway stations. "Everybody has to start somewhere," Nader said.

"So where did you start?" she asked.

"U of T," said Nader. "The *Varsity* . . ."

"I didn't know you went to U of T," Cyril interjected.

"Then a chase job at *Canada AM*. That one nearly finished me. Showing up for work at four in the morning. Been where I am the past five years, with a year off to study Arabic. Just back."

Megan laughed. "Very cool."

Cyril wandered to the kitchen where there were many bottles of wine arrayed with plastic glasses on the countertop. He opened the refrigerator, which was packed with beer. On the table there were plastic-wrapped trays of sandwiches. He felt his cheer disintegrating. Leo had planned a celebration party but nobody was coming. He'd planned to drink only wine, to pace himself for what he expected to be a long and lively evening. Pointless. He poured a stiff Scotch from the bottle he'd brought with him. Then he returned to the brightly lit living room.

"There you are," said Leo. "You missed my little announcement."

"Oh?"

"You've inspired and motivated me." He raised a glass. "Here's to my buddy Cyril. And here's to me."

Cyril raised his glass, then sipped. "What are you talking about?"

"I'm hanging up the old hard hat," Leo said. "Been accepted at U of T. Finally going to finish that degree I started six years ago, but quit when I discovered I could make more money in construction than my tenured profs were earning for boring me to death. Anyway, I'm going to take another crack at the books, if it isn't too late."

"What field?" Nader asked.

"Economics. What did you take?"

"History," said Nader. "Been thinking of going back for my master's."

"Cool," said Leo.

Cyril toasted Leo, gulped his drink and drifted back into the kitchen and poured another. Off the kitchen Leo had a small desk and a chair in an alcove. Cyril sat, thinking that if he hadn't been impulsive Gloria would be here right now—a bright spot in a deadly scene. He considered texting. Or even calling. Then he felt an unspecific wave of anger. Gulped his second drink. To avoid pouring a third he went into the bathroom, locked the door, and sat on the edge of the bathtub studying his hands.

"Shit," he said out loud.

Eventually he became aware of the increased frequency of door-knob turns and rattles. Finally a voice. "Somebody dying in there?"

"Yeah, yeah. Just a sec," he called back. Stood, flushed, ran the tap briefly and then unlocked the door. There were three people waiting outside in the hallway.

"You okay, man?" one of them asked. Cyril didn't recognize him.

"Yeah. Good."

The apartment was now packed with people and lit only by wavering candles and a stove light in the kitchen. There was a din of voices, loud music playing in the living room.

Okay, he thought. Went into the kitchen and poured a glass of wine.

In the living room, Leo, Neil and Scott were in a corner working on a joint. Leo was talking through his teeth, eyes pinched shut. Cyril demurred when Leo waved the joint in his direction. He wondered if Nader was still there.

He found him sitting on the side of Leo's bed, deep in conversation with the reporter, Megan.

"Sorry," he said, and began backing out of the room.

"No, no, no," said Nader. "We were wondering where you got to."

"I was just telling Nader that I've applied for an internship at the *Star*," Megan said. "He tells me you started as an intern recently."

He sat. "I lucked out," he said. "Now I get to work with this guy."

"I'm hoping for something like that," she said. "My goal is to work on their jihad project."

"Their what?" Cyril asked.

"I probably shouldn't have mentioned that," she said, flustered. "But this is off the record, right?"

"Of course," said Nader. "So what's the jihad project?"

"You know. Young people getting recruited . . . but I shouldn't say any more."

"No," said Nader. "Probably you shouldn't."

∾

"So, what do we make of that?" Cyril asked.

Nader was driving. It was just after midnight. The party was in full swing when they'd made their excuses and left. "Work day tomorrow," Cyril had explained. Hardly anybody heard and only Megan seemed chagrined.

"Make of what?"

"The *Star* working on our story."

"I'd be very surprised if they were working on *our* story. Probably another newspaper feature about homegrown radicals. Old story, been done. Being refreshed now by the Syria thing. I doubt if they have a news hook."

"Like we do . . ."

"Like we hope we do."

"I feel pretty confident."

"Good."

Cyril lapsed into a silence.

"I could fall in love with this vehicle," Nader said. "If you were serious about selling it I hope you'd talk to me first."

"Absolutely."

At a red light Nader said, "This Megan. We should keep in touch. I have a hunch she'll get that internship. She gave me her number. She said she really wants to be in television. She certainly has the look. In any case, it would be nice to know what they're getting up to at the *Star*."

"I think she was kind of taken by you, Nader. You two looked good on a bed."

"Nah. She's young and ambitious. I think you should take the initiative. You have more in common."

"What does that mean?"

"Work-wise. You're just past the internship stage. I think she'd be more comfortable talking to you. I'm older, and with me she was just asking questions. And of course you have the car."

"How old are you, Nader?"

"Getting up there. Twenty-eight going on twenty-nine."

"Jeez."

"Who knows where it could go, you and Megan."

"Nah. I'm still a bit shell-shocked by my last relationship."

"That's another plus. You need some kind of transitional diversion."

"Maybe. Did you find her attractive?"

"Very."

"Okay. So *you* should go for it."

"Nope. I'm saving myself for a nice Muslim virgin. Or seventy-two."

"All those virgins in paradise?"

"Sure hope so. Very few left in this world."

He pulled over outside the St. George subway. "I'm going to leave you here. You'll be okay the rest of the way?"

"Sure. It's just a few blocks. But are you sure you're okay, Nader?"

He laughed. "You're starting to sound like Suzanne. This 'are-you-okay' business."

"I hear you. But what do you really think?"

"About virgins?"

"Come on."

"Our story? I think we've got the goods. If by a bizarre coincidence this guy you met at the café is the security contractor, that's major. But I also think our story will never see the light of day."

"What the fuck, where's that coming from?"

"I'm tired, Cyril. Can we talk about this another time?"

"Yeah, sure. But, Jesus."

"Come on. It's just a story, man. You'll get used to it. For every one that goes on television there are a dozen weeded out for a hundred reasons."

"Not this one, buddy. This one's going to fly."

"I hope you're right. I really do."

He reached across and squeezed Cyril's hand. "You're good people." And then he was gone into the darkness.

∽

Cyril woke to a memory. He'd met Gloria at one of Leo's parties. She'd arrived as someone else's date. It was a noisy party, a volatile mix of students and construction workers. The music was cranked. Retro heavy metal stuff. Leo loved his metal. AC/DC. Iron Maiden. Cyril could barely make out what Gloria was telling him. Something about her dad. He led her away from the crowd and she hesitated when she saw that he was taking her into a bedroom. But he'd grabbed the chair from Leo's desk, flipped it around and sat, arms folded on the back, which was like a fence between them. She'd been touched by this reassuring gesture and not long afterwards, she emailed. *Would love to pick up where we left off. Coffee sometime?*

They'd been talking about fathers and absences and how even amicable absences can become estrangements as people change, and how absences that are initially painful evolve into a certain kind of freedom. Liberation from responsibility, was how she put it.

Gloria's dad had been out of her life since she was four or five. He'd been a freelance magazine writer, a name that everybody knew. Which was what kept him alive for her until one day she realized that he was just another presence in a crowd of memories. She was in law school when he died unexpectedly after a game of tennis. At his memorial everyone had remarked about how fit he'd been.

He noticed his BlackBerry blinking and hoped it might be Gloria. But it was a low battery warning. He attached the charger, then after just a hesitation, he typed: *Just in case it matters, my feelings haven't changed*. He paused before sending it, realizing that it was three-twenty-five in the morning. What the hell. Send.

He felt anxious then, remembering the Bald-Headed Bastard, the intimacy between them as they'd jogged past him in the park.

For distraction he removed one of his father's journals from the row of twenty-two he'd neatly shelved. 2001. He turned to September 11. His father had written at the bottom of the page, after obscure jottings about his day of lawyering: *WTC, Pentagon . . . now it is a war.*

He put the journal back in its proper place, turned off his bedroom light. When he turned over to lie on his side, he saw that the BlackBerry was blinking again, a tiny red eye winking at him.

The message was from Gloria: *It matters.*

～

Hughes stood, hands braced on his desk. He looked weary, as if he'd been there all night. "Got time for a coffee? I'm desperate for one."

"Sure," Cyril said. He noticed the two Arabic diaries in the clutter. "I see you've been reading the journals."

"Yes. I want to talk about that."

Walking to the elevator Hughes asked: "What did *you* make of the meeting with Savage and the lawyer."

"Doc doesn't seem as interested as he was in what we're doing."

Hughes laughed. "You'll learn the pattern. Initial enthusiasm becomes ambivalence that has very little to do with the story. It's just positioning. You shouldn't let it bother you."

"Positioning for what?"

"For cutting the project loose if things don't pan out or horning in on the glory if it turns into something big. Leadership 101."

They found a table. Hughes was quiet for a moment, then he said, "I gather you didn't know your father very well."

"I didn't know him at all."

"Too bad. He'd have had a fascinating tale to tell if he'd ever decided to write it down."

"So you've read both journals?"

"As best I could. I got the gist, which I suspect was all we were supposed to get."

"So, there's nothing in them?"

"Well, nothing definitive. But there's enough to place him in or near events and people that we know about and that's what's intriguing and frustrating. There's just enough to make you want a whole lot more. Like the smell of food to a hungry person. Where he begins writing he's in a little village I'm familiar with. Kfar Matta, the one I mentioned in the Chouf Mountains. He's a Christian and, from other clues, it's clear that he was close to senior people in the Phalangist forces."

"So?"

"Kfar Matta is a Druze village. The Druze were at war with the Phalangists in '83. So what was your dad doing among the Druze? Your old man somehow manages to get a ride out of the Chouf with the Israelis and he eventually ends up at the marine base, south of Beirut. How does all that come together?"

Cyril shrugged.

"One possibility is that he had some kind of special connection with the IDF. When we go back to my office I want to show you something interesting I found in the 1983 diary. Your father led a charmed life. He left the Chouf just before a bloodbath. He left the Marine base just days before the terrorist attack that killed hundreds of them."

"I guess the charm expired in 2007."

"It looks that way."

~

The intriguing item in the 1983 diary was a faded note that had been taped to a page.

"Do you mind if I take this out?" Hughes asked.

"Go ahead."

Hughes carefully removed the note and passed it to Cyril. "It's in Hebrew. Did your father know Hebrew?"

"I have no idea. What is this?"

"I got a friend to translate for me—it basically authorizes the holder to pass through an Israeli checkpoint on September eighteenth, 1982."

"Okay."

"That was the day the world found out what had been going on in Sabra and Shatila on the sixteenth and seventeenth. A horrific massacre of civilians. Maybe two thousand. Mostly women, kids, old people. The note is signed 'Charon.' That's all. No indication whether it's a first name or a last name. No indication of military rank. Just 'Charon.' First I thought it was 'Sharon,' who was Israeli minister of defense at the time and my heart stopped. Now that would be a story. But, alas."

"But who's Charon?"

"Right—who indeed, and why was your father going into the camps on that particular day? I doubt if we'll ever know, unless, of course, we find this Charon. Which is unlikely."

"Do you know who he was?"

"Only what I was able to find out from an old IDF intelligence contact. Apparently it was a code name for somebody in the very dark side of Israeli counter-terrorism operations. It might have been more than one person. He or they specialized in bombings. Car bombs, buildings, booby traps of all kinds. There was a rumour that Charon might have had something to do with murdering Elie Hobeika."

"Hobeika."

"Yes. By the way, I couldn't find any direct reference to Hobeika in either of the journals. But my Arabic is pretty rusty. You might want to send them out for a professional translation." Hughes picked up the two diaries and passed them across the desk. "On the other hand, you might just want to put them back on the shelf and leave them there. Sometimes a secret is an act of kindness."

"What about this note?"

"Keep it some place safe. It might become important to our story."

Cyril folded the note and placed it in his wallet.

32.

He still had a couple of hours to kill before meeting Nader at the Only Café. He opened his text messages and stared at the two inscrutable words: *It matters*. How to interpret *that*. He scrolled back. His message couldn't have been more clear. *Just in case it matters, my feelings haven't changed.*

He thought of calling her but then decided to let it lie for now. Don't risk distraction before what could be a crucially important visit. The strategy was Nader's. He would attend Friday prayers at the Danforth mosque, then drop by the Only Café coffee bar for a social chat with Cyril. If Ari happened to be there, they'd leave it up to him to come to them.

The place had a back entrance, through a laneway patio. The day was overcast and cool and the patio was deserted. Inside was quiet, two regulars sipping an early beer; young coffee drinkers peering at their laptops. Cyril ordered an Americano and found a seat near the front windows. Soon he saw a trickle of men in shalwar kameez hurrying back to their shops and offices and homes. By leaning close to the glass he could see Ari in his usual place, on a bench, ankle over knee, puffing on a cigarette, a coffee mug beside him on a window ledge. A large, sleepy middle-aged man with nothing on his mind but his retirement savings.

The sidewalk became busier, a throng on both sides of the street, individuals and small groups, talking, listening, hands clasped behind them or hidden in the folds of clothing. A thin, swarthy young man in a track suit, wearing a boxy ball cap, paused near where Ari sat, lit a cigarette. Was that a nod, an acknowledgement from Ari? A secret sign? Would Cyril even have noticed if he hadn't harboured so many troubling suspicions? A reminder: control the imagination; hold all speculation up to honest scrutiny. He produced his notebook, started writing down the thought.

"Making notes for the novel?" It was Nader, smiling. "How's your coffee. Want a refill?"

He put the little notebook in his backpack. "Just had a thought about jumping to conclusions," he said.

"Excellent thought. I'm getting a coffee. Why don't we sit outside, at that little table? I'll find you there."

He picked up a *Metro* tabloid, walked out scanning the front page, was startled to see a byline: *Megan Spencer.* A story about urban transit problems with a nice tight lead. He sat, then remembered Ari. Stole a glance in his direction but he wasn't there.

"Your man is inside now," Nader said, setting down two mugs. "He's standing at the bar talking to some young guy. Do you think he saw you?"

"I don't know," Cyril said. "I was reading this." He held up the paper. "Is this the same Megan?"

"Ah. The very one. She mentioned she was doing a transit piece."

"Have you seen her since?"

"Yes."

"Aha."

"Aha yourself."

"She writes well."

"She's very bright for nineteen."

Cyril set the paper aside. "Nineteen is the new twenty-nine."

Then he realized that Ari was on the sidewalk and that he'd noticed them. He waved and smiled. Ari approached.

"We meet again."

"Yes. I forgot you're usually here on Friday afternoons. This is my friend Nader Hashem."

Nader stood, extended a hand. Ari grasped it. "Hashem?"

"Yes, and you're?"

"Just call me Ari. So Hashem . . ."

"Sometimes when the spirit moves me I go to Friday prayers. The spirit spoke today so Cyril and I decided to hook up here afterwards. Funky little place, isn't it?"

"Can I get you a coffee?" Cyril asked. Ari looked doubtful, checked his watch.

"I think not," he said. "I just had one." But he sat down.

"So Nader. Iran, I'm guessing," Ari said.

"Good guess."

"And you were born in . . ."

"Toronto. A fairly common story. Family found itself on the wrong side of the revolution in '79. Bailed. Got here somehow. And you?"

"Born in Montreal. Family got fired up by the '67 war. Moved to a kibbutz in what I quickly learned to call Judea. I'm sure you learned your politics the way I did."

"No better cure for politics than to hear your parents arguing."

"For sure."

"I keep reminding myself of that when I hear people getting worried about radicalization."

"Of course radicalization doesn't originate in the home, does it? Mostly the media, the Internet, other influences."

"Totally."

"And what do you work at, Nader?"

"I work with this guy. Television."

"Interesting. I apologize but I rarely watch."

"No apology necessary. And you?"

"A gentleman of leisure. A bit of import-export. Mostly living off my savings and a pension from the Zionist entity." He smiled.

"Import-export?"

He lit a cigarette, blew the smoke toward the passing traffic. "Olive oil. Footwear."

Nader nodded, sipped his coffee.

"Boring stuff. I could probably make a lot of money on more interesting things if I cared about money. But I lead a simple life. Plus I've had all the excitement I can handle, as Cyril will explain. Won't you, Cyril."

"To be truthful, I don't really know much I could tell."

"I keep confusing you with your dad. A terrible loss."

Nader said, "You knew Cyril's dad?"

"Briefly, yes. We were only getting to know each other when he went out east. But given our age and where we came from, there was a lot we could assume without much explanation. This isn't uncommon among people like me and Pierre."

Nader said, "Maybe that was why I tuned out so much at home—nobody bothered filling in the background."

"But you're obviously observant? In general, but also religious. Right? But I'm surprised, for a Shia to be going over there? I'd have thought the Imam Ali mosque . . ."

Nader chuckled. "Impressive. Dad was secular. My mom's people followed the Sunni tradition."

"Religion fascinates me, all of them. Obviously you too."

"I wouldn't go that far. Maybe religion is just my way of firming up an identity that I rejected before I understood it."

"So true. So many of the problems in your community today, with the young people, started exactly there. Rejecting values, identity, then trying to reclaim something more meaningful than the bullshit that passes for youth culture nowadays. If you don't mind me saying so."

"Partly true," Nader said. "Actually I don't have a problem with secular culture. I hope I didn't give that impression."

"No. I was just rambling. I spend too much time by myself, thinking and worrying. I should spend more time among young people and less time reading about the misfits. Maybe it's why I'm sitting here."

"Well, I'm glad you are," said Nader. "So you used to have a government job in Israel?"

"Everybody in Israel works for the government, one way or another. But yes, I was a career soldier."

"Interesting time to be a soldier."

"Yes. My first excitement was in Lebanon in '78. You wouldn't have heard of it. Operation Litani. That was the thing about your dad, Cyril—so long after the fact, we could talk about things we remembered, sometimes controversial things, but with the perspective that comes with growing older. Hardly a day goes by when I don't think about how I'd love to talk to Pierre about what we're seeing now. Syria. Iraq."

"So what's your take?"

"I only know what you guys know, maybe less. I'm just following the news from a great distance. And not even much of that because, all due respect, I don't really trust the news. I guess all old soldiers feel that way, more or less."

"So you're a soldier for decades. You must have got pretty high up."

"Unfortunately not. I was on the intelligence side of things where promotions don't happen very often. Not so intelligent on my part? But you know the old cliché about military intelligence."

"Intelligence . . ."

"Don't go jumping to conclusions. Do I look like James Bond?" He laughed, produced the pack of cigarettes again. Shook one out, studied it.

"No. My work was pretty much like yours as journalists. Trying to find things out. Writing reports. Analyzing what other people find out. The big difference, you guys figure out what happened after the fact. My job was finding out what *might* happen so other people could prevent things or manage consequences. I wish it had been half as exciting as the movies make it seem. I'd be rich now. Or dead."

"But don't you miss the involvement?" Nader said.

"Honestly? Some days absolutely. The common cause. The game

aspect. But it's thankless work. Nobody knows about what doesn't happen so nobody gets credit. That's the way it was in my time, anyway. No glamour, no rewards."

"I never thought of it that way," Nader said.

"These days," Ari said, "politicians and television experts make hay from terrorism and security. A fucking joke, excuse my French. All that politicking and publicity is theatre at best. At worst, counter-productive. Like Crocodile Dundee and his big knife. I always laugh at that scene. You don't ever want the other guy to know about your knife until he feels it. How I figure it, anyway. Maybe I'm wrong. But it's a fact—security consists of negative outcomes. Fuck-all happen-ing, or as an old mate of mine used to say, 'fuck-nothing' happening."

He butted his cigarette in an ashtray. "I'm talking way too much. The peril of spending too much time alone. I must go now."

He stood, shook hands with each in turn. "Thanks for indulging an old soldier." He seemed to shuffle as he walked away.

Nader was smiling. "Look at his back and shoulders. The hips. He's built like a weightlifter. And what he said about the knife. Who knew?"

"I can see him and my father."

"Way, way too likeable."

∾

Maybe if Cyril's father had died the way that normal people die, withering with age or some slow affliction, or struck down by some unanticipated stroke of fate, he'd have had a better understanding of death as a particular event as opposed to the continuation of an absence that he'd long ago accepted as a tolerable condition of his life. Cyril had never seen a corpse, let alone his father's. Maybe if he'd seen his father's lifeless body that would probably have done it: the primeval shock of seeing someone who had recently been vigorous, mysterious, productive, now emptied out of thought and memory and possibility—pale and cold as marble.

There had been no hard *evidence*. Only words: *There's been an accident on the boat. Your father is missing. We must be prepared for the worst.* But for Cyril there could be nothing worse than the gnawing feeling in his gut, the enormous hole in everything after Pierre's dramatic exit from his son's life on May 26, 2000. Nothing could be worse than that, the cold dark endless autumn where there should have been a summer.

And then one afternoon—could it only have been months ago? It felt like years, the final confirmation that his father was deceased. *Deceased? You mean dead? Yes.* A bone and a bracelet offered as proof.

~

That night, after his and Nader's meeting at the Only Café, he told his mother, "I've been talking to this guy Ari."

"Ari?"

"The guy Dad met at this little bar in the east end."

"He's Lebanese?"

"No. Israeli."

"I can't imagine what there'd be to talk about with him."

"I believe he thinks Dad committed suicide. He knows that he was having trouble at work, that he had cancer . . ."

"Things I never knew."

"And he mentioned something strange, about a marriage problem."

"First I've heard of it."

"It was the one thing that rang false . . . like he was making it up."

"Or maybe mixing your father up with someone else he knows. It's been five years, after all."

"Could be."

"Mother of God. If there was one thing solid in his life, it was that marriage, it pains me to say."

"Okay, though. Here's the thing: what was he doing vacationing on the boat with Lois here? What was that all about?"

"It had something to do with work. At least that's what Lois told me at the time. He was having trouble at work. And—okay, I don't want this to get around—she said that he was going to have to take the fall for some big scandal in the company. That the lawyer, Ethan Kennedy, the one we met, was behind it somehow."

"Ethan?"

"You could ask her. And Cyril—I hope you don't think this is me butting in—I really think you should try harder to be nice to Lois and especially to little Peter."

"Let's have a drink, Ma. What'll it be?"

"Let's go for the stuff underneath the sink."

~

"Lois, it's me. Cyril."

"How are you? How is the car? You're loving it, I bet."

"Yes. It's transforming my image. I'm a totally different person."

"I hope not. I kind of like you the way you are."

"I wanted to ask about the lawyer, Ethan."

"Ethan Kennedy."

"What do you make of him?"

"He and Pierre were good friends. He's always been helpful with the legal stuff. I think he knows more than he's prepared to talk about and he doesn't want to tell me everything he knows."

"My mom says Dad was about to quit or to be fired and that this Ethan was somehow involved."

"It was more complicated than that. Let's just say that Pierre was prepared to sacrifice his job to help the company through a controversy."

"What kind of a controversy?"

"You can look it up yourself. Some people were killed during a strike in Indonesia and Pierre was the person in the hot seat. He did nothing wrong. This was all corporate politics. Okay?"

"Where did it happen?"

"I don't remember all the details. It's been a while. Google 'Puncak.' And 'New Guinea.'"

"Puncak?"

"P-U-N-C-A-K. And aren't *you* turning into the journalist?"

"Okay. Let me ask this then. Were you and Dad having . . . marriage difficulties?"

"Where did you hear that?"

"From someone who probably doesn't know what he was talking about."

"And who . . . ?"

"It just seems strange. You're pregnant in the big hot city. And he's off on a boat somewhere. I mean, you couldn't have been too thrilled with that?"

"He went out there for just a few days. A week, max. Then he was coming home. He was on the phone every few hours. He was over the moon that I was expecting. Does that sound like marriage trouble to you?"

"Sure doesn't. I gotta run, I'm at work. Someone's walking toward my desk. Talk later."

∽

Hughes grabbed a chair and wheeled it into Cyril's cubicle, sat, leaned his elbows on the desk, picked up a sheet of paper, looked at it, dropped it. "You're well?"

"What's up?"

"Well, you're about to get a lesson in the reality of institutional journalism."

"Which means?"

"Which means our project is off."

"Off?"

"Killed."

"Dead?"

"Something like that. I have no doubt that we are onto a situation that's real and important so there's always the chance that something will break and it'll be back on the agenda. But for now we'll have to find something else for you to do."

Cyril felt nothing. Perhaps it was shock or, maybe, at some deep level he had expected this.

"You don't have to worry. You're on contract now. There will be other stories." He stood to leave.

"Who killed it?"

Hughes paused. "Savage, under pressure from legal. They don't kill stories. But they present you with certain realities that leave you hanging out there if anything goes wrong. Not many managers like to be in that position and I don't blame them. So, we move on."

"And Suzanne . . . ?"

"Think 'rock' and 'hard place.' If legal is the hard place, Suzanne is the rock. Right about now I expect Savage is wishing he'd picked another line of work."

He walked away laughing without humour. *Hah*. *Hah*. *Hah*.

~

Cyril called Nader's cell, let it ring until he heard the voicemail prompt.

"I guess you heard. Call me."

~

He sat for maybe five minutes, mind stumbling from thought to thought. If it's a real story and we're certain that it's true, why can't we just tell it? Let the other side try to prove it isn't true. If Ari is who Suzanne and Nader suspect he is, a spy who is also a provocateur, shouldn't people know? Shouldn't the people he works for know about his background, what he's up to? Who *does* he work for? What do I do next?

He opened up his browser, looked up the number for Draycor's head office, made a note of it. He studied the number for what felt like a long time. A phone number his father would have known by heart because it was the most important telephone number in his life. He dialled.

"Could I have Ethan Kennedy's office, please?"

He listened to the ring, the answer. He asked to speak to Mr. Kennedy.

"Who's calling, please?"

"Tell him Cyril Cormier."

Kennedy picked up. "Cyril, yes. I remember, from . . . our meeting about estate matters. What can I do for you?"

"I want to explore his request about the . . . memorial."

Silence.

"You knew him. You think that he was serious about that?"

"I wouldn't have an opinion one way or another. The document reflects his wishes at the time. You can draw your own conclusions."

"When you and he prepared the document, did he give you any idea who this person Ari is and what was their connection?"

"I didn't ask."

"I see. Well, that was the reason for my call."

"I'm sorry I can't be more helpful."

"No problem. Oh. One other thing. Lois, his widow, mentioned that Dad was about to leave the company. What can you tell me about that?"

Silence.

"That he was about to quit . . . or that he might be fired," Cyril said.

"There was no thought of him being fired. I can tell you that much. Yes, there was one brief conversation about . . . an amicable separation. It was discussed briefly and for the first time on the day he . . . on the day before he died."

"So he wasn't going to be fired? And why was he supposed to take the fall for that incident in Indonesia?"

"Cyril. Look. I'm going to have to cut this short. But I'll tell you this much. Your dad and I were friends. I don't think that it's a secret anymore that there were things happening in his life that had nothing to do with his work. Stressful things that . . ."

"Like?"

"Like his health, for one."

"Okay. What else?"

Silence.

"What about his early life in Lebanon? Did he talk to you about that?"

"Cyril, listen. Things happen in a life. We move on, try to forget them and, gradually, they become kind of abstract. But now and then they flare up again. You know what I mean?"

"I suppose."

"I'm not basing this on anything he told me. But I found something on his desk when I was removing files and his personal effects. I kept it because I didn't see its relevance to either the company or the family. It was just a business card but . . ."

"A business card for what?"

"A law enforcement outfit you probably know about. INSET."

"I've heard of it."

"An Inspector Nicholson. The name rang a bell—it was on the list of people he wanted to attend that memorial, the so-called roast. I'll fax it to you if you'll give me a number. It'll be up to you what you do about it—if anything. And I'll ask you not to disclose where you got it. Understood?"

"Yes, thanks."

"I understand your need to know things. But it's been a long time now. Your dad died in a terrible accident. It was a terrible loss. But you have a lot of life in front of you, a future to be concerned about. Sometimes mucking around in the past is not a good idea."

"I hear you. But just one more thing: what do you know about the accident?"

Silence.

Then Kennedy said, "A propane tank blew up. It happens."

"I see."

"You never heard that?"

"Maybe I just blocked it out of my mind."

"Be well, Cyril. If there's ever anything I can do, just let me know. Okay?"

"Will do."

∾

Nader was surprisingly relaxed, leaning on top of the padded privacy barrier beside Cyril's desk.

"I guess you haven't heard," Cyril said.

"Heard what?"

"They killed our story."

"Correction. *They* don't want *us* to *tell* our story. Nobody can kill a story, Cyril. Remember that."

"Is there a difference?"

"A big difference. Unless we find out that our story was never a story in the first place. I'm still on it, whether they want to tell it or not."

"Fair enough."

"Are you with me on this?"

Cyril stood. "I'm with you."

They shook hands.

"So what's this handshaking?" Suzanne was standing behind them, hands on hips. "Never mind. Savage's in fifteen minutes." She walked back toward her office.

∾

Of all the people in the room, Cyril, Nader, Hughes, Suzanne and Savage, it was the boss who seemed most ill at ease. "This is never an easy call . . ."

"Never mind that," Suzanne snapped. "Whose call is it? Really."

Savage sat up. "My call. Okay?"

"It's a chickenshit call, Doc, and you know it."

"Mind your fucking manners, Suzanne. Remember who you're talking . . ."

"Let's cut the hierarchical horseshit, Doc, and talk like the colleagues I thought we were."

"Colleagues don't start conversations by hurling insults."

"Okay. I take it back. Honestly. Let's start all over again. You talk."

"Shut the door."

She did, then sat on the arm of a chair. She reminded Cyril of a large cat, crouched to pounce.

"Hughes," Doc said, "you tell me the story we'd put on TV if your fairy godmother delivered all the goods."

Suzanne rolled her eyes. Hughes laughed. "Oh, I don't think it would take a fairy. It would only require a couple of credible flesh-and-blood sources and maybe a document of some kind."

"Just tell the story . . ."

"Our government security establishment has turned to a foreign intelligence agency to recruit a specialist to manage the infiltration of the local Muslim community. We have reason to believe that he and his agents are acting as provocateurs, either deliberately or inadvertently doing more harm than good."

"So who *is* this spook?"

"We think we know but we can't say yet. I think we can do the story without naming names."

"I disagree. But let's just say it really is this dude you guys say hangs out in a bar not far from a downtown mosque. Correct me if I'm wrong. He's a Canadian citizen, right? Okay, he worked for IDF intelligence, maybe on the dark side. Maybe the very darkest. But he's one of us, folks. Probably working for *our* government. You say he's an instigator? I say that's subjective and impossible to prove. At worst it's paranoid. Even if we had his contract in our hands, so what? Nader, you're being very quiet."

"Only because I see your point."

All eyes turned to Nader.

"Is that it?" Savage said with a laugh.

"No," Nader said. "But do you really want my perspective?"

"Of course."

"Okay. There's a war. Young people everywhere are interested in the drama. Some of them are turned on by the cause. Or a lot of different causes. We call them radicals, Islamists, terrorists. Personally? I call them idiots, most of them. They're dangerous. Mostly to themselves. Anyone who stirs them up or encourages them is dangerous to all of us." Nader stood then. "If I can be excused, I have a meeting I can't miss."

"Story-related?" Doc asked.

"Maybe. If there is a story, right?"

At the door, Nader said: "For the record, I believe our angle is a story, whether we tell it or not."

"Wait," Doc said. "What is *your* angle, in a nutshell."

"My angle? Certain people are exploiting the idiots to win public support for an extremist political agenda here at home."

Doc flushed, and his voice was tight: "That isn't a fucking story. It's a theory."

Nader smiled. "Like evolution? Like global warming? Like relativity?" He left.

Doc spread his hands wide and sighed in resignation: "See folks? There's my problem."

EIGHT

NADER

33.

Nader is sweet, smart and funny—that's how Megan Spencer saw him anyway. Cyril agreed with her but could tell that she had deeper, more complex feelings for his friend. They were in the little Dark Horse coffee bar on John Street ostensibly to talk about the challenges of interning at a major media employer. She'd been accepted by the *Star*. She wanted pointers, practical advice. But from the outset it was clear her mind was really on Nader.

"He's quite the enigma," she said smiling.

"He is indeed," Cyril said. "So when do you start?"

"On Monday."

They'd nursed an Americano each as Cyril tried to tell her what he'd learned in his brief internship phase: pay attention to *everything*; consider everyone to be important until each person you

345

encounter demonstrates that he or she is *not*; don't worry about sounding green or even stupid—they expect that anyway; arrive early, stay late; above all, take every bit of praise or kindness with a grain of salt because it's usually delivered to make the futility of internship more palatable; expect nothing more than a free drink or a farewell lunch at the end. Hope for a glowing letter of referral. Try not to pass out if you get an offer of employment, act like you expected it, deserve it, earned it. Be alert, friendly. Admire, but don't suck up.

"Nader says you had a job in a matter of weeks."

"Pure luck. I arrived as they were launching a special project and I was interested, and I seemed to be—and they were totally out to lunch on this—informed about the story, maybe even connected somehow. Anyway, they took me on for what I consider to be a six-month trial. Probation, if you like."

"The story—young jihadists?"

"Sort of."

"But you mentioned a connection to it?"

He laughed. "I'm in the right demographic. Young, male and Arab . . ."

"You?" She was leaning back now, eyes wide.

"My dad was Lebanese, came here as a refugee in the eighties. Cormier wasn't his birth name. He changed it legally. Long story. I'm still trying to figure it out. My dad didn't talk much—to me, anyway. In any case I was genuinely interested in the subject and they could tell."

"Wow."

"Well. Interesting, maybe. But a long way from 'wow.' How's the coffee?"

"I'm okay . . ."

"I'm going to get another one."

"Oh all right. Me too."

"So," Megan said when he came back. "I'd say the luck was having Nader on your side. Right?"

"Hmm. I wouldn't say he was on my side."

"He thinks very highly of you."

"If you say so."

Soon she disclosed that she and Nader had been seeing one another since Leo's party. Just as friends. Coffee. A drink ("He's the only person I know who doesn't seem to need alcohol"), they'd been to a couple of movies. "Have you seen *Waltz with Bashir?*"

"It's on my list." She didn't seem to know Cyril's middle name— it was interesting that Nader hadn't brought it up, or thought better of it.

"Amazing movie," she said. "The point of view of some Israeli soldiers about the invasion of Lebanon in 1982. You've heard about that, I imagine."

"Yes."

"I've been reading up on it. A lot. The destruction. The PLO, etcetera. The massacres. You say your dad was Lebanese?"

"Yes."

"Well, then you'd know."

"There's a lot to know."

"You can say that again. But that movie, it really puts you into it. It's all kind of animation. Really interesting technique. And it leads up to this huge massacre of refugees where it suddenly goes actuality. Frigging blew me away."

"How did Nader react?"

"He didn't say much. His people are Iranians, right?"

"Yes. His father, anyway." He was about to say *but his mom was Palestinian, from Gaza*, but he caught himself. If Nader hadn't mentioned it, he wouldn't.

"We had a drink after that one. I really needed one. He kind of filled in the background, the Lebanese politics and stuff. There was a lot to take in. I was just reeling from the film. But I could tell that it bothered him, too, but he doesn't talk much about himself, does he? Do you find that?"

"That's fair. Nader is very serious about things. But what I like about him is that he doesn't take himself too seriously. Rare in our line of work."

"That's for sure." She sipped, looked away, then smiled. "Is he involved with anyone by any chance?"

"No." Cyril was now laughing. "Not Nader."

"You make it sound like he's gay or something."

"No. Not as far as I know. You can relax."

"But there's something about him. Right? What do you think?"

"I think you take him as he is. What you see is real. Like you said. Smart and funny. I don't know about the 'sweet.' But I know he's deep. And he's true blue."

"Yes," she said. And he could hear the wistfulness. "So I can safely assume he's single? No significant other?"

"Not that I know of."

"Family?"

"Yes. Close, I gather. But he doesn't talk about personal stuff much to me either. He's all business."

"I just have this feeling. And I don't know why I'm telling *you*. But you're a good listener." She reached across and squeezed his hand.

"I have this feeling that I could get awfully fond of him. You know what I mean?"

"I know what you mean."

"And I keep thinking about something my dad told me once. Dad is a clergyman, by the way. Anglican priest, if you can imagine. Anyway—he says it's important that the guy you fall for should be single. But what you should *really* watch for is something that's harder to detect. Some guys aren't just single. They're *singular*. Maybe Nader's that way. What do you think?"

"I don't know what that means."

"Okay. A single guy is unattached by choice and, more often than not, temporarily. A *singular* guy is unattached in spite of himself. How Dad explains it is that they're usually idealists. It never really made sense until I started thinking about Nader. And where we might be going, or not going. Idealists tend to be going somewhere by themselves."

"How old did you say you were?"

"I never said." She blushed deeply.

Cyril was suddenly aware of the surroundings, the aromas, the banging, hissing, scouring sounds of coffee preparation, sirens blaring, honking outside on the street, human movement, human sound. Voices, words that were meaningless outside the context of emotional engagement. And suddenly he felt the presence of his father.

"I've probably kept you too long," she said.

"No," he said. "What you're saying is important. It's just a lot to take on board."

"I know," she said. "I don't know what came over me." She grasped his hand again.

He looked away. And that was when he saw Gloria standing by the cash.

He stared, hoping for some extrasensory connection that would cause her to look his way. He detached his hand from Megan's.

"Someone you know?" she asked, following his gaze.

"Yes," he said. "Sorry. It's someone I haven't seen in a while."

And he realized by Gloria's intense focus on her wallet, the furrows on her brow and how she deliberately deposited her change, bills in one compartment, coins in the little pocket that had a corner of its flap permanently creased so that it would never lie flat when she snapped it shut and tried to fold the always-bulging wallet, and how she brushed the hair back from her face as she turned abruptly toward the exit without looking, that she'd seen him. And she was gone, smiling thinly at some stranger who squeezed past her, looking for a place to sit.

"Excuse me a sec," he said. And he headed for the street.

But she was nowhere to be found.

∽

It was difficult to focus after that. He wandered aimlessly along the harbourfront. Stopped in a pub he'd never heard of, ordered a pint. Drank half of it. Left. Tried calling Nader. No response.

He bought a newspaper, checked the movie listings. Nothing worth seeing.

He sat in the little park where he'd seen her running with That Other Fellow. Tried to read an editorial about Syria but nothing that he saw or thought had any context. Tried to read a novel but kept having to go back to find the storyline.

He thought: maybe if I just called. Or if she answered, what then? Explain? Explain what? Or better still, send a text. Better? Why better? Less exposure. Chickenshit, in Suzanne's words.

Fuck it.

He went home. Mercifully Aggie was out. He poured a drink. What would the singular idealistic Nader do? Pour a Coke? Maybe he'd smoke pot. Or would crawl onto a prayer mat, top of his head toward Mecca, arse to the rest of the world. Lose himself that way.

It was a stiff drink on an empty stomach.

He felt improved enough to go to bed.

Removing his clothes he put a handful of change on the dresser. It always drove him *crazy* when the goddamned coins would tumble out of his pockets, scattering everywhere as if alive and fleeing. Checked his inside jacket pocket and found a folded sheet of paper.

The fax. Photocopied business card, front and back, from Kennedy. *Ronald J. Nicholson. INSET*. A handwritten phone number. Placed it face up beside the coins on the dresser, not to be forgotten. In the morning.

Awaiting sleep he reviewed the Megan theory of singularity and it made too much sense to be ignored. It explained so much about his friend. Of course. Nader wasn't able to commit to anything but ideas. Theories, Savage pointed out.

Is singularity a deficit? Or a gift.

Just before sleep claimed him he thought of Gloria again. She was his proof: Cyril's emotional paralysis didn't come from singularity. It was the opposite. *I'm not like Nader. I'm not like my father.* And now, as clarity dissolved, he was insisting: *I'm not like them at all. I'm a different species altogether.*

34.

The sidewalk on University Avenue was thronged with lunch hour people hurrying. Cyril stood waiting close to the curbside, next to a lamppost, eye on the doorway to the nondescript sandwich place that Inspector Nicholson had recommended. He was still doubtful that the cop would actually show up, but he kept watching anyway for a big man in a suit.

"You'll know me when you see me . . . I've got 'cop' written all over me," Nicholson had told him on the phone.

How matters would proceed if Nicholson showed up, he didn't have a clue. But he felt he also didn't have a thing to lose, so what the heck. Meet the guy. Bring the conversation round to where he wanted it. He'd called Nader to let him know and maybe get advice. But Nader wasn't answering and hadn't called him back.

On the phone Nicholson had been courteous but cool. "You work where?"

"Television news. But I'll be honest, I'm pretty new at it which is why they have me gathering mostly background stuff. Like how INSET works, structurally . . ."

"That's all online . . ."

"Yes, I've been to the website. But also, the practical aspect. Historically, of course."

"Historically."

"Well, I was hoping that somebody could walk me through a particular historical scenario, like the Toronto Eighteen from back in '06. Canada's nine-eleven that never happened." He managed what sounded like a chuckle.

Silence.

"Tell me your name again. I'm sorry. The memory."

"Cyril Cormier."

"Cormier."

"Yes. Actually, I think you met my father once."

"And your father was?"

"Pierre. Pierre Cormier."

Silence.

Cyril thought that Nicholson was gone but then he heard a sigh. "Cyril. Let me tell you something. And before I do, every fuckin' word that comes out of me. Every syllable. Off the record. Okay? You got that?"

"Absolutely."

"And you aren't recording this, right?"

"No way."

"Okay. In this line of work there is no distinction between what's historical and what's contemporary. We aren't talkin' about ordinary crime, like homicide or some holdup. Criminal conspiracy is a different kettle of fish. Terrorism? We're talkin' about a criminal phenomenon, a *culture*. And what makes it hard is that nobody in that mindset thinks of himself as a criminal, or what he does as crime. Hell. Most of them think they're saints. Martyrs."

"Completely agree with everything you say . . ."

"So what I'm *sayin'*, Cyril, is that there's no way we can talk about the Toronto Eighteen, or Eight, or Eight-Fuckin'-Hundred, without talkin' about what's going on right now. Not because I'm worried about my job or all the rules and regulations. It's because I'm worried about the country. Simple as that. We just don't need that shit and no way I'm gonna say anything to jeopardize what folks are doing to prevent it happening."

"Totally agree. And by the way I've had this conversation, more or less, already . . ."

"With who, if I can ask?"

"Well."

Silence.

"You'll understand if I'm not comfortable saying who."

Nicholson laughed. "Good for you."

Silence.

"Okay," Nicholson continued. "Let me say this. Because it is a culture, deep and wide, we have our feelers out far and wide and deep. We first picked up on the Toronto thing on a website out of Edmonton, if you can believe it. Following some nutcase out there, we noticed a lot of what seemed like young people buying into this guy's line and looking at the videos this guy was putting up. Eventually we had the eighteen on our radar. What bothered me was that most of these were ordinary kids from normal families. A bunch of guys making misery for themselves and their parents."

"A BOG," Cyril said.

"A BOG. Yes. By the way, where did you hear that expression?"

Silence.

Nicholson chuckled. "My oh my. You don't have to answer. I can pretty well guess."

～

Cyril spotted him a block away. Nicholson was tall and had the appearance of an athlete who had long since given up the physical activity but not the calories. He had close-cropped silver hair that was thinning at the front, slightly fleshy lips, frameless glasses. He had style, dressed in a well-cut grey suit, pale yellow shirt, charcoal tie with a subtle pattern of tiny yellow crowns. Lawyer shoes with tassels, feet that were surprisingly compact. Cyril suddenly felt awkward in his cargo pants and black T-shirt, denim jacket and Blundstones.

Nicholson paused in front of him, checked his wristwatch, studied the passing crowd. Produced an iPhone, scrolled briefly with a thumb then walked to the door of the sandwich shop and peered in. Cyril waited until the door closed behind him, watched through a window until he saw him take a seat in a far corner of the shop. Took a deep breath, pushed through the door.

They made eye contact and nodded at each other. Cyril noted that Nicholson wasn't smiling. But he stood and they shook hands.

"We go over there and order and they'll bring it to us," he said. On the way to the counter Cyril said: "I really appreciate you taking the time to meet . . ."

Nicholson said: "We'll talk about that. What do you like? Everything here is good. We get drinks over there." He pointed to a cooler.

∾

They were seated, waiting for their orders. Nicholson was doodling on the tabletop with an index finger, then he raised a hand, looked hard at Cyril. He had deep hazel-green eyes that never seemed to blink.

"I'm afraid this isn't going to take long, Cyril. It was probably a mistake, me agreeing to meet you here. But anyway. Here comes the food."

Nicholson picked up his wrap, gnawed the end of it, sat back, studied Cyril, smiled for the first time. "Shit. If anybody knew that I was here, my ass would be in a sling, man."

"I really appreciate—"

"Never mind the appreciating. Just understand where I'm coming from. This government we've got in Ottawa these days. From the cop perspective? Fabulous. But they go too far in some ways. Police work is a two-way street. I don't much believe in letting public affairs do the talking for us working guys. We work for the people so we talk to the people. You guys in the media—talkin' to you is talkin' to a whole whack of people in one go. It's part of the job. With ground rules, of course."

"Of course."

He *slowly* peeled back the wrapper, chomped off another bite. Chewed thoughtfully.

"But basically, having given it a lot of thought, I can't talk about the Toronto Eighteen or any aspect of any investigation, past or present. As I might have mentioned, it's all one big investigation. Everything we do is connected. What'll you have to drink?"

"I'll go with you."

Nicholson picked an orange juice, Cyril a Diet Coke. "Let me get this," he said.

Nicholson smiled. "Uh-uh. Don't get me wrong. Thanks. But it's the rules now."

∾

The food and drinks were almost gone. They were sitting, conversation stalled. "Did you ever smoke?" Nicholson asked.

"No."

"You'd be wise not to start. You never get over it. Like right now. What I wouldn't give for an Export A. What I smoked for years. Actually I might have a coffee. You?"

"Sure. But let me get it."

"No. You stay where you are. We can talk about something neutral. Like the East Coast, eh. You didn't know my roots are back there? Like yours." He stood, walked away to get the coffee.

Cyril watched him go, trying to remember how much he'd told Nicholson about himself. East Coast? Then he was back, carrying two mugs.

"I know what you're thinking," he said. "You're thinking: how does this guy know where my roots are?" He laughed, set the coffees down.

He sat, studied Cyril for what felt like a full minute, tapping his forefinger on the tabletop.

"I met your father once, quite a while back. I went back to my notes. He told me he was a refugee from Lebanon who ended up in Cape Breton. It was interesting. My folks came from the East Coast, Cape Breton, I'm pretty sure. I think we could have made a connection, him and me. He struck me as a straight shooter."

"What was the reason for your meeting?"

"He approached us. He thought he had some information we might be interested in."

"Can I ask what information?"

"Ask away, but you won't get an answer. He passed away shortly after I met him."

"June 2007."

"I think so." He looked away. "See that guy over there?" He waved at a man who was busy behind the sandwich bar. "He's from Lebanon. Great people. Hard workers. So what year did your dad come over?"

"Early eighties."

"Yes. It's coming back. They've been through a lot, the poor Lebanese. I talk about it sometimes to Sami there. Everybody's battleground, Lebanon. And now you've got your Hezbollah in there." He was shaking his head, a sad expression on his face.

He put his mug down, laced his fingers together in front of him on the table. "I'm gonna be straight with you, Cyril. I think you and I kind of understand each other. You haven't been in the media long enough to get sneaky. And I've been a cop long enough to know an honest person when I see one. Being two-faced is probably the worst part of both our jobs. Anyway. You'll find that out for yourself."

There was a longer silence then. Sami showed up at the table with a coffee pot. "Okay. Just a bit," said Nicholson. "I'll be pissin' like a racehorse all afternoon. But it's great coffee, Sami. This is my friend Cyril."

"Nice to meet you," Cyril said.

"Cyril here has Lebanese connections through his dad. What was the name when he was over there, your dad?"

"Haddad," Cyril said.

Sami smiled at him. Filled his cup. "I haven't seen you here for a while, Ronny. Keeping busy?"

"Never stops," said Nicholson.

Sami walked away. Nicholson watched him go, then turned back to Cyril. "I got the impression that your dad was part of stuff in Lebanon, the war and all. Knew certain people. How up on this are you?"

"Barely."

"Your dad must have talked, eh?"

"Never about Lebanon. Nothing."

"Nothing at all?"

Silence.

Nicholson studied the tabletop, frowning. "Because there's a name ringing a bell in my old forgetful head. I remember because I knew he was kind of a bad guy but he had a girly name. Ellie, I think."

"There was an Elie Hobeika in the civil war."

"That was the name. Your dad indicated he was part of this guy's crew for a while. But there was a falling-out. Does this ring a bell?"

"He never talked about Lebanon."

"And if I recall, he told me something about some bar here in Toronto, called the Only Café—a name you'd remember, eh—and a guy who hangs out there who might have had something to do with a hit on this Hobeika guy. Does this make any sense to you?"

"I was twelve when Dad moved out of our home. I didn't have much contact with him after that. So this is all news to me. Interesting, though."

"So he never talked about any of this? Guy murdered in Lebanon? Some mystery man in a Toronto bar?"

"He never mentioned a thing."

"Anyway. It's all ancient history now, isn't it."

"Yes. I guess." *In this line of work there is no distinction between what's historical and what's contemporary.*

"So I guess it was an accident that took your father. A boating accident?"

"That's what it looked like. Though they only recently confirmed that he was dead. There was no body."

Silence.

"So he never mentioned some guy in a bar in Toronto?"

"Not to me."

Sami was back again with his coffee pot. Nicholson waved him off but Cyril let him top up his mug. Took a deep breath. "So, Ron. Can I call you Ron?"

"Of course."

"Thank you. Just for obvious personal reasons, I'd be curious to know anything you can tell me about my father. Anything he told you about Lebanon. How he died. It was an explosion. I don't know much more than that."

"I can check about his death. There would be a file."

"And this guy in a bar. You just reminded me of something. My dad left a list of people he wanted at a memorial, if anything should happen to him. Now that I think of it, your name was on the list. And a guy named Ari."

"Harry, hmm."

"No, Ari. Do you know anybody named Ari?"

Nicholson was silent. He took another sip of coffee.

"There's a rumour that our security people have spies in the mosques," Cyril said.

"Well, I wouldn't know anything about that, but it would make sense."

"And that this Ari . . ."

Nicholson leaned back and laughed. "Cyril, I'm going to stop you right there."

"Are you telling me you never heard of Ari? Dad didn't tell you anything about Ari?"

"I didn't say that, Cyril. And it doesn't fuckin' matter, does it? Your dad is dead."

"I'm only trying to understand what happened to him."

"And you think this Ari might have been involved?"

"I don't know."

"Look, Cyril. There probably isn't a whole lot more to know. I remember once years ago, in Moncton, New Brunswick. Some restaurant guy blew up. Right away, all kinds of speculation. A mob hit. The guy was in the restaurant business. Owed money. Going bankrupt. Etcetera. But the poor guy had a propane cylinder in the trunk of his car. Sat there all through a hot day in July. Him looking forward to a weekend at the cottage, probably. On the drive home. Boom. Simple as that."

"I often wonder whether there were witnesses."

"Witnesses."

Silence.

Nicholson said, "That would be a stretch. It was early in the morning, if I remember rightly. In the middle of nowhere."

He stretched in the chair. Clasped his hands behind his head, eyes on the ceiling, rocking slightly. "I think one guy was mentioned. A kind of down-and-out chap. Lived in a little trailer near the wharf. He might have been a messed-up war vet, scrambled by booze and dope. Nothing comprehensible to contribute, as I recall. Funny how things come back."

"Do you remember his name?"

"I do, actually. The name stuck. Beaton. Yes. That's what it was. Beaton. As in defeated. That's how I remember it. You run into people like that. Beaten down by life. No fault of their own."

"Beaton."

"Beaton. I'm pretty sure I heard he'd passed. But you want my advice, Cyril? Let it go. You're a young guy with a bright future. Let it go."

∽

He went to the office. He was at his desk, staring into space when Hughes found him. "Take a few days, Cyril. Step back. This is never easy, walking away from a story you believe in. But trust me. We're not giving up on it. It's just that we're going to have to set it aside for a bit and address a couple of other things that are more achievable in the short term. It's how it works nowadays."

"Okay. I'm thinking about going to the East Coast. Maybe check out where my father spent his last few days."

"That's a good plan. Get a bit of closure, maybe. Get some distance from the rest of us for a bit. But don't be gone too long, right?"

"Right."

"Have you been in touch with Nader?"

"Not since the meeting with Savage."

"Well, if you're talking to him, tell him I need to see him."

"I'm sure he'll surface. Look. I should tell you I talked to a cop. Off the record. I wasn't—"

"What cop?"

"I found out about him from a friend of Dad's. I wasn't trying to go over anybody's head."

"Don't worry about that. Who was the cop?"

"A Mountie with INSET named Nicholson."

"How did he know your father?"

"The funny thing is, they all did, it seems. INSET, CSIS. I think it's because of Ari, at the Only Café. And Hobeika. I have this funny feeling about what happened to Hobeika and what happened to my dad. So, anyway, I'm going to go east. If nothing else just see where it happened."

Cyril was at the door when Hughes stopped him: "Cyril . . ."

"Yes?"

"Watch your step. Okay?"

"I hear you."

35.

Route 19 runs along the west coast of Cape Breton Island. If you imagine a seated crop-tail dog, Route 19 follows the curved back from just above the stub of the tail to the nape of the neck, roughly south to north. That was Aggie's description, anyway. They call it the Ceilidh Trail, "ceilidh" being a Gaelic word for "social gathering." He remembered Pierre teasing Aggie, "It's the Gaelic word for 'drunk.'" That was when they still seemed fond of one another.

"So New Waterford would be down around the dog's asshole," Pierre had said once, in front of Pius Lynch.

"More like his balls," the old man said. "And they're big ones, and you'd better not forget it, boy."

Cyril was studying a tourist map at an information centre, where the causeway from the mainland connected with what was once an island in the real sense of isolation and remoteness. He followed the road with his finger, through places with names like Troy, Creignish, Judique, and Port Hood, until he found Mabou. How odd, he thought, that he had no memory of the place, though he knew he'd visited there when he was small.

From Mabou he traced a small secondary road along the edge of what looked like a long inlet from the sea. Mabou Harbour. Mabou Coal Mines.

"It's gorgeous there," the woman at the information desk exclaimed. "But I'm biased. I grew up near there."

"Would you know somebody named Beaton down there?" Cyril asked.

She laughed. "Beaton. Half the place is Beatons."

It was Thanksgiving weekend. The hillsides were flushed with deciduous yellows, reds and apricots flaring wildly against the grim brooding of the evergreens. St. Georges Bay flashed and foamed for as far as he could see. He stopped twice to take pictures on his cellphone and considered mailing them to Gloria. Reconsidered.

Aggie had been harsh when he told her he was going. "For me he died three times. The last time really didn't register."

"For fuck sake, Ma."

"Don't you dare use that word in front of me."

But she told him how to find the harbour, and the old homestead she and Pierre had rescued and restored back in the early days, and where to find the hidden key.

"You should stay in a motel. Or one of the nice bed and breakfasts. There'll be nothing in the house but bats and *bocans*."

"Bockans?"

"Ghosts."

On the road approaching Mabou he finally recognized the soaring hills from a spontaneous Thanksgiving weekend years before. Saturating warmth of summer lingering beyond its shelf life; the shock of the chilly, musty farmhouse, the grudging doors and windows. Summer quickly disappearing with the falling sun. A grumbling search for sheets and blankets. Pillows. A crackling fire. Mummy and Daddy curled around their toddies on the chesterfield, soft music from a violin. The little boy between them, soaking up their body warmth and the tantalizing smell of woodsmoke, spice and alcohol. Sleep deliciously descending.

It was the red shoe that caught his eye, a painting of an old-fashioned shoe on a hanging oval sign out front, and the name: The Red Shoe. It was a pub and it was busy, judging from the cars along the road that ran through the little village. He parked.

A pamphlet on the table told him there was an autumn Celtic music festival in progress across the island. It would explain the chattering clientele, mostly made up of people passing through or visiting for the entertainment. Sad music filtered softly from an unseen system.

He studied the menu. He wasn't hungry, but the beer was tempting and he realized that he'd be hungry later. He told the waiter he'd need a minute or two. "By the way, I'm looking for a guy named Beaton."

The waiter smiled. He was close to Cyril's age. "I'm a Beaton," he said. "There's no shortage of us around here. What Beaton in particular?"

"I don't have a first name."

"Ah."

"He knew my dad a few years back."

"And your dad?"

"He wasn't from here. But he was, um. He was killed in an accident near here about five years ago."

"Oh jeez, that's . . . we have a lot of that here. The roads, people who don't know them very well."

"It was an explosion. He was on a boat."

"Okay. Yes. I remember hearing something about it. I was away at university. It was on the news, I think. Let me ask."

He walked away. Cyril was suddenly exhausted, maybe from the early start, the flight, the long drive from Halifax.

The waiter returned, nodded back toward where he'd just been: "That guy might help. His name is Willie. They call him the Bulletin. He knows *everything* that goes on around here."

"Is he a Beaton?"

"He's a Campbell."

"Not from here?"

"No. From Mabou Ridge. But he knows everybody."

He could see a red-faced middle-aged man wearing a flat tweed cap rising from a table on the other side of the room.

"Thanks. I'll have a club sandwich and a pint of that . . . Keith's. And whatever Willie drinks."

"Willie doesn't drink."

"Ah. Okay. I just assumed."

"He used to, but he doesn't anymore. He hangs around here for the gossip."

Willie came toward him slowly, pausing to exchange greetings and smiles with other customers. Cyril stood. They shook hands solemnly. They sat. Willie leaned back, hands folded on his lap, and studied Cyril carefully.

"I didn't catch the name."

"Cyril. Cyril Cormier."

"Aha. Cormier."

"I live in Toronto. But I probably have relatives around here on my mother's side. Her mother's people were MacDonalds, from a place called Mabou Coal Mines."

"Right, right, right." He was nodding. "Martin mentioned something about your father."

"Yes. About five years ago. An accident. He died at Mabou Coal Mines. He was on a boat in the harbour."

"I remember. They were saying it was strange. Early morning and if I recall correctly, no remains. So he was your father? Some people were doubting that he was even on the boat."

"Yes. But it was confirmed recently. They found a body part."

"Right. In a lobster trap. Leonard Rankin found it. Bizarre."

"Yes."

"So what can I tell you?"

"Well, actually, I don't know. I basically just wanted to see where it happened. Maybe put some things to rest."

"Of course. I can see that. Well, you just follow that road down by the church and keep going about three miles. And then there'll be a dirt road on the right. Another three miles and it'll take you to the coal mines."

"Why do they call it the coal mines?"

"Well. Because they used to mine coal there."

"Okay." Cyril laughed. "So it won't be hard to find the harbour."

"That'll depend."

"Aha."

"So your mother's people. Do you happen to know what MacDonalds?"

"No. I'm afraid not. She left here young, lived in New Waterford. Got married. Eventually moved to Toronto."

"And her name was what?"

"Lynch. Agnes Lynch."

"Jesus. Not Aggie Lynch. We went to school together. She was ahead of me. But I remember her. She was kind of a dish. You don't look a bit like her. I'd say you more resemble the French side. So what, Cormier?"

"I'm afraid I don't know much about them."

"Isn't that the way now. Your mother's people were from the coal mines, but before you get to the little harbour there."

"Where exactly?"

"You can't miss it, on the lower side of the road. Pretty rundown now. I could take you."

"Thanks, but I think I can find it. There was a guy down there, though, at the coal mines, who was talking to my father just before the accident. His name was Beaton."

"Right. You'd have to be more precise. The place is crawling with Beatons."

"All I know is that he was living near the wharf. In what was described as a trailer. He might have been a war vet."

"Oh. Him!"

"You know him?"

"Angus? Of course. Everybody knows Angus."

"I'd heard he might have passed away."

"Oh merciful God no. Far from it."

"Okay."

"Very much alive, is Angus."

"And could you tell me where he lives."

"I could. In West Mabou."

Cyril laughed. "How many Mabous are there?"

"That depends."

"And can you tell me how long it takes to get there?"

"That would depend."

"On what?"

"On if you were on foot or in a car. Or if you got lost. Anyway, just drive back out the way you came. You can't miss it."

And Willie walked away laughing to himself, already structuring the latest bulletin.

∽

The boy who answered the door seemed to be about seventeen. "I'm looking for Angus Beaton," Cyril said.

"Yes," the boy replied. He had one hand on the doorknob, the other on the door frame, a barrier.

"Is this where he lives?"

"Yes."

"I wonder if I could speak to him."

"He isn't here."

"When do you expect him?"

"It's hard to say."

"Okay. I can come back. Could you give me a phone number so I can check first? Save a wasted trip."

"*Maaaaawm!*"

The boy turned and disappeared into the house, which seemed new, a bungalow perched at the end of a long hillside lane. A woman appeared, maybe in her forties. Saw him and stopped. She folded her arms. She bore an uncanny resemblance to Suzanne. The appraising look, the thick, dishevelled auburn hair, bunched carelessly, reading glasses perched like a tiara. She was standing in an archway leading into what was probably a dining room.

"Yes?" she said.

"I was hoping to speak to Angus Beaton," Cyril said.

She leaned a shoulder against the archway, shoved both hands into large pockets on a smock she was wearing.

"You're young," she said.

Without thinking he replied, "Well, I guess that's relative."

She laughed, straightened up. "I guess I asked for that. I meant you're young for military."

"I'm not military," Cyril said.

"Ah," she said. "So you are . . . ?"

"My name is Cyril Cormier," he said. "My dad and Angus Beaton were friends."

"So your dad was in the army with Angus."

"No."

"Well, Angus isn't here anyway and I'm not sure when he'll be back."

"Okay. Could you give me a phone number so I can check with him before I try another time?"

"He doesn't carry a cellphone. But I'll give you the number here." She recited it, then said, "Wait. I'll write it down for you."

∿

He parked on the road. The hill below, descending to the seashore, was steep. He could see the back of the roof and second storey of his mother's house. The gate fell over when he unlatched it. It obviously had not been opened in the six years since his mother's last visit. She'd planned to sell the place, but changed her mind. Or just didn't get around to it. Or tried to forget about it altogether after his father died.

He found the key where she'd told him to look for it, under a brick on the front door step. He had to force the key into the lock but it wouldn't turn, probably rusted and corroded from the relentless caustic winds of winter. Afraid it would break off in the lock, he surrendered. He walked around the place. It was in desperate need of repairs and paint. He peered through windows, trying to remember warmth and light and life.

He turned his back to it, breathing deeply the aromatic air. Late wild flowers somewhere, decaying apples in the flattened grass, the scent of spruce, a freshness that had its own sweet presence. The sun was melting on the edge of the sea, pooling and running in a silver path toward the shore.

His father spent his final days out there. It had been June. There might have been lilacs and the scent of roses when he'd return to land, if in fact he did. His father loved the water. It reminded him, he said, of boyhood. What boyhood? The wild rose bushes Cyril now saw everywhere would have been in bud. Ash and birch and maples on the hillside in fresh leaf. Once upon a time Pierre had loved this place, loved Aggie, loved Cyril. He had a sudden memory of his father standing exactly where he was standing now, arm draped over Aggie's shoulders, silent, both of them, just watching the sun melt down.

He turned back to the old house. Even five years earlier it would have been unwelcoming and he could understand his father's preference for the boat. He'd never seen the boat, though he knew it was large enough to live on. Pierre could have gone anywhere on that boat, but he chose to stay in the little harbour. He obviously felt safe here. Nobody would have thought of looking for him here. Nobody here would have any reason to cause him harm. The boat blew up. Probably propane. It happens. The body disappeared, a conspiracy of wind and tide. Probably.

It had been wishful thinking, the notion that he could stay here, in the house where his mother spent her childhood. "You'll have to vacuum," Aggie said. "The flies, they'll be everywhere. Every fall the place filled up with flies. And probably the mice will have taken over. You'll have your hands full for a whole day, I'm telling you. If it was me going, I wouldn't give it a thought, with all the nice places to stay and you earning a salary. Finally."

She was right. It annoyed him how often she was right. She had a way of making what was right and logical sound querulous and therefore aggravating and unacceptable. It was at the essence of their struggle.

"You don't get it, Mom. It's more than just a place to stay. I'm surprised you can't see that."

"Well, you can do what you want, but mark my words."

He tried to remember the name of one of the little inns and bed and breakfasts he'd seen along the way. He couldn't. He'd have to drive back to the village, go door knocking. He considered continuing on to the harbour to take a look. But it was getting dark and he felt a sudden sense of dread. He decided to call Angus Beaton, set something up for tomorrow morning, maybe at the harbour.

Beaton answered. When Cyril told him who was calling he went silent. Cyril waited for a moment, the discouragement gathering around with the cool gloom of the October evening. "I was hoping to meet up," he explained. "Maybe sometime tomorrow, if you have a few free minutes. I heard you spent some time with my dad, before the accident. I just wanted to meet you, I guess. Nothing in particular . . ."

"Where is it you're staying?"

"I was just on my way back to the village to look."

"You'll not find anything this late. The place is filled up for the Celtic Colours."

"The Celtic Colours."

"It's a music festival. They have it every fall."

"Okay."

"Where are you now?"

"Mabou Coal Mines. My mom's old place."

"You might as well come here," he said. "There's a rec room in the basement, if you don't mind sleeping on a pullout couch."

"Ah, no, I couldn't. It would be too much trouble."

"Well, it's up to yourself. But you'll be welcome. I don't suppose you ate?"

"No, not yet."

"Well, come along. We'll set another place. We can talk about the sleeping arrangements when you get here."

"Ah, but . . ."

"You know where we are. We'll expect you."

∾

Angus Beaton was tall and broad-shouldered, with a substantial paunch. His handshake was firm, his eyes cautious. He led Cyril straight to the dining room. "We usually eat in the kitchen, but you're a visitor."

"I hate to be putting you to . . ."

"Never mind that. Can I give you something before we eat? I don't touch it myself but Maureen likes a little nip when there's an excuse."

"Well, maybe."

He turned toward the kitchen and called, "Maureen, where did you hide the Scotch?"

"In the usual place."

He walked toward a small hutch. "You'll be having one yourself," he shouted.

"Sure," Maureen called back. He produced a bottle and two glasses, poured generously.

∾

"The food is nothing special," Angus said when they were at the table. "If we knew you were coming . . . when did you arrive?"

"Just today."

"First time?"

"Well, when I was just a kid."

The boy, Bradley, was uncommunicative. He ate quickly.

"Slow down," his father said.

"Are you using the truck this evening?" Bradley asked.

"I had no plans. Where were you thinking of going?"

"Just to Kevin's place for an hour. Okay?"

"You know you can't be on the road after midnight."

"I won't be that long."

"I'll be up."

The boy rose from the table, gulping a glass of milk, turning to leave. Halfway to the door, his father called him back. "Where's your manners, goddammit?"

"Oh. Sorry." He smiled, came back and reached out to shake Cyril's hand. "It was nice meeting you."

∼

Cyril and Maureen had a second Scotch after dinner while Angus cleared the table. She fetched a photo of their daughter, Melissa. She was twenty, in first-year university. Very athletic. Played varsity field hockey. She was stunning, Cyril thought—how her mother must have been twenty, thirty years earlier.

Maureen told him she was a nursing supervisor at a senior citizens' establishment in Inverness. She loved the work, relating to the old folks who had so much history and wisdom.

Angus came back with a pot of tea. "I don't suppose either of you two boozers . . ."

"Listen to him," Maureen said.

Cyril said, "Actually, a cup of tea would be great."

~

"Life is queer," Angus said after Maureen had left them. "Your poor father wouldn't believe what you're in the middle of here. Me and Maureen and Bradley. Melissa off in university. A nice house. Me a teetotaller. It was quite a different scene five years ago." He shook his head. "I was pretty down and out when I met Pierre."

They talked then, and they were still talking at eleven when Bradley returned, stepped into the room, but backed out wordlessly and went to bed.

The words were still flowing a half hour later when Angus finally stood up and stretched, yawned, and said, "We can continue this in the morning, if you're up for it when we go down to the harbour. I go back there now and then, just to remind myself."

~

Before climbing into his temporary bed, Cyril checked his BlackBerry. He couldn't remember having gone so long without trawling for texts and emails, browsing through the news. There was nothing in his inbox.

He sat on the edge of the makeshift bed and composed two messages, but he agonized before he sent the first one. Finally: *Hi I need to talk to you. It's kind of important. xoxo*

Then to Nader: *Hey brother, where are you? I'm on the East Coast. I might be onto something.*

36.

He woke up frequently to look for messages, but also to compulsively return to the reconstruction of events from details Angus Beaton had provided from the year he'd spent in a tiny, dilapidated travel trailer near the wharf at Mabou Coal Mines.

Gloria had responded with surprising promptness: *Whenever.* But whatever excitement her cryptic message might have caused was lost in the frustration he was feeling over Nader's silence. It had been days now with no call or text.

Then he'd drift again, into the recurring thought: how life goes off the rails. Crisis, catalyst for change. Explains everything. Then he'd doze and dream and be awake again, wondering if he had really slept or if the dream was part of a memory that was inaccessible.

Angus Beaton, he thought, was a crisis master. He had survived so many crises he now spent much of his life helping others deal with crises of their own. Mostly struggling military veterans, or often active-duty soldiers arriving on his doorstep unofficially. Word gets around about someone who will listen, someone who had been to the dark places. The local legion had a grant and paid him a stipend to be available to the haunted walking wounded.

The crisis that reconfigured Angus Beaton's life had started with a game. A *stupid* game he realized in retrospect. Grown men being careless little boys. Cyril later couldn't remember all the details, as he'd been listening for openings to steer the conversation back to his own agenda.

At one point Cyril had asked: "Do you mind if I take some notes?"

"Don't know what's worth noting," Angus said. "But go ahead. Whatever turns your crank."

"So, this game?"

"Oh. I don't like talking about it and for a long, long time, I didn't. Then I realized I had to. Bored guys farting around in a very dangerous place in Afghanistan. Kind of a race. Anyway, one day I lost two good people."

He lit a cigarette and walked to the door, opened it, stood there, blowing smoke out into the still darkness. Spoke to the night. "I was in charge so. There was a court martial, naturally. But the guys stood up for me. Long story. I didn't do such a great job of standing up for myself. From then on it was administrative duties. Which was probably wise. Then I was out of it."

His second crisis was arriving home to an empty house—Maureen and the kids up and gone. "I got pretty crazy after that. It was during that phase I met your dad. I probably wouldn't have met him at all. He kept pretty much to himself and I would spend my days alone, too, digging my grave with a bottle opener. But I couldn't sleep at night and I got the impression he had the same problem. Though he never said much. I just know he wasn't much for the booze.

"This night I'm wandering around the wharf, completely wired. I decided to have a look at this new boat. It was all in darkness so. It must have been about three in the morning. And I'm standing there having my smoke and I realize there's this guy sitting down there and he's watching me. Not saying anything. We exchanged a few words and I left, feeling kind of stupid. Later I discovered we probably had a lot more than insomnia in common."

Then there was a long digression about the failure of his marriage and how Pierre had listened. It was good talking to him. It was a rare experience for Angus, a stranger listening and being really interested.

"But, funny thing. I don't think I'd have gone back to the boat at all to talk to him if it hadn't been for the two guys I saw snooping around one day while he was out on the water."

Cyril made a note: *Two guys snooping.*

"Local guys?"

"No. They were cops."

"Cops?"

"Plainclothes cops, but I could tell by the car they were driving. A big old black Crown Vic with tinted windows and those lights you never see until they start flashing at you. They were cops all right. But they weren't from here. I knew all the ones from here."

"So you told my dad?"

"Yup. He seemed to take it all in stride. Like he was surprised, but not overly. So I just let it go. Anyway that was when we started talking. Eventually he told me where he came from originally. And that, in itself, was revealing."

"Revealing how?"

"Lebanon. I'd never been there but I knew enough to know I never wanted to go—certainly not soldiering. I met some Irish fellows once. Jesus, but the stories. Somalia was bad, but I couldn't imagine Lebanon. The Israelis, eh. Run right over you. And you couldn't do a thing about it. And then of course the Syrians. I had a bellyful of them on the Golan Heights."

He lit another cigarette, walked to the door, pinched off the ember after three quick puffs.

"Okay. So there was this morning when I figure, looking back, I hit rock bottom. I don't know whether I was sleepwalking or what. At first I thought I was in a dream but I wasn't. I'll show you in the morning—there's a breakwater down there. I was out on the end of it, in a wind would blow your hair off. And the waves pounding. I was soaked. Not a clue how I got out there, never mind how I'd get back.

"And it just came to me in a flash: I'm not meant to go back. It's all over now. I was that close."

He was staring hard and Cyril couldn't read the look.

Angus stood suddenly and walked into the kitchen. Cyril could hear a tap running. He was gone long enough that Cyril thought that perhaps he wasn't coming back. He made a note: *Breakwater. Storm.* Then Angus returned, sat rubbing his hands on his thighs.

"So there I am. Close as I think I'll ever be to the other side without actually crossing over. And I felt . . . *happy.*" He looked away. His hand was shaking as he lit another cigarette. Cyril watched the smoke curling upwards, the ash growing.

"And then your old man showed up. I have no idea how he got there. I seem to recall he was kind of crawling over the rocks until he got close enough and then he stood up and reached out. I tried to wave him off but he got hold of my hand somehow.

"I'm going to tell you, Cyril . . ." He halted, struggled. Cyril picked up an empty tea cup, held it out. Angus flicked the ash from his cigarette into the cup. "I'm sorry. Anyway, we're standing there and he has ahold of my hand. And he kind of steadied me. He had some kind of a grip, your dad did. For a lawyer. And we helped each other off the rocks. And he didn't let go of me until we were aboard his boat. We had drinks. That's about all I remember specifically. I know we talked."

"You talked."

"Yes. And I'm ashamed to say it was pretty well all about me."

"Okay. And that would have been when?"

"I think Sunday morning. I was supposed to go out with him on the boat the next day but I overslept and I missed him. I wasn't much for boats anyway, so I didn't think he'd mind."

"The accident was Tuesday morning."

"Yes. About seven thirty. It was a miracle there were no other boats in the harbour at the time. It was lobster season and they go out early. It was one of the reasons they were saying it was deliberate."

"Deliberate?"

"The timing. Like he wanted to do himself in without hurting anybody else. The fishing boats were all out, right?"

"I suppose there were other ways, if he wanted to. I mean, going to the trouble of blowing up a boat?"

"Yes. That was what the cops were saying. That, and there being no body. They thought maybe he'd staged everything to cover up a disappearing act."

"What did you think?"

"I didn't know what to think. I was kind of in shock, right? So I did what I normally did. Numbed out on booze and pills. But I remember the cops and their theory."

"These cops would be Mounties?"

"I presume so. The same two that were looking at his car earlier on. Of course there were other Mounties, too, in uniforms. But they were mostly concerned with trying to find a body. They were sure of what happened. They were blaming a propane tank—I told them he'd cooked supper for me and he had a propane stove."

"You have doubts?"

"I'll show you something in the morning."

"Okay." Cyril made another note: *He wants to show me something.*

"The plainclothes guys seemed more professional than the others.

Lots of questions, mostly what he might have told me about himself. Which wasn't much." Angus settled back. "Odd, remembering. I thought they'd have been more interested in the fat guy."

"Fat guy?"

Cyril wrote: *Fat man?*

"Yes. Some stranger around the wharf the day before. But then I thought, maybe he was one of theirs. But why so much interest in some Toronto lawyer on a boat in a place like that?"

"This fat guy, what do you remember about him?"

"Well. He was in a car up on the gravel road for the better part of the Monday afternoon. Just sitting. As I was driving out, on my way to town, probably the liquor store—he was out by the back of the car. He had his back to me. It looked like he was taking a leak as I drove by, turning so I wouldn't see what he was doing, right? So I never saw a face. I recall thinking, 'That guy is as broad as he is long.' And I kept on going. But he was still there when I came back, sitting in the car."

"Where was my father's boat?"

"Out. Sometime between six and seven I heard it coming in. Then a few minutes later it went out again, which I thought was strange. I didn't notice when it came back the second time. I fell asleep, I guess. But I was up later. Maybe ten o'clock and it was there. There was a light on. I remember now, I'd picked something up for your father while I was in town. A bag of ice, I think. I started over with it but when I got close I could hear voices."

"People talking?" Cyril was writing: *Boat in, 6 to 7; out again; back by 10. Voices.*

"I thought so," Angus said. "But it could have been your father talking on a phone. Or it could have been a radio. It was just one voice I heard. But I turned back. And I saw that car near the end of the wharf."

"The fat man's car."

"Yes. But it was gone by three a.m. when I was on my usual stroll. There was no sign of Pierre. No lights on. Boat dead quiet."

"Could the fat guy have been somebody from around here?"

"Could have been. But the car was a rental."

"And you told these policemen all this. The car. The stranger."

"I did." Angus yawned. "I wish I could tell you more," he said. "Maybe when we're at the harbour in the morning, things will come back. But I'll tell you something, Cyril. That explosion woke me up in more ways than one."

∽

Cyril had a feeling that he'd seen the harbour before. Perhaps on calendars or postcards. Or it could have been an image surfacing from childhood memory. There was a solid wharf and a floating dock embraced by boulders. They were stopped on the road above the harbour. Cyril pointed down. "The famous breakwater?"

"Imagine me standing out on the end of that in a southeaster. Wind must have been gusting to seventy knots. Wild."

"And the car with the fat man."

"Right where we're sitting now," Angus said. "I drove right by him."

"He was here all afternoon?"

"I seem to recall it was near three when I headed for town. It was after five when I got back. I'm sure I had a *sgleo* on at the time, though, so I can't be precise with time."

"What's a sklow?"

"A glow."

"I see."

"Let's go down."

They parked and walked along the wharf. Angus showed him where he'd put the little trailer he'd lived in for a year, even through the winter.

"I was some glad to see that spring in 2007. A few days there I thought I was going to blow away. But the thing was easy enough to heat. And people would check in on me. Make sure I had food. Your dad's boat was tied up there. Near the end of the wharf. The fishing boats would be behind it, or over there along the floating dock."

"But you say they were all out that morning, the fishing boats."

"Yes. It was near the end of lobster season."

"And the noise woke you, I guess."

They stopped. Cyril was trying to imagine.

"Well, yes. I'm pretty sensitive to sounds like that. Explosions. Helicopters. They get me every time. Anyway, that morning I thought I was back in Kandahar. Was almost glad to look out and see smoke over the wharf. Then thought, *holy Jesus.*"

"What did you see?"

"Just smoke, really. Some flames. The cab was gone totally. The hull was already filling up with water. The ropes were keeping her from sinking altogether."

Cyril paced.

"Look at this," said Angus, pointing with his toe. The timbers supporting the wharf were charred. Cyril felt a first wave of grief, was suddenly afraid to speak. Angus placed a hand on his shoulder, squeezed.

"I know," he said. "I know." Then he walked away, seemed to be inspecting one of three fishing boats.

In a while, he came back: "I want to show you something else if you're up for it. What have you got on your feet?"

Cyril lifted a foot.

"Good," said Angus. "Good, sturdy boots."

~

The wharf was in the lee of a long, bald hill that was fringed with tamarack and wild rose bushes, a few stunted spruce trees. It took them half an hour to climb a rough pathway up the side of the hill.

The sky was hanging low with dark, glowering cloud. "I wouldn't be surprised if we get an early snowfall," said Angus. "It isn't uncommon to get snow for Hallowe'en."

Cyril barely heard him as he struggled to keep up. Gloria or no Gloria, he thought, I have to get back into running. Here I am, struggling to keep up with this old man, a smoker.

"Okay," said Angus. "Here we are."

They were nowhere, from Cyril's point of view. Halfway up a hillside.

"Come," said Angus, and he followed him off the path through a clutching bramble. "If you have your eyes open you can find blueberries in here in late August, which was what I was looking for when I came up here two years ago."

He stopped and pointed toward a bush. Cyril could see a rusted object near it, half-buried in leaves and deadfall.

"Go look."

Cyril hesitated. He knew what he was looking at—a squat propane tank, the kind you see on barbecues, recreation vehicles and boats. He approached it cautiously, leaned over, and pulled it up from the debris and carried it back to where Angus stood.

He dropped it on the ground. It rolled and when it came to rest he could see the faded lettering. *Miriam*.

"Who have you told?" Cyril asked.

"Nobody," Angus said. "I didn't think that anyone was interested until you showed up."

∼

He called Hughes. Hughes answered. Hughes always answered, first ring as a rule.

"Have you heard from Nader? I need to get in touch with him."

"Take a number."

"What does that mean?"

"What did you find out in the east?"

"I'll tell you when I'm back. What about Nader?"

"Nader seems to have disappeared."

37.

He thought of trying Megan but he didn't have her phone number. His departure from the coffee shop had been, to say the least, abrupt. After failing to catch up to Gloria he'd returned to the coffee shop only to find that Megan, too, had disappeared.

He texted Leo: *I need a number for Megan Spencer asap. It's life and death important.*

He sat back and waited, cellphone in his hand. He entered Megan's name in the search box, just in case. Nothing. Then the phone rang.

It was Leo. "What's up?"

"You wouldn't happen to have a number for Megan?" he asked, struggling to be casual. "I need to get in touch."

"You dog," he said. "After me just reassuring Gloria."

"What the hell are you talking about?"

"Whoa, whoa, whoa," Leo said. "Don't go getting shitty with me. I didn't ask to be sucked into your personal drama."

"Wait. Wait. Wait. I'm sorry. I need to get in touch with Megan to get in touch with my friend Nader. The guy who came with me to your place, the night of the party. He and Megan have been seeing one another. It's a long shot but she might know how to reach him."

"You can't?"

"I don't have time to explain. Do you have a number for her?'

"Hang on."

Leo returned, recited an email address and a cellphone number. "Look. Before you go, about Gloria."

"What about her."

"You should call her."

"I should call her? Leo, there's some other guy. I'm cool with that. But don't go jumping to conclusions about Megan."

"Another guy? No way. I asked her flat out, Cyril. Her life is all lawyering, man. 'All work, no play' was how she put it. And I could tell she's hurting, man. The way she tried to sound okay about the woman that she saw you with."

"A woman?"

"In some coffee shop."

"That was Megan and it was business."

"Holding hands?"

"Hardly holding hands. Megan is a toucher. What can I say? But this is stupid."

"You got to call her. If it matters to you, you got to make the first move."

∼

"I'm calling for two reasons," he said, when Megan answered. "First, to apologize for running out on you—I can explain. But I really, really have to find Nader. He seems to have disappeared. Have you spoken to him lately?"

Silence.

"Megan, this is important."

"Why are you asking me?"

"When did you last hear from him?"

"I hear your bosses killed the homegrown jihadi story."

"Where did you hear that?"

"Is it true?"

"Megan, a story can't be killed. Postponed, suppressed, ignored, yes. That's exactly why I need to get hold of Nader."

"When did you last talk to him?"

"I haven't seen him or heard from him since the meeting you've obviously heard about. And you could only have heard about that from Nader."

Silence.

"So help me here."

"I'm afraid I can't."

"You can't? You won't."

"Both."

"What the fuck . . ."

"Cyril, I'll say this much, even though I know I shouldn't say anything. It's beginning to look like Nader is becoming part of *our* story. So if you find him, you should strongly suggest that he check in. People here are anxious to talk to him. Okay? Now I gotta go."

"Megan, what are you talking about?"

"Get him to call me."

"Get *him* to call *you*?"

But the line was dead.

～

It was a long shot but he found a number for the Only Café.

"Is Ari there?"

"Who's calling?"

"Cyril Cormier. He knows me."

There was a long pause. "No, he isn't right now."

"Let me give you a number. Ask him to call me, please."

～

He stood in his bedroom window and stared out at the massive maple in the backyard. *A survivor*, he thought. He knew there was a time when the maples and the elm trees were as ubiquitous as poplars in the city and the countryside. No more. What's the secret of survival? According to Angus Beaton, it's all about determination, will and discipline. At least for humans. But it must be more than that. Avoiding the consequences of decisions and actions by other people— the will or whims or mental health of people with more wealth, more power, people who need the security of having more.

Maybe not so much determination as luck, being in the right place at the right time. When you're on the sunny side of power, you win.

Otherwise you lose. Tree, mountain, river, conscious organism—
you get in someone's way and suddenly you're gone.

His phone rang.

"You were trying to reach me?"

He recognized the voice but hesitated.

"Sorry, I should have said, it's Ari. How are you?"

"Great. Thanks for calling. Look, this is going to sound strange.
I've been away and I was wondering if you've seen my friend Nader
lately. I introduced you . . ."

"Yes."

"He seems to have dropped out of sight and some people are getting worried."

Long silence. Cyril waited.

"I'm not sure I . . ."

"It was a long shot calling you, but he mentioned that he might
drop in again to the bar, someday after prayers, continue the conversation. He found it interesting."

"Well, he hasn't been here. I could ask around."

"Don't go to any trouble. By the way, I was planning to drop by
one day soon myself. I've just come back from the East Coast. I went
to see where my father died."

Silence.

"I thought maybe seeing the place, maybe talking to some people
even though I never really . . ."

"And did it help?"

"Well, yes, actually."

"Sure, come on by."

"When would work for you?"

"I'm flexible."

"Tomorrow evening?"

"Why not."

~

That night Aggie blurted, during their nightcap, that Gloria had called when he'd been out of town.

"Gloria called? Here? And you didn't tell me?"

"She didn't call for you. The world does not revolve around you exclusively."

Gloria had called her to apologize for the books left on the doorstep, Aggie told him. She was sorry that she hadn't tried harder to be Aggie's friend. She could have used a mother substitute in the city. She knew that now. Aggie said she had been very touched by the phone call and had admitted she'd never given Gloria much encouragement, hadn't really given her an opening for friendship. The call had ended warmly. The possibility of lunch had been raised.

She must have known I wasn't here, Cyril thought.

"I think I'll strengthen this," said Cyril, holding up his glass.

"Oh, what the hell," Aggie said and slid her own glass across the table.

~

Later. "I didn't plan to bring it up," Aggie said. "But I've been thinking. All the mysteries. It's why you had to go down east. All the unanswered questions because of people's little secrets. I'm fed up with secrets. I get really angry thinking about your father and all the secrecy. Was it really necessary?"

"I guess we'd have to know what he went through during the war."

"I knew more than he realized but I never questioned him. I always thought the day would come when he'd tell me more."

"You knew what? How?"

"I'm not half as stupid as people think," she said.

"Nobody thinks . . ."

"It's always a big mistake to think someone is stupid just because they don't say much. Of course, some people are thick as milkshakes. Be that as it may. But I always knew more than they gave me credit for. Father Aboud would hint at things and I read up on it and put two and two together. And eventually I realized maybe there are things that I didn't want to know for sure. Sometimes we're better off in the dark."

"So fill me in. Like, something specific that the priest told you."

"The one thing that I took to heart was that a day would come when Pierre was going to need me. When 'his burden got too heavy for him alone,' was how Father put it. Old age wasn't going to be easy for us, he said. Little did he know."

She looked away, toward the clock. "My, my. Look at the time. Okay, I'll have one more and you can tell me about the trip. The old house must have been a treat."

"It's derelict," he said, pouring. "I couldn't even get the door open. I stayed with someone I met, someone who remembered Dad. But what about . . ."

"I suppose there are a few there who would remember from the good days. It was a lovely house once. And all the work that went into building it. It's a shame, but isn't that the way with all the things we do?"

"Yes."

"Life seems short when you're getting near the end of it." She gazed toward the ceiling, the kitchen light reflected a sparkle just below her left eye. She rubbed at it and then she took his hand.

"Mom, you're hardly near the end of anything, you're only, what . . ."

She smiled, squeezed his hand. "Talking about secrets," she said. "I suppose it's time I told you mine."

"Oho," he laughed. "You have secrets?"

"Strictly speaking," she told him, "your mother is a bastard."

He leaned back in his chair.

"I know what you're thinking, but don't you dare say it. I might not be the biological daughter of Pius Lynch but by God . . . and I'm going to have another one, so." She drained her glass, tapped it on the table. He got up to pour.

"Lighter this time," she instructed. "And anyway, to hell with Pius Lynch and to hell with tomorrow."

Such a simple story to have burdened so many lives. But in her time a scandal too sensitive for acknowledgement above the threshold of a whisper. Her mother's unexpected and unwanted pregnancy. The only alternatives to shame an orphanage or exile. She lived as her mother's sister until she was seven when Pius Lynch, who had been her mother's husband for five years then, finally adopted her, gave her his name.

"He was a good father," she said. "He wasn't a nice father, but not many were in those days. Being a nice father is something new, at least the way I see it."

When she was fourteen her mother sent her back to live with her grandparents in Mabou Coal Mines. There was a convent school nearby and it had a comprehensive program for training secretaries and stenographers. Shorthand, typing, bookkeeping. It was what girls did in those days. Girls came from all over to be educated there by nuns. Most got good jobs afterwards. Aggie got a job in the town of New Waterford, at the high school, moved back in with her mom and Pius Lynch.

"I couldn't wait to get out of New Waterford. Coal. My God. It darkens people in more ways than one. My grandparents never forgave my mother. The nuns knew. Everybody knew. And Pius Lynch, in his own good way, never let me forget that I owed him. Big time. The day Pierre said we were moving to Toronto was the best day of my life.

"It's queer, isn't it, the way everything works out."

She was finished talking about it. Without her secret she now seemed not so much relieved as empty.

~

He was wakened by the telephone. He fumbled, finally picked up. "Yeah."

"Nicholson here."

He sat up, checked the bedside clock. It was ten in the morning.

"Ronny Nicholson. Is this a bad time?"

"No, no."

"After we talked I checked around and I came up with the first name for that witness. Angus. Angus Beaton. And I gather he isn't dead after all. Sad case just the same, PTSD I understand. I doubt if he'd remember anything useful. Our people found him unreliable five years ago."

"Actually, I've been down there already. I talked to him."

Silence. Then: "You don't waste any time. How did you find him?"

"I just asked around."

"Yes. But how was he? Mentally wise?"

"In good shape. We had a good talk."

"I see."

Cyril was wide awake now, brain in gear. "He was quite helpful. He told me basically what he told your people. Including the description of the possible *other* witness."

There was a long pause, the sound of paper rustling.

"I wouldn't know about that. It wasn't my file. But I never heard of another witness."

"A stranger who was there the day before the accident, who seemed to be waiting for my dad."

Silence.

"He was around most of the Monday afternoon. Just watching and waiting. Later, his car was seen parked down by the wharf."

"So, what did he look like, this guy?"

"Beaton only saw him from behind. But he described him as a fat man. 'Broad as he is long,' was how Beaton put it."

Nicholson laughed. "That could be a lot of people. Doesn't give us much to work with."

"I agree," Cyril said. "Oh yes, and Beaton also found the propane cylinder, the one that we thought blew the boat up."

"Shit. Couldn't have been much left of that."

"It was intact. Actually, it still had propane in it. I could tell when I picked it up. What do you think?"

He'd made up the last part. He waited. Nicholson sighed deeply, cleared his throat.

"Like I said, it was someone else's file. I'll ask around. I'll call again if I hear anything. But Cyril . . ."

"Yes."

"You should be careful with this stuff. From here on in, let's just keep this between ourselves. Okay?"

"That's probably wise."

"Oh, and by the way. Your friend, Nader Hashem . . ."

"What about him?"

"I don't suppose you have a number or a way to get in touch?"

"No, I don't."

"I figured. You have a good day."

∾

Ari was in his usual place at the café but suggested that they retreat to the back patio where there was privacy and the privilege of smoking. It was early evening, mid-week, and the patio was practically deserted. The act of standing up and sitting down seemed like work for Ari. He seemed heavier.

"So you went east. A trip I must make some day, I've heard so much about the coast. It must have been quite a moment to see the place at last. It was your first time?"

"Yes. First time. So you've never been?"

"Never east of Quebec City." Ari's face was blank. He patted his pockets, removed a pack of cigarettes, found matches, lit one. He blew out the match, dropped it in a flowerpot.

Cyril was no longer sure why he was there. He realized what he was really feeling: a loss of confidence. It was not an unfamiliar feeling. Maybe gullibility. What if what you're hearing is someone's best approximation of reality, of truth? Is everyone a liar? What if Ari really was his father's friend, a confidant?

Then he remembered something Nader told him: Empathy is admirable, important, but in certain lines of work it isn't always helpful. Where was Nader anyway? And who is *Nader?*

What if this man was what he seemed to be? A pathetic human being. Angus Beaton saw someone who was fat. So what? Cyril had

seen a hundred seriously fat people in his travels, in the airports, in
the pub in Mabou. He'd seen a fisherman on a boat in the harbour and
he, too, was broad as he was long. Nicholson was right, not much to
go on—fat.

"We should have something," Ari said. He began the struggle to
stand.

"Let me get it," Cyril said quickly and was on his feet. "Beer?"

"Why not. Something dark."

Paying for the beer, Cyril found a slip of paper in his wallet, a page
torn from someone's notebook, folded. Waiting for his change he
spread the scrap of paper on the bar. The note was indecipherable and
then he realized: the Hebrew note. How could he have forgotten? He
folded it and slipped it into his shirt pocket where he could reach it
easily. He felt the revival of something that resembled clarity, and
with it a trace of fear.

∽

"So what did you find out on your haj?" Ari was smiling, now relaxed.

"Haj?"

"Your trip east. I've heard it called the transplanted Maritimers'
mecca."

Cyril laughed. "I met some people who remembered Dad and saw
where my mom had spent quite a bit of her childhood. Had some
memories of being there as a kid, when my parents were still together.
It was interesting."

"You were their only child?"

"Yes." Then he thought: why not. "Though I have a half-brother.
My father and his second wife, they had a little boy. Born after my
dad was gone, though. Dad never saw the little guy."

Ari studied the beer glass. "I'm glad to hear that. I recall it was something that was important to them. Another child." He drank deeply, sighed. Lit another cigarette. "I hope the smoke doesn't bother you. You never smoked?"

"Not tobacco."

Ari laughed. "Yes, of course. Something on my—what is it called—my bucket list, to 'smoke grass,' we used to call it. I never did."

"I never took to pot or cigarettes," Cyril said. "The inhaling. Made me feel congested. I think my dad was once a smoker."

"I suppose," Ari said. "In a war, most people smoke. The fatalism."

"I don't know much about my father's war. As you know."

"What's admirable is your effort to find out. If more young people understood the reality . . ." He shrugged. "The movies. The videos. The games they play at. I worry, the impressions they take away."

"I agree."

"Which is why I'd like to help you. I admire your effort to find out. I'll keep trying to remember things."

Cyril patted his shirt pocket, then removed the folded note. "Maybe you can help me with this. It's probably nothing. I found it among my father's things." He placed the note on the table, unfolded it, smoothed it. "Someone said it's Hebrew."

Ari reached for the note. He picked it up and held it at arm's-length, squinting. Then he patted various pockets on his jacket until he found reading glasses. He slowly unfolded the glasses, installed them. Frowned.

"My, my," he said, smiling. "Your father was a pack rat. Where did you find this?"

"Dad kept diaries. This was taped to a page in one of them."

"Do you know what this is?" He was carefully removing his reading glasses, folding them.

"No."

"An interesting document. You might want a translation."

"Please."

"It's what you'd call a 'safe conduct.' Permitting someone—your father I presume—and some other people, to pass through a military checkpoint. It's interesting because of the date on which it was written, and where, and because of who wrote and signed it."

"What was the date?"

"September eighteenth, 1982. In Beirut."

"And the signature?"

"Mine."

Ari unfolded the reading glasses and put them on again, held the note up. "Charon." He laughed, shook his head and repeated: "Charon, my, my."

Cyril struggled to keep the shock from showing in his face.

"Sharon? Like the prime minister?"

"No. Charon with a 'C.' In my former occupation, a name is like a politician's shirt. You wear it for a while, it gets soiled, it starts to smell. People notice. So you change it. Sometimes more than once a day." He shrugged. "What was it that Shakespeare said? So I've had many names. Charon was one of them. It's not so unusual."

"And the date?"

"Yes. The date. Quite significant." He removed his glasses, folded them, returned them to a pocket. Then he carefully folded the note and put it in his pocket with the glasses.

"Actually," Cyril said, "I'd like to have that back . . ."

Ari raised a hand, palm toward Cyril: "Don't worry. You'll get it back. But you must understand that I should check this out, for both of us. I'll take very good care of it. It is important. To both of us."

"No, let me have it, I'm sure there's a photocopier here, I could . . ."

Ari laughed. "Such a worrier. We must have more faith in one another."

"You should understand I—" he produced his BlackBerry. "Here, just for a second, I'll take a picture with the phone."

"There is no need for pictures with phones. It is yours. You will have it back. Here's the problem, Cyril. All I'm asking for is just a few hours. This note raises important questions. And I should remember but I don't: one, where was I that day and what was my authority, to write such an instruction. You see, it was not an ordinary day, September eighteenth, 1982. And number two, and perhaps most important, from your point of view—why did Pierre need such a note on such a day, to enter such a place?"

"What place?"

"The camps. September 1982. The time has come for explanations. But I need to clarify my memory, Cyril. You will find as you grow older that memory is not to be entirely trusted. I have notes and certain documents from the time. When we speak again, I'll know my facts." He gulped his remaining beer, put the glass down, suppressed a belch. "You mentioned diaries."

"Yes."

"Also interesting."

"I've started studying them. But they're cryptic."

"Yes, of course. Something else we can compare. Maybe I can help you fill in certain blanks. There is a diary for 1982?"

Cyril hesitated, mind racing. "I'll check. It would be in Arabic."

"If you find it, bring it. I read Arabic. All very interesting, Cyril, as you will see in due course. Now I must leave."

He stood, reached for Cyril's hand. They shook.

Cyril watched him go. The shoulders were slumped, he thought, the whole body slack, no longer the strength that Nader had noticed, the strength of a weightlifter. Just another fat old man. Cyril retrieved his BlackBerry, saw there was a text waiting.

It was from Nader: *Imperative. Stay away from TOC and A. Important. Will explain soon.*

38.

Hughes was late to work the next morning. When he arrived, Cyril followed him into his office and shut the door behind him. Hughes looked annoyed, stood behind his desk, waiting.

"Is everything okay?" Cyril asked. "Maybe I should come back?"

Hughes sat. "Is that why you trailed me in here? To find out if I'm okay? Well, if you must know . . ."

"I've met Charon."

Hughes stared. "What are you talking about?"

"I met Charon."

"How the hell do you know that? He just walked up and introduced himself?"

"Something like that."

"Cyril. Get out of here. I don't have time . . ."

"He admitted who he was and that he wrote that note. The Hebrew note that allowed my father to enter the Shatila camp."

"Let me guess . . ."

"Yes. Ari at the Only Café. Also I'm glad you're sitting down. I think I have a witness who can place him in Mabou Coal Mines at the time my father died."

"Mabou Coal Mines?"

"Where it happened."

Hughes leaned back, scratched his head, studied the ceiling. "Anything else?"

"Yes. I've heard from Nader."

"No shit!"

"I'm serious."

"Okay, where the fuck is Nader? It's a matter of some urgency . . ."

"He didn't say. But he told me that he'd be in touch again. But look, I might have made a serious mistake."

Hughes was nodding. "Now, finally, something that I can believe. Let me have it."

"I gave the Hebrew note to Ari and he kept it."

"You didn't make a copy?"

"No."

"It never crossed your mind to make a back-up copy?"

"No."

"You didn't think to use your fucking smartphone?"

"I did. But he wouldn't give it back."

"I see."

"He said he only needed it for a few hours, he wanted to check something."

"Sure he did."

"Look. I've been thinking. Why would he spontaneously admit that he was Charon and that he wrote that note if he had something to hide from us."

"That's a valid point. But you should lay low just the same and, for sure, avoid him for a while."

"But I need to get the note back."

"Well, think about it. If he gives the note back, maybe you're right. He's nobody. But if he is who you think he is, you are never going to get that note back. Trust me."

"He thinks I still have something that he wants. So I'm pretty sure I'll be seeing him."

"He thinks you have what?"

"A diary for 1982."

Hughes leaned back, laughed. "Very good. For a moment I thought you were a total idiot."

Cyril stood to leave but Hughes said, "Sit for a second. We should talk."

He sat.

"I've had some strange inquiries about our Nader." Hughes's unblinking stare, the cold appraisal, was something new. "You wouldn't be holding out on me?"

"Inquiries from where?"

Hughes stared off into the distance. "It seems he was bonking some young one at the *Star*. Revealed some things to her. Now the *Star* is trying to track him down. You know anything about this?"

"Bonking? I doubt very much. But I do know he met an intern there and was helping her adjust—"

"Okay. I'm going to assume you're on the level here. According to a source I have over at the *Star* this intern bailed on Nader because she found some of his religious attitudes and political views to be, her word, scary. This ring a bell?"

"No. I'm surprised that anybody is going to take seriously a nineteen-year-old out to make an impression on her bosses."

"Agreed. But Suzanne has had a call from someone in RCMP security. And *they're* trying to find our guy too. So, if he surfaces, you'll let me know. Okay?"

"So what about Charon?"

"What about him?"

"What if this is all about discrediting Nader . . ."

"We still don't have a story. Even if your man Ari admits he's Charon. Okay? Them's the facts."

"What if he really did kill my father."

"We don't know that. And, more important, even if he did, we don't know why. And I think we can be pretty sure there are people who don't ever want us to know why." He shrugged. "I don't want to seem cold, Cyril. I know what you're going through. Somebody killed my father and I spent a long time trying to find out who and why. I never did. Eventually I admitted to myself that, in the big picture, it didn't really matter to anyone but me. That was my first journalism lesson."

Cyril stood up to leave. "Then you'll understand that it might be a while before I let go of this. Story or no story."

"I understand. Always listen to your gut. But don't expect anybody else to."

∽

Cyril's phone was ringing when he got back to his desk. Ari seemed to be out of breath, as if he were walking as he talked on his cellphone. "I promised I'd get back to you about that note."

"I appreciate it."

"We must get together. It is very, very interesting, what I've been able to dig up. Your dad, my friend, was a very interesting man. There are things you should know. Important things."

"I could meet you anytime."

"How about tonight. But Cyril, we shouldn't meet at the usual place. I have this feeling that I'm being watched, followed even. Maybe I'm paranoid. But maybe it's a little dividend from all my years of following and being followed. You develop certain instincts."

"Okay."

"Have you heard of Cherry Beach?"

Cyril laughed. "Yes. But isn't that a bit—"

"I agree, but we'll be safe from prying eyes. The only people who go there in the evening are lovers and addicts. And, of course, cops at the end of their shifts. But we don't have to worry about them. It will be much too early for the regulars. This won't take long. So nine o'clock. I'll have interesting documents to show you. What will you be driving?"

"A black Mustang."

"A Mustang? Nice. I'll be watching for it. And you'll bring that diary? For 1982?"

"And you'll return that note?"

"Of course. As I promised."

~

Cyril had very little experience with fear. This is not to say that he had never been afraid. As a child he was plagued for many years by sleeplessness and anxiety and was prescribed medication for a brief spell. His doctor assured his parents that the boy would grow out of what was just a phase. To everyone's relief, he did.

And yet, the feeling that he regarded as anxiety never entirely went away. Now, preparing to head off to Cherry Beach, he wondered about the slightly nauseous sensation in his stomach, an unfamiliar weakness in his legs and arms, a lightness in the head. It was like somewhere in his system there was a circuit breaker that kept tripping, bringing movement, physical and mental, to a standstill. This was new, beyond anxiety.

Imperative. Stay away from TOC and A. Important. Will explain soon. But Nader had gone silent again, hadn't explained why Cyril should stay away from the Only Café, stay away from Ari.

There was a section of their basement where he and Aggie had stored what became known to them as "Daddy's stuff." There were banker's boxes full of documents, large cartons full of clothing, winter tires for a long-gone car, items of furniture and a disused set of golf clubs. Cyril selected a nine-iron, hefted it briefly, and then carried it to the car, placed it by his side in the front car seat— feeling somewhat silly as he did so. Afraid of some old fat guy, for God's sake?

He deliberately arrived early. The parking area at Cherry Beach was as deserted as Ari had predicted. The configuration of the harbourfront gave him the impression of being on an island. The glittering city rose before him as if thrust up from nowhere on the edge of Lake Ontario. His nerves settled. He reminded himself of the logic he had presented to Hughes. Ari had admitted he was Charon, that he wrote a note that revealed he was a person of authority near the scene of what had been a war crime for which nobody had ever been held criminally accountable.

Why would he have done that if he was dangerous?

Cyril replayed in his head his last conversation with Ari. The ease of his acknowledgement. He was Charon. He wrote that note. End of mystery. Ari had volunteered to review his records. He wanted to be helpful. *We're both in this together*, he seemed to say. He wanted to deliver context. Cyril remembered a feeling that was close to empathy, maybe even pity, watching Ari walk away, all traces of his past identity as soldier, spy, provocateur, commando, killer, *whatever*, lost within an unimaginable burden of lard, laziness and redundancy. What was there to be afraid of?

His phone rang.

"Where are you?"

"Who is this?"

"Come on, man. You know who this is. Where are you?"

"Jesus H. Christ. You're asking *me* where *I* am?"

"Goddamn stop playing games. Where are you?"

Silence.

"I'm at Cherry Beach."

"Cherry Beach. What for?"

"I'm meeting someone."

"Leave now."

"You know what? Fuck you."

"Cyril. I know what you're up to. Leave. Now. Come and talk to me."

"And where might you be?"

"Figure it out. Drive anywhere. Now."

Cyril saw headlights. The approaching car drove by the entrance to the parking lot. But then he saw the brake lights. *Fucking Nader. Why am I listening.* He started the engine. He left his headlights off until he thought he was close to the exit, then turned them on. The two cars passed each other on the narrow roadway. Cyril looked resolutely straight ahead, and then he tramped on the accelerator. The Mustang howled and fishtailed.

"Why am I doing this?" Cyril said aloud as he raced along the Lake Shore toward the centre of the city.

∽

Even sitting in the shadows Nader wasn't hard to find. It was a section of King Street that was busy only in the daylight hours, during lunchtime or right after work. In the evening it was deserted.

"Yo." Nader was smiling. He had a glass of Coke in front of him. He slid the pint of beer across to Cyril. "Thanks for coming."

Cyril started laughing and realized he couldn't stop. He laughed and laughed. *Thanks for coming?* Nader was studying his wristwatch. *You must be kidding.*

"You are such an asshole," Cyril said.

Nader frowned, said nothing. Cyril drank half the glass of beer in a single gulp.

"Nader, what did you say to Megan that freaked her out?"

He raised his eyebrows, studied his glass for a moment, then laughed. "We can talk as you drive," he said, and stood.

"Where are we going?"

"Not far."

In the car, Cyril struggled to contain his anger. Nader's call and his panicky response had aborted what could have been the best opportunity he'd ever get to learn the story of his father's flight from Lebanon, the crisis that had consumed him in the spring of 2007. Cherry Beach had been his last chance.

"You fucked up what was probably my last shot at the truth, my friend. Thanks a lot."

Nader was nodding as Cyril seethed, staring straight ahead, rubbing at his jawbone. His hand was resting on the shaft of the golf club. He picked it up.

"And this was for what?"

Cyril said nothing.

"Maybe you were going to hammer the truth out of him." Nader laughed. "Somehow, I don't think that would have worked with this guy."

"He thought that I still had something he wanted. I was that close," Cyril said. "It was worth the risk."

"He thought you had what?"

"It doesn't matter."

"Finally, the truth. It doesn't fucking matter."

"What? You're saying the truth doesn't matter?"

"I'm sick of talking about truth," Nader said. "We've been talking about truth for three thousand years and we still don't know what we're talking about."

"So, what did you say to Megan?"

"Something like that, that we waste a lot of precious time on abstractions, like The Truth."

"Come on."

"I'm serious." He shook his head and sighed. "So what else have you learned about our friend Ari?"

"Just that he went by the name Charon back in the seventies and eighties. Maybe even more recently. And that he and my dad were involved somehow in the Sabra and Shatila massacre. But you knew that all along. Right?"

"Very good. How did you find that out?"

"In my father's diaries Hughes found a note that was written in

Hebrew. Dated September eighteenth, 1982. Signed Charon. I showed it to Ari and he admitted he wrote the note to let my father enter the Shatila camp. For what reason I'm not sure. He's up front about it. I was hoping he'd tell me more tonight at Cherry Beach."

"You were impressed by his candour?"

"To tell you the truth, yes . . ."

"Where's the note?"

"He has it."

Nader laughed. "You gave it to him, right?"

"Yes. I was at Cherry Beach to get it back. He was going to fill in the background."

"Of course he was."

"You're saying he was setting me up."

"So why did you take the golf club if you didn't suspect that yourself? Come on."

"So you're saying I'm gullible."

"Candour, out of context, always works. He got what he wanted. He thought you had something else incriminating? He was going to get that, too, one way or another."

Silence.

"Maybe he was on the level," Cyril said.

Nader laughed. "Maybe you were about to have a serious accident. Like your dad."

Cyril sighed. "Okay, let's say he did it. How would he have been able to find exactly where Dad was?"

"Good question, Cyril. And the answer is obvious."

"And it is . . . ?"

"That Ari is part of something larger than we will ever get a handle on."

They drove in silence. Nader hefted the golf club then dropped it into the back seat.

"What about you?" Cyril asked.

"What about me?"

"Do you know how many people are looking for you? Do you know why?"

"They're idiots and they won't find me."

"Hughes? Suzanne?"

Silence.

"The police?"

Silence.

Cyril broke the silence. "So what now?"

"All things will be revealed."

"And in the meantime?"

"In the meantime, I will disappear. And, in the short term, so will you. It's necessary, for both of us."

"Come on."

"Trust me. There must be somewhere you can go, somewhere nobody knows about. Maybe back to the East Coast. That would be poetic, wouldn't it."

"And what about him. Ari, Charon? If he's so fucking dangerous."

"He'll be taken care of. You'll get a message when it's safe to surface."

"What does that mean—taken care of?"

"Cyril. There's a war on. Forget about Osama and nine-eleven, the Arab Spring. We're at war. It's been coming for a hundred years and it could last another hundred. And here's a scoop: The people we call the bad guys? They're gonna win. As things are beginning to unfold, they can't lose. There are a billion people listening. To them."

"It's too big to be a story. That's what you were trying to tell Savage."

"Here's reality, Cyril—the only truth worth anything is what's happening. And the only way to know what's happening is to be part of it."

"Where will you be, Nader?"

"Pull up here," Nader said.

"St. George subway station," Cyril said. "What is it about this place?"

"From St. George station you can go anywhere in the world, Cyril. North, south, east, west. Take care."

He opened the car door and before he left, he paused briefly, as if he had a final thought. But then he slipped out, closed the door gently, vanished without another word.

∽

The policeman was rapping on the window with a flashlight. "You can't stop here. Move on."

He started the car, moved slowly down the block, away from the entrance to the subway station. He parked again. He no longer knew where he was going, where he could go. He checked for messages. There were none. He called his mother.

"Mom. I won't be home tonight. I'll probably be away for a few days."

"Away?"

"If anybody asks, I'm overseas. I'll touch base later and Mom—I love you."

"So where *will* you be?"

"I don't know yet."

"Cyril. Are you sure you're all right?"

"I'm okay."

He hung up and scrolled through his contacts until he found Gloria's number. He hesitated, but only briefly.

"This is Gloria."

"Hi."

Silence.

"It's me."

Silence.

"You're at work?"

"Yes. Where are you?

"Out and about. Can I come home?"

There was a pause that was long enough for the germination of a thought, a sensation of an idea clicking into word forms, syntax, slipping toward the tongue: *Maybe this is a bad idea . . . sorry if I'm putting you on the spot.*

"I won't be here much longer. Do you still have your key?"

"No. I forgot it . . ."

"Why am I not surprised? Do you mind waiting in the lobby until I get there?"

"I'll be waiting."

~

It was a Saturday morning. He stared out over the dismal city, rain streaking down the glass balcony door. Plants carefully arrayed along the railing were already dead. He remembered how he'd placed them there back in springtime, carefully packing the tiny shoots in the pots, visiting the gardening store and asking for advice about the most nutritious potting soil, an antidote for the boredom he'd endured before the start of his internship. And of feeling marginally improved by what he considered a small act of creativity. Now they were with-ered, dead from neglect as much as anything.

The weather channel informed him that the temperature was plus-two degrees Celsius. There could be sleet. He couldn't watch the news channels anymore. He didn't trust what anyone was telling him. He was bored by movies. He couldn't stand sports. Everything he saw and heard seemed false, fabricated, performed.

He'd started reading three highly recommended novels. He'd even started writing one—the story of the past six months. The novels failed to hold his interest, but they succeeded in persuading him that he didn't have the talent or the discipline to write one of his own. And what had really happened in the past six months? What could he say for sure? Would anyone believe him? Would anybody care? He'd slept a lot that week, far too much he knew.

He was waiting for a signal of some kind, a sign that it was safe to face the outside world. But he realized, that Saturday morning, that he really didn't care what anybody had to say about the outside world, the unseen perils of the present, the chaotic narratives of his-tory as shaped by academic storytellers, the media manipulation of reality and motive, trying to explain what happens, the menace of what hasn't happened yet, all from the sanctuary of detachment. He'd envied Gloria as she dressed for work, even though it was the weekend.

My weeks don't end. When was it she had told him that?

He decided to go out, brave the sleet and whatever peril waited for him there.

The only way to know what's happening is to be part of it.

But everything boils down to just one word, he thought. Power. The power to get what everybody wants: wealth, security and sex.

Isn't that what it would mean to be "a part of it"? To play the game to win a portion of the prize. Power, survival.

He felt the chill of bitterness, the memory of abandonment, though he could never have explained why he would feel that way. It was, after all, he who had disappeared, who had turned off his phone except for swift and furtive checks to see if there was any word from Nader. Now he felt there never would be a message, that if a signal came at all it would be from somewhere unexpected, in some surprising form.

He watched the rain pissing down. Piss, piss, piss. The wind was stirring. The weather was worsening as predicted by the cheerful weather woman in the skirt that was too tight for television. He felt sorry for her. TV makes everyone look fat. Nobody likes to look fat. Nobody fat likes to be stared at. He killed the television picture. He grabbed a coat and ball cap and headed for the elevator, turned on his telephone as he was going down. Nothing.

About a block from the apartment building he could feel the vibration in his pocket. The display told him it was Gloria. "Hey."

"Just giving you a heads-up," she said. But before he heard another word he saw the car slipping quietly along the curb, slowing to a crawl beside him. Tinted window sliding down. He killed the phone and bolted toward a shop doorway. The door was locked.

The voice behind him, loud, authoritative: "Hey, whoa—come back here." He thought he recognized it. Hughes?

He bent down, walked toward the car. Hughes was frowning at him through the drizzle on his glasses. Suzanne was behind the wheel. She leaned forward, waved.

"Jump in," said Hughes. Cyril complied, after looking nervously up and down the sidewalk.

"How did you know I'd be here?"

"Elementary investigative journalism. *Cherchez la femme*. We located Gloria and asked her. She told us. Where were you going?"

"Coffee and a muffin."

"We need you at the office. We'll grab something on the way."

"Wait. I can't go there yet."

"And why not?" Hughes asked. "Last time I checked you were working for us."

"I've been told to lay low, sort of like witness protection, until I'm told it's safe to surface. I don't know how to explain."

"Who told you."

"Nader."

"We figured."

The car was now moving out into the traffic. "I haven't been given the green light yet."

"Consider this the green light."

"It's about that guy at the Only Café. Suzanne, you were right about him. Stop the car."

She accelerated. "He doesn't matter anymore," she said. "Now we can do the story and we need you to help us tell it."

"You talked to Nader?"

"No."

"Well, where is he?"

"Nobody knows," Hughes said. "Best guess? He's gone to war. Whether to fight or to cover it, we don't know. I doubt if he knows yet."

"Is Nader part of our story?"

"Perhaps."

"But what about Ari. Charon. What about him?"

"We'll explain when we get you to the office."

"Something happened to him."

"Yes."

"Dead?"

"That's one way of putting it."

Cyril was shocked by a sudden sense of loss—his father's killer but also the last connection to his father's distant past. "Does anybody know who did it?"

"It seems he had a heart attack. He lived alone. A two-room place on the second floor of a tailor shop, not far from that bar. A young guy who used to work at that café found him. Also an Israeli, we understand. I guess they knew each other."

Cyril managed to laugh. "A heart attack. And we're supposed to believe that?"

"It's official, Cyril. It doesn't matter what we believe. He's dead. Cause of death, a heart attack. More important, we have our story now."

"Okay. But what makes it a story now when it wasn't a week ago?"

Hughes didn't even turn around. "Dead people don't sue," he said quietly.

"And Nader?"

"Forget about Nader. He's gone."

The wind was now aggressive, rain lashing the windows, braids of liquid distorting everything outside, the wobbly, wavy world only intermittently clarified by the rhythmic sweep of windshield wipers. All sound now the inside hum of mechanism, thunder in his head, the hiss of outside traffic.

"You're very quiet back there," said Hughes.

"Yes. Just thinking."

"I can imagine."

But the image in his mind, for no reason that he could easily have explained to them, was of a house abandoned on a hillside a thousand miles away, and of a sloping meadow long since reclaimed by skimpy juniper and stunted spruce, finally surrendering to a rocky shoreline and a sprawling endless roiling emptiness beyond. And the whitened veils of winter that increased the darkness and the loneliness. And even in the laggard spring, the howling northeast wind that, according to his mother, always stirred the dust of decades, the detritus of past lives, the ghosts of long-departed people, of bats and mice and their excretions. It would be on days like that, she'd say, you'd always dream about away.

"You okay?" Suzanne asked. She turned slightly. He looked away. She turned the car onto University.

"I think it finally sank in," he said. "My dad is dead." Silence.

"Nader said something interesting."

Silence.

"That the only way to know what happens is to be a part of it."

Silence.

Hughes sighed. "He's an Arab, Cyril."

"I'm as much an Arab as he is."

"If you say so."

A car horn, urgent. Suzanne braked and swore quietly.

"You spoke to him?" said Hughes.

"Yes."

"And?"

"Nothing. He'll figure it out, the right thing to do. And do it."

"And you?"

Silence.

"It's all highly overrated, I think."

"What is?" Hughes asked.

"What we do."

"I hear you," Suzanne said.

The rain slashed horizontally. The wipers doggedly responded. Swish. Swish. Swish. Suzanne turned on the radio. The car filled up with talk.

"Turn it off," said Hughes. She complied.

Silence returned, interrupted only by the swish of wipers, hiss of traffic.

"Pull over for a minute," Hughes instructed.

She signalled, edged through the traffic until she reached the curb-side, stopped. They sat in silence.

Hughes sighed. "It's up to you, Cyril." He was staring straight ahead. "I understand. It's okay."

"Yes," said Cyril. "Thank you."

"Where will you go?"

"Home."

"Where's home?"

The car windows were fogging rapidly. There was only the sound of rain spattering, the surge and splash of traffic. "Yes," he said. He wiped the window with a sleeve, peered out. "I guess I have to figure that out too."

He opened the car door and struggled out. He stood for just a moment in a sudden gust of wind and rain. And then he started walking.

ACKNOWLEDGEMENTS

~

This work of fiction is based on real events.

I have drawn extensively on the work of journalists who risked and occasionally lost their lives covering the civil war in Lebanon. I am indebted, in particular, to the journalism of Robert Fisk, who lived and worked perilously in West Beirut throughout the worst of the turmoil. His encyclopedic account of the war, *Pity the Nation*, was an indispensable source of insight and corroboration. A seminal scene, the murder of the woman at the clothesline on the morning of September 18, 1982, was inspired by his reporting of the horrifying spectacles he witnessed that day.

I found useful detail and texture in Robert Hatem's controversial memoir, *From Israel to Damascus*. The report of the Kahan Commission of Inquiry into the massacre at Sabra and Shatila, September 16-18, 1982, offers rare, if incomplete, forensic accountability by those responsible. Many of the scenes in this novel have been reconstructed from my own experience as a reporter making periodic visits to Lebanon between 1982 and 2005. On one such visit I witnessed the immediate aftermath of the Sabra and Shatila atrocities in

September 1982, and reported them for the Canadian Broadcasting Corporation.

I am indebted to many people for their work and for their patience as I thought and spoke and wrote my way through a complex and, at times, emotional reconstruction of a murky and still-unresolved chapter of the history of the Middle East. I reserve my deepest gratitude for my editor and publisher, Anne Collins, whose help was indispensable in my shaping of this story/commentary on the tragic history of a vital country, Lebanon.

Special thanks to Helal Endisha and Andre Mekhtfi. And profound appreciation to Tal Regev, bartender/cook/resident-mystic, and James O'Donnell, proprietor, at The Only Café.

Linden MacIntyre
Toronto, January 2017

LINDEN MACINTYRE's bestselling first novel, *The Long Stretch*, was nominated for a CBA Libris Award and his boyhood memoir, *Causeway: A Passage from Innocence*, won both the Edna Staebler Award for Creative Nonfiction and the Evelyn Richardson Prize. His second novel, *The Bishop's Man*, was a #1 national bestseller, won the Scotiabank Giller Prize, the Dartmouth Book Award and the CBA Libris Fiction Book of the Year Award, among other honours. The third book in the loose-knit trilogy, *Why Men Lie*, was also a #1 national bestseller as well as a *Globe and Mail* "Can't Miss" Book. His previous novel, *Punishment*, was a *Globe and Mail* national best-seller. MacIntyre, who spent twenty-four years as the co-host of *the fifth estate*, is a distinguished broadcast journalist who has won ten Gemini awards for his work.